# VISEGRAD

A NOVEL

# VISEGRAD

A NOVEL

Duncan Robertson

New Europe Books

Williamstown, Massachusetts

Published by New Europe Books, 2022
Williamstown, Massachusetts
www.NewEuropeBooks.com
Copyright © 2022 by Duncan Robertson
Cover art by Alexa Fermeglia
Interior design by Knowledge Publishing Services

ISBN: 978-1-7345379-3-2

Cataloging-in-publication data is available from the Library of Congress.

First edition

10 9 8 7 6 5 4 3 2 1

# VISEGRAD

A True Story of Debt Collection,
Unrequited Love, and Wet Feet

D. Ryely

"The real tragedy of the Visegrad thing was that it happened to us. Otherwise it would have been sort of funny."

—Lear

# Part I

# 1

I stayed up all night and supervised the destruction of McKayla's and Lear's passports in the morning.

It was important that the passports retain no information pertinent to security status or dates of entry, but be kept whole, in order to pass muster with the embassy. McKayla and Lear had tried ripping out pages, smearing them with ink and expunging them with bleach.

I sat on the counter and drank black *pivni*, watching McKayla use kitchen tongs to dunk the passports into boiling water.

In their bedroom, Lear was dividing their possessions into individual piles.

They were to be backpackers on their way out of Visegrad, headed to Krakow and Prague, respectively. To this purpose, McKayla was already in character and dipping the passports in boiling water as a version of McKayla, a graduate student. She stewed the laminated pages and, whenever she brought them out, hissed disconsolately through her teeth.

Lear hadn't done as much background work as McKayla, and so was dividing their possessions into individual piles as a version of me. Character work is about absorbing extraneous information, spending time with a personality, and sort of drinking that personality in.

"You're crazy staying behind," he said. "Get out while you can, is what I think."

"What good will you do here by yourself?" asked McKayla.

"There's nowhere for me to go," I said. I attempted to light a backward cigarette.

McKayla watched me struggle for a moment, then plucked it from my mouth, turned it around, and replaced it between my lips.

"What did he say?" called Lear.

"He said he's got nowhere else to go."

"Budapest," said Lear. He appeared in the door, clutching handfuls of lingerie. "You need this?"

"Yes," said McKayla.

"What do you mean, Budapest?"

"I mean," said Lear, pointing to himself, "Krakow," pointing to McKayla, "Prague," and pointing to me, "Budapest."

"I don't think I could live in Budapest," I said.

"Rye," said McKayla, "Whoever you think you're protecting, in the end you'll only hurt yourself."

"Is that working?" I asked, indicating the passport.

"I don't know," said McKayla. She frowned. "I don't think so."

"Then it's my turn," said Lear, and tossed her lingerie into the bedroom behind him. She lifted Lear's passport from the pot so we could examine it under the hot white fluorescent light over the sink. The passport steamed. Its entry stamps were faded but their dates were still legible.

Lear cursed. He snatched her passport from the kitchen counter and prepared to burn it.

"Stop," cried McKayla.

He hesitated, lighter flickering beneath its blue, laminated corner. "Why?" he asked.

"Don't you think it's illegal to burn them?"

"So what?"

"Well, won't we get in trouble if we show up with them at the embassy, burnt like that?"

"I don't think burning is any worse than–" Lear yelped. He yanked his thumb from the lighter's hot flint and nursed it.

McKayla turned to me. "Rye, what do you think? Should we burn them?"

"What will you say happened?"

"See?" said McKayla. "See?"

Lear gave a betrayed grunt, then said, "Accident."

"What kind of accident?" I asked.

"I don't know," said Lear. "Workplace accident."

McKayla snorted.

"I don't want you to feel like we're ganging up on you here," I said, "but what kind of workplace accident do you foresee McKayla having?"

"It could fall into an incinerator."

"An incinerator?" McKayla drew a sharp breath. "Like, in what capacity do you think I might be dangling my prize possessions over an incinerator?"

"Not dangling," he said. "It could have fallen out of your pocket. Besides, nothing else worked and we tried everything. You'll have to come up with a reason why it got burned." He thrust the lighter back under the passport. McKayla swore and grabbed for it. He held it at arm's length, balancing on the balls of his feet.

Then she relented and all three of us watched the passport smolder.

After a while, Lear yelped and stuck his thumb back into his mouth.

"Good," said McKayla. She bent to retrieve the little book, nudging him out of the way. He lost his balance and brushed against an enormous pyramid of long-neck, half liter *pivni* bottles that took up part of the apartment. The whole apparatus shifted precariously. We held our breath. A soldier leaned out of formation and fell, shattering on the kitchen floor.

"Whoops," said Lear.

McKayla opened her passport. "Not a scratch."

"What do you mean?" asked Lear.

"You can't burn it." She stepped back so we could confirm her diagnosis.

"What do they make these out of?" I ran a finger along the soot that had accumulated at the bottom of the page, and it came away, exposing the date on a Vlodomerian Defense Forces' Heightened Security Status stamp. "We should be using this material on the space shuttle and in levies and on the aspirations of people who give up their childhood dreams."

McKayla snapped her fingers. "Wait here." She stomped out of the kitchen, pulverizing a shard of glass.

"Where would we go?" asked Lear.

I leaned against the kitchen counter, then jerked awake as my beer began to slip from my hand. I took another drink.

Lear regarded me coolly. "Jesus, would you take it easy?"

McKayla returned with a bag of large and fashionable dimensions. She rummaged through it, discarding used tissues, lip gloss, and Colin Having's ragged copy of *The Dim Corona of Lazlo Nawj*.

She brought out a small bottle of nail polish and shook it. She unscrewed its top and removed the brush, placing it on the counter.

Purple dots rained on the laminate.

McKayla rolled back one sleeve, loosened the joints in the fingers of one of her hands theatrically, picked up the bottle and poured it across the open passport. She clamped it shut. "There."

"How'll we explain nail polish?" asked Lear.

"We'll say the bottle broke in my bag."

He deflated, shuddered, shimmied back and forth and gasped for air. He looked around as if awakened from a trance. "That settles it. Let's go."

While McKayla doctored her passport, I watched Lear pack, drinking more and eating clumps of wet speed from a plastic baggie.

Lear and McKayla had already made an appointment at the American embassy for that morning, where they received temporary passports and their new passport numbers. The woman who issued them was a tired-looking embassy worker in her forties. "It's been a bad week for theft," she said. "This must be the tenth temporary passport I've issued, today. It's some sort of counterfeiting ring, so hold on to these."

"Theft," said Lear, snapping his fingers and turning to McKayla. "We didn't think of that."

McKayla jabbed him in the ribs, so he sat bolt upright.

When Lear recounted the meeting, he lifted his shirt to show where McKayla had poked him, exposing yellow and purple fingerprints. I looked reprovingly at McKayla, who shrugged.

"We almost got in trouble again," she said, "When they asked where they could ship the passports, we told them Prague and Krakow. We were the third couple she'd seen heading in opposite directions."

"Maybe someone should tell them," I said.

"Yeah right," said Lear. "And get run in for crimes they haven't named yet?"

"Looks like it's finally working, at least," said McKayla.

"Looks that way," I said.

"Still staying?"

"Sure," I said.

"They're adults," said McKayla. "They have to take responsibility for their own choices."

"Imagine if everyone thought that way."

"Everybody does," said Lear.

"Maybe that's the problem." I sat down on the couch in the living room among crumpled blankets. It was the couch I had woken up on the day after the police raid on the El Matador Café.

Outside the weather was damp and cloudy. "Rye," said McKayla, "come with me."

"You don't mean that," I said. "You just don't want to feel guilty about leaving me behind."

We sat still and listened to the sound of each other's bad breath.

Lear cleared his throat. "Don't wanna miss the bus."

"That's right." I nodded.

McKayla was booked on an overnight coach to Bratislava with the intention of catching a train to Prague in the morning.

We stopped on the second floor of our prefabricated apartment complex. I unlatched the stairwell window and held it open while they lowered their possessions onto the corrugated metal roof of a shed in the courtyard. One by one, we climbed out, balanced on the sill, then dropped onto the shed.

We left through a side entrance and walked to the international bus terminal, where we waited in the drizzling rain and I tried to think of something to say.

"Want to help me with a math problem?" asked McKayla.

"Okay," said Lear.

"A bus leaves for the Slovakian border traveling one hundred kilometers an hour. If a white van full of assholes also leaves for the border, traveling at a hundred and fifty kilometers per hour, how much of a head start will the bus need to make it to the border before the van full of assholes can catch up?"

"About fifty minutes," I said. "Give or take."

Her bus pulled in.

"Cross your fingers?"

I crossed my fingers and showed them to her.

McKayla hugged me first, then she held onto Lear and they kissed each other a long time while people moved delicately around them to stow their baggage in the bus's luggage compartment. She waved goodbye from the window, wiping away tears.

I cried a little too and I was glad it was raining.

Lear just stood there, jaw set, bracing against some huge invisible force, the lump in his throat moving up and down like a glottal piston. Then she was gone.

"Let's get drunk," I said.

"Okay," he said.

I suggested we go someplace we had all loved, but the only place open was the Gouged Eye, where the electricity was out and the taps didn't work. We huddled together in the candlelight and sucked on the necks of warm beer, taking a little more wet speed. The neon eye on the sign outside was turned off, so the street was undressed in the gray weather, festooned with dog shit and cigarette butts.

We were in the city of Visegrad, that new ancient, beautiful ugly scene.

# 2

I was born in Please Leave, USA. It was not originally called that. They started calling it Please Leave after white people moved there. An ethnographer pieced together what it meant from the anglicized Paiute around the turn of the century. By then, everyone had got so used to the name that no one cared what it meant.

If you grew up in Please Leave, you didn't even think about it. It had an almost Celtic ring, so you could be forgiven for thinking the whole town was named after one family of overabundant Scotsmen. I found out what it meant in seventh grade, when Mr. Harbor told our fourth period English class. I couldn't believe it. Nobody else seemed surprised, so maybe they already knew.

It wasn't a real city but it wasn't rural either. Its population didn't shrink or grow so much as it increased or decreased in proportion to everything else. Please Leave had three colleges: one Adventist, one liberal arts, and one community. It had wineries and cattle and branch locations of commercial banking subsidiaries housed in squat brick buildings.

Most people never left. I made it farther than anyone else I ever knew.

By the morning after the police raid on the El Matador Café, I had made it all the way to McKayla and Lear's couch in the gypsy quarter of Visegrad, where I woke up to McKayla saying, "I told Deddy he could have the apartment while we were in Ukraine."

"Deddy?" said Lear. He looked at her across the table. "Wouldn't it be safer to lock a bunch of feral dogs in here?"

"Sure, if you think the dogs will water the plants." McKayla was studying Vlodomerian, seated diagonally and facing away from Lear. She took a bite of toast and marinated cheese.

"The other day he took a shit behind the bar at the Gouged Eye. Did you know that? I'm saying, you'd better make sure he knows not to take a dump on the kitchen table."

"I'll tell him," said McKayla.

"I've nearly shit in here a couple times actually," he said, "even though I never had the faintest inclination."

"I said I'd tell him," said McKayla. She dabbed a flake of *hermelin* from the corner of her mouth.

"You know how many times I've thought I was in the hall bathroom, when I was really squatting six feet in the air with my pants around my ankles? Only at the last minute, do I realize I'm standing over a bowl of fruit."

"Sounds like a near miss."

"Misses," corrected Lear. He set down his tablet. "It's happened more than once."

She took another bite of toast and cheese. He took a long drink off the top of a mug of coffee.

"I think you're funny," I said.

Lear jumped. "Jesus Christ, who let *you* in?"

The blankets on Lear's couch were perpetually strewn over the body of someone no one else remembered letting into the flat. After I moved in, I took to yanking back the mound of duvets, prepared to shout at whichever liquor-sodden unnecessary was curled against its cushions. You could never quite rid yourself of the suspicion that a body was buried in that apartment.

"We did. I told him he could sleep on the couch." McKayla looked at me and smiled.

I screwed up my face. "I lost some motor function and was not sure what part of the city I lived in."

Lear gave a woeful toss of his head.

He was an athletic West Texan, not as good at any one thing as at being himself. McKayla was a Trustafarian from Ohio, whose parents had operated a regional chain of home furnishing stores that folded in 2011. What they had in common was that they enjoyed terrific sex that caused everyone, roommate(s), vermin, neighbors/neighbors' pets, to flee or cower until the ruckus had subsided. We had met, really met, the previous night during the raid on the El Matador Café. This was in Visegrad,[1] which, if you are at all a citizen of the world, have set even one toe out of the brown paper bag you were jettisoned into post-birth/graduation/marriage, you would know it is one of the great cultural cities of Central and Eastern Europe—rivaling Krakow, Kiev, Prague, Budapest, Berlin, and Vienna—and overshadowing those other cities to which it is often unfairly compared: Sofia, Minsk, Belgrade, Bucharest, Zagreb, Lviv, and Ljubljana. The city

---

[1] In Thom Elliott's excellent *Surviving Eastern Europe*, he opens the topic of Visegrad thus: "Visegrad, pronounced, [ˈviʃɛɡraːd], [ʋiʃɛɡraːd], or [viˈʂɔɡrut]— spelled Visegrad, Vyšehrad, Visegrád, Wyszogród, Višegrad and Вишгород (Vyshhorod), in Vlodomerian, Czech, Hungarian, Polish, Bosnian and Ukranian/ Ruthenian respectively—is the largest and capital city of Vlodomeria: officially the Vlodomerian Republic, formerly the southernmost part within the Oblast of Western Volhynia and the Wołyń Voivodeship (styled Vladimir-in-Volhynia), and variously titled, or within territories titled, The Kingdom of Galicia and Vlodomeria, the Principality of Halych, Austrian Galicia in New Cisleithania, Galician Beskidy, Subcarpatho-Ruthenia and Transcarpatho-Ukraine.

Visegrad is from the Old East Slavic meaning "high seat" or "high place," so named for the city's ancient castle, Vlodo's Seat, or "*Visegradgrad*" in Vlodomerian: literally, "High Castle Castle," but which can be taken to mean "Visegrad Castle" in the same way that "Peter's peter" can be taken to mean "Peter's penis" and is not indicative of any kind of nesting doll situation in which one man named Peter is subject to, or somehow couched within, another man named Peter.

The Vlodomerian Republic is perhaps the least likely of all the states to emerge in the post-Soviet era and is characterized by a tangible sense of cautious optimism that it will be allowed to continue to exist." (415–16)

was uninhabitable in winter, its natives cold and distant, its cuisine inedible. And it was, for a time, the absolute hippest place in the universe, eclipsing the suburban popularity of East Portland, Williamsburg, Shoreditch, Canal, St. Martin and the Mission. This was the product of some unusual circumstances that made it possible to live there without a visa.

How I first met McKayla and Lear has been obscured by the frequency and the inconsequence of those meetings. We were all in circulation, and had met in passing sometime before the police raid on the El Matador Café when all three of us sheltered behind the same enormous black velvet portrait of Tupac Shakur.

"I'm Rye," I whispered to McKayla.

Lear poked his head out from behind her as I shook her hand.

She said, "We've met."

A police raid is exactly the kind of experience that forms lasting connections.

Visegrad Police tended to raid all the expatriate bars on the same night, once every couple of months, going from dive to dive and collecting would-be detainees in a sort of quasifascist pub crawl. I say *quasi*fascist, because these raids never led to the detention of anybody. Detention led to expulsion and expulsion precluded the levying of additional fines, all of which ran contrary to the interests of the state.

What happened after you extracted from one of these bars, assuming you did not have a large velvet portrait of Tupac Shakur to shelter behind, was you attempted to bribe an officer, asking, "Is there a fine I can pay now?"

If you were stupid or nervous or just unlucky about this, asking it in the wrong way or within earshot of the unit's Foreign Police officer, the second thing you did was march to an ATM. At the ATM you were made to extract a much larger amount of money, which constituted a fine levied against your person.

This fine was for failing to produce a passport, which you were required by Vlodomerian law to carry at all times.

The fine was about 33500 Vlodomerian *grivni* (VRG), roughly equivalent to 120 USD (112 EUR, 84 GBP, 100 VRP), not an unreasonable amount given that the Vlodomerians had you on an expired visa and could put you through the wringer, which might result in you paying the cost of a last-minute plane ticket back to Wherever You Came From. If you couldn't afford the plane ticket, the government in Wherever You Came From would extract the price of the ticket, with interest, once you were squared away on good old WYCF soil.

Even if you had your passport, which you never did, it was better to pretend that you didn't and pay the 33500 VRG. If you produced the passport and verified your extralegality, you became the subject of a lot of angry discussion in Vlodomerian. Then, as likely as not, you would be released. But there was a fifty percent chance of total catastrophe.

Fines levied for failing to produce a passport acted as an unofficial tax on the expatriate community; we had our own doctors, restaurants, coffeehouses, theaters, dentists, insurance agents, newspapers, and beer halls. We lived with every conceivable luxury and convenience of home, except we were excluded from all workings of government, almost every aspect of Vlodomerian commerce, and felt, always, as though some debt were piling up in our absence that was to be ruthlessly extracted from us on our return. For about half of us this was literally true, since many Americans could not pay the debts we had accrued in college.

McKayla's education had been paid out of her trust, but Lear had attended school without the benefit of financial aid and had large unmanageable debts he neglected. Yet, whenever serious money was spent, rent, nights of particular largesse, Lear was McKayla's sponsor. He worked tech support for a company that believed he resided in El Paso. This made him practically a millionaire on the Vlodomerian scale, but also meant he worked

American business hours, 4:00 PM to 1:00 AM CET, which turned him into a blood quaffing maniac just getting started at two in the morning, and was always running into people on his stagger home who were on their way to Saturday lunch.

I had come to Visegrad from Prague from Chiang Mai from Please Leave, arriving late and leaving late at each like a bad guest at a good party, digging into the couch with a small audience that did not want to be rude after everyone else had gone to bed. Habits or thoughts or facts of life built up on me all the time, and the only way I could shake them loose was by selling my possessions and moving to another country where I did not speak the language.

I had followed a Spanish girl from Prague to Visegrad. She was the sort of European that enjoyed funny Americans in the abstract and was a great fan of Woody Allen, who I am nothing like. A few weeks after she left Prague, I received a slurred voice message asking why I wasn't in Visegrad to kiss/be kissed.

I never extracted the kiss, receiving no more than a worried hug at the bus station, but the relation of this story endeared me to strangers whenever I answered the fourth inescapable question of Visegrad icebreaking protocol. The fourth question was "Why did you move to Vlodomeria?" The others were, 1) "Where are you from?" 2) "What did you study?" and 3) "What do you do?"

"She never even gave you the kiss?" asked McKayla.

The raid had ended, and the El Matador had shuttered for the night, so we had resolved to tie one on at the Galician Whale, which was hosting a survival blowout.

"Not even a peck?" asked Lear.

I shook my head. "I don't think I'm the sort of guy you kiss when he's expecting it. In fact, based on personal experience, when I'm expecting to be kissed I might be the least attractive man on the planet."

"She didn't even touch it?" asked Lear.

"Not a grazing elbow," I said.

"She didn't tease you till you were just one big, chafed nerve?"

"No," I said indignantly, "she did not."

"She didn't ambush you in the stall when you went to the bathroom, so you had to sit there and take it?"

The walls in the Galician Whale were painted to look like ribs.

"The trick," said McKayla, "is to stop him before he says something that he keeps you up all night with, telling you how he wishes you'd stopped him saying it."

"Wow." I rubbed my eyes. "I wish someone would do that for me."

"Take her," said Lear. He shooed her towards me with his hands. "I can't afford her." Neither could I, really. McKayla did not work tech support or teach kindergarten or bar-back. She was a dreamer, an artist/photographer/poet waiting to be discovered by other artist/photographer/poets. Occasionally, in the most dire of circumstances, she could be persuaded to au pair at incredible rates for turgid Vlodomerian businessmen, which she despised doing. She was otherwise occupied with waiting to begin her life as she had envisaged it before her slide into destitution. She called this state "accumulating personality."

When I asked her the third question of the four inescapable questions of Visegrad icebreaking protocol (What do you do?), she told me, "I'm taking some time for myself, thinking about applying to graduate school in the fall." This caused Lear to grunt and roll his eyes, which caused her to lean in and kiss me while Lear was in the bathroom.

"Maybe next time," she said, "I can tell you what you look like when you're expecting it."

It was this sort of response to inescapable Vlodomerian icebreaking questions that convinced me to spend the night on her living room couch after Lear had nodded off in the Galician Whale (he had not slept the day before). And so there was no confusion on returning home, McKayla roused him to bang out a percussive symphony that was, in volume and rhythmic diversity, the equivalent of Deco Kulpa's Vlodomerian Rhapsody, displacing a squadron of pigeons that began to fight or copulate around the skylight window overhead.

I found, lying there among the blankets, that I did not care.

I did not care that the Spanish girl had not kissed me, or that McKayla had done so only to get back at Lear, or about the awful racket the pigeons were making, or that I was on the wrong side of my Schengen Area visa, or that I had no prospects and no one in the country on whom I could rely.

This feeling, which began as not caring, was the feeling that things could no longer go on as they had, that the presence of McKayla and Lear represented a colossal shift away from who I had been, and that the suspicion I had entertained as I disembarked from my international coach at the Visegrad bus station, shoes sticking to the floor beside the overflowing toilet, would prove correct; I was brimming with potential. I was funny and intelligent and attractive. And since no one knew me, how could anyone prove that this was not so? Of paramount significance was that I was among brave and interesting people, so I could no longer be the man that drank alone in his filthy apartment and received only worried hugs from Spanish women that he had endured ten-hour bus rides to harass. Instead of that pink ghost I would be, at last, the person I was destined to become.

# 3

The doorbell rang. We all looked at each other. Nobody wanted to get it. We could sense the *visegradišag* (ˈviʃεɡraːdεʃaːɡ, 1: Visegrad-ness 2: the stuff of Visegrad) out there, lurking. One of those things most difficult to convey about the special conditions in which we lived was the *visegradišag*: that everything, buying bread, recycling, riding the tram, came with a surreal associated cost that was impossible to anticipate and could range in consequence from mild discomfort to soul-shattering alienation, forcing you to withdraw from the human experience and curl up in bed with plastic trays of precooked meals that you nurtured toward palatability with streams of your own panicked tears.

This was not just the result of being foreign and not speaking Vlodomerian, Rusyn, Slovakian, Hungarian, Polish or Ukrainian, any of which might penetrate the field of disdain Vlodomerians raised whenever they detected a hint of English, but of Visegrad, which seemed to attract weirdness on every level: local, political, personal, historic. Everything was subject to its influence, so that the most Visegradian quality was practiced nonchalance in the face of Visegrad itself.

Doorbells were its horsemen, and Visegrad doorbell protocol always involved calling ahead and letting the phone ring a few times before hanging up, so whomever you were visiting could poke their head out and confirm your presence to buzz you in.

An apartment's doorbell announced the means by which the real Vlodomeria, the immutable, dangerous, weird Vlodomeria, infiltrated your life: a troop of Galicians that could not be dissuaded from believing that your flat was an after-hours *kazyno* bar, demanding beer and inadequately cleaning up after themselves in the toilet: hatchet-faced repairmen, buffeted in on clouds of Vlodomerian profanity that ripped out all your copper wire: serene, dopey-eyed faux-Krishnas that sought to baptize you into the Actualization Method and International Restaurant Chain of Supreme Master Nam Ha Simpkins—in winter temperatures that, however much you were the sort of person with the time and patience for spontaneous baptism, made the question of being repeatedly dunked in a rain barrel a matter of self-preservation (plus, one of the Simpkinsites would sneak into your kitchen and throw all of your meat, honey, and diary-stuff out the window).

"I'll have to excuse myself from answering," I said as the doorbell rang again. "This is not my apartment, and I would hate to presume."

McKayla looked from me to Lear.

"Rye," said Lear, gazing sympathetically at me from the table, "I want you to feel at home. We just met, but I think of you as family."

McKayla looked from Lear to me.

"I don't want to," I said.

"Me neither," admitted Lear.

"You sheep," said McKayla. Someone began pressing the doorbell repeatedly and in rapid succession. "Cowards." She stood up. "This is typical of your whole chromosomally-encumbered sex."

"Our sex?" asked Lear. "Okay, Virginia Woolf, why don't you do it?"

There came the angry rap of knuckles on the door itself. McKayla rounded on Lear, and he brought his hands up as though to catch a punch. "You'd like that. You'd prefer this task, too, was lashed to womankind, knees buckling under the accumulated weight of male ineptitude." There was another flurry of bell-ringing, more angry knocking.

"Maybe it's reinforcements from the universal sisterhood," I said. "Maybe when the door opens you'll be clasped to the bosom of breathless suffragettes."

"I don't know why you're smiling," she snapped at Lear. She sat down and gave me an irritated look. "I can't believe this is how you're paying us back for the hospitality we've shown you."

"Hospitality? If your idea of hospitality is to let a guy sleep on your couch, just so—"

The pounding returned, now with ferocious kicks against the base of the door and frustrated slaps to the doorbell which conveyed its abuse only faintly. We stopped talking to listen as the action crescendoed in a half-hearted attempt to break down the door. There was a final blow, then silence.

"Ah," said Lear, "it must not have been important, since he gave up."

McKayla nodded. "We once had a guy smoke us out with dead brush he collected from potted plants on the landing."

"We sure let him read the meter," said Lear. "He earned it."

A loud clattering came from the skylight, and we all turned toward the first crystal spell of the Visegrad spring. Something had displaced the roosting pigeons: they flapped and toppled across the red tiles, leaving airy tufts of gray feathers. Then came the noise of a body sliding down the roof.

"Out," commanded McKayla. She abandoned her laptop, toast and cheese. Lear ran to the door and threw on a jacket.

"Hasn't this one earned it?" I asked.

Lear began stuffing his feet into his shoes. "Anyone that wants to talk to us this badly must be dangerous."

A loose shingle flew past the window and exploded in the street. "C'mon," hissed McKayla.

I attempted a sit-up, which I was unable to perform. I leaned to one side with a pained expression on my face.

"What're you doing?" said Lear.

"I have a cramp," I said. "I don't know why you're upset. It's not like they can get in."

I heard the squeak of friction against glass and looked up. A face was staring in at me, upside down. It was at once perverse and familiar: hideously ugly, and yet the ugliness of its features was like my own, hair long and greasy, nose bulbous against the windowpane, irises wide and black from chemical dilation.

There was a flicker of mutual recognition. I resisted the urge to undo the latch.

"Rye!" warned Lear. Shrinking, I turned and grabbed my shoes. Then I ran into the hall, down the stairs, and into the street.

We did not return to the flat that day, but drank in an imitation Irish pub called the Fubliner, all resplendent in fascimile Irish trappings and served by a bartender who was really, actually from Letterkenny, but who lived in a state of caricature, maintaining a cereal commercial brogue whenever he worked, six hours a night, four nights a week.

Visegrad was brimming with people who explored these lines between parody and originality, originality and self-indulgence, self-indulgence and irony, irony and the jagged edge of derision.

We took turns sleeping in tall booths that looked like stained mahogany but were in fact reinforced cork with vinyl stickers pasted along their backs and sides. We drank super dark Slovak lager beneath a poster of the doors of Cornwall and an outsize flag of Côte d'Ivoire.

By the time we left it was nearly three o'clock, which was the perfect hour to look for The Greatest Bar in the Universe.

The Greatest Bar in the Universe was difficult to locate, because it had no fixed address. It moved from place to place inside a larger bar called Bunker, and even there it was difficult to track down, since Bunker was spread out over several buildings.

Bunker had another thing going for it, which was that by the time the foot traffic had died and the lads had retired, regurgitating and drug addled to writhe sweatily in their lice-ridden hostel beds, there could be found, in the darkest recesses of its labyrinthine interior, novelty. Not jaded, twenty-first century, age-of-spectacle novelty, but music and conversation and people fleeing in all directions from fireworks indoors and fights between Galician body builders. Also, the novelty made it sort of hard to navigate.

Also, there was a drug named after Bunker, called "bunker," that was just MDMA cut with speed+.

Visegrad substance abuse protocol dictated, sort of by default, the taking of bunker in Bunker.

It was just so in Visegrad that there was a substance abuse protocol: a lot of beer and heavily stepped on cocaine for getting to know somebody, LSD for midnights in spring after thunderstorms, dexedrine for paperwork, DMT during excursions to ruined castles, endless spliffs and Romanian semiweiss for beer gardens, 25I-NBOMe and cigarettes when sunbathing on the *strand*, psilocybin mushrooms for crisp days in fall, dissociatives to phase out the longest chilly finger of Vlodomerian winter and, in the throws of January, nothing would suffice but great quantities of heavily steeped tea. There was also always, always, a drink. There were Czech pilsners and Slovak microbrews. There were shots of *palinka* and *slivovitsa* and *horilka*. There was mulled wine, grog, elderflower radlers, artisan cocktails painstakingly constructed by Visegrad hipsters. There were several rungs of digestive aids from Becherovka to Unicum to Balsam. There was acid Hungarian white wine and Portugese *kalimotxo* and honest-to-God Galician mead called *medivka*.

Bunker's upstairs, which was about the size of a twin turboprop, was decorated all around with newspapers and magazines on rods and buntings in Vlodomerian colors. A picture of Danylo Nawj[2] was hung up behind the bar, a brace of silk peonies supporting his great personage as if he had already ascended and was gazing judgmentally down from on high as we walked past.

We secured six doses of bunker the substance from a man who sat playing with his phone on the toilet, then abandoned the claustrophobic foyer and descended the bar's first flight of stairs. The steps led to a wine cellar that had been a rallying point for Vlodomerian anarchists, where a lot of them were shot by the police. It was filled with foosball tables and restored stand-up arcade machines.

We took a second short stairwell to a narrow channel and, there, we sat down and ate our drugs. After that there was nothing to do but wait and grin and dig finger-shaped gouges in the dimly lit tac barrel around which we sat.

---

[2] "Twenty-first century Vlodomeria owes its existence to Danylo Nawj, a benevolent if hard-nosed social reformer that survived corrective labor in the '70s, feigned docility on his return, then thumbed his nose at Brezhnev in a profane essay titled "The Stagnant Pond." The method of his subsequent escape, inner tubing to the Adriatic, had previously been called *sabadšaghåjodzka*, which roughly translates to *«freedom-boating»* but after photographs of Nawj emerged, sun-bespectacled in a Hawaiian shirt, relaxing among a little flotilla of rubber tires and sipping from a coconut (rumored to have been taken in the swimming pool of Tito's mega-yacht, the JRM Peace Ship Seagull) it was subsequently called *piåkorutoz a Fuggodzki*, or *«boozecruising the Curtain.»* During his years in exile, Nawj translated several classic works of fantasy and science fiction into Rusyn and Vlodomerian, and wrote tirelessly of Vlodomerian self-determination. He returned to Visegrad in 1991 and helped topple the Yanukovych regime. From there, he was washed into the newly created Vlodomerian executive, where he implemented policies that not only brought the country abreast of its neighbors, but, for a short time, left its post-Bloc contemporaries choking in the dust. He abdicated in 2008, clad in his signature Hawaiian t-shirt and returned to work in the lucrative field of children's fantasy. The entire industry had stalled in his absence, since the public was unwilling to read new volumes in anything but the definitive Nawj." *(Surviving Eastern Europe,* 427-8)

# 4

The problem with Bunker, as the name suggests, is that it comes on like an artillery strike executed at the competitive military-industrial level. It was designed this way in hopes of catapulting users straight into empathogenic euphoria, so they might skip any nervous conversation, and begin wiggling around on the dance floor or making forays into dubious sexual territory.

McKayla looked at me, eyes streaming. "Maybe we need to go further in."

She was speaking of Bunker the bar, of insulating ourselves from bunker the substance by going further underground.

"I dunno," muttered Lear, "dunno if I can extricate myself." Lear had wrapped his legs around the barrel and was bracing against the curved wall of the low vaulted ceiling, receiving gravities of force.

"Sure you can," she said. Her mascara was running down her cheeks in cruelty-free rivulets. "Tell him, Rye."

"You can," I said. I put my head on the barrel and looked up at her. Her face was clenched so tightly around her skull it seemed as though her delicate orbital bones might snap at any moment. I released a train of flatulence, actually drawing breath to fill the vacuum as it passed through the entire length of my intestine and out of my anus. Chairs scraped as the room behind me was abandoned.

"Don't worry," roared Lear. "These guys had it coming. Everybody has it coming." A troop of Ruthenian Poles eyed us as they retreated to a safe distance.

"What a terrible thing to say," said McKayla. "We'd better get out of here."

"We can't leave," I said. I was rolling my head back and forth on the barrel. "Bad enough to poison the air, but to pursue those that my evacuations have evacuated—"

"Hey," said McKayla, loosening, "I think I'm—" She looked groggily around. "*P-ew*, Rye. That stinks."

"*P-ew?*" challenged Lear. "*P-ew?*" He produced a series of noises from deep within his throat, attempting to unstick an insufficiently lubricated morsel of derision. "What a cliché." He deflated, shivered dramatically, and sat up. "Me too. I made it through. I'm alright."

"Rye?" asked McKayla.

Saliva pooled from my open mouth. I straightened up and my head snapped back, so drool flew across the narrow gallery. "Yes," I said, "I'm out of the woods entirely."

McKayla and Lear exchanged worried looks. "Are you sure?" asked McKayla.

"Sure, I'm sure." I snorted. "Absolutely. Absolutely over the river. You're such a mother hen. We should call you Mom." Lear cringed. "Maybe I'm a little wobbly," I conceded. I drained my glass. "All I need is another drink; I'll be right as rain with another drink." I banged my knee as I rose, felt hot points of attention on my retreating back as I stumbled away.

Hunching, I descended a third stairwell, which led to a bomb shelter of the shallow, World War II variety—a parallel set of stairs rising from its other end. These led, in turn, to a courtyard sunk two stories below street level.

I had reached the first of several dance floors, which was bordered on one side by a cavernous bar and whose top was cut from a single cross section of oaken wood that had been brought through the door from outside—evidenced by its silhouette in new mortar.

"One beer, please."

The bartender frowned.

"*Vejke pivni, prosivem,*" I said, Vlodomerian unintelligible under the vaso-dilatory barrage. The bartender took my plastic cup and filled it with beer that was also called "Bunker" and that, if consumed in immoderate quantities, left an orange residue on the tongue.

"What's your name?" asked a voice.

A man was standing to my left.

He had Asian features and almost no accent. He was short, with a cowlick.

"Rye," I said, surprised.

"What do you do in Visegrad, Rye?"

"I'm on holiday," I said. I took my cup of beer, feeling with a shudder the departure of bunker's psychedelic delivery mechanism. I remembered that I had not paid, and glanced curiously down the bar after the retreating staff.

"What do you do when you're not on holiday?" asked the short man.

"I'm a writer," I said, "but not a very successful one." I scrounged in my pocket for the price of a *pivni*, then thought better of it.

"Really?" asked the short man cheerfully. "Is it possible? Such a handsome young man, and strong." He touched me lightly. "And a writer."

I discovered I was blushing. "What do you do?" I asked. There were no other customers at the bar, so I was standing alone with him under excruciatingly bright lights.

"I work at the government immigration office," said the short man, "helping people with their status. If you ever need any sort of help," he produced a card, "don't hesitate to give me a call."

"Thanks," I said, "my friends are probably looking for me."

"Are they beautiful writers too?"

I shook my head and moved away. I was relieved. There was something unsettling in his confidence, since it did not reflect any outward sign of intelligence or physicality, was only hinted at by his brilliant white teeth. But in every sense he had seemed a normal man, could have been a tourist from San Francisco or Sydney or London. It was simply how he had behaved. And he had only been the third person, ever, to call me beautiful.

I returned to the barrel in the narrow gallery and found it abandoned. I stood there a moment and then, reasoning that I would have met McKayla and Lear had they passed me at the bar, went out to the courtyard. I found them beneath golden lights strung around the budding canopy of a carob tree.

They had collected an extra body that belonged to a very tall, very thin man, who I recognized as the bartender of the Gouged Eye. His name was Deddy, which was short for Dead Rockstar. He was so thin because he shot dope all the time and never ate. He wore tight pants and a tight tank top and a large feather boa. He had pickled himself, so that he looked less forty-five than a badly used thirty-two—having stalled in a mid-twenties version of his personality due to a lot of sexual validation.

He swung his hand out from the end of his arm like an ax.

"Rye," I said.

"I remember," said Deddy. You could not really get in or out of the Gouged Eye without some sort of protracted bartender/patron interaction.

"Do you think that's The Greatest Bar in the Universe?" asked Lear. His head was craned back and he was staring at the budding carob, hung about with golden lights.

The GBU didn't just move, it was possessed of a wisp-like ephemerality. You could try unsuccessfully for hours to get back to the place where you had last seen it, only to discover that it had been replaced with an empty parking lot, and then get caught up in an argument with someone and follow them into the bathroom so you could whittle away at their self-esteem while they urinated only to find that the toilet stalls were crammed full of interesting attractive people, that all the linoleum was replaced with rounded pieces of seaglass and the bathroom windows opened on the shaft of a freight elevator with stairs and platforms that had been set up like scaffolding, people laughing and singing and smoking on little trellised balconies beneath paper lanterns. Or you might be waiting around having a drink, and the GBU would wash into the room. Then, unless you were careful to distinguish yourself from the chaff, you could be buffeted along on this wave of coolness into the night. Worse, the GBU might actually spontaneously erupt all around you, and everything would be going beautifully, a lot of people hanging on your every word, and you would say the wrong thing and the GBU would suddenly retract, so you were stuck holding the bag, exposed as some asshole that wanted strangers to like him—watching third person as the trip played itself out in a crowd of fashionistas and their moneyed boyfriends who were intent on discovering whether you possessed some yet-untapped kernel of personality they might regurgitate in order to appear interesting and psychologically dynamic. Then there was no hope but to run like a maniac for the nearest exit.

"No," I said. "It's a tree."

"No, that's it," said McKayla.

"It's a carob tree, I think."

"Not the tree," said Lear, "the window."

The first story window glowed invitingly, four stories up. The courtyard was two stories beneath street level, and Vlodomerians had the abominable habit of calling the second floor the first floor, which is something I could never truck with. I could hear the babble of muted conversation through its double-pane glass.

Suddenly there came the sound of someone struggling with a latch, and a door swung out into mid-air. A man stepped from the door onto the boards of a catwalk, which was suspended between one end of the courtyard and the other. He walked nimbly across the catwalk and disappeared through a door on its other side. When he returned, he was rolling a keg of beer. Twigs snapped off as they met with the aluminum barrel, bar patrons recoiling instinctively as he passed overhead. He stopped at the door beside the window and rested the keg against its sill. Disembodied hands reached out, pivoted it and lifted it over the frame. He went inside and shut the door behind him.

"I know where that is," said Deddy. We all looked at him.

"Yeah?" asked Lear.

"Uh-huh," he meditated, "I can get us there." Then he set off, rolling, hands in his pockets and backbone pitching to avoid full drinks and lit cigarettes.

We followed him through the bomb shelter, past the excruciating light at the bar—now crowded by customers—to a pair of lifeless escalators that led to another bomb shelter of the apprehensively deep, extraordinary-feat-of-engineering Cold War variety.

I stared down the escalators, which descended at a sharp angle. "Are you sure you know where we're going?" I asked.

"You have to go down to get up," said Deddy. He hopped onto the steel barrier between the escalators and slid to the bottom, braking against the rubber handrails with the heels of his shoes and bouncing over the occasional stump of a prohibitive obstruction so as not to tear the seat of his pants. Nodding thoughtfully, McKayla finished her drink, placed its empty plastic cup on the top of the rail and began to slide. Lear shrugged, held his beer to his chest, and shot after.

I watched them go.

I stood for a second, rocking back and forth on the top step and staring down into the dimly lit shaft. I mustered my available courage, then clambered down the escalator.

A troop of ascending women leaned over the handrails to chuckle at each other's sotto expressions of alarm as I blundered past.

When I arrived at the bottom, I said, "Hi, sorry."

Deddy said, "No sweat," and lounged away.

"Try not to offend him," said McKayla, "he can be very delicate, as in he has delicate sensibilities." I nodded dumbly and Lear snorted.

Lear had spilled a lot of beer on himself bouncing over the occasional stumps of prohibitive obstructions and was looking unhappy about it.

A circus tent was permanently installed in the center of the Cold War bunker for which Bunker and thus the beer, Bunker, and the drug, bunker, were named. The tent was heated, and contained three bars and a dance floor. It was lit by LED advertisements and luminous strings affixed along the edges of platforms and support pillars.

An elevated promenade enclosed it on either side, which was designed to accommodate rows of small businesses or huddles of Soviet citizens asphyxiating on radioactive dust.

"This way," Deddy said. He jumped onto the abandoned metro track. We followed him down the track through an access door, climbing a set of stairs past an empty bar. We entered a maintenance corridor, and a man shouted at us from an open doorway. We climbed another set of stairs and at last heard the mounting chatter of conversation.

There was a glass door on the landing, painted gray. Deddy leered at us and pushed it open.

To our horror, we were greeted by the interior of a clean and well-appointed franchise themed restaurant.

"Jesus Christ," said Lear.

"What the fuck is this?" demanded McKayla.

A Vlodomerian girl bounced over to us. "How many?" she asked.

"Four," said Deddy.

"Just hold on," said Lear, he raised a hand as though wading upstream through a torrent of the girl's entreaties. She looked around the empty restaurant, menus knocking rhythmically against her chest. "What exactly are we doing here?" he asked. "I mean, what is this?"

"We're out of *pivni*," I said. We all spent a moment thinking about that.

McKayla turned to the hostess and asked, "Is there another bar around here?"

"Another bar?"

McKayla coughed and cleared her throat. "It's not exactly a normal bar, it's sort of a floating bar. Have you heard of the, uh, Greatest Bar in the Universe?"

"The big party."

"Yes," said Lear, "the big party."

"Follow me," she instructed.

I felt my feet positioned squarely atop the springboard of optimism. We followed her to the back.

"Four beers?" she asked.

"Yes."

She held open a door and we filed in.

The pale faces of a dozen men looked up at us. The room we had stepped into was lit only by the organic semiconductors of ultra-high-definition OLEDs. The televisions showed sports coverage from all over the world: water polo and women's tennis, speed skating and team handball. It was these that had illuminated the first-story window as we sat beneath the carob tree. People around the table budged up to make room.

"I'll be right back," said the waitress and shut the door.

It stank in there.

"But that keg they rolled across the catwalk," began McKayla.

"Oh," said a man. "That's next door." His face was turned away from us, trained on coverage of Mixed Doubles curling.

I coughed. "Would somebody please open a window?" I asked.

"Nailed shut," said the same man.

"Ah," said Lear.

"Maybe we should just go," I said.

"Without a drink?" asked McKayla, as if I had suggested we leave behind our feet. Deddy said nothing.

"Why don't you have a seat?" said the man.

He turned and I saw, again, the greasy red beard and bloodshot eyes of the person who had stared hypnotically in through the skylight of the apartment.

# 5

"**I**'m Wilder," said the man. He offered McKayla his hand, and—leaving it untouched—returned to watching television.

I conveyed to McKayla that we were not to use our real names by stepping hard on Lear's foot and saying, "I'm Dominik Joos, but I think we've met." In retaliation, Lear kicked me and I suppressed a yelp. Wilder looked at McKayla, who held his hand, then at me. "This afternoon," I explained, "through an apartment skylight." Behind me, Deddy seemed instinctively to retreat under his attention.

"Deborah," said McKayla, smiling, shaking the hand.

"Rye," said Lear brightly. Christ, what's the point of using a fake name if you're just going to take someone else's?

"Deddy," managed Deddy.

"Deddy," said Wilder, pointing at Deddy. "Rye," he pronounced, pointing at Lear. "Deborah. Dominik."

"Thas-right," said Lear, affecting a drawl I did not possess but which was no consolation whatsoever.

Wilder scratched his nose.

"Something the matter?" asked McKayla.

This is what liars do, they double down on a lie with total disregard for its consequences. Wilder let go of her hand. "You're not Lear Fadder?" he asked.

"No," I said.

"I was looking for him. We need to have a conversation."

"I slept in his apartment last night," I said. "I was just waking up when I saw you giving me the hairy eye."

"I knocked."

"Yes," I said. Terseness puts people on the defensive, compels them to do the rhetorical heavy lifting. The beer arrived, foamy and yellow, in the unappetizing way that bad beer always is.

The only match on TV that anyone was watching was Mixed Doubles curling, and only Wilder was paying attention to it. The others were not watching their screens, but staring straight ahead, listening to our conversation. "You like curling?" I asked.

"No," he said. There was a tittering around the table. It was the first time I thought that maybe they all knew each other.

"Y'all' know each other?" drawled Lear.

Wilder surveyed the room. They were each instantly glued to the televisions they were not watching. "Yeah," he said.

I cleared my throat. "So why are you watching curling?"

"Mixed Doubles curling will fill the time slot at five o'clock Eastern Time on Friday, during the next Winter Olympics."

"Oh," I said.

"Five o'clock Eastern Time on Friday is when Wall Street goes to the bar."

"Do you work on Wall Street?" asked McKayla. She was sitting beside me, on the outside, and, when she leaned past me, I could smell her perfume and the beer on her breath.

A seam opened between Wilder's nose and chin. "No," he said. "I'm sort of a bookmaker."

"Oh," said McKayla, "you bind books." His smile widened, filling the room, pieces of errant meat vibrating between his yellow teeth.

"Bookmaker as-in booky?" tried Lear. Deddy fidgeted, producing a flatulent complaint from the wooden bench on which he sat.

"That's right," said Wilder. "And, by the time the Winter Olympics roll around, I'm gonna be the only bookmaker with a complete working knowledge of Mixed Doubles curling."

"Okay," I said. "Why's that?"

"During the five o'clock time slot on Friday three years ago, more than forty million dollars passed through internet bookmaking clients; now the five o'clock time slot is Mixed Doubles curling and I intend to be the go-to-man, the absolutely ruling personality on the ins and outs of Mixed Doubles curling. I just need to get a little capital together first." Everyone shifted, as though they had just realized they were sitting on their wallets. "That's why I was wondering if you were Lear Fadder," Wilder said. "I need to talk to him about some money he owes me."

Lear showed no sign of surprise.

"Is there something you want me to tell him?" I asked.

"Alright, sure," said Wilder. "Tell him, the longer it takes, the worse it's going to be."

Lear crossed his arms. "That sounds sorta like a threat."

"No," said Wilder. "It's a fact, a fact of compound interest."

"Ah," said Lear.

"Ah," echoed Wilder. "And what do you do?" he asked.

"Dominik," deflected Lear, "is a writer."

I did a double take.

"No," laughed Wilder.

"I am," I said.

"Alright," said Wilder, as though he did not believe me, "whatever."

I heard the squeak of glass on wood and saw that Deddy was absentmindedly grinding his empty mug into the table. "Well," drawled Lear, "we didn't mean to crash your party." McKayla stood.

"No?" asked Wilder.

"No," agreed McKayla, "we thought this was the GBU."

"What's the GBU?" asked Wilder.

"The Greatest Bar in the Universe," said McKayla.

"Sounds made up. What's your name, again?" he asked.

McKayla hesitated, trying to remember. 'Deborah,' I thought at her. 'Your name is Deborah.' "Everybody calls me Dee," she said. She sidled out from behind the table to stand by the door.

"I guess any of you could be Dee," said Wilder. "Except Rye."

"Not me," interrupted Deddy. "You couldn't call me that. If you're going to say my name, say the whole thing."

"Alright," said Wilder. "Alright."

I finished my half liter of Superlite Corporate Dystopia Brand lager.

"Dominik," said Wilder. "Let me just ask you something. Are you rich?" The people sitting around the table eyed me with renewed interest.

"No," I said.

"You want to make some money?" Without waiting for my reply, he fished a card from his wallet and passed it to me. It read, "*Wilder Bright*" on one side, and "*THE AMERICAN CONCERN*" on the other.

I would not say that I was poor.

I could not say it, because I was not. I had made my nut by writing in an esoteric genre of fiction, which was more of an oeuvre, and which was called Fantasy Gangbang.

The defining feature of Fantasy Gangbang Fiction was that, during the climax of the story, a group or groups of supernatural creatures (minotaurs, djinn, elves) took turns penetrating or simultaneously penetrated the protagonist's body. Most of the time the creatures were werewolves. I didn't know a lot about fantasy gangbangs when I started, and so I had done a great deal of research—struggling for a few months, making ten dollars here, twenty dollars there, pulling my hair out over how a person might be ravished in mid-air by a flock of pterodactyls. At around forty titles, I found my niche, which was Fantasy Gangbang parodies of Literary Fiction with names like *The Young Woman and the Sea and the Mermen,* and *A Room of One's Own In Which to Have Sex with Goblins.* Fantasy Gangbang parodies of Literary Fiction came in at about 3,500 words a pop. I produced a book and reskinned it to make it gay, every five days. That meant a new title every seventy-two hours. I sold them online, so people could download them straight to their e-readers and enjoy them in the comfort of their own homes.

It transpired that platforms for direct-to-e-reader content made their recommendations based on genre tags. And, since I was the only prolific writer of Fantasy Gangbang parodies of Literary Fiction, I was the subject of much algorithmic promotion.

In Prague, I had been making just shy of two thousand dollars a month, but by the time I met Lear and McKayla it was closer to two and a half—nearly all of it from my back catalog. It was breaking my heart.

I wanted to be writing Literary Fiction *without* gangbangs of almost any kind.

I had already written a book of that sort, and, whenever I described it to anybody, they would say, "That sounds complicated," which meant that it was not the kind of thing they were likely to read. Then I'd say, "I'm still hoping it finds an audience," which meant I was doing my best, but nothing was happening.

If you are a young writer or painter or musician, doing your best and nothing happening is the majority shareholder of the hours of your life. After a couple years of doing your best and nothing happening, you start to have violent fantasies in which it doesn't matter that you're not being validated by success because you have become a ruthless mafioso.

That was why I had begun writing Fantasy Gangbang parodies of Literary Fiction in the first place, because I felt that as long as I was making money, I was a writer—which I had always longed to be. I had also begun to feel that writers who did not support themselves by lavishly describing chupacabra glans were pretenders and hobbyists canonized by a political and economic system of New York elites that had lost their grasp on what people read and how. This made me feel new and important.

I drank a lot while I worked. Sometimes I worked in bars and sometimes I purchased two-liter bottles of cheap beer and sat in my apartment. When I was too drunk to write, I watched TV. When I was too drunk to watch TV, I drank until I fell asleep. In the mornings I washed out the two-liter bottles and placed them in a loose plastic bag under my sink. Then I went for long expansive runs to work off the beer, which caused me to disgorge the contents of my bowels with dramatic force.

I worked between noon and five PM and seldom had a drink before four-thirty, and never went a day without drinking.

I had bad cramps because I was so dehydrated after running and drinking so much. The cramps would wake me up in the middle of the night, and I would writhe in my sheets. Sometimes I would shake a little or was sick, but the cramps were the worst thing. I also had nightmarish farts that followed me through the world and were a symptom of my poor behavior. Mostly, I was paralyzed by my fears of being exposed as a pretender, one of those reptiles of tastemaking that can be found everywhere hip people waste their time. I was like McKayla, waiting for some dire or transcendent circumstance that would reveal me to other people but might never arrive.

# 6

Wilder spent that week lurking around McKayla and Lear's building, hands stuffed in his pockets, collar pulled up around his neck. They got in and out through a second story window, which meant clambering onto a shed with a corrugated metal roof and exiting through the courtyard of an adjacent building.

It was hard work, and it made it impossible to visit them without breaking a sweat. Consequently, I hung out in the bars near their flat and attempted to goad them into coming down for a drink. It was no surprise that Wilder saw me through the window at the bar in His Cups one day after he'd spent the afternoon surveilling for American-esques.

His Cups overcharged for beer in a city where the price of beer was sacrosanct.

It was the measuring stick by which we determined the relative value of everything else: weighed in VRP, Vlodomerian *pivni*, instead of VRG, Vlodomerian *grivni*, because it was easier to use beer for back of the envelope math. The American dollar stood at 1:280 *grivni*, while the conversion rate for *pivni* was a neat 1:1.2. Thus, five *pivni* was six USD and ten *pivni* twelve. Or, one *pivni* was 335 *grivni* was a dollar and twenty cents. That was important because everything in Visegrad seemed to scale to units of 335/1. One subway ticket was 335 *grivni*, so was one slice of pizza. A shot cost 670 and a double shot about 1000, which was also the cost of a take-away meal. Dishwashing fluid and bottles of extra-virgin olive oil and cans of coconut milk, negligible by the American standard, produced groans of remorse when their real value was tabulated on the *pivni* scale.

The proprietors of His Cups had the gall to charge their patrons about 1.2 VRP for a drink, or a dollar and forty-four cents.

"You know," said Wilder, as he sidled up beside me, "when the revolution comes, these animals are going to be first against the wall." The bartender glared in our direction. "Cut your eyes at me again," he warned, "and you'll be lucky to make it that long," The bartender didn't know what this meant, and the softest shade of pink entered his complexion. "Beer," explained Wilder, then to me: "You have to show them who's boss."

I shrugged.

"Alright, so you're a writer, so sue me. A guy has the right to be a little suspicious." I was plugging away on a small laptop of Chinese manufacture, transmitting *The Wasteland: Supermutant Gangbang* to a server farm in Guangzhou as quickly as I was writing it. "Dee, right?"

"Dominik. People call me Dom."

"Wilder," said Wilder. We shook hands—"Bright. Have you given any thought to my suggestion?"

"What was your suggestion?"

"I guess that depends," said Wilder, taking a sip of beer. "It depends on how adaptable you are, how flexible."

"You want me to write about Mixed Doubles curling?"

He laughed. "No. God, no. I was thinking something more in the short term."

"Leg-breaking?"

"Alright," said Wilder, "just what kind of guy do you think I am?"

"You threatened the bartender."

Wilder made a face. "He's Vlodomerian." The bartender was Galician; he had Galician features, which is not to say that all Galicians looked the same, just that there was a certain look some Galicians had that you could spot from a mile off. If I had had to describe the look, I would have said it was like Andy Warhol but physically enormous.

In Vlodomeria, the deepest ethnic fault line was between these Galicians and the Vlodomerians proper; the Galicians were Slavic, and part of a loose confederation of ethnic groups resistant to Westernization that included Ukrainians, Serbs and some Hungarians (Hungarian nationalists were not Slavs but subscribed to a political/cultural identity of white Turanism), but there were more Vlodomerians than Galicians, and their *de facto* allies were Ruthenian Poles, Romanians, Croats and, of course, Hasidic Galitzianers. The neutral parties were Gypsies, expatriates from the Anglo Sphere, East Asian immigrants, and Africans (usually of Nigerian extraction). Tensions were constant. The Galicians resented the Vlodomerians—who were generally richer, more urbanized, and could frequently be heard saying, "Everyone in the country is Vlodomerian. The country is called Vlodomeria, after all"—but had a deeper feud with the Ukrainians, who still occupied the historical Galician capital in Halych and thought of Galicians as a wayward little brother ethnicity. As a result, Ukrainians spent a lot of time in Visegrad tiptoeing around the subject of Ukrainian supremacy. Ukrainians and Galicians both resented the Poles, though not especially the Ruthenian ones, with whom they had enjoyed an even more storied back and forth than they had with the Galicians (Galician serfs had turned on Polish noblemen during an uprising against the Hapsburgs, massacring them until the Austrian military was obliged to step in on their behalf). The Ruthenian Poles, in turn, were embittered toward the Vlodomerians, due to feuds derived from Polish–Czechoslovak border conflicts during the interwar period. Of similar scope was the rift between Slovaks and ethnic Hungarians, which stemmed from their shared border in the Carpathians and some laws in that same region that, for instance, made it illegal to sing in Hungarian in public. Yet, for reasons surpassing understanding, Hungarians and Poles shared a fierce sense of camaraderie, perhaps out of a mutual distaste for Czechs. The Balkan Peoples did not seem to mind anyone else, but despised each other. Romanians loathed, and were loathed by, Hungarians, Moldovans and Galitzianers. Galitzianers didn't like anyone, but especially disliked Lithuanian Jews (Litvaks), who they called 'crossheads' for their detestable habits of assimilation.[3]

"Weren't you worried he'd take it the wrong way?" I asked.

"Who," asked Wilder, "Danylo over there?" He nodded toward the Galician bartender. "He's a lamb. Aren't you, Danylo?" The bartender frowned. "Hey, want to have a lot of fun for free?

---

[3] The Vlodomerian linguist József Magfalvy said of these divisions in his classic, *Vlodomerian Ethnography*, "It must be from the problems and frustrations of nearly understanding one's own neighbor that the worst prejudices are derived. It is harder for a Vlodomerian to hate a Galician, who cannot be understood but occupies a special place in the fabric of life (much like it is difficult to hate the village idiot, though he is occasionally beaten out of frustration) than to hate a Hungarian who so nearly speaks Vlodomerian but whose speech is rife with Turkish contaminates." (54) It should be noted that later in *Vlodomerian Ethnography* can be found the passage, "While all the peoples of Vlodomeria are vibrant and important, none have been more civilizing than the Germanized Vlodomerians, Hungarians and Austrians to who we owe the very idea of nationhood, and none more prolific than the Jews, whose quickly growing number is a threat to the independence and welfare of all other peoples." (336) Perhaps a more pragmatic and contemporary guide to ethnic divisions can be found in Thom Elliott's *Surviving Eastern Europe*, which states, "Just as it is a shock to discover the variety of white ethnic groups that inhabit all parts of Eastern Europe and are proud of their distinctive traditional costumes that seldom amount to more than variations on the theme of embroidered linen frocks, it is a shock to discover that they guard these differences jealously and are capable (with little or no provocation) of swearing up and down that, however slight the differences in a neighbor's embroidered linen frock, they and their embroiderers should be expunged from the record of history. The greater the number of similarities between the embroidered frocks in question, the louder the calls for genocide." (19) In the section devoted to Vlodomeria, specifically, Elliott writes, "Conversations about race in Visegrad are never fruitful. They are easy to avoid, since Vlodomerians never raise the subject." (407)

Stand at the top of the metro and shout, 'Hey, Danylo!'" The bartender began to walk purposefully in our direction.

"Want to hear another?" asked Wilder.

I shook my head.

"Know how to make Helen Keller less useful?" I stared at him. "Teach her Rusyn."

The bartender hit Wilder on the nose with a left-hand jab. He sat down, dazed, clutching the bar to keep from falling onto his back.

"Sorry," said the Galician. He nodded apologetically at my laptop. I looked down to see that my glass was overturned and that my keyboard was filling with beer. Its screen snapped off.

"Alright," said Wilder. He got gingerly to his feet, holding his nose. "Alright, whoops."

I turned the laptop over and began to remove the small black screws that held its bottom in place. I opened the wet casing, disconnected the ribbon clip to my keyboard and pulled out my hard drive. Everything was drenched.

"That one's on me." said Wilder. He quaffed his beer, blood dripping from his nose into the glass and producing inky clouds of brown. When he was finished, he belched and wiped his mouth. "Where to now?"

The Gouged Eye sat at the very bottom of a north-south gutter set between two short hills, which was the very bottom of Visegrad too. All the music and beer and dog shit rolled downhill into this gutter. It was the only topographical feature east of the Volodymy.

Halfway there we stopped at a National Tobacco Distributor so he could buy cigarettes. He offered me one and we smoked together, walking the steep, cobbled streets and venting clouds that hung in the air beneath gas lights in the wet atmosphere of early spring.

Then Wilder began to talk about how he made money.

# 7

Cigarettes could be purchased in Visegrad only at National Tobacco Distributors, due to the machinations of the leader of the Vlodomerian Togetherness Party, Vidor Kárbon.

Kárbon was short, about five-foot-five, but he had a strong body and thick, expressive eyebrows that magnified his emotions. The emotions they magnified most were those associated with humoring someone who is explaining something you know how to do before doing it yourself.

He had been a student activist during the political unrest of the 90s and later helped to form a coalition of conservative interests who had been forced to bide their time under the charismatic Nawj. After Nawj left power, the Togetherness Party formed a united front against the fractured Vlodomerian left, and installed Kárbon as their *Premiér*. In return, Kárbon helped them establish a super-majority in the *Soim* and began rewriting the constitution.

Spoken Ukrainian and Polish were outlawed in public buildings. Education budgets were slashed, as was social welfare. He nationalized tobacco and distributed the contracts to party loyalists. He banned all prayer in school, except Christian prayer, which was made mandatory. He posted large billboards in the Vlodomerian language (which twenty percent of Vlodomerians could not read) that proclaimed immigrants unwelcome and

Vlodomeria to be a white nation. In a sense, the country belonged to him.[4]

But it was the anti-globalist, protectionist, nationalist and isolationist policies of Vidor Kárbon that predicated our living there.

In order to extract funds from Brussels, it was necessary that Vlodomeria appear ready to leave the European Union at a moment's notice, and, to this end, Kárbon had spearheaded a piece of legislation called The Togetherness Heightened Security Resolution. The resolution said that, as long as there existed a threat to Vlodomerian security, Vlodomerian Defense Forces could exercise their sovereign right to protect citizens by elevating the rate of random checks at their nation's borders. Since the day of the resolution's passage, the rate of random security checks had been elevated to a rate of 100 percent.

On the off chance no one had done anything that might possibly be construed as a threat to Vlodomerian security, the Twitter account @DeathToVlodomeria would tweet, "*Smrt' Vlodomer*," or "Death to Vlodomeria," in Vlodomerian. The tweets were shown to originate from an IP address within the Togetherness Party's Headquarters, but when responding to the question of how outside threats to Vlodomeria might come from such a place, Kárbon furrowed his eyebrows and said, "Is it not apparent, the reason for the tightening of security controls on

---

[4] On the topic of Kárbon, Leybl Gorie, the ethnic Galitzianer philosopher and critic, has written, "He was as every fascist, a bully; he believed that the world must be comprised of bullies, that compassion and forbearance were pretenders to action; he believed in a system of bullies, that men must clamber up and down each other like ladders and that the only force mightier than the self-interest of others was his own self-interest, which became—to him—the measure of his will." (*My Poor Country*, 13) Thom Elliott writes, "Reports that Kárbon is a Hitler or a Stalin are exaggerated. The Togetherness coalition was formed and its grip assured, not just by the unscrupulous methods of its core political engine, but by the votes of agrarian constituents pining for a return to a more conservative time that never existed. He rules by the disenfranchisement of the young and the dogged obedience of the elderly. He is the executive to a Curmudgeonocracy." (*Surviving Eastern Europe*, 415)

our fragile nation, when there are signs of our government's complete infiltration?"

During elevated random security checks a small red stamp was placed in your passport that showed your dates of exit and entry. Of course, this system was actually implemented in order to prevent African and Middle Eastern migrants from passing through other parts of Europe in order to reach Vlodomeria, which none did.

It didn't make sense to pass through other parts of Europe to get to Vlodomeria, because all the other parts of Europe were wealthier and safer and more hospitable than Vlodomeria. It had once made sense to pass through Vlodomeria to get to other parts of Europe, but after The Togetherness Heightened Security Resolution it didn't make sense to do that anymore, either. So the elevated random security checks were effective only in keeping migrants out of a country they did not want to enter.

What made the difference to us, was that these border controls turned Vlodomeria into the default extraction point for expatriates that had overstayed their welcome in Paris, Vienna, Athens, Berlin and Prague, since the Vlodomerian Defense Forces ignored Schengen entrance and exit dates in favor of the small red stamps. There were no controls on the way out of Vlodomeria, but, in accordance with the principle of least action, men and women stopped commuting from their apartments in Paris, Vienna, Athens, Berlin and Prague, and rented apartments in Visegrad, instead.

It was also these anti-globalist, protectionist, nationalist and isolationist policies that allowed Wilder to make money, because he made it by collecting the student loans of other Americans. He bought the debt at a rate of about one half a cent on the dollar, and never at a rate of more than five cents. He did not tell me how he purchased these debts, exactly, but he did tell me that the debt was so cheap because the debt holders had moved abroad and were years delinquent.

It was supposed to be impossible for Wilder to buy individual debt like that.

He made his routine collections through a dummy application on the Play Store, which disguised payments as tokens users could exchange for loot boxes. The loot boxes contained only valueless cosmetic alterations to the dummy application's UI, and were a form of legalized gambling that helped explain the large amounts of money changing hands. Wilder deposited the proceeds in a bank in New Hampshire.

"Why New Hampshire?" I asked.

We stopped and waited for a streetcar to pass. It sparked along its hanging guide cables, soft interior glowing warmly. I could see the Gouged Eye's neon sign, a punctured iris bleeding hot jelly.

"Tax reasons," said Wilder.

"It's not illegal?"

We reached the door in silence. Wilder stood a little straighter as he turned to watch me think. For a moment, he seemed dignified and academic, hair miraculously free of his face. I detected only the faintest echo of his fulminating curiosity before he doubled over and stomped out his cigarette on the pink cement. He spit. The long tresses of hair bounced back across his forehead and the neon light shone on the drying blood around his mouth. "Who knows?" he said.

# 8

The Gouged Eye was a place where excessive consumption of every kind was not just permitted but encouraged: not to get ripped and laid, but because its customers relished their addictions. These were the professional tier quasi-functional monstrosities, the early-induction-into-The-Hall-of-Famers of suicide in public.

Deddy waved to me as I walked in, stopped, and retracted his hand as he saw Wilder, then leaned over and said something to a man at the bar. Without looking up or speaking, the man stood, made his way to the bathroom, and climbed out the window.

"Was that Ken Paulsen?" asked Wilder. The whole bar was eyeballing us now, dark red badge in Wilder's beard and mustache.

"I dunno who that was," said Deddy.

"Alright," said Wilder. He grinned. "Try and do somebody a favor. *Horilka* and a *pivni*, please."

While Deddy poured, I asked, "Why me? I mean, if you've got such a sure thing, you're making all this money—"

"I just wanted to keep you abreast of the opportunity."

"That's why you got me eighty-sixed from His Cups and destroyed my computer? To keep me abreast?"

"Galicians are animals. Also"—he cleared his throat—"I should tell you, I bought Lear Fadder's debt." He punctuated this confession with a meaningful look.

"What's that got to do with me?"

"I thought you might want to help him, since you know him. At the same time, I thought you might help yourself."

"You got it all wrong. I just met the guy."

"Yeah?" asked Wilder.

"Sorry I can't help you," I said. "I wouldn't know where to start."

"Rye," called Lear.

He was standing at the far end of the bar, waving. He recognized Wilder and hesitated for a moment, hiccup in the motion of his elbow magnified by the arc of his hand.

"He likes to announce himself," I said.

Lear slouched forward. "Wilder," he drawled.

"Rye," confirmed Wilder.

Lear said, "I thought you were working."

"I was. There was an accident involving my laptop."

Wilder scratched his head. "The indirect result of me antagonizing a Galician."

"Ah," said Lear, "Galicians are a lotta savages."

"I'm glad we see eye-to-eye on Galicians," said Wilder.

"I can't stand Polacks either," said Lear, "or Gregorys."

A 'Gregory' is what we called a Vlodomerian. It was an expatriate habit imported from former Czechoslovakia, where expats called Czechs Gregorys because Czech rhymes with Peck. Also, it should be made clear that Gregory was a byword for a specific subset of Vlodomerians that we came to identify with Gregory-ness. That is to say, many Vlodomerians were kind and open-hearted, and not Gregorys at all; but Gregorys, no matter their points of origin, seemed universally possessed of a special quality that many Vlodomerians had in spades. This was the suspicion that you were about to make their life more difficult in some undiscovered way, that you were fighting the urge to break into their apartment and track mud all over the place. You had to forgive them this, since, we all agreed, it was the product of life in the *visegradišag*. As far as we were concerned there were Galitzianer Gregorys, Ukrainian Gregorys and Polish Gregorys. There were Chinese Gregs that worked in Beijing and Indonesian Gregs that lived on paradisiacal islands and British Gregorys from Hull. But Visegrad had the greatest concentration of Gregorys in the world, even more than New York City.

The Vlodomerians, in return, called us "potatoheads," because we couldn't pronounce their word for potato. The Vlodomerian word for potato has a special elegance that the Anglo tongue cannot replicate.

Whenever you tried to order chips or fries in Vlodomerian, you could spot a Gregory because they made a face like you were pelting them with bits of ground up complex carbohydrates. The Vlodomerian word for potato was *brámbörly; brámbörly* may not look like much, but Vlodomerian is a difficult language. The total number of letters in the Vlodomerian alphabet is approximately fifty-three, *approximately* because *x* and *w*— usually *ł*—exist only in loanwords, which would, with their inclusion, bring the total to fifty-five. It contains five sounds that are not used in English, and has many more that are, but are not given letters: four *o*'s, four *u*'s, three *i*'s, three *y*'s and only a couple of *e*'s, which is to make up for its immoral plethora of *a*'s (of which there are six). It has one letter, *kk*, which is never sounded, but whose existence has become a political question in the debate over the inclusion of Vlodomerian in the Finno-Ugric language family.

Once you have trained eye and mouth to read and make these sounds perfectly, *perfectly* because it is an incomparably phonetic language, you must begin learning grammar and vocabulary.

"I'd take a Gregory over a Hun," said Wilder.

"Really?" asked Lear.

"Sure," said Wilder, "Hungarians are a race of subhuman monsters."

"We're in back," said Lear.

"One second." Wilder raised his little glass of *horilka* into the light. We clinked and shot. Then he tucked his hands into his armpits and flapped his elbows.

Lear led us to a pair of small tables, set away from a large projection screen that played turn of the century music videos. McKayla sat by herself, nursing her drink and glaring daggers at a slew of Nazis that were kicking back, having a pretty good time. They were not white supremacists with shaved heads and overalls, but actual jackbooted Waffen-SS with helmets shaped like coal scuttles.

Visegrad was cheaper for film crews to shoot in than Prague, Budapest and Bucharest, each of which was cheaper than Paris, Berlin and Rome; spring was the season for shooting and, like starlings returning to the field, costumed extras had descended on the city in the uniforms of the Gestapo, Stasi, NKVD, and—worst of all—Iron Trout: Vlodomerian fascists that had massacred Visegrad's Galitzianer Jews in the last days of the German occupation.

It was not uncommon to round a corner on your way home through some old neighborhood and find the entire street decorated with gigantic swastikas set on four-story banners of evil crimson. To round such a corner at night, bloodstream thick with psychotropic flotsam, always gave one a special shock.

How, when Visegrad was the frayed tip of this raw nerve, could it be that men regularly paraded through the city dressed as the perpetrators of humanity's worst crimes? It was simply that the Iron Trout had done their job so well that there were very few Galitzianers left to voice their objections.

McKayla glared at the actors as they leaned back with their jackboots unlaced, helmets in their laps, smoking long filter cigarettes. The longer they sat there, talking happily amongst themselves, the more incapable they seemed of noticing McKayla, and the more McKayla seemed unable to differentiate them from the genuine article. After half an hour, an actor wearing an *Oberführer's* uniform finally leaned in and said, "Excuse me." Lear and I held our breath. We had been pretending not to notice McKayla's protracted seething, hoping that the costumed extras would receive a call and return to set. "We are doing something to offend you?" he asked.

McKayla made a noise like she was dislodging peanut butter from the roof of her mouth. "I think it's in bad taste, is all."

The Waffen-SS exchanged looks. "We are actors," explained the *Oberführer*.

"I know that," said McKayla.

"I mean," he said, hesitating, "we are not actual Nazis."

"That's no excuse," said McKayla. "You shouldn't be walking around dressed like that without taking people's feelings into account."

The Officer laughed. "I mean we are not *völkisch* or something like this. I am a socialist. I hold two advanced degrees. Mikel is an anarchist," he pointed to a man in a greatcoat who waved gingerly. "Béla is a homosexual and a member of the Visegrad Actor's Union. David is Jewish."

"Then you should know better."

"I think we're all sorta on the same page, politically," said Lear. McKayla rounded on him and the Waffen-SS grinned.

"You know," said Wilder absently, "I always wondered what it'd be like to kill a Nazi." A piccolo blast of giggles erupted from the man named Béla. Wilder, who sat facing away from the actors, turned. As he did, he disrupted the air in the folds of his clothing, so his smell wafted through the room.

The laughter trailed off and died. They examined his face and the blood on his chin.

"We are just actors," repeated *Herr Oberführer*.

"Alright," said Wilder, "I don't think that counts."

"What does that mean?" asked *Oberführer*.

"It's more like big game hunting, like hunting rhinos and lions. You know, nobody that goes to Africa and hunts lions is ever upset they're bagging big game on a fenced reserve. They're not dressing up in grass skirts and using spears, is what I'm saying. They do it because they love killing lions. I think that's what it'd be like to kill a Nazi. Americans have a cultural mythology around killing Nazis that's wired into our reward system from watching too much TV. Killing Nazis is more American than a Super Bowl-winning pass to a cowboy liberating the French on the Fourth of July. Does it really matter if it's some poor old lion, all busted up, all spoiled, not even knowing he's a lion anymore? For that kind of gratification I'd kill a Nazi even if he was a house cat."

One of the Nazis had turned very pale. Everyone was quiet for a few seconds, then *Herr Oberführer* said something in German and the actors got noisily to their feet and left.

Lear was sporting an insane grin, as though the expression had been fired into his face at point blank range.

Wilder cleared his throat and relaxed. Even the smell abated.

"I hope you're proud of yourself," said McKayla. Then, realizing what she had said, became frozen in admonition.

"The secret," said Wilder, "is not to be outraged. I don't know what the point of outrage is. The secret is wanting to hurt somebody. You don't have to lay it on thick; knowing when someone or something wants to hurt you has been instrumental to the development of animal life. I'm pretty sure you could browbeat a starfish if you went about it in a really genuine way."

McKayla finished her drink and stood up. "I'm going to apologize," she said.

"You'd better hurry," said Wilder.

She glowered at Lear, who was just now returning earthward, blushing with the heat of atmospheric re-entry. Then she left, walking through the light of the projector so that for a split second she was vividly illuminated on one side of her body.

# 9

McKayla had come to Visegrad to urinate on the grave of Francis Bukovni, who had been "boss of the country" during the extermination of its Galitzianer Jewish population.

She had resolved to urinate on the graves of those people she thought responsible for disproportionate human pain and suffering.

This habit, which had begun as a hobby of convenience on the gringo trail through Costa Rica, El Salvador and Guatemala, was at once a passion and a purpose, a compass during the years prior to the evaporation of her trust, and a perpetual source of novelty. It helped to separate her from a posturing sea of contemporaries. In urinating on the graves of despots, moments had to be seized, discretion practiced. Costumes were sometimes required to disguise a funnel in her crotch or tube around her leg.

She did research wherever she went, so as to find monuments or graves worth despoiling. She showed a remarkably balanced reading of history to this effect, and not only left a puddle at Hitler's bunker, but deposited small, wet stains on the cement walls on the mausoleums of Lenin and Mao.

She defiled the altar in the Temple of Caesar, the sarcophagus of Napoleon under the Dôme des Invalides, and the small cordoned-off slab in the floor of the Basílica de la Santa Cruz atop Franco.

She pissed on Andrew Jackson at the Hermitage, on the colossal monument to Genghis Khan on the Steppe, and the extant tomb of Pope Innocent III in the Holy See. She discreetly sprinkled King Leopold in Brussels and made water near the Terracotta Warriors in memory of Qin Shi Huang. She went Down Under to slash the graves of Royal Mounted Police, stopping on the way to mark the final resting places of Tikka Khan and Pol Pot. She watered the flowers for Ahmed Sékou Touré beside the Grand Mosque at Conakry, and, for Cromwell, the hedgerows beside Westminster Abbey.

She had selected Vlodomeria partly because so many evil men were buried there, and it lay within arm's reach of Poland, Slovakia, Hungary, Romania, and—beyond—the killing fields of Ukraine and former Yugoslavia.

She was having a hard time with her current squeeze, Bukovni, because she could not find out where he was buried. Like many fascists, the location of his remains had been intentionally hidden to stop young antisemites from erecting shrines and conducting pilgrimages.

She had run into a similar problem with Prince Asaka Yasuhiko, who had perpetrated the Nanjing Massacre. In the end, she settled for baptizing the greens at a golf course on the Izu Peninsula (golf and Roman Catholicism being his late-life obsessions). But she had only been satisfied by a special overlap in the Venn diagram of Japanese stodginess and historical irony. Plus, as far as she knew, Bukovni had had no hobbies.

The records she needed were only available in Vlodomerian, and only upon special request. The special request was a byzantine and highly sensitive matter to be conducted in Vlodomerian and according to an obscure Vlodomerian protocol. She had toyed with the idea of hiring a graduate student in order to expedite the process, but had been unable to justify the expense. Instead, she whiled away her Sundays scouring Web 1.0 articles on white nationalist websites for the details of whichever pit it was, exactly, Bukovni had been pushed into after being strangled with piano wire.

She had searched the graveyard nearest to the building where the execution had taken place, but found only Bukovnis whose first names were not Francis. Once, excited to find the grave of a "Bukovni F." who had died ten years before the dictator's execution, she peed on it just in case.

After she had exhausted her options, there was nothing left for her to do but to try and learn Vlodomerian, which was impossible.

When speaking about Vlodomerian, one must always exercise discretion and sensitivity, since, to many Vlodomerians, the inclusion of the Vlodomerian language on the Finno-Ugric sapling, its independence from the massive Indo-European pan-linguistic canopy, is a matter of pride and identity and—sometimes—life and death.

In 1847, for instance, a crudely worded letter published in *The Ruthenian Kopek* suggested the suppression of the Slavic question by Vlodomerian linguists and proposed that the chairs of the National University of Visegrad were either secret Jews, in which case they were naturally opposed to Slavic unity, or so distracted in mutual physical gratification that they had failed to consider the possibility of a Slavic-Vlodomerian connection, in which case they were negligent homosexuals. When Germanized academics held a conference the following year to lay to rest the possibility of such a connection, disenfranchised Galicians, Ukrainians, and Ruthenian Poles raided the building where the conference was held, and the whole panel was paraded into the Market Square where they were found guilty of over-analysis and hanged. Retributive policing action carried out against the city's slavophilic element continued through the next year. Afterward, members of each group vowed not to look Vlodomerians of the alternative linguistic opinion in the eye during evening toasts. This was not ideal, since it was necessary for everyone to glance around to find out who was, or was not, looking in their direction. As a result, whenever taking an aperitif Vlodomerians tended to engage in heated political debate.

By the middle of the twentieth century, however, strong opinions became associated with agitators and saboteurs. Bukovni had even substituted his false eye with an upturned prosthesis—iris and cornea skewed radically up and to one side to give the impression he was looking in all directions at once. The secret of which of Bukovni's eyes was real remained closely guarded until his strangulation and, accordingly, all portraits of Bukovni were done in profile—facing forward, nose beak-like.

Before Bukovni, during the collapse of the Austrian government and the subsequent leftist putsch, it was dangerous for Visegradians to take the conservative linguistic position. When the famous intellectual József Magfalvy was murdered, he was found with a clipping from the *Gazeta Visegradi* pinned to his chest, the following passage circled in corrective red ink, "*The suggestion that Vlodomerian might be influenced by Rusyn or Polish is like the suggestion that a man might have a little canine ancestry because he has stepped in dog shit.*"

It remained unsafe for Vlodomerian linguists to express their reactionary opinions until the failed uprising of 1938, after which the tide of the Rutho-Ugric war turned under the Hungarian occupation. During this period the language was officially relabeled "Subcarpatho-Magyar." And it was then that all the surviving critics of the long-dead Magfalvy were routed and neutral parties forced to sign affidavits. When the Red Army first held the city in 1944, the affidavits were used to justify reprisals, which included the hanging of the corpse of Attila Vovk, who had died of pneumonia while crouching in a wine cellar. Hence the Vlodomerian expression, "*Holot mént nyelvsznk*," or "Dead as a linguist."[5] The whole argument was finally put to rest through the cumulative efforts of Bukovni, who inflicted brutal purges on the Visegrad intelligentsia, and the Soviets, who found it to be a "disconcertingly ethnic question, not in keeping with the historic and economic spirit of international workers' solidarity," and so tasked the Vlodomerian State Protective Authority with stamping it out.

The VSPA spent a lot of time in dark alleys trying to trick people into recognizing the notation system of the International

---

[5] In *Surviving Eastern Europe* Thom Elliot writes, "Vlodomerian's closest sibling is Hungarian, which has been attached—along with Vlodomerian, Mansi, and Khanty (these last two being languages of less than 20,000 combined speakers along the Ob river)—somewhat unconvincingly to the Finnic languages: the Ugric branch of the proposed Finno-Ugric tree. In actuality, the origins of these languages are hopelessly muddied, and nobody is sure where they might have come from. Unlike Hungarian, which takes many loanwords from Turkic languages (mostly foodstuffs like "apple" and animals like "monkey" but also a few grammatical eccentricities like "[to] there"), Vlodomerian borrows many of the same words from Rusyn and Polish. This is unfortunate, since Slavic words have a habit of cramming consonants into places they don't quite fit. To make matters worse, Vlodomerian, like Hungarian and Finnish, has vowel harmony, which means that once you use an open vowel in a word, like the e-acute (the *é* in "hé," not the plain Vlodomerian *e*, which is also open, but sounds more like the *e* in "less" or "bed"), you must continue using open vowels and only open vowels for the remainder of the word. In Vlodomerian, many parts of speech are replaced with prefixes and suffixes, so whole lexical chunks are compressed into single words like glutinous German compounds. In English, it would be as if the presence of the open 'é' in 'tree' were to transform the vowels in adjacent case pronouns, as well as the vowels in any prepositions with poor enough judgement to be hanging around the noun, to open *é*. So the sentence "all over our tree" becomes "eell eeveer eer tree" Hungarian vowel harmony can be very pleasing to the Germanic ear, whereas Vlodomerian pitches up and down wildly, giving the impression that it is being spoken from inside the drum of a broken washing machine." (460–1)

Phonetic Alphabet. "Comrade, what sound do you think this upside down 'e' makes?" That sort of thing.[6]

When proposing a toast in Visegrad, today it is customary to pick a person on the opposite side of the table and to stare unblinkingly over their right shoulder.

---

[6] Three years before his assassination, and writing with uncharacteristic clarity on the topic in *Notes on the Rutho-Ugric War* (1912), Magfalvy confessed, "I wish I had never involved myself with the […] question [of Vlodomerian's linguistic origins]. The most a man can ask is either the cooperation of his bowels or a life free from political entanglements. Accordingly, as I have aged, my interest in the Vlodomerian question has depleted. I am not totally convinced that it is not kept afloat by secret Jews." (7)

# 10

When we arrived home from the Gouged Eye, McKayla wasn't in the apartment. "She's a big girl," said Lear. "What if something happens to her?" I asked.

"Nothing'll happen to her," said Lear. "I'm going to bed."

"Okay, cool. I'll see you soon," I said.

I found her in a *kazyno* bar, feeding 50 *grivni* coins into a video poker machine.

She was drinking a glass of flat beer and smoking cigarettes while pushing coins into the machine. Whenever she wanted beer she would touch her glass against a surly Vlodomerian's, who would oblige her by tilting his glass into hers. He had a forehead of tremendous width.

"Hi," I said.

"Hi," she said.

She took a silver *grivni* from a pile at the base of the machine and inserted it into the coin slot. It rattled, beginning a loud chain reaction.

"I was worried about you," I said.

"Oh yeah?"

The Vlodomerian with the remarkable forehead glanced in my direction.

"Yeah," I said.

She took a drag off the filter on her smoked down cigarette. "You found me. Where's Lear?"

"He said you could take care of yourself."

She inserted another coin and pulled the lever. "Hey, I guess that's what love is."

"What?" I said. "What is it?"

She turned to look at me. For a moment I felt thick and pale as she peered up from the glow of the video poker machine, hair on the moon of my face, fat on my chest, stomach pressed against the wet bunches of my shirt cinched tight by tubes of denim so that my body shot upward from the stalks of my pant-legs, a crustacean eye staring back at itself through the light of a smoke-filled room.

"Do you know how Lear and I met?"

"No," I said.

"We knew some of the same people in college, basically."

"Oh."

"Basically. We knew some of the same people that would skinnydip at the entrance to a flooded mine. They were all swimmers. Did you know Lear swam?"

I shook my head.

"Well, he did. These swimmers found a big, flooded elevator or mine shaft—I don't know how—and they would drink beer and hold freediving competitions. Someone had some real equipment and marked the inside of the shaft, 'fifteen feet,' 'twenty feet,' whatever, so they could toss flares to the bottom and take turns seeing who went deepest."

"Cool," I said.

"Yeah, cool," she said. "So the key to freediving is to save your air. You're kind of playing chicken, seeing how far you can go without running out of air. The really good guys used to 'kill themselves,' like someone would say, 'Hey, Bob, why don't you shut up and kill yourself?' and they'd have to chug a beer and get a flare. That usually meant there were one or two of the others in the water so they could get them back if they blacked out. It was like a rite of passage with these guys, including Lear. He's done it three times I think."

"Wow."

"Yeah, so I was a pretty good swimmer, had been a lifeguard in high school but never competed. I was talking about wanting to swim more at a party one night when this guy who was hitting on me said, 'Why don't you come swim with us?' I'd heard about the mine and thought maybe I'd try it one day and blow everyone away with my lifeguarding skills. And I was drunk, so I said, 'Okay,' and afterward we all piled into a flatbed and drove out there.

"I don't know if I noticed Lear at first. I probably did but like how you notice someone on the street. Then the guy I'd been talking to said, 'Hey, you're that girl that wanted to swim. I thought you said you wanted to swim. Blah blah blah.' Daring me, y'know, because he thought I'd get cold feet now that I knew I'd have to do it naked, which was not really the problem. The problem was the guy, who I had started not to like. He had picked up on that and it was how he knew I wouldn't let him call me chickenshit.

"So I dip a toe in, and it was cold—I mean, ice cold in the middle of summer. But I had started actively hating this guy who wanted to see me naked and everyone was already watching me, so I took off my clothes and they dropped a flare.

"I executed this perfect, perfect swan dive, and I was in really good shape—running every day, plus yoga, plus I don't smoke yet so I was flying past markers for twenty, twenty-five, thirty feet when I realized that I was killing myself, swimming for the flare. I blacked out way down there, below thirty feet.

"Holy shit."

"The next thing I know I'm on my back, all these kids crowded around like crying and asking me if I'm okay or gagging because it turned out I'd just thrown up in Lear's mouth. He'd gone down and pulled me out—jumped in as soon as he realized I was going for the flare."

"And after that he asked you out?"

"No," she lit another cigarette and the Vlodomerian next to her fit a big silver *grivmi* to its slot and pulled the lever. "I went out with that guy I hated. Later, I saw Lear flip a cop and asked him out."

"He flipped a cop?"

"Like a jujutsu thing. The cop had it coming, believe me."

"Okay."

She looked at me and blew smoke. "Would you have jumped in?"

I glanced around, sensing a trap. "I don't swim," I said. "I don't think I'd have gotten far enough to save you, or, if I had, I'd have drowned same as you. Maybe if I was a better swimmer, I'd have dived in."

"No one's a good enough swimmer. Have you ever tried to swim with another person's body? It's not like in the movies. Half the time people panic and end up pulling down the person saving them. But Lear didn't sit there and do the math, he was already in the water. I'm not judging you," she said quickly. "It's just that Lear's not like us. He's incapable of making the decision of whether or not to jump. It never occurs to him that there's a decision to be made, actually. At the end of the day, people like us are all sitting around, waiting for people like Lear."

# 11

Wilder was let into the building after he knocked on the security door and a woman came down to tell him he was not the sort of person to be let in.

Lear and McKayla had been paranoid about Wilder getting in and finding out who Lear was, because Lear owed him so much money, so they had gone door to door reciting speeches translated piecemeal from English to Vlodomerian, pleading with their neighbors not to buzz strangers into their prefabricated Soviet-era housing block. When that hadn't worked, they had run through the stairwell at two in the morning collecting right sneakers. This, McKayla and Lear's acquisition of thirty-ish dilapidated tennis shoes, transformed the apartment into a hyper-secure facility where Vlodomerian matriarchs peeked through their doors to estimate height and jot notes on coloration.

Suspicion never reached McKayla and Lear directly, but they were indicted on the grounds that they were foreign. And, though they had gone door to door only days prior, they were visited by a procession of Vlodomerians that were convinced one or both of them had not grasped various aspects of doors or door locking procedures.

"Yes, at the night," their neighbors insisted in tremulous English. They jabbed imaginary keys into invisible locks. "Yes, at the morning."

The woman that let Wilder into the building was an elderly Gregory who was well-known to us, since she was easily distinguished by a large mole on her cheek. The mole was not only remarkable in size, but for a single black hair that curled down around her chin.

She could be observed at all hours of the day, standing in the stairwell, motionless except for the hair, which curled and uncurled like an insect's proboscis.

McKayla and Lear believed that the hair functioned like an antenna, but instead of picking up radio waves, it responded to fluctuations in air temperature. Lear said it was accurate enough to detect a draft from two hundred meters. And, whenever we opened a window, it had to be resealed before it could lead her to the apartment. It was a time frame that shrank as she became increasingly suspicious of our activities. By spring, Lear had its receding dimensions accurately pinpointed so that he could close the window just as she made the landing. Then she could be seen through the peephole, casting around, willing the impotent hair to make evident the direction of her next victim.

Wilder demonstrated to this woman that he should be let in by not understanding a word of Vlodomerian, after which she resolved to bring him to us, so that we might make clear that he was unwelcome.

After all, it was this kind of thing—some stupid potatohead without a key or understanding of apartment buzzers (maybe they didn't have them in America)—that had cost her a pair of tennis shoes she had been nursing toward disintegration since the fall of communism.

We were playing cards, window slats casting horizontal shadows over the table, when the doorbell rang.

"I don't think I've got it in me," said Lear, "to explain to one more Vlodomerian that I know about doorknobs."

"Don't look at me," said McKayla, drawing a card. "I've developed chronic dimple pains from prolonged bouts of polite smiling."

"I'll get it," I said. "I've always been unclear on whether you close a door before you lock it."

I looked through the peephole and saw our human barometer. She stood in the hallway, arms crossed, mole hair flaccid.

I undid the latch and turned the knob.

As soon as the door opened, Wilder's foot shot between it and the frame. I yelped and tried to push it closed, but Wilder slammed his shoulder into the wood and it buckled. The Gregory behind him withdrew, hissing.

"Ah-ha," said Wilder. We were face-to-face through the opening.

"Ah-ha, what?" I kicked at his shoe. He was heavier than me and much stronger. He heaved, and I lost my balance.

I toppled backward as he barged in, nearly tripping over me as I scrambled to my feet.

The matronly Greg began to shout in alarm and Wilder put up his hands. "*Jätzé*," he said. *Jätzé* is Vlodomerian for "game," and is the word from which the Milton Bradley/Hasbro property is derived. He cuffed me on the shoulder and I looked up at her, follicular windsock rigid with fear.

"*Jätzé*," I confirmed. It would not do to involve the police. I did not want to pay a bribe.

"*Jätzé?*" she asked, disbelieving.

"*Jätzé*," we confirmed. Her face clouded. Anger replaced alarm.

A voice from downstairs shouted a question.

"*Jätzé*," she remonstrated. Then she did the matronly Gregory equivalent of storming off, which was taking the stairs by gripping the rail and inching her foot onto each proceeding step one at a time.

"I knew it," said Wilder. He looked savagely down at me. "I knew you were lying."

"What are you talking about?" I got up and dusted myself off.

"Are you ready to quit fooling around?" he asked.

"Who's fooling around?"

"I tried to come to you as a man. I always try and make it easy. When you consider the service I'm going out of my way to provide."

"Service?"

"Flying halfway around the world on the prospect of what? And, you think, you meet somebody—"

"Look," I said, "if I've done something to offend you, you better spit it out. As far as I can tell, you're the one that owes me an apology since you keep trying to break into my friend's apartment."

His jaw dropped. He poked me in the chest.

"Hey," I said, "that hurts."

"Still?" he asked, poking harder. "You still won't admit it?"

"Admit what?" I took a step back.

"That you're Lear Fadder!"

"Lear Fadder?" I asked. It took me a few seconds to process what I was being accused of. I guess I shouldn't have been surprised, since I was the only person he'd ever seen in the flat. "I'm absolutely not Fadder," I said. "In fact, you don't have to take my word for it. He's in the next room playing cards."

Wilder followed me from the foyer to the kitchen, where all evidence of McKayla and Lear had vanished. A game of solitaire was laid out on the kitchen table. The extraneous beer bottles had been disappeared. One of the apartment's slatted windows was open, on the basis of which I reasoned that they must have climbed onto the roof.

"I'm sorry," I said, "he must have climbed onto the roof."

"The roof?" said Wilder. Disbelief was etched all over his face.

"Look," I said, "this whole thing is a big misunderstanding. I'm not Lear."

"I don't suppose you could prove that by showing me your passport."

"Carrying around your passport is sort of a liability, isn't it?" Wilder glared at me. "You must be the worst liar I ever met. As a professional, I find this whole thing deeply embarrassing."

I looked around the apartment. "How much does he owe?"

"You," said Wilder, "owe me one hundred and ten thousand dollars, but because I have acquired the debt at very little cost, I am willing to settle for about twenty."

"Twenty dollars?" I asked hopefully.

"Twenty thousand."

"I was afraid of that. Listen, I can't make a dent in a financial obligation of that caliber, but—seeing as he owes you—you're welcome to take anything from the apartment."

Wilder frowned and looked around. The thing of greatest value in the room was the TV. He walked over and examined it.

He unplugged it from the wall, sniffed, and lifted it from its seat. It was the only television with which I had any sort of regular correspondence and I felt a pang of remorse letting him take it. "Wait a second. What happened to cutting me in on this, whatever you call it?"

"That offer expired. I thought you must be broke. If you were broke, you wouldn't be able to afford this." He thrust out his chin, indicating Lear and McKayla's spacious digs. "Now I know you're lying about that, too, or making enough to pay me by writing." He waddled toward the door, power cable trailing behind him.

"Then why offer?"

He hesitated. He glanced down at the top of the television, reflecting momentarily on its value. "I take points off the back of my associates' collections," he said. "The thing is, there's too much uncapitalized debt in this city for one person. Once somebody's on the teet, it's better than nothing."

"How much teet are we talking?"

Wilder shook his head. "It doesn't matter. You're not qualified. Desperation is my chief qualification."

He shifted the television and turned toward the exit.

I wondered what Lear would do, which, of course, would have been to climb out the window at the first sign of Wilder. Then I thought of McKayla staring up at me in the light of the video poker machine.

"It's all Deborah's," I said. "It's not my apartment, not my TV. That's why I don't care if you take it. I'm a terrible boyfriend, ask anybody."

Wilder put down the television and squinted at me. "Is that so?"

"Yeah," I said. "Her real name's McKayla. We're really embittered and competitive—only together for the sex." I heard a noise of stifled indignation from out on the roof.

"Are you really Lear Fadder?" he asked.

"Absolutely," I said.

He sighed and scratched his chin. "Call me." He changed his grip on the television again, and, with an uncharacteristic deficit of energy, hauled it from the apartment.

I shut the door and locked it behind him. When I came back into the kitchen McKayla and Lear were climbing in through the window.

"Why'd you give him the TV?" demanded Lear. McKayla didn't say anything but walked up and hugged me, sliding her thin arms around my stomach and pressing her head against my chest.

The SEC man sat upright from the blankets on the couch.

"Jesus Christ," said Lear, "who let you in?"

# 12

When Wilder worked alone he anticipated 10 percent. If you were working under him, he made closer to 5 percent, and took the remaining points out of what you owed him. Everyone who worked for Wilder owed him something. He was acquiring debt from all over America at a rate of 3–5 percent, so when the system worked, he was making a 300–2,000 percent profit, which is the single largest margin I have ever heard of. Or, to put it another way, it was a higher return than the Spanish crown saw for discovering America.

If you had the right clients, you could pay him back and make a killing at the same time.

On average, people in Visegrad made an annual wage of 15,000 USD, or 13,300 Vlodomerian *pivni*, but an expat could survive on about 12,000 USD, or 9,000 VRP. The name of the game, therefore, was to get as much of that spare 3,000 USD (2,500 *pivni*) as possible, without structuring a payment plan that would cause them to cut and run. If a client had an inheritance coming or a wealthy sibling, you might adjust their payments accordingly, but, in general, with an average student loan debt of 18,000 USD (15,000 *pivni*), and Wilder expecting 5 percent plus the 5 percent you owed him, there was a difference of about 1,000 beers you might squirrel away into your own pocket.

Often, your ability to earn depended on the size of the debt you were collecting. For example, if you secured a client with a student loan of only 7,500 *pivni*, you could get them to pay about a third of the principal (depending on how you rated his income and any potentially liquid human relationships). However, if your client had attended private school there was a chance he/she was sitting on a debt closer to a hundred thousand. Then you were screwing the pooch on shit creek; Wilder would still want his 5–10 percent, and you had to get ten grand (or 8,333 *pivni*) out of the poor bastard just to break even. You either structured a plan with a low rate, maybe 4 percent per annum for 3.3 years, and hoped his/ her degree in Movement at Sara Lawrence had prepared them for career advancement at whatever English immersion school they were slaving away at, or you brought them in as a collector, taking 5 percent out of their end, the same way Wilder took 5 percent out of yours.

Wilder was amenable to this mostly because he had no legal right to be collecting debt over state lines anyway, much less on the other side of the Atlantic. If a client had all the facts, they could usually get him down to around 4 percent, from which Wilder might still be making a tidy profit. In this way, the rest of us were Wilder's means of taking out insurance against himself.

Even if you structured a debt to be paid down over the course of multiple years, like you did with a really bad client, you didn't see dime one unless Wilder got what he was owed.

Another problem was turnover, not of the product, which never expired, but of clients.

Americans spent an average of fifteen months in Visegrad. Assuming a population of 60,000 anglophone expatriates, of which the Americans comprised roughly half, and of which half had student debt; at any given moment there was a quarter of a billion dollars of debt moving through the city. The population of debtors refreshed itself completely every two and a half years, meaning that a whopping 108,000,000 USD left the country every 365 days. That's 205 dollars a minute.

The more time clients had to pay out their contract, the more likely they were to cut and run before meeting their financial obligations. Once out of the city, clients tended to discontinue payment immediately, which was part of the mentality that had brought them to Visegrad in the first place. Accordingly, we rated debtors on the basis of their perceived likelihood to bolt. More important than ratings, though, was an associate's ability to accurately gauge a client, since it reflected the associate's ability to earn for themselves and everyone upline on their income stream.

We rated clients albatross, goose, and swallow. Albatross clients had the lowest flight risk, a rating usually reserved for expatriates with children in school, high-paying contracts, or Vlodomerian spouses. Geese sat nearer the center of the bell curve, and could be expected to migrate within a period of a year to a year and a half. They were usually young professionals working at multi-nationals. The lowest rated debtors were swallows, young men that were unlikely to put down roots or live in the city longer than nine months. We identified them by sub-tranches that were S, double S, triple S, G, double G, triple G, A, double A, and triple A—with triple A being the highest and S being the lowest. There were a lot more swallows than albatrosses, so the whole curve was skewed radically left on the x-axis.

The *Arable* application Wilder dummied up did not just facilitate payments, but helped motivate associates to make their collections. It accomplished this by employing game design elements. The game design elements were these: you were an impoverished farmer in a third world country; you had to feed your family or they would starve; you fed your family by cultivating plants; you cultivated plants by opening new accounts with new clients.

Once a client opened an account, a tiny, pixelated seed appeared in a patch of dark earth outside your house. If the client made payments, the tiny, pixelated seed sprouted. With each payment, the sprout grew. Eventually, the sprout turned into a plant you could eat.

The catch was that as your farm grew, your children multiplied, so you had to cultivate more plants, otherwise they would die of starvation. To check the UI, you had to name your children, since Wilder had found that associates were more likely to keep up-to-date on their collections when they named them themselves.

Naming your children was one of the only things you had control over. You could name them anything as long as it was under thirty-five characters. Everything else was a reflection of how much the client paid, and if they paid on time.

You were allowed to leave your farm, but only to visit the farms of others; when you passed through your front gate, a dialogue prompted you to input the username of the person you wanted to visit. There was no option to just nose around a village somewhere, and there was no list of users. Someone had to give you their name, or they had to be downline on your income stream: a client's client, since the usernames of clients appeared on their corresponding plants.

Once you were on another person's farm, you could admire their yields and the plumpness of their children.

When a client didn't pay, the plants died and your children began to starve. When your plants were sick, it was how you knew to put the screws to somebody.

There were also badges you could earn, and non-user characters that, if selected, vomited word bubbles. The word bubbles said things like, "On difficult ground, keep always on the march," and, "Deal with brute nature. Be cold and hungry and weary."

You could do one more thing in the Arable UI, which was to leave an invitation for another user to visit your farm. All a user ever needed was your username to visit you, so that was all the invitations ever said.

# 13

The SEC man wanted to discover how Wilder acquired individual debts, so he could bring whomever Wilder was working with in America up on charges of conspiracy to commit extortion and for violations of the Debt Collection and Management Reform Act. He took me into his confidence about all this after he spontaneously generated among the blankets on the couch.

He was my first client. He was albatross rated, Triple-A.

His Triple-A rating was an unintended consequence of his plan to discover the means by which Wilder acquired individual debts.

"I'm determined that you take me on as a client," said the SEC man. "Of course, I'm telling you all this in confidence."

I called Wilder and agreed to meet him during his workout. Wilder liked to take meetings amid demonstrations of power and during our meeting he was seated on a low-cable row machine, doing loud reps of 130kg in a crowd of other associates who were listening and waiting their turn to speak.

His partner, Doc June Sr., was reclined on an elevated bench beside him. Doc June was a long-boned man and thin. His arms and legs escaped an inch or so from the track suits he always wore at their sleeves and cuffs. He had gotten the idea to make everyone call him Doc June *Sr.* even though "Doc" was a nickname and not his first name, because he wanted to impress upon his unforeseen progeny that they were to become doctors like he was—though, he admitted, not doctors of history.

He had opened his first hostel in Vlodomeria just four months after the Orange Divorce, his second two months before the inclusion of Vlodomeria in the Schengen Free Travel Agreement. In between, he had spent a lot of time developing his brand.

Doc June Sr.'s brand was one of poor behavior without consequence, no matter how degenerate, as long as its perpetrators were solely under the influence of alcohol. The sale of narcotics was not something Doc June morally objected to, but left him in the lurch with various bodies of law enforcement. "Bribery isn't free, that's why it's bribery," he was fond of saying. He did not extend this line of thinking to the fire code, due to differences in cost versus risk.

Doc June Sr.'s idea was to make his brand of poor behavior without consequence integral to the experience of Visegrad. He said that, while his guests may not have known it, they wanted the Doc June Sr. brand experience, because it was an experience free of judgment, an experience during which they could ritualistically sodomize their friends on Saturday night and return to work on Monday without giving it a second thought.

So Doc June Sr.'s brand was also to let British people drink beer out of each others' assholes and smoke each others' pubic hair in cigarette papers. These squadrons of jocular haircuts were always slightly miffed when their antics were met with less than total enthusiasm by the proprietors of kebab stands or elderly couples walking home from the opera.

To maintain the illusion of poor behavior without consequence, Doc June Sr. had purchased a neighboring establishment, which had signaled the beginning of a course of vertical integration that included the acquisition of four additional hostels, three bars, a nightclub, two tattoo parlors, a boat on the

Volodymy, and, ultimately, the Visegrad School. All would become extensions of the Doc June branded experience.

The experience had already existed, of course, as drinking coffee had existed before the franchise coffee shop. All Doc June Sr. did was create a space in which the experience of poor behavior without consequence could be packaged and distributed with peak efficiency. If visitors found the experience to their liking, the Visegrad School facilitated long-term residency permits by teaching students the Visegrad School Methodology, preparing them to one day teach other students and providing legal employment. The school was housed in an old manufacturing plant, which the Vlodomerian State Consumer Electronics Manufacturing Facility had used to manufacture diverse microwaves and stereos and TVs. The minuscule R&D team that worked at the plant had reverse engineered consumer electronics from the West, which resulted in some brilliant practical adaptations. These adaptations had been catalogued and preserved in a garage off the main building, the Museum of Vlodomerian State Electronics Manufacturing. It continued to operate as per an agreement with the building's lease holder, who was the son of two thirds of the minuscule R&D team, and who spent his days sitting in a folding chair by a china plate, waiting to charge Visegrad School students to use the bathroom.

There was very poor class attendance at the Visegrad School, but since it was only nominally a school and the Visegrad School Methodology only nominally a methodology, it made no difference.

It went: you paid Doc June for your room, for your drinks, your tattoos; you paid him for the chance to meet the people you slept with, who were paying him too; inevitably, you paid him for your job. You paid him for your right to live in the country.

"But why stop there?" Wilder had asked. And Doc June Sr. had become the second largest holder of unpaid American student loan debt.

I told Wilder about the SEC man at a dull roar so as to be heard over his grunts and the plates of the low-cable row machine.

Wilder finished his set and wiped off his forehead. He put two fingers out for Doc June's cigarette.

Doc June passed the cigarette to him and Wilder took a drag. "Alright," he said, "he'll never figure out how I acquire individual debts. In fact, I'm so sure of this, I'll buy his uncapitalized debt at a fair rate, which, because he says he's going to stay in Visegrad until he's figured out how I acquire individual debts, is triple-A."

I scratched my head. "He told me all this in confidence." There was snickering in the peanut gallery. "I don't think it would be right letting him go, a lamb in the wilderness."

"Be that as it may, the offer stands. I'm going on the record here, as extending that offer to whichever associate is in a position to accept it." Doc June sat up and looked around. His eyes were powered separately from the rest of his apparatus, which never seemed to shift entirely out of first gear. The others were eyeballing me, too. "Anything else?" he asked.

"No," I said, "but thanks for putting a target on my back."

"No problem," he said.

The SEC man was in his early forties and very together. He kept his clothes clean and, when they wore out, he gave them away and bought new clothes. He had a watch on all the time. He had deep pockets. He had the keys to a car in his deep pockets and a large fine telephone and a minimalist wallet and a pair of sunglasses. His pants were too tight and whenever he needed something from his deep pockets, he took everything out and fished around for whatever it was he needed.

To us, his car keys and fine telephone and wallet and sunglasses were humiliating manifestations of the permanent tourist class to which we were also consigned. It was not that he was more moderate or reserved. He drank as we drank. He ate more, certainly. What made him embarrassing, but not intolerably so, was that he bore no outward sign of secret life.

He had a fantastic, glowing smile, and it was Lear's espoused belief that he had self-mutilated to achieve it—bludgeoned to death some interior spark of individuality.

I did not see evidence that there had ever been a spark of any kind.

He adored sports, which none of the rest of us followed. He could not believe that none of us knew the quarterback for the Ravens or the centerman for the Canucks or the power forward on the Suns. He loved to talk about politics, and, during election season, railed ceaselessly against his political enemies. He ignored the substance abuse protocol, so, while the rest of us buckled under the combined weight of its psychedelics and opioids and barbiturates, he needled us ruthlessly:

"Hey, if you had to guess, how do you think Wilder acquires individual debt?"

In certain states that kind of question felt like he was poking holes in us to collect our sap; it was impossible to shake the feeling that, though we knew nothing about Wilder, couldn't possibly understand the convoluted mechanics that made up the foundation of the Arable app, the information the SEC man wanted was somehow leaking out of us. We would have told him anything, just to make him stop.

Once, Lear dove across a table in the Galician Whale and attempted to throttle him, scattering his valuable possessions. The SEC man jumped back and laughed, unable to parse Lear's wrath from jocular ribbing.

"How can you ask us that goddamn question?" Lear batted the SEC man's sunglasses across the bar. "You know we don't know. You just want to drive us crazy!"

"Drive *you* crazy," giggled the SEC man. "How do you think *I* feel? I can't leave here until somebody tells me."

"You'll let me know when that is, won't you?" I asked.

"Stop laughing," said Lear, which just made him laugh harder.

At first, the SEC man was a lot of questions, little questions with deceptively simple answers. Answers like, "No thanks," and, "Could you, like, possibly, like, instead of asking your questions, like, go walk in traffic?"

Then, at the end of that spring, someone poisoned him by slipping upwards of 100umg of lysergic acid amide in his beer and disappeared him from the hospital. After that he was just the one big question.

# Part 2

# 14

By four-thirty the sun was down. Lear and I were in the Gouged Eye, stone drunk. The drunker we got, the more exposed we were to the fact of McKayla's departure.

It was a terrible predicament and a whinge as old as time.

If we had been born twenty thousand years ago we might have been drawing pictographs in the dirt, working it out over bowls of fermented berries that women had chewed up and spit out and let sit in the sun—getting the stink eye, of course, because the bowls of fermented berries were for ritualistic consumption, but us feeling they ought to make an exception on account of our grieving—communicating through grunts; first, something like, "What's the point of opening up to people when they're just going to let you down and you'll end up getting hurt?" Lear grokking, shooting back a growl in the neighborhood of, "That's true but you can't forget the good times. Just because something ends badly, doesn't mean you should discount the good times. Besides, what are you going to do, stop putting yourself out there? Live on the edge of the forest like Mog? Mog, who has to chew and spit and leave in the sun his own bowls of fermented berries? Mog, who doesn't even have time to hunt or make war, he is so busy preparing for winter?" and me shaking my head, giving him, "Well, maybe Mog has a few things figured out. Sure, he's a little muddier than the rest of us, but talk about freedom. I bet nobody ever makes him feel like this," then Lear grunting and slapping his bare chest like, "Mog? Mog's got it figured out? The guy who is always goofing around with that tiny spear and animal gut and arched branch, saying he's going to make a self-throwing-spear?" and me, "You're right. I guess I'm feeling down. I don't know what to think,' then Lear knocking two rocks together for emphasis, 'But, Mog? Mog? Really?"

Instead, we were drinking to stave off our dread realizations, eating speed to sober up.

What was needed was the tender exchange of mercies, something exactly her shape to wedge between us. We were grinding our teeth, chewing holes in the cheek flesh around our molars. We had to wait it out, and, once we had done that, she would still be gone.

"This is a real crock of shit," said Lear.

"Crock of shit," I said. "From where do you think that's derived, the 'crock' part, I mean?"

"A crock is like a big earthenware pot."

"How big? I thought maybe it had something to do with crocodiles."

"It's not a crocodile's worth of shit, if that's what you're thinking."

"I was thinking, like, if you loaded one to the brim and swung it against a wall, so it left a wet explosion like a bluebottle fly."

"You're a scatological goblin," said Lear. "And not as smart as you think."

I puffed out my cheeks and leaned back, crossing my arms.

"I'm sorry," he said, "I dunno know why I said that."

Finally, a chance for reconciliation, an act of compassion. I wondered if I blamed him.

"Don't—" he began. He was bent all the way forward and down and I was leaning all the way back. "Don't use it as an excuse. Don't pretend it's not so bad. Don't chalk it up to our not being able to hack it or make the grade."

"I never thought that," I lied. "I loved you both."

He gripped the bartop, knuckles white, cuticles blood-pressure red. "I'm trying to protect myself. You've got to protect yourself."

"Uh-huh," I said.

"Promise?" He bent around the column of his spine to face me in the candlelight, no fat on his face, veins in his neck standing up like the arteries in his forearm.

"Promise what?"

"Promise you'll protect yourself."

"Sure," I said.

He nodded jerkily and took a swig of beer. All that and not a melodramatic bone in his body. He wiped his mouth. "Let's go."

His backpack was loaded and everything. I helped him get it on before we went out.

While I was holding the door, he turned to the bar and announced, "Just as likely, I'll be back. If I'm not, if I don't see you, count your lucky stars. You're the worst bunch of people on the planet. I wish somebody would lock these doors and start a fire." They toasted him, *pivni* glinting in the candlelight.

We took a night bus out to the suburbs and walked from the last stop to the D1 motorway.

Lear had a big cardboard sign that read "*Krakkó*" in black marker. I sat away from the headlights, on the access guardrail, watching him thumb traffic.

A van pulled onto the shoulder and I stood up for a farewell embrace. Not wanting to keep the van waiting, he simply turned and waved.

I waved back.

Over the sound of passing traffic he called, "See you when I see you." The passenger-side door unlatched as someone held it open with their fingertips.

"Good luck," I shouted.

He shrugged and climbed inside. I watched the van pull away, honking as it got up to speed. First, it was a boxy silhouette, then a pair of taillights reflecting on the road surface, then indistinguishable, lost in the vapor of traffic.

I walked back in the direction of the city, beer subsumed by an amphetamine buzz.

My pleasure centers were burning out and my hangover was kicking in. The irreconcilability of the day's events with its stimulant payload created the illusion of physical distance, as though I were witnessing everything second-hand.

Suburban micro-districts loomed out of the freezing mist, German and English franchise grocery stores squatting at their feet like colonial outposts at river mouths. The apartment blocks turned into row houses. The row houses became pre-war *bérletek* with gated courtyards. Compounds of the nouveau riche huddled around the castle. It was an age of private zoning accords.

The wind off the river was freezing cold. I had run out of wet speed to eat and beer to drink, and I marked the homeless jealously where they reclined on the finest benches.

The lights were off at the Gouged Eye, the street outside our apartment empty. I climbed into the building through the back.

The door to the flat was open.

Its lock had been broken out from the wall. I listened carefully, and, after a long time, went inside. My feet crunched on broken glass.

Someone had shattered the great pyramid of bottles in the kitchen. I checked the bathroom and the bedroom. All was ransacked and lifeless.

The windows were open and a faucet dripped into the pot McKayla had used to boil Lear's passport. It was their place. Without them it was empty. What possessions they left behind had been tossed.

I felt alone and sickly tired. My head lulled. My eyesight was going in and out. I went to the bathroom and had diarrhea.

Afterward, I poured myself a glass of water.

Two days since I had slept. It was in allostatic overload and I was going to cry, there, in the empty kitchen. I took a breath and released the first sensuous moan of despair and fatigue.

Colin Having spontaneously generated among the sheets and blankets on the couch.

## 15

My second client was a double-S rated leper from Flagstaff who was already losing his mind to the *visegradišag*. I had to fight McKayla and Lear for his second S and am still proud I got it.

To make the determination of whether or not to pitch a prospective client, you first had to find out their full name and point of origin, so as to do a credit check. Then Wilder would acquire their debt through some means that the SEC man wished to discover.

We had to tread lightly, because, even though our product was a once in a lifetime opportunity, it was also, technically speaking—under the most pedantic legal definition—usury.

"Why give them the opportunity to be paranoid?" asked Wilder. "Why let them get worked up?" We were at dinner in a kosher place called the Weeping Menorah. He took a bite of pickle and a forkful of boiled egg and chewed them together with a slab of goose neck.

This was the incredible thing Wilder had tapped into. Not only was he apparently the only person with access to this information, for almost six months he was the only person with a pitch. He wasn't just prospecting; he was selling us pickaxes.

"What you need, more than to be clever or ruthless, is to learn to prostrate yourself. Can you do that? Can you work on your knees? It's not a job for people that stand on principle. It's work of relative merit."

"I can," I said.

"I hope so," said Wilder.

The next day I spread a blanket in a park with a view of the castle and invited McKayla to come sunbathe and picnic.

She emerged from the gypsy quarter in sunglasses and a bikini bottom that appeared in flashes from the hem of an open blouse, like something a girl that has sorted through her lover's closet wears to breakfast. After a while, she took off her top and began reading.

"I need a popsicle," I said. "Do you want a popsicle?"

She looked at me. Her legs were kicked up, ankle bones grazing, toes flexing indecisively. One eyebrow emerged suspiciously from behind the frame of her sunglasses. "I could eat a popsicle."

By the time I returned, McKayla had collected a pair of athletic twenty-somethings with shaggy hair and a lot of tanned skin. She was shrugged defensively up over her novel, which was a translation of Lazlo Novak.

"I love Novak," said one. I detected the lilt of phantom consonants that sometimes close the vowels of the people of Australia.

"You're Australians?" I asked. "Either of you go to school in the States?"

They looked at each other. They shook their heads.

"Get out of here," I said.

They crossed their arms.

"She's not going to sleep with you. She hates Australians; Australians killed her mother."

"Boating accident," wailed McKayla, "on the Great Barrier Reef." She took a racking breath.

"Ohr nor," said one.

"You always say it's going to be such a g'day. Well it's not."
She rolled over. "It's not a g'day; it'll never be a g'day again."
She moaned. A brace of dewy teardrops spattered her heaving
chest. The Australians beat a hasty retreat, sporting inappropriate
physiological responses.

"Wow." I handed her the popsicle. "That was amazing.
How'd you cry like that?"

"I just stopped, like, not crying. Did it seem real? Maybe
I should be an actress." She eyed the popsicle, which was pink.
"Where's yours?"

"You know what would make you feel better? A nice big
kielbasa."

By the time we had attracted my swallow-rated leper,
McKayla had accrued and/or consumed the big kielbasa, a bottle
of cola, half a bottle of red wine, a pack of cigarettes, a banana,
and a stuffed pink bear I had purchased from a junk *potrivjn* across
the street.

He appeared to have been attracted by, as much as anything,
the Novak book, because he was expounding on his beliefs about
its influence on subsequent texts. When McKayla saw me she
made a face she thought he wouldn't see. He did, and began talking
even faster, afraid that she would get up and leave.

As he was bowling through the phrase, "The thing about
Vlodomerian literature and the accumulation of its critical
esteem—" I held out my hand and said, "Lear Fadder, San
Antonio." Introducing myself as Lear was a necessary precaution,
since Wilder might meet any client.

"Colin Having," he said. Then, as though he were slightly at
pains to reveal his points of origin, "Flagstaff."

"They read a lot of Novak in Flagstaff?" asked McKayla.

Colin frowned. "Maybe, but it's a real mixed bag. I went
to school in Vermont anyways. I liked Vermont a lot and that's
where I read Novak. I've read all his stuff, actually."

"Even *Staring Eyes?*" asked McKayla.

"I lived and breathed *Staring Eyes* for two weeks in the fall of my junior year. The falls in Vermont have a special quality. Have you read *The Dim Corona of Lazlo Nawj*?"

"I don't think so," said McKayla, who prided herself on the breadth of her familiarity with Novak.

"Oh," said Having, "well that's not surprising. It's been overlooked. I'm the only person I know that's read it. You can borrow my copy."

"What's it about? Maybe I read it and forgot."

"Ah," said Having, "it's about a middle-class accountant whose sister dies and he has to adopt her children, and his wife is cruel, and he transforms into an anthropomorphic wrench, but that's alright because people use him to open hydrants and tighten lug nuts."

"Sort of like *A Living Dog*," asked McKayla, "but a wrench instead of a toilet brush?"

"Well," said Having, "part of the reason *Dim Corona* enjoys so little critical esteem, and why *A Living Dog* enjoys so much, is Novak's dangerously sympathetic treatment of action as character."

"Where did you go to school?" I asked.

"Champlain University."

"I have a cousin that went to CU," I said.

"Really?"

I nodded. "Beautiful campus."

His eyes took on a distant quality. "Next to the lake," he said. "I always thought, 'Having, how will you ever live without the lake?' Was her last name Fadder, your cousin?"

"My mother's side. When did you graduate?"

He frowned. "Twenty-twelve."

"She would have been before your time. But I wrote my undergraduate thesis on *A Living Dog*. I'd love to hear more about this overlooked Novak, this *whatsit*?"

"*Dim Corona of Lazlo Nawj*."

"*Dim Corona.* Would you like to get a drink?"

He nodded. "What is it you do in Visegrad?" There we were, already at the third inescapable question of Visegrad icebreaking protocol.

"I'm writing," I said.

"What sort of thing do you write?" he asked.

"Short fiction," I said, "exclusively short fiction."

"You're published?"

"Sure," I said. "I support myself through my writing."

We had begun to make our way across the grass, so McKayla had to pack up the blanket and the food wrappers and various bottles and cigarettes and, cursing, abandon the teddy bear on the side of the hill. She caught up with us as we began our descent into the gutter, fixing her polka-dot bikini where it was escaping between her imprinted buttocks.

"I can't believe I met you," said Having. "I've only lived here two weeks and I'm already meeting real writers. I know there are writers in Vermont, but—"

"I bet you thought I'd be offended by that sort of thing," interrupted McKayla.

Having peered at her, curious.

"What sort of thing?" I asked.

She glared at me. "You think you're so goddamn smart. Well, I've got news for you, it's nothing to be proud of."

I rubbed my fingers together and considered whether it was really nothing to be proud of. I said, "McKayla and I are dating."

# 16

We bought Having drinks in The Mausoleum of Electric Teeth, nestled into the hill on the far side of the gutter. It was an okay sort of place whose spookiness did not really live up to the title of mausoleum, but compensated with great tubes of luminous neon and xenon that ran across the roofs of tunnels and wrapped the domes of antechambers in tongues of 60 mA orange and cerulean.

It had been hollowed out so various Soviet flunkies of esteem could be interred there. After the Orange Divorce, the Visegrad Executive Committee had dragged out the corpses and reburied them in unmarked graves.

Above our heads stood a statue dedicated to the enduring liberty of the Vlodomerian people. It was a statue of an Eastern Galician general that had bludgeoned a lot of crusaders to death, even after his eyes were gouged out (it was for this personage that the Gouged Eye was also named). The general was leaning on his great hammer, and, where his eyes should have been, there was unworked material with the word *SLOBODZSÁG* carved upon it (Slobŏdtʃːaːg, 1: liberty; 2: vacation). His right hand was raised up and it clasped a feather, which he held as though it were a torch.

"I'm a bit of a writer myself," admitted Having. He sat beside a window that had been excavated from the hill. Looking past him, I could see the lights in the windows between the crenellations of Vlodo's Seat.

"Really?"

"Or I was," he said dully. "I'm the victim of a conspiracy. The conspiracy has affected my self-esteem. As you know, it is very difficult to do good work without self-esteem."

"What do you mean conspiracy?" asked McKayla. We had previously resigned ourselves to Having's arcane literary speculations, and this talk of conspiracies was decidedly more juicy.

"It's like I've been marked for death by a cabal of high-ranking government officials," said Having, "except instead of government officials it's a group of household pets, and instead of murdering me they're murdering my poetry."

"Okay," said McKayla, "what does that mean?" After we arrived at The Mausoleum of Electric Teeth she had donned a sweatpants/sweater combination that she had been carrying with her in a bag of gigantic and stylish proportions. It was no problem bringing the bag everywhere, she was so used to it. At the time, a lot of women were being deprived the use of pockets. They were closing in on the pockets of men, too, making them smaller and smaller, which is why the SEC man was always regurgitating the contents of his.

"It started at a wedding in the Finger Lakes. I had written this piece, this long serious piece, you know what it's like to get the nod from a friend or somebody to speak at funerals and weddings because you're 'the writer?'"

"I dunno," I said. "Mostly, I just shoehorn myself into the lineup at funerals and weddings."

"Six of one," said Having. "Anyway, poetry was, *is*, my forte. I'm not a prose man by nature. And I wrote this long serious piece, this *epithalamium* for their wedding."

"Epithalimum?" tried McKayla. "Say that again."

"*Epithalamium*, a ballad that consists of invocations of blessing and predictions of happiness, interrupted from time to time by the ancient chorus of Hymen."

"Uh-huh." She took a drink.

"It was a beautiful, sunny day and I was feeling optimistic about the *epithalamium*—how it would reveal me to be sensitive and talented to a lot of bridesmaids. But as soon as I arrived, I found out the bride had asked someone else, someone I'd never heard of, to read before me. She was this yoga instructor, and she had written a few sort of cute, sort of funny lines of pop poetry. In college we used to call it uh—"

"T-shirt copy," I said.

"That's right."

"We called it that too. Like, don't get stuck writing T-shirt copy."

"Well," continued Having, "the yoga instructor wrote a speech about how the couple were in love and were the same kind of dinosaur and didn't have to hide their farts: everybody smiling, laughing. All of a sudden I'm looking at my eleven paragraphs of invocations of blessing and predictions of happiness, interrupted from time to time by the ancient chorus of Hymen with a more critical eye. I don't mind telling you, doubt starts trickling in, starts making itself known. I start to wonder if the eleven paragraphs of invocations of blessings and predictions of happiness interrupted from time to time by the ancient chorus of Hymen is a bit much, now that there's been this talk of not hiding farts and being the same sort of dinosaur. But too late. It was time for me to read, and it was the only thing I had on me."

Having paused for dramatic effect, we leaned further in.

"The sun was beating down on the wedding party, everyone had just finished lunch, and it was getting unreasonably comfortable for a wedding."

"Uh-oh," I said. "People started falling asleep?"

"No," said Having. "You'd think, but no. Adrenaline: my reputation in the balance—and these bridesmaids. All of a sudden, I'm belting it out to the rafters. I'm rainmaking. Literally. Clouds are gathering on the lake behind me, thunder rumbling in the distance. Then"—Having sunk back into his seat—"a pug in a bowtie came barreling out of nowhere, shot across the audience, barking. The whole wedding collapsed into fits of laughter, *fits*. Even the preacher laughed until he was drooling." McKayla covered her mouth.

"Terrible," I commiserated, "but that's not really a conspiracy, is it?"

Having sighed. "The same thing happened at my grandfather's wake, right in the meat of my tenderest reminiscences. And twice in Burlington with two different girls I thought I might love, at two different poetry nights."

"The same dog?"

"No," said Having, "different dogs. All dogs may be involved in the conspiracy."

"Why don't I give you something to read now?" coaxed McKayla. "You'll see there's no conspiracy. There can't be."

Having tucked his arms into his sides. His knees drifted up toward his chin and his elbows protruded birdlike from the tenting vertebra of his spine. "It has to be something I care about. I have to want it to be well received, to be taken seriously." He rocked there, fetal, like a gastropod that had been poked with a stick.

McKayla looked at me, surprised.

"Lear," called Lear as he walked across the room, dyed 60 mA orange.

Colin jerked. His chin bounced as his extremities unspooled over the sides of his chair.

"Ah," I said brightly, relieved I had not attempted any conciliation, "this is Rye."

"Y'all look like you've seen a ghost," drawled Lear.

"Apparently we might," said McKayla.

"Colin Having," said Having, "Flagstaff via Burlington. They're not ghosts, they're corporeal."

"I thought he might have gone to school with my cousin in Burlington at Champlain University."

Lear made a small motion with his hand for me to take it easy. Colin stared at the table. "What business are you in?" asked Lear.

"Teaching," said Having. Lear's eyebrows knit with displeasure. Then Having said, "I've just come from Taiwan."

"Yeah," said Lear brightly, "I hear Taiwan's good money."

Having nodded slowly. "What do you do, Rye?"

"I work for an outreach program," said Lear.

"What kind of outreach?"

Lear sat down and signaled for beer. "We settle debts for folks whose domestic interests are what we call balance-sheet insolvent. And sometimes also people whose cash-flow puts them at risk of balance-sheet insolvency. You know anybody from your TEFL training could use a hand, feel free to send 'em my way."

"Insolvency?" asked Having.

"You know, outstanding loans," said Lear.

Having stiffened. "Maybe I know someone like that. If that's what insolvency means."

"Sure it does," said Lear. He appealed to McKayla, who nodded obliquely.

"And how do you get people out of insolvency?"

"We buy their debt at a reduced rate. Not as cheap as it might be, because when you're buying a specific debt, the holder knows you're interested in settling."

"How not cheap is it?"

"We can usually get it down around ten," said Lear.

"Ten percent?" asked Having. "Ten percent of the principal?"

I cleared my throat. "Rye," I sang, "I don't mean to burst your bubble, but I'm almost certain I've never heard of anyone resolving balance-sheet insolvency at below fourteen." Lear was trying to downsell, knowing that he would have an easier time keeping Having on the line at ten than at twelve or thirteen.

"Fourteen percent?" frowned Lear. "Why, just t'other day I'm sure I managed it for under eleven."

"No," I said, "I know the case you're thinking of. It was thirteen: prime numbers."

"Twelve and a half," said Lear.

"Deal," I said. "That was the deal I remember you making."

Having cleared his throat. "I know somebody, a friend of a friend, who might be interested. I don't think he has enough money."

"They have payment plans," I said. "Or they did for me."

"You did this?" asked Having.

"Sure. And good thing. I was at the very brink of balance-sheet insolvency."

"So," said Having slowly, "if my friend were to pay in installments?"

"As little as one percent per month," said Lear.

"One percent," said Having, "just a second." He picked up again as he produced the flat, brick-shaped burner all expatriates owned, its corners practically virgin from not yet having been used to pry open bottles of *pivni*. He ran the primitive converter application on his phone, which required the manual input of exchange rates.

"It's 279 Vlodomerian *grivni* to the dollar," said McKayla.

Having flushed, his face shining darkly in the Xenon blue.

"Am I to understand," drawled Lear, "that you don't know anybody verging on insolvency, but you, yourself, are delinquent and have cleverly misdirected your concerns to hash out whether you might take advantage of my professional services?"

"Maybe," said Having. His eyes were trained on the tiny screen. "Let me see." He stopped. He started over. He arrived at the number again and cleared his throat. "Maybe," repeated Having.

The ground rumbled beneath our feet.

There was a muffled sound of an explosion.

Trickles of dirt fell from the ceiling and the neon tubes flickered dramatically.

Frantic, I looked around, convinced that some pressure or boiling point within The Mausoleum of Electric Teeth had been reached, that some interior valve had not been discharged which should have been vented by Having's 'yes.' "What have you done?" I shouted.

Having recoiled in terror.

"There!" Lear pointed through the haze of initials carved onto the plexiglass window overlooking the Volodymy.

A fiery crown bloomed from the ramparts around Lodo's Seat, fingers of streaking orange tipped with gold. Debris fell onto the red earthenware roofs beneath the castle.

"A bomb," said Having.

Then, from above, came a sound like rending metal that drowned out everything. We craned our necks toward the statue's feet. There was a hanging half second, then a deafening crash. The ceiling cracked, which freed a great neon chandelier from its anchors. The chandelier plummeted to the floor, tubes shattering.

"Another bomb?" shouted McKayla.

"It's the liberty statue," roared Lear.

He was right. The arm which held the feather had been in disrepair and had shaken loose. It had fallen, squashing a jogger who had been all decked out in breathable moisture wicking exercise equipment.

It was the death of the jogger that was more dangerous than the attack, since the AP article everyone's parents emailed them did not read, "*17 Dead in Visegrad Blast*," but "*18 Dead in Visegrad Explosion, British Among Casualties.*"

To make matters worse, Lear ended up paying 10 percent instead of 12.5 percent, a number we settled on in one of those moments of compassion that follow mutual trauma. As a corollary, Having became our friend, and I spent several days a week pretending I was Lear—Lear pretending he was me.

## 17

A girl was being pushed around by three tall men in black at the tram stop across from the Gouged Eye.

The girl spoke in a thick Spanish accent, asking why the men were doing what they were doing. What the men were doing was pushing her down, and when she tried to stand up, saying something in Vlodomerian and pushing her down again.

"Shouldn't we do something?" asked McKayla.

Lear and I looked at each other.

"What are they saying?" I asked.

"They're asking her why she doesn't speak Vlodomerian."

My belly button itched.

I have made mention of some obvious defects I possess, and I have perhaps stretched credulity with some of these, but one aspect of my person needs no embellishment. Only my belly button transcends unpleasantness and aspires to the grotesque.

The work of a top-notch belly button man is to guarantee that his patients undergoing umbilicoplasty do not end up like me. Instead of a neat balloon-knot of pale flesh, the proverbial 'outie', I have a spare orifice, I know not how deep. It may extend to sulfurous hell, which would explain its aroma.

It must be specially dried. It must be swabbed with antiseptic cotton.

There is no sensation more ominous than to be crossing the street in a civilized country and to feel the sudden itch of an optimistic strain of bacteria that has escaped the vault-like depths of my navel to combat the hostile environs of the stomach plateau, sparse dark hair above the pubis like grass on the Eurasian steppe. Then some brave finger must spelunk there, descend to the knuckle and scrape out its contents to be cured in the baptismal sun.

To these tiny organisms I am a cruel and personal God.

The Spanish girl stopped trying to get up and lay on the pavement between the tram stop and the street. She had beautiful, olive skin.

Vlodomerian bystanders had retreated to the sidelines and turned away, looking up the gutter in the direction from which the tram would arrive. All the way up the gutter, the buildings had been decorated with Vlodomerian flags. There was a lot of this nationalistic stuff after the bombing.

I'm not saying that you can't hang a flag, if you love a flag, just that there were flags on every building.

I remember Kárbon's eyebrows on TV. Not a drop of sweat on his forehead. Not a man concerned with problems of the belly button.

He stood beside the parents of the squashed jogger while their son was interred among other victims of the bombing. The father loomed over the mother while she addressed a row of television cameras from the statue's base. "If it was up to me, I'd tell them I'm sorry," she said. "I'm sorry about what happened in your country, and I'm sorry you had to go and blow something up somewhere, because someone lied to you, because someone told you that hurting us would make you happy," and now the tears ran along the lines of her mouth in beading streaks. "I'm sorry my son liked to keep fit and I stuffed him when he was home last. I'm sorry he was never happy at home and that he wanted to go and see the world. I'm sorry Bill read him *The Adventures of Tintin* when he was little and that he loved the computer. That's what he was doing, in the first place." She stopped and whimpered, and just when she seemed on the verge of breaking down completely, she said, "I'm sorry you think you could ever change anything by killing *An*-Dee. I'm sorry you'll never be brave and clever and strong. You can't get that with bombing can you, you filthy Pakis?"

The father pushed her away from the microphone and, over the noise of her sobs, said, "We *are* sorry."

For hatred to dabble in truth is dangerous, but when hatred exalts in it, their combined mass, $T(h)$, makes them both (the hatred and the truth) subject to certain laws of repetition, certain undefined laws that allow for the transfer of dense packets of information at the speed of word of mouth. Word of mouth, or $m/W$, has never been accurately measured, though it has been hypothesized that it is equal to the time it takes to find out a person has been sleeping with someone they shouldn't be.

In this case, the super-dense, super-fast wave of truth(hatred) had enough stupidity, $s=.5*T(h)*(m/W)^2$ (this is in mouths over words times hatred times truth, $h$ and $T$ in the mass of greeting cards needed to articulate truth and hatred in Frutiger typeface on both inside pages but not the back), to strike nearly everyone west of Dresden deaf, dumb, and blind in all matters involving Vlodomeria. And, instead of joining the fraternity of cities marred by acts of terrorism, the country was enveloped by those places where terrorism could be expected to happen.

The super-dense, super-fast wave had two effects on me, personally.

First, it bestowed a sudden windfall of credibility. After three or four years of failing to publish anything but Fantasy Gangbang parodies of Literary Fiction, a few people had begun to treat my work with less than total seriousness. The squashing of the jogger made me seem exotic and dangerous.

Second, I tended to condescend more easily. This was not entirely my fault, since I received, or was tagged in, footage of the apology sixteen times in the three months following its debut on BBC Yorkshire. I felt a responsibility to present the minority opinion, that blame for the death of the jogger lay with Vlodomerian passivity in the face of crumbling infrastructure.

*"In the case of a car crash,"* I wrote, *"even one that has resulted from attempted suicide or murder, the tragedy does not insulate car manufactures from liability. Safety must be taken into consideration. The presence of seat belts and of airbags and such, the ability of a vehicle to withstand impacts from the rear, back and sides."*

When the men realized that the Spanish girl had given up trying to stand, the largest of them picked up her bag and overturned it. It looked like she was a student to me, with all the papers flying out. He shouted something in Vlodomerian, then bent over and sorted through the pile of her stuff. He grabbed something and thrust it triumphantly into the air. It was a tampon, white in its bright plastic wrapper.

He held it to his nose and took a big whiff.

"It's a tampon," I said, marveling at his stupidity. I looked around.

Colin Having stared back at me, pale-faced. Beside him, McKayla was looking down and away, as though she was listening very intently. Lear was clenching and unclenching his fists.

There were a couple Vlodomerian Defense Forces officers monitoring the situation with good-natured curiosity while everyone else pretended nothing was happening. The VDF were everywhere now, leaning against doorways with their hands resting on the barrels of their rifles, smoking cigarettes. Sometimes they wore jaunty hats and blue jumpsuits. Sometimes they wore helmets and, under their helmets, balaclavas, so they were sweaty and squinted in the light.

They did not step up raids on the expatriate haunts or recommit themselves to passport control. They were this unflexed muscle.

"You've got to expect a little juvenile brutality," I said, and tossed my cigarette into the street. I held open the door to the Gouged Eye and they ducked in—first, Having, then McKayla, then, more slowly, Lear, glaring at me as though it was my fault what was happening with the Spanish girl across the street.

## 18

"**J**esus, there's no end to them," said Lear. Tourist season was afoot, and we were in a bar called Garden. It was tit to elbow in there.

The mustached warblers were in the city just then. They had migrated north from Africa and one was fluttering around a knot of elderflower boughs that drooped over the patio, dappling us in shade. Lear and McKayla were arguing over a triple-G client named May Mazur, a divorcee we'd met while corralling a group of S-rated English teachers.

English teachers traveled in flocks composed entirely of other English teachers who had been brought into the country around the same time by the same companies and who had gotten their Teaching English as a Foreign Language certificates together. If you could keep them all in-country, you could make a lot of money off teachers, but you had to watch for signs of restlessness and trade them off as quickly as possible if you noticed the faintest indication they might scatter. As soon as you lost one, you had about four weeks before you lost the rest (except one teacher that wouldn't get the memo and you would kick yourself for trading while they hung around and paid off their loans to Doc June Sr. who would look at you like you were the sickest gazelle).

May Mazur had been sitting one table over, scoffing.

May scoffed compulsively.

She scoffed when she thought something objectionable was being said, whether it constituted opinion or fact. Lear said she scoffed compulsively because she believed that rightness was constant and immutable and that the verisimilitude of her personal rightness justified extraordinary cost. Lear said she kept a running tally of moments in which she had gotten one over on somebody by backing them into a corner.

Example,

Colin Having: I think Venerated Actor is really outdoing himself-

May Mazur: *scoffing*

CH: -really passing gracefully into old age without tracking dog shit all over his filmography-

MM: *louder scoffing*

CH: -not appearing alongside any CGI supporting characters so as to lend fading star power to some newly acquired IP-

MM: *scoffing that verges on mean-spirited cackling, scoffing that asks, 'How could you be so naive, baby Colin, orphan to reason, Mister Having?'*

CH: -or any Baby Boomer cash-in romantic comedies co-starring close contemporaries or less relevant actresses from his hungry prime-

MM: *seizing with derision, now, grinding her ass into the seat of her chair so Having's ignorance wouldn't jettison her skyward*

CH: -or any weird screwball comedies, written, directed, produced and starred in by a comedian that habitually writes, directs, produces and stars in-

MM: *vibrating, teeth gnashing, eyes rolling with the untenability of what Having is saying, its implications and the consequences of its escape into meatspace*

CH: Are you alright, May?

MM: Why do you ask?

CH: You were scoffing.

MM: Was I?

Colin Having said that May Mazur's intention was never to uncover the actual stuff of rightness, but to appear closer to rightness than anyone else.

It was difficult to tell, because, again, this was going on at the level of compulsion.

McKayla theorized that May Mazur was trapped in a reactive mode, which made her some sort of victim. That's how McKayla thought about almost everyone, given adequate remove. In any case, she did nothing to stop Lear quoting the *Bhagavad Gita* whenever May Mazur was behaving like an anthropomorphic toothache.

Lear quoted the *Bhagavad Gita* so somebody would ask, "Why are you saying that about becoming death, destroyer of worlds?" and then he could say, "First woman to split the hair." Then, because it was a running joke, people chanted along with him while May raised her voice and pretended not to hear.

We met in the Ritual Sacrifice, a post-Goth, post-Witch House electronic Grindcore bar. A Serbian ran the place, but he couldn't even play the music that was its guiding cultural touchstone, it was so goddamn awful to listen to. The music was just an excuse for him to coat the bathroom stalls in *ero-guro* and curate a collection of expensive English language board games. Of course Punk and its counterculture equivalencies in the twenty-first century would expire among people that painted their nails black and couldn't resist a game of Settlers of Catan.

Lear was describing the conspiracy we believed in to the S-rated teachers, who were lapping it up, when May Mazur began scoffing.

"You alright, lady?" drawled Lear.

"What's that?" asked Mazur.

"You were sorta coughing."

"I was?"

"You were," said McKayla.

"Well, since you asked, I have some concerns about what you're saying. For example, I don't think—but I don't want to be rude. Do you mind if I sit down?" All of the sparrows made faces.

"That depends," said Lear.

"On what?" asked Mazur.

"The nature of your concerns," said Lear.

I had a sliver of smoked pork knee behind my back left molar, where slivers of pork knee tended to accumulate. I was picking at the sliver with my whole hand, so my thumbnail could get between tooth and swollen gum. McKayla reached out, took my hand and lowered it gently to the table.

"What he means," said McKayla, "is that he doesn't want to invest in a, like, prolonged interaction with you when he's got nothing to go on, as far as the validity of your concerns. Your concerns are sort of up in the air, because of how you raised them."

"Listen," said Mazur. "I was asked if I had problems. I didn't even broach the subject, just answered whether or not I had them. That's a fact."

"No," said Lear. "I asked if you were okay, because you were coughing."

"Wow, I can't believe you choose to remember it that way." She came over and sat down at our table and was on us that entire night until early that morning while we tried to bag the teachers. After that, whenever one of us managed a, "How's everybody's credit rating, just out of curiosity?" she scoffed uncontrollably.

"Is this the sort of thing we should be talking about?" asked May. "If we were potato farmers in a fly-over state, maybe. We're here, on the other side of the planet. It's a litmus test; only a certain kind of person makes it this far, so why hamstring ourselves talking about applying for mortgages?"

As soon as we'd passed the threshold when promises no longer held any sort of residual value in the sober light of day, when the teachers were so nauseous they were no longer even stealing looks at McKayla, Mazur asked the third inescapable question of Visegrad icebreaking protocol and then jumped on the hook at five o'clock in the morning.

I believe she did this so that we would be forced to continue spending time with her.

It was hardest for McKayla, because May believed in the same conspiracy she did, which made her a sort of political ally by default.

In Visegrad, political ideologies and personal philosophy had been more or less subsumed by large, unsound conspiracy theories that were constantly being fleshed out over glasses of *pivni.*

Wilder was an anarcho-capitalist, whose conspiracy involved neo-liberals and academics and the media.

Colin Having was a paranoid and a socialist, whose conspiracy involved the bourgeoisie and nationalists and dogs.

The SEC man was a corporatist, whose conspiracy involved conspiracy theorists, lazy millennials, and poor people with unclean opinions that he would not cop to hating.

Lear's conspiracy theory, and soon my conspiracy theory, was the theory of sogginess.

The theory of sogginess was that the primary motivation behind all conscious and unconscious human impulses was to get indoors and dry off one's feet. Accordingly, life was divided into three states: sogginess, whose defining characteristic was having a lot of cold water around one's feet: unsogginess, when one's feet were dry and one might go shopping or invent the number zero: and unsoggification, a period of indeterminate length between sogginess and unsogginess that involved wiggling one's toes by a roaring fire.

A presupposition of the conspiracy of sogginess was that there was no such thing as *soggification* (despite the existence of rainy days and mud and unexpectedly deep puddles), but that sogginess was a baying constant of the universe. As a result, Lear felt that there was very little that anybody did that was worth getting worked up about—short of them lining you up against a wall (and even then, you were usually too late).

Once, McKayla asked Lear, "Why, if everyone wants to dry off their feet, don't they go through life killing each other for the chance to get indoors and take off their shoes?" to which Lear answered, "They do."

Part of the conspiracy of sogginess was that all other political opinions, ideologies, and conspiracies were developed to compensate for a deficit of personality, which you only had time to do if your feet were dry. That's not to say there's anything wrong with compensating for a deficit of personality. Shining examples are forged from deficits of personality: bodybuilders, armchair gourmands, novelists. But it was that part of the conspiracy theory that McKayla and Mazur most vehemently objected to.

McKayla thought we were just being contrarian, which, talk about drawing a line in the sand. And Mazur thought we were the ones compensating for a deficit of personality, which, talk about diminishing returns.

McKayla and May believed in the conspiracy of assholes, which was that people like Lear and me were in a conspiracy to let the world get rotten, because we had it pretty good and thought it was too much work to make it any better. It was a good theory, probably sogginess's strongest competitor, but even if May Mazur was on your side and arguing in a way that wasn't oppressively pedantic—wasn't screeching the rhetorical equivalent of a thousand tiny insect bites over recitations of the *Bhagavad Gita*—she was rabid with tedium.

Our disdain for competing theories and ideologies was the disdain of young men for a world that was in no hurry to throw open its doors and usher us in. This was not necessarily a problem. As Lear pointed out, young men were not a group you wanted ideologically engaged, especially if you wanted to keep a lid on ethnic cleansing. He often cited Doc June as an example of this, who was not particularly young but whose stance on ethnic cleansing was, 'only when necessary.'

Doc June was a Korean nationalist whose conspiracy involved all kinds of enemies of the Korean race.

"What do you want to do about Mazur?" asked Lear. "She's missed two payments. If she's delinquent another week she'll be junk. No one's going to touch her for months, and we'll look like we don't know what the hell we're doing. We'll be lucky to trade Having if this keeps up."

The digital bean sprout that corresponded to Mazur's rating was languishing in the shade of the SEC man's jackfruit tree. Our progeny, Lil' Mistake and Boy is Birth Control Expensive, were looking peckish.

"We shouldn't trade Having," said McKayla. "Having's one of us."

Lear did some Mazur-esque scoffing. "He's not following us around because he likes us. He wants to get you drunk and drag you into a room at a party and discourse about Modernism."

Having was making his payments just fast enough to produce the odd potato.

"It's true," I said. "He's definitely some kind of pervert."

"How can you tell?" asked McKayla.

I leaned back. "I was very nearly a pervert myself. Sometimes I think I could still swing it … if I would get serious and stop procrastinating."

"You really should," said McKayla.

"I find the prospect of all that boot leather and lubricant exhausting."

"You sound repressed,"

Lear shook his head. "That's easy for you to say. Do you know the energy it takes, hoisting you halfway to the ceiling? I didn't know anything about bondage before we met, now I'm a nautical encyclopedia."

She blushed.

"I don't see any way around it," I said. "We'll have to do the unthinkable."

They both looked at me.

"Threaten her physical well-being?" asked Lear hopefully.

"Go see her where she lives and ask for the money."

# 19

Lear and I hid around the corner while McKayla knocked on the door to Mazur's apartment.

"Why are we hiding?" I whispered.

Lear scrunched up his nose and put a finger to his lips.

Footsteps came to the door on its opposite side and we heard a neutral "McKayla."

"I was worried about you," said McKayla.

Mazur unbolted the lock and slid back the security chain.

Lear moved quietly to the door and, as soon as it opened, shot his foot out between it and the frame.

"No," said Mazur.

She tried to push the door closed, but Lear had wedged his foot in there. It slammed on his toes and he screamed. He was wearing sandals.

He hopped up and down on his good foot, blood spattering the parquet floor.

"Well, why'd you put your goddamn foot in there?" shouted Mazur.

"Let us in," pleaded McKayla. "He's bleeding."

Mazur groaned.

She saw me and I gave her an apologetic wave. "Do you need stitches?" I asked Lear. "Does he need stitches?"

Lear turned balefully to me, then hobbled through the foyer, stopping in the hallway to examine a row of cardboard boxes. "What're those for?" he asked. He was holding his foot, so blood was running over his hand.

"Are you moving?" asked McKayla.

"To Germany," said Mazur.

"What?" said Lear. "Since when?"

"Come into the bathroom and let me see your foot."

While McKayla put water in the electric kettle and went hunting for tea, Mazur ran the tap in her bathtub and examined Lear's toe.

"You can't leave," said Lear.

"Close the door," said Mazur. I closed the door. "Lock it," said Mazur. I locked it. "Listen, I know you're not who you're pretending to be."

I retreated to the corner.

"What d'ya mean?" asked Lear.

"You can drop the accent," said Mazur. "You're lucky I haven't spilled the beans. And you," she said, rounding on me, "should be ashamed of yourself. I found your writing."

"How'd you manage that?" I asked. I hadn't written anything since the assassination of my laptop. When someone asked what I did, I told them I was teaching.

McKayla rapped gently on the door. "Can I come in?" She tried the handle. "Why's the door locked?"

"Force of habit," called Mazur. "This needs stitches. I can bind it but I don't know if it'll stop bleeding." I could see, now, the jagged chunk of flesh that had been unseated from Lear's baby toe.

"And your debt?" asked Lear, no hint of his affected drawl. Mazur splashed the toe with water.

McKayla knocked. "Open up, please."

"We're negotiating," shouted Lear.

"I did some research," said Mazur. "I don't know how you managed to get hold of my debt specifically, but I know that you couldn't have paid more than a dollar out of every one hundred."

"That's hundreds of dollars," I said.

She scoffed. "The reason the cost is so low is because no one expects me to pay it."

"Listen," said Lear, "it's owed. We own it; we'll sell it. Then someone else is going to come for the rest."

"Collectors," said Mazur. "I can deal with debt collectors. What makes you different is you're pretending to be people's friends."

Lear took a plastic bottle of conditioner from the corner of the tub and chucked it at the mirror over the sink, which cooperated by fracturing spectacularly.

Mazur looked at Lear. She held the heel of his damaged foot in the palm of her hand.

"Everyone okay?" asked McKayla.

"Here's the deal," said Mazur, "forget about me and I forget about you. Otherwise, I'll tell that rich creep you drag around"— the SEC man was due to be poisoned on Thursday of that week—"what sort of people you really are. And Having." She turned to me. "Don't forget Having. He thinks the sun shines out of your ass."

We supported Lear between us as we exited Mazur's apartment, leaving dark stains on the concrete.

"She's not going to pay?" asked McKayla.

"No she's not," said Lear. "We better trade her. She's moving to Berlin or whatever part of Germany has the highest concentration of *fraulein*s with enormous nests of frozen hornets where their genitals should be."

# 20

I noticed that we were being followed after the men who were following us got cold feet.

It wasn't their fault. They were just unlucky and thought I'd made them. I hadn't, really. They were on the roof of the building opposite, and I was sitting in the window, bobbing my head and staring at them. I was doing this because the windows in the apartment were a different thickness in different places, so had a funhouse mirror effect.

The people following us were staked out exactly where the glass was most warped and where bobbing my head was most interesting.

To them, it must have looked like I stopped working and suddenly made them, then began to make them in more and more minute detail. After about a minute of peering and bobbing, they got cold feet and a trio of flesh-colored balls disappeared from the roof of the building. I had been staring at them, in particular, because I had mistaken them for the most interesting feature of that building, which was because they were the heads of the people following us.

I didn't put two and two together à la being followed, until the day the SEC man was disappeared from the hospital. When Lear found out what had happened at the hospital he said, "Maybe this has something to do with the people following us." And in the same moment it occurred to me that they must have seen a lot more than my head bobbing.

Lear had made them, actually made them, when he was riding black: riding without a ticket. Lear never bought a ticket, and liked to sit where he could see people waiting at the stop when the tram pulled up, so he could watch for the public transportation gestapo. If the public transportation gestapo got on, he got off and waited for the next tram.

He only barely made the people following us, because he was eating a lot of pharmaceutical-grade smack called paramorphine to deal with the pain in his foot.

Right away, at the first stop, the public transportation gestapo got on and Lear got off. Naturally, the people that were following Lear got off too.

When Lear boarded the next tram, the public transportation gestapo was already on board, so he pretended like he'd forgotten something, patted his pockets and made noises of self-reproach, then limped back onto the platform. The people following us had no choice but to pretend to have forgotten something as well, and stepped onto the platform after him.

The three of them stood alone at the tram stop, Lear processing, pharmaceutical-grade dope gumming up the works until he hit on the idea that they were riding black also, even though they were two middle-aged, bald, heavy-set surveillance-professional-types. Lear had never considered that particular demographic as tending to ride black, but he knew better than to pigeonhole his fellow passengers.

As the third tram lurched into the bottom of the gentrified gypsy quarter, sparking and complaining as it applied its brakes, all of his suspicions were put on hold by the apparition of the transportation gestapo for a third time.

Lear surrendered. He got out a badly worn but still legible ticket and inserted it into a little machine. No sooner had the little machine validated his ticket, then a faint alarm bell went off in his head, barely audible over the paramorphine. The alarm was going off because the two heavy-set surveillance-professional-types had just gotten out their own tickets to be validated in a little machine at the other end of the tram.

Lear thought maybe the people following him had likewise been exhausted by the transportation gestapo and surrendered, but, when they followed him onto a connecting bus, they validated more tickets. This seemed to suggest that they were not the sort of people who rode black, at all.

Lear rationalized. He rationalized that they were probably as suspicious of him as he was of them, that he was not being followed but that it only appeared that way because he was preemptively following them somehow. You or I might call this going to the same place.

Just as the tram was about to depart the next stop, Lear dismounted. So did the people following him.

That clinched it and made him late to meet us at the hospital.

The hospital was on the other side of the river, way behind the castle, on the way to the airport. The city government had been making noise about extending the metro out there but lacked the jurisdictional cojones.

McKayla and I had agreed to meet every Thursday in order to visit the SEC man until he was discharged. Lear promised too, but never came.

That was fine with me, because I privately relished the idea of meeting McKayla alone, week after week, while Lear failed to show up, it being like a signifier for the ways in which we were different, despite the fact that Lear was my friend.

Usually we waited for Lear at the front desk, just to be polite, but that day we went straight up to where they had put the SEC man after he tried to cut out his implant.

The SEC man believed his implant had been in the divet formed by his pelvis, below his abdomen and above his thigh. He had gotten in there pretty deep—deep enough to scrape bone—

before they broke down the bathroom door. He did this with a razor he'd disassembled. It could have been worse, only you had to share hospital rooms with a lot of elder people in Visegrad, and the elder people he was sharing his room with had figured out he was up to something.

Vlodomeria had a staggering suicide rate that was entirely due to the prevalence of suicide among elder people. They would refuse to go to the hospital for their entire lives and once they went in they would stop eating or slash their wrists or walk out and jump in front of trains. There were always a lot of sons trying to read the minds of their geriatric fathers, in those crowded Vlodomerian hospitals.

While he cut out his implant, the old men yelled, *"He's too young to kill himself! Someone help!"*

Beforehand, whenever we'd gone to visit the SEC man, he'd been sort of pale and wistful and hadn't spoken much, but after he cut out his implant he talked nonstop.

The SEC man would only talk to us, but his psychiatric specialist convinced us to record everything he said.

"They're going to disappear me," he said. He always used that verb in the direct/active sense, and, after they disappeared him, we did too. His insistence that someone was going to disappear him was part of why we felt comfortable giving recordings of everything he said to his psychiatric specialist.

"I know you're recording me," he said. "It's okay. I forgive you." He was totally paranoid.

"I wish I could do something," his psychiatric specialist told us. He had a big mustache, a push broom. "Maybe I could, if I were allowed to move him. They take patients' rights very seriously in this country."

The first time we went up to see the SEC man after he cut out his implant, I couldn't handle it; to get into the ward we had to put blue plastic bags on our shoes and I broke mine over and over until McKayla made me take off my shoes and put them over my socks. When we got into the room, the SEC man was too tired to keep his eyes open. He was woozy from the surgery to repair the damage to the divet between his thigh and his abdomen. We thought talking was a side effect of the anesthetic, but the next time we visited him his psychiatric specialist gave us the recording device.

Then, on the day that Lear made the people that were following us, we didn't wait for Lear and went straight up and found his room empty.

We squeaked around in the blue plastic bags looking for a doctor that spoke English.

We found a doctor who said, "He is getting well in the getting well room."

"Which getting well room?" asked McKayla.

"Normal getting well room," he said.

We made inquiries. We had his full name and his alien registration number and a notarized photocopy of his state identification. He had given McKayla these for when he was disappeared.

The Gregory at admittance kept saying, "šenki *nüla*," which meant "nobody."

"Nobody, huh?" I said. I got out the notarized copy of the SEC man's ID and slid it toward her and she looked at it for a long time. She took the phone off its hook and held it to the big linen slope of her bosom while the notarized photocopy accessed some subroutine level of her brain. Then she ineffectually chipped away at what to do for a few seconds, and keyed in an extension. When she saw we were listening, she shooed us back from the desk.

We stood in the middle of the hall and waited for something to happen.

An incredible Vlodomerian woman arrived. Vlodomeria women are incredible, I hope I've mentioned. Everywhere has incredible women, of course, but Vlodomeria had a lot. This one had splotches of dry blood on her scrubs that had turned the color of baby shit. She had incredible hair that was tied up in elaborate braids. "You are looking for the American?" she asked, bags under her eyes, lips chapped—overripe.

"Yes," said McKayla.

"Voom," she said.

"Excuse me?" said McKayla.

"Voom," said the Vlodomerian. "He went voom."

Big converging lines like chevrons on the bridge of McKayla's noise. "He disappeared?" asked McKayla.

"Men came and voom," she said, "disappeared." She shook her head. "I apologize."

She turned and walked back through the double doors at the end of the hallway.

The Gregory at admittance stared at us, daring us to resume our inquiries.

"Sorry I'm late," said Lear as he came in.

McKayla collapsed into a vinyl chair that was coming apart at the seams. "It doesn't matter," she said, "someone disappeared him."

"What?" said Lear.

"He's not here anymore," I explained, "someone came and took him."

Lear observed us critically, scratching his chin. "Maybe this has something to do with the people following us."

The SEC man claimed that he'd figured out Wilder's means of acquiring individual debt. He said that, while poisoned, he had flashed on our conspiracy of sogginess, which he had never understood. He said that we did not understand the theory either, but that it had large, important ramifications.

He claimed that, as a result of finding and extracting the tracking device, which had been no bigger than a grain of sand, he knew that his insights were correct.

His insights were this. Wilder was acquiring individual debt directly through the highest levels of the American government.

The American government held so much student loan debt and so little of it was being paid off that it was being sold abroad. It was being sold abroad to give the impression that the debt was still worth something.

The SEC man said that the tracking device had been implanted in his pelvis while he was under the influence of a powerful hallucinogenic substance, which had been slipped into his drink at a Washington St. bar. He said he had only been able to recall this in the altered state which resulted from his poisoning.

The SEC man said that he had been dispatched to Visegrad in order to give the impression something was being done to discern how Wilder acquired individual debt. He said that his progress was being carefully monitored through his tracking device, which had been implanted by a man with whom he had had a torrid love affair. He said people were made of single unbroken threads, one per person, that wrapped around and around their bodies starting from the interior of the small intestine and radiating in diagonal loops out of the anus, over the arms and legs, until they were spooled back into the mouth and through the intestine.

When I told Wilder and Doc June Sr. that someone had disappeared the SEC man, Wilder asked, "Is he making his payments?"

"Someone is," I said. "It's probably to throw us off their scent. Like when they leave your car at the airport and use your credit card to buy plane tickets."

"Who's they?" asked Doc June.

"I don't know," I admitted. "Is it true, though? About how you acquire individual debt?"

"You sound just like him," said Wilder.

"How would you know? Nobody saw him except McKayla and me. And Rye."

"I thought Rye never came and saw him," said Doc June.

"Rye gets credit, because, even though he never actually saw the SEC man, it's not like he knew they were going to disappear him. As far as I'm concerned, Rye checks all the boxes insofar as having done the legwork. It's only on a technicality that he never visited."

"If you're so sure someone disappeared him," said Doc June Sr., "why don't you sell me his debt?" He had an overbite and he stuck out his bottom jaw when he thought maybe you were noticing.

"Yeah right," I said.

"Why not? You've just been telling me someone's disappeared him." He leaned back and lit a cigarette. "Anyway, keep this disappeared thing under your hat."

It was good advice. I knew something no one else knew, which was that my triple-A client would be worthless inside a month, his uncapitalized debt a beater in an overnight lot, graying and accruing parking tickets in bright red waterproof slips never to be paid off. But it felt wrong letting him go to Doc June or Wilder, burning anyone I knew personally, so I sold him to an associate I'd never met for a handful of geese. The associate had weaseled my username out of somebody and dropped his own into the mailbox of the Arable UI. When he neglected to ask why I was selling the SEC-man for so cheap, I told myself he had it coming for trying to lowball me in the first place.

# 21

I will never forget the woman I met in Portland, Oregon, who had the Vlodomerian for, "Excuse me, this is the incorrect change," tattooed on her neck.

Discounting the words for hello—*sé ya*—and the words for goodbye—*hú lö*—and the country's preferred expletive—copulate with your mother while employing for these purposes a dog's genitals—"Excuse me, this is the incorrect change" was the most frequently uttered combination of words in the Vlodomerian language. This was at least partially due to the fact that the *visegradišag* deprived Vlodomerians of a sense of time.

The American sense of time, which is most tellingly reflected in that axiom, "time is money," considers free time the favored entrant in any contest among time's varieties.

If you are a family man, free time is spent with your children. If you are an ambitious man, free time is spent improving the margin by which free time is earned, since free time is the best metric of success. If you are a rich man, all your time is free, which is why Americans equate wealth with liberty.

It is not out of the ordinary for some people to take a hiatus from free time for years, during which it is tallied up and held in trust, where it does not accrue interest. This is an accepted practice among people who prefer to pool their time in case they get lucky and die before spending it.

In contrast, if you are Vlodomerian, a large quantity of free time is spent arguing over exact change. It is, of course, a reflection of poverty, but it is also a reflection of a people's tolerance for indignity, that oft maligned brother of humility. Vlodomerians are born into a world that oozes indignity; in Visegrad, it seeps over the pavement so you track it in on the soles of your feet. Their negotiating for change is not a sign of pettiness but of resilience.[7]

---

[7] Symon Warclowtz, the great observer of Vlodomerian life, famously illustrated the phenomenon thusly, "I saw right away what my baker had in his young mind. Though he was a very good baker, he was—as many good bakers are—a lousy banker (this is a pun in Vlodomerian, where weights of silver are called 'floursacks' or *léstšak* ['listʒaːk] and a banker is sometimes called 'floursacker' or *léstšakõ* ['listʒaːkøː] while bakers are 'floursellers' *léstšalkõ* ['listʒaːlkøː]) and I knew that he was going to deprive me of my one-half *grivna* note in change. While he was busy counting the change twice, discerning the margin by which he might comfortably short me, I saw my opportunity and snatched a one-half *grivna* bill from his hand. 'Wait, Mr. Warclowitz ... I was not done counting out your change!' he protested. 'I have the count myself.' I said. 'Goodbye, my friend!' I turned and left with my five rolls and a cake of sweet poppyseed bread, for which I paid four *grivni* and an additional half *grivna* altogether, each roll being priced at one half *grivna* and the cake of sweet poppyseed at two *grivni*. As you can see, I certainly had the correct change; I have an excellent mind for numbers, and can tell you the exact change of everything I bought for years afterward. Did that satisfy the young man? Of course not. He followed me out of the shop, turning the sign in the window as he left. 'Mr. Warclowitz,' he called, 'you have made a mistake and your counting is incorrect!' 'It is fine,' I called back. 'You may keep whatever extra change you have coming to you.' 'It is not extra change that is coming to me, but an amount that exceeds the correct change, which you have taken, I'm sure, by accident!' 'No, no,' I said. 'I have an excellent mind for numbers. I was returned five and a half *grivni* from my ten *grivni*. The cost of the rolls was a half *grivna* each, and the cost of the poppyseed sweet bread was two *grivni*, making the sum four and a half *grivni* with a remainder of five *grivni* five.' 'You must have misread the sign,' said the young baker. 'The price of poppyseed bread is always two and a half *grivni*.' Now the villain was revealing himself! Who, I ask you, in the autumn of 1926 in Visegrad, being of sound mind, would pay two and a half *grivni* for a roll of poppyseed sweet bread? 'You must have misprinted the sign,' I said. 'It clearly gave the price at two *grivni*.' I was doing him the favor of not discussing his mis-step of attempting to extort a half *grivna* from me with his fantastic tale of a two and a half *grivni* poppyseed sweet bread. 'That is not the case,' said the exceptional villain. 'I have not changed the price of poppyseed bread in a year and it has always been two and a half *grivni*.' 'Then some little mischief maker must have spit on his thumb and blotted the price, probably

I asked the girl in Portland, OR, if she spoke Vlodomerian in Vlodomerian.

"I'm sorry," she said, "I don't understand."

"Oh," I said, "I thought, because you have Vlodomerian on your neck, there." I pointed.

She looked down her chin. "My grandfather was Vlodomerian," she said.

"I lived in Vlodomeria for years. I thought maybe we knew some of the same people."

"Oh," she said. "What does it mean?"

---

hoping to make trouble between gentlemen such as we.' 'If that were true,' said the young man slowly, 'then the price has been constant, you have only been mistaken in your reading it, just as I suggested.' 'Aha!' I said, having succeeded in my ruse, 'but then the sign blotting must have occurred under your purview!' 'Please,' said the fink, 'do not go until we have resolved our disagreement.' I looked around. I had arrived back at my apartments, five blocks from the bakery. The young baker had followed me all the way home. I realized that to go to such lengths for a half *grivna*, even while there were customers assuredly waiting outside his shop, this baker must be brimming with the patriotic Vlodomerian quality. I went into business with him immediately and we have been close friends ever since, though he occasionally calls in debts that have accrued an additional half *grivna*... very mysteriously."

# 22

After they disappeared the SEC man, we took it on ourselves to do some digging.

We began with the SEC man's psychiatric specialist. We didn't know his name, but there was a log in the ward of the hospital where the SEC man had been. Lear paid the Gregory at reception so he could take pictures of it.

She kept looking at Lear's foot, since Lear was wearing a second-hand plastic brace.

He had seriously considered seeking professional medical attention for the toe, but the reason he was bribing the Gregory at reception to photograph the logbook was that someone had disappeared the SEC from the hospital, and he would have had only himself to blame if he were disappeared under similar circumstances.

He had already lost his job working IT: had gotten loaded and forgotten to turn on his VPN, at which point various higher-ups cued up his recorded customer service care interactions and discovered they had degenerated to the level of heavy breathing. This was sort of a ten-strike situation for Lear.

It's never the habit that puts you in a bind, but the extra pressures generated by the habit. The pressures up your chances of experiencing a lapse in judgment like letting your baby toe go black and the rest of your foot get all inflamed so you can't go anywhere but just sit around eating through your supply of pharmaceutical-grade smack. This is because, when you have a habit, a lot of time is spent getting high or trying to get high, so the seriousness of a habit corresponds to how well you believe yourself to be doing while the habit continually squeezes in on your functionality; that is to say, when you're at your lowest (excepting when you are subject to those special rules which govern life at the Infamous Nadir) you sort of think everything is going swimmingly—must, in fact, constantly reassure yourself this is the case—whereas, when things are going swimmingly, you possess neither the time nor the inclination to make such reassurances, because you have a diverse laundry-list of things to do that does not include the habit.

Some people are so cognizant of this habit(time)denial relationship as to tie one on or toke up only when they can't afford it, utilizing the correlated guilt as a barometer of relative health, which is just another form of denial, really.

It could have been worse; pharmaceutical-grade smack was not Lear's weapon of choice.

Lear's weapon of choice was speed, which was part of the reason that he and McKayla had sold all their shit and left Austin, because, at the time, Lear had been operating on about an hour of sleep in order to work two part time jobs and steer a guerrilla noise collective that stratocasted in huge empty open-air parking garages, which acted as natural amplifiers for their drony/shoegazy electric guitars.

They could be heard for miles, playing for fifteen to twenty minutes in the middle of the night. Anything longer and the risk of police intervention was too high, which—apart from being wrong for the overall creative direction of the guerrilla noise collective—could have dire consequences, since everybody was high on marijuana or methamphetamine, usually both, the latter of which Lear was selling in order to afford more and more expensive equipment. This had, long before his life in Visegrad, led to his acquaintance with a system of accounting that was not dissimilar to how we used Vlodomerian *pivni*, but used American Les Paul Guitars, instead (as in, 'That Oldsmobile is about 4 LPGs).

We found the name of the psychiatric specialist and the address of a private clinic.

The address belonged to a big, prefabricated housing block without signs. The signs should have said *"Getting Well Recovery,"* which was supposed to be the name of the private clinic. But the front door was open, and we took it as an indication that people were in and out.

"If this is a hospital, where's the elevator?" asked McKayla.

Lear's plastic brace made a noise like a big, soft fingernail tapping every time he took a step.

"Yeah," I said. "I mean, it's called 'Recovery.' Recovery denotes people in wheelchairs, right?"

"You never know," said Lear. He was gritting his teeth, vibrations shooting up through his heel every time the brace made its big, soft fingernail noise. "This is our only lead."

I supported him with one shoulder in his sweaty armpit and, at the landing, I let him go. Lear lurched over to the door that matched the address, while I puffed out my cheeks and looked around. It looked like a regular apartment to me.

He reached for the knob and tried it. It was locked and he rang the bell.

"I don't think this is it," said McKayla.

Lear raised his hand to press the bell again, but before he could, the door swung open.

May Mazur said, "Did you forget something?"

Her face paled and, without thinking, Lear stuck his cast between the door and the frame.

The reason May Mazur opened the door was because she thought we were Dead Rockstar, who had just left and was waiting out of sight around the corner.

Deddy had heard us coming up the stairs, was halfway down when he heard our voices. Shrinking, he had retreated before us. There was probably nothing in the world that could have made him show his face, which constituted copping by implication to a vast spectrum of shit he was getting away with, except that we stopped at May Mazur's apartment where she opened the door and that Deddy and May Mazur were deeply, hopelessly in love.

He came from behind, shrieking, trying to get past me to protect Mazur from Lear.

May Mazur was slamming the door over and over on Lear's cast, and Lear was screaming in pain. His foot was about halfway into the apartment. McKayla was pushing against the door, trying to stop it from slamming but managing only to cushion the blows as they rained on the plastic brace. In the meantime, Deddy was trying to incapacitate me by hitting me hard enough that I pitched over like someone knocked out in an old movie, but was too thin from never eating and shooting dope.

I put my arms up and staggered backward, which put me between him and May Mazur, who was shouting his name. She was shouting his name in time with slamming the door, going, "Deddy, Deddy, Deddy," which was punctuated by fluctuations in a single iterate howl disgorged by Lear.

I was only dimly aware of this situation because Deddy kept hitting me in my face, trying to get past me. I only registered it was Deddy doing it, because May was screaming his name. Finally, McKayla pushed through the door to subdue May Mazur in order to stop her slamming it on Lear's cast. She immediately found herself in a one-sided death match, shouting, "Stop, stop," while May Mazur shouted, "Deddy, Deddy, Deddy," and whipped stuff at McKayla and ran around the apartment she had been hiding out in while Deddy shot dope and never ate.

She and Deddy had been in love for long enough that it was Deddy who had spilled the beans to her about The American Concern.

She had steamrolled into the Gouged Eye one night and found him on the patron side of the bar, sort of puddling down by the floor. They were a match made in heaven: Deddy's infinite powerlessness and May's deep-rooted obsession with control. Her ex-husband had also been a user, a drunk not a junky, until her enabling had resulted in his wrapping their SUV around a telephone pole in the early hours of a Greenbay morning. Deddy, on the other hand, gravitated toward sexually predicated care-giver/care-receiver relationships, which was how he sapped women of their dignity and financial independence. The women he dated almost always wound up strung-out by osmosis.

Deddy was an order of magnitude above Mazur's ex-husband on the scale of self-destructive behavior and May Mazur an order of magnitude above Deddy's next most resilient victim in terms of tolerance for accumulated baggage.

I kicked Deddy in the leg, connecting mid-thigh. His foot shot out from under him, no mass or support system to redistribute the kinetic payload, and he slammed into the floor.

I bent down.

Blood was leaking from my soft face and falling in his hair.

I got a handful of the hair and pulled him up to look him in the eye. He spit in my face—a wad of mucus that plastered one lid completely shut. Then I availed myself of some really strong feelings of frustration and violation and confusion I was experiencing.

Afterward, I dragged Deddy inside, where Lear had been processing some similar emotions.

McKayla was holding a dish towel to her face, because May Mazur had gone for a kitchen knife, which had settled the question of whether to negotiate.

I remember standing there, dragging Deddy by the ankle, thinking I had never seen a man hit a woman.

"I think he's got a concussion," said May.

"Don't worry about him," said Lear, "worry about me." He was speaking without his accent again, something menacing in the flat suburban quality of his language.

"It's going to scar," said McKayla.

"We'll go to a plastic surgeon," said Lear.

"What if they disappear me?" asked McKayla.

"You can't let him fall asleep if he has a concussion," said Mazur.

I put a finger in Deddy's face. "Follow my finger," I said.

He spit onto his chest.

"He seems okay to me," I said.

"Why aren't you in Germany?" asked Lear.

"Like you don't know," said Mazur.

"Don't know what?"

"Like you don't know why I'm not in Germany."

We looked at each other. "We don't," I said.

"If you don't know, then how come you knew where to find me?"

"We're looking for the SEC man's psychiatric specialist," I said.

May Mazur blinked, the motion of her right eye constricted by swelling. Her scalp was bleeding where Lear had beamed her with an ashtray. "I don't know anybody like that."

"This was the address in the logbook at the hospital," said Lear. "The address of his practice."

"If he's got a concussion and he falls asleep," said May, "he could go into a coma."

"He's fine," I said. "Why aren't you in Germany?"

# 23

May Mazur had attempted to fly from Visegrad to Berlin, direct.

She had arrived at the airport with everything she was capable of fitting into an enormous, cheaply made set of plastic luggage. Everything else, she shipped to her new apartment and never saw again.

She had printed her boarding pass from a little machine in the departure hall, and afterward the little machine had told her to stand in line to check her luggage.

She gave a Vlodomerian air hostess her passport and boarding pass, and said, "I'd like to check some luggage."

The Vlodomerian air hostess said, "Wait one second, please." She placed a call on the phone behind her desk.

"Is something wrong?" asked May.

"No, nothing is wrong," said the air hostess, pressing buttons on her keyboard.

May Mazur noticed a man walking all the way down the inside of all the ticket kiosks. Vlodomerian air hostesses were pressing themselves against their consoles as he walked by, and he was stepping up onto a conveyor belt occasionally, but not even thinking about leaving the kiosks so as to walk unimpeded. He was some kind of management.

"What's the problem?"

"No problem," said the air hostess.

The man arrived. "Please come," he said. "You must please come with me."

The man led May Mazur to a room with a desk and two chairs.

"You are here more than ninety days in the time not less than one hundred and eighty," he said.

"That's alright," she said.

"For more than ninety days you need the work visa."

She looked around the room, which was featureless except a big mirror, like on TV. "I don't have one," said May. "But I'm leaving."

"You must have the form with the employer signature, if you have the work visa."

"I'm not under contract," said May. "I don't have a work visa."

"Do you have the employer signature?"

"No," said May Mazur. "No work, no employer, no employer signature."

The man got up and left.

After a while, May Mazur stood up as well. She tried the door and found that it was unlocked. She poked her head out.

Two men stood in the hall. They stopped talking and looked at her. She went back inside and sweat bullets.

The man returned with a piece of paper. "Were you attempting to leave?"

"No," she said.

He put the piece of paper on the table between them. It was a form, all in Vlodomerian, still hot from the photocopier, hot smelling, sharp on each side from having just come off a ream of paper. She pointed to it. "What's this?"

He tapped a line at the bottom of the page. "For the employer signature."

The skin on the back of his hands was red from contact dermatitis.

"I don't have an employer," she said. "I don't have a work visa."

"You are here more than ninety days in the time not less than one hundred and eighty days."

"I know," she said, "but I have no visa. I'm illegal."

The man frowned.

"Listen," said May Mazur, "you know migrants, right? You know what a migrant is. Well, I'm one. I'm migrating now. If you have to deport me, deport me, but my flight leaves in an hour."

"You're an American," the man said.

"I'm an illegal alien."

The man shook his head sympathetically. "You have the work visa more than ninety days."

He pushed the paper meaningfully toward Mazur.

May Mazur pushed it back. "You're not listening," she said. "I'm in your country illegally. You have to deport me. Whether I'm an American or not doesn't make a difference. I broke the law."

The man pushed the piece of paper back. "Employer signature."

"Please," said May, "listen very carefully. I don't have an employer. I don't have a job. I'm a drain on your country's resources."

"Until taxes," said the man. He pointed at the unlocked door. "Now leave."

May Mazur scowled at him. She collected her cheaply made plastic luggage and pulled it into the hall, cheaply made wheels already wobbling. She returned to the baggage check.

There was a line and she had to wait.

The sweat had spread all over her body, down the back of her spine around the soft pockets of fat at her waist.

She got to the front of the line and a different Vlodomerian air hostess called her over. The Vlodomerian air hostess took one look at her passport and picked up the phone behind the desk.

"No," said May Mazur. "You don't have to call anybody."

The man began to walk all the way down the inside of all the ticket kiosks.

"Forget it," said May.

She took her passport and went and sat on a toilet in the bathroom near security where people poured liquids from their carry-ons down the sink. She called Deddy and his phone went straight to voicemail. She got up and left the stall and poured her shampoo and conditioner and body wash and perfume down the sink. She got some looks for pouring out all that stuff.

She got looks again for her cheap plastic luggage, while she was hauling it through security.

She showed her boarding pass to a transportation agent, who said, "Not check anything?"

"No," she said. "I'm going to carry it on." He looked at the ticket on her phone. "No time," she said. "I'll have to pay."

The man made a face. May's sweat was making a Douglas fir on the cloth of her shirt.

"Okay," said the man.

She passed through the metal detector.

She collected her cheaply made luggage and walked to the terminal. Her flight was departing from concourse C.

She crossed the food court, found her gate, and stood in line.

She had to explain about the cheaply made plastic luggage and pay an arm and a leg in fees.

As soon as her boarding group was called, she handed her ticket to an air hostess, who took her passport and scanned it.

The air hostess returned the passport and May Mazur walked onto the plane and stowed a piece of cheaply made plastic luggage.

She sat down and relaxed. She wondered absently what it had all meant while she flipped through the in-flight magazine.

There was an announcement over the PA in Vlodomerian.

The other passengers groaned.

The flight crew gave each other significant looks.

She checked her watch. They had missed departure and she had to use the bathroom.

When she stood up, a Vlodomerian air hostess approached her from behind and told her to sit down.

"I need to use the bathroom," said May.

"Please return to your seat," said the air hostess.

May Mazur looked around. The other passengers watched her curiously.

"Please," said May, "it's an emergency."

"Wait until we're airborne," said the air hostess.

"I can't," said May. "I'll pee."

The air hostess shook her head, then craned her neck toward the cockpit. She pointed at May like, "This is the one."

When May turned to follow her gaze, there he was—some kind of management—flanked by officers of the VDF, arms resting on the barrels of their automatic rifles.

# 24

Wilder was eying the crowded square from the balcony of the Superior Mind.

In the Superior Mind there were plaster busts of philosophers on wood columns that were painted white and some great potted plants. Every now and then a person following me would point to us from the street and dart into the building, only to reemerge, scratching his head.

In order to gain entrance to the Superior Mind you had to key the café from an interior door and give the pass phrase, which was distributed every week via old listserv software running off a primitive VM/CMS mainframe on a turn of the century laptop that was installed inside a water feature.

"There's a picture of this place in the dictionary under 'Ivory tower," I said. "I mean, who needs the pretensions?"

"I do," said Wilder. "We can't all be artists."

"You only lack the self-indulgent impulse and the blind encouragement of friends and family."

"I indulge myself a lot," he said.

The square turned slowly. The tourists, their misshapen bodies jammed into leisurewear, shuffled and sweat as they drank in the open. There was an enormous clock in the center, which had been reconstructed in 2005. Along the outside of the clock were rings of parading figures that completed one rotation by the minute, hour, day, week, month, year, century. The tourist conglomeration outpaced the minute wheel, traveling in the direction it was turning.

"Why don't they ever walk the other way?" I said. "They could see the whole thing twice as fast."

"I always imagine these people with their mouths full of Shrimp Louie," said Wilder.

"That's funny." I took a drink. "Can I ask you something?"

"Shoot."

"Have you heard of a client named Mazur?"

"Triple swallow," said Wilder. "She's with Deddy."

"I guess you know Deddy," I reflected.

"He gets around."

I could have kept myself from making a pretty bad mistake right then.

"May tried flying out of Deco Kulpa but got bounced." I said. I stifled a belch.

"She what?" asked Wilder.

"They wouldn't let her on the plane, and when she got on the plane, they wouldn't let the plane take off."

"How much did they want her to pay?"

"Nothing. I don't think they wanted a bribe. They just wouldn't let her leave the country. You read Vlodomerian?" He wobbled a hand. "They gave her this."

The paper was a page-long formal notice. It bore the Vlodomerian seal beside the insignia of the Togetherness Party, a stylized patriarchal cross and leaping trout.

"What is it?"

"It's new stipulations on travel. It says that anybody on a work visa needs their employer's signature to leave." I pointed to a blank space at the bottom of the page.

Wilder cocked an eyebrow. "Good thing you don't have a work visa."

I signaled the waiter. "*Pivni*," I said. "Neither did Mazur."

Wilder kept his eyes on the paper. He produced his scarred expatriate burner and navigated through his contacts. "Excuse me," he said, and left to stand at the other end of the balcony with his phone against his ear.

The waiter returned with our drinks, took a pad of paper from his breast pocket and tore a sheet from the pad. He put the sheet on the table and notched it twice. This was Visegrad bill tabulation protocol.

Despite their paranoia, Vlodomerians were a people that would never conceive of replacing such a sheet and marking it differently. That or they didn't care.

Not caring was a way of life in Visegrad.

What was the point, the logic went, of busting your hump, so some Russian, German, Ukrainian, Pole or Austrian could make an extra buck? It was incompetence as sport that bordered on open revolt. It even had a name. They called it *rábotånélkülišégetlen*.

*Rábotånélkülišégetlen*, "rábotå" [rɐˈbotə], Vlodomerian for "work," derived through Rusyn from the proto-slavic "orbota," meaning slavery, also from where "robot" is derived in English—though, by way of the Czechs and not the Carpathian Ruthenians——nél [neːl] from the Vlodomerian adessive case, and -kül /ˈkɤl/, a variant of the Old Vlodomerian *kívül*, literally "with" and "[in] out," or—as in this case with the additional "-i," the Vlodomerian adjective suffix—"without-ish," plus šég [ˈʃɛg], a noun forming suffix, much like "-dom" or "-ness," but then reversed by "etlen," a harmonic variant of the privative suffix to express "lack" or "absence:" all together "work-un-without-ish-ness," or as I always thought of it, "not without workingness."

And it really *was* a sport.

Every place in Europe had an obscure sport over which its people claimed peerless mastery. The Finns had the triathlon.

The Macedonians had team handball. In Visegrad, the holy sport was *rábotånélküliśégetlen* and it was played every day, all day, by any Vlodomerian that was receiving any kind of wage, and many who were not.

The only measure of skill in *rábotånélküliśégetlen* was the establishment of a position of *elérhetetlenśég* or 'unapproachability.' Unapproachability in *rábotånélküliśégetlen* was the economic and social position of anyone that was not doing a lick of work, but had arranged things to make it look like they were absolutely busting their hump.

*Rábotånélküliśégetlen*'s closest living relative was *capoeira*, the Brazilian martial art that combines elements of dance, acrobatics and music. Like *capoeira*, rábotånélküliśégetlen was invented as an act of rebellion, but was designed in such a way as to show no sign of a rebellion taking place. Despite this, players of *rábotånélküliśégetlen*—everyone in Visegrad and many people in the surrounding countryside—instinctively recognized one another and sometimes made very bold gestures of admiration for each other's style of play. Danylo Nawj was famous for applauding great players of *rábotånélküliśégetlen*, often saluting them during his stint in the Vlodomerian *Soim*, saying, "I defer to Representative Such-And-Such as to the correct course for the betterment of the nation, since he humbles me with his position of *elérhetetlenśég*."

Similarly, Nawj claimed to have discovered his first VDF Chief of Staff in the mailroom at Land Defense HQ, concealed by reams of paper, behind which the future Chief spent every afternoon for fifteen years repeatedly scribbling her signature on a blank sheet of paper with an empty pen, and listening to soccer over a tiny receiver she had jury-rigged from a sardine tin.

"I am very confident in the selection of Franciszkak Sącz as Chief of the General Staff of the Vlodomerian Defense Forces," he proclaimed. "Had she been any more qualified, she would have been impossible to locate."[8]

"I just talked to somebody I know at Togetherness," said Wilder, having returned from placing his call.

"Wow," I said, "you know everybody."

"We've got nothing to worry about with this signature thing."

I took a sip. "That's reassuring."

"Uh-huh," he said. He picked up his beer and held it to the light. Vlodo's Seat towered on the other side of the Volodymy. Construction crews had cordoned off the blast site and there were puffs of dust where they were excavating. "Have you heard of the tunnel at Łupków?"

"No," I said.

"There's a long tunnel in Łupków that comes out in Slovakia. Before the Schengen Agreement, expatriates used to take that tunnel and get their passports stamped when they crossed to the other side."

"But even if I got stamped," I said, "I'd still have more than ninety days out of the last one hundred and eighty, which is illegal."

---

[8] In *Surviving Eastern Europe*, Thom Elliot writes, "Do not confuse *rábotânélkülišégetlen* with sloth. As any Western observer that has lived in Visegrad can tell you, *rábotânélkülišégetlen* is often very difficult. Many Visegradians work extraordinarily hard in their young lives to find a job that dissatisfies them, makes misuse of their talents, and lacks the potential for advancement, since these are the most important preconditions for what they call, 'unapproachability.'" (421) The word *"rábotânélkülišégetlen"* makes its first appearance in Lazlo Novak's masterwork, *A Living Dog*, and is one of the reasons it is considered the defining Vlodomerian work of the twentieth century. In it, he wrote, "It was N's greatest aspiration to be *panno* Lawoz's toilet brush, since he believed her incapable of defecation. It was perhaps that mistake that galled him most, not because he had been disappointed by *panno* Lawoz, but because he perceived all the signs in himself of a great player of *rábotânélkülišégetlen*. Unfortunately, he had soon acquired a work ethic and it was too late." (1)

"Alright, but in order to determine that, the border guard would have to do some serious math."

"What do you mean?"

"To determine that you've spent more than ninety of the previous one hundred eighty days in Visegrad, the border guard will have to look through your passport and find the previous exit date. If that exit date is within the last ninety days, he'll have to find its corresponding date of entry. Then, if the difference between the day you're attempting to exit and your last entrance date plus the difference between your previous exit date and your preceding entrance date is more than ninety days, but, also, only if those ninety days were in the last one hundred eighty days, he knows you're breaking the law. Now," he said, "off the top of your head, you arrived in Visegrad on April tenth and you're leaving June twentieth, how many days could you spend in Visegrad without going over your visa?"

I stopped and thought. I checked some math on my fingers. "April, May, June: twenty days?"

"Nineteen," said Wilder, "but close enough. So put yourself in his shoes. It's the middle of a workday. You figure you need nineteen more days out of the last one hundred and eighty to determine if this potatohead is legal. You're flipping through their blue passport, trying to read the stamps. There's a line of fifteen people and before you arrive at the number, you find another exit and entrance stamp. These new dates are only ten days apart, what do you do then?"

"I probably wouldn't make it that far," I said.

"Most don't. It's one thing to detain someone on an expired visa when they're going through a booth at the airport and the VDF is right there with guns, but when you've got a flashlight under your chin and it's just you and a bunch of tourists—"

"I get the idea."

"So here's what I'm proposing: go see the tunnel at Łupków, you and your girlfriend and whoever."

"Whoever?"

"Anybody that might need a little encouragement. Anybody with feelings of insecurity—maybe that cowboy you hang out with—and reassure them. If they get the new stamps, they won't worry about being flagged for overstaying their tourist visas."

"Will that really work?" I asked.

"Sure it will," said Wilder. "It's a funny kind of people you deal with in this job. Some people just want to feel like they're getting one over on everybody."

# 25

Having was excited that we had called him and felt that a day trip to the countryside was exactly what he needed. "I'll compose a poem for the occasion," he said.

"Swell," I said.

We headed west toward Strelsau, then south to agrarian Jassel, and, finally east, before taking a hairpin turn into tiny Šagor.

I kept glancing at the wet gauze around Lear's toe, barely visible inside his cast. Once we were underway, he doled out tablets of paramorphine.

He had got the paramorphine off his cousin, who had brought them in on a scrip. Unless you actually shot your dope, it was easier to get a befuddlement going on this pharmaceutical-grade stuff than on anything else, and for the depressive user, the golden honey-coated-high chaser, your options were smack from Pakistan or little pills from Purdue Pharma.

"Six *pivni*," he said. "Money first."

It was hard to begrudge him that. Him sharing the paramorphine was his way of getting out from under the habit, rushing toward the finish line and withdrawal.

We produced our colorful billfolds, even McKayla.

Then we were careening along the Vlodomerian countryside, air buffeting in through the window, dozing in our compartment. The terrain on the foothills of the Tatras curved, track rippling on the fat heads of drumlins.[9] The cupolas of a Galician church came into view, tiered shingle roofs that peek-a-booed from unlikely angles after you had long since given up hope of ever seeing them again. In those moments you had to pity the narcotic teetotaler, as, on the mornings you were doubled over vomiting, he pitied you.

We were practically non-responsive on arrival, and it was just in the nick of time that McKayla read aloud the name "Šagor" off a sign in the station. The train warned us of its imminent departure with the chiming of a bell and we dismounted in a huff, babbling and checking our pockets to make sure we had retained our wallets and cell phones.

We found a bus to Łupków and, from the bus stop, hiked to the tunnel, which was secreted away in a national forest reserve.

At the entrance to the park there was a wooden kiosk that sold beer and kielbasas, and where Vlodomerian and Polish hikers sat at picnic tables.

A sign beside the kiosk read, "*túra tunelni, 11:00, 13:00, 15:00.*" It was just after four o'clock.

McKayla approached a man turning sausages on the grill. "Are we too late for the tunnel?" she asked.

Hikers perked up at the sound of English. The cook gazed obstinately at her, then shouted something in Rusyn.

---

[9] In *My Poor Country*, Leybl Gorie writes, "It is best to think of the peopling of Eastern Europe as a heat system. In the West are the Carpathian mountains, the Tatras and the boundary of the Carpathian basin. They abut the system in a semi-diffusive barrier. At some point in the East there existed a very great quantity of random action or entropy, the khanates, the Xiongnu up through the Golden Horde and the Timurid Empire. As these peoples radiated west, they were dispersed by rivers and mountains. They reflected and refracted, pockets collecting in Kiev and Samsara and Kazan. By the time they reached Subcarpathia they had mostly dissipated. Those that penetrated the Carpathian basin were the Magyars. Vlodomerians are even less than this. We are the particles that have passed through the barrier and reverberated out again, bombarded forever, a ship in the eye of an eddy in the eye of a storm." (53)

A boy in his late teens emerged from the souvenir stand. "Yes?" he asked, wiping his hands on his apron.

"Are we too late for the tour?" asked McKayla.

He continued to wipe his hands. "You visit tunnel?"

We all nodded.

"Five thousand," said the man with the sausages. He held out all the fingers on one hand. The sign read, "*sprzedaż 2200.*"

Lear pointed at the sign. He of the kielbasas shook his head. "Five thousand," he said.

I did some quick math. Five thousand was a lot of *pivni*.

Colin Having bit his lip and made a disconcerted hum. "It's a little more than I can spare," he confessed.

"Rye will spot you," I said. After all, we had just paid him for the paramorphine.

Lear tapped the sign and drawled, "Two thousand two hundred."

"*Zbyt ciemno*," said the man.

"Too dark," said the Galician teen.

"*Napfényzk* hour-ákig," said McKayla, which meant something like, "We know you've got us against a wall, here, but I have learned this much of the gibberish spoken in your country so cut us some slack," though not in so many words. This set off a chain reaction of excited conversation among the hikers sitting on the benches.

The younger boy turned beseechingly to the man with the kielbasas.

"Four thousand," he said, adding, "special price."

"Two thousand two hundred," insisted Lear, but the rest of us ponied up.

Lear stared at the painted sign until it was his turn, and paid for himself and Having while casting his eyes around as though expecting to be ambushed. After that, we argued over change while the Galician kid collected his tour guiding equipment.

The equipment consisted of a bright yellow hat (so we would not lose him in the crowds), an umbrella, and a dog-eared brochure in broken English.

It was tough going. We were not in hiking condition, not physically, or, thanks to the hardworking lobbyists at Purdue Pharma, mentally. We were sort of rolling along behind our guide, helping Lear as needed, taking the uphill stretches in low gear while the young Galician shouted passages from the brochure.

Suddenly, Having remarked, "I don't think I thanked you."

"Thanked me?" I said. "Thanked me for what?"

"It's just, I know I can be hard to take in large doses."

"Huh," I said. I did not want to reinforce any particularly brutal self-deprecations but also did not want to be complicit in an outright lie. It is necessary to insulate yourself from another personality's introspective moments or else find yourself confirming all sorts of things you believe about them—that they know you believe about them—and that they believe about themselves, but which they will nonetheless wave in your face like the corpse of a household pet you've flattened while backing down their driveway.

"I can be a little cloying, a little over eager and sensitive," said Having.

"I never noticed."

McKayla glanced back at us under her armpit.

"I can put unfair demands on peoples' time and attention."

"You like to have an audience," I said. "Who doesn't like an audience?"

"See, that's what I'm talking about," said Having. He was beaming at me, as though I had just said something tremendously kind. "When I bought my ticket to Visegrad, I never imagined I'd meet someone like you, someone who's already so accomplished. I have to admit that I'm jealous, but I feel now that I have this opportunity, an opportunity to—I guess the word I'm looking for is blossom. Do you know what I mean when I say blossom?"

"I think so."

"I've always felt that I haven't been in quite the right place or had quite the right friends to be the person I really am. As strange as it seems, I've never really felt like myself." He stopped on the trail and I stopped beside him.

"Yeah," I said.

"I think that might be the reason I moved abroad in the first place. I saw all these people living incredible lives and I asked myself, 'Why can't that be me?' And you know what I figured out?"

"What?" I asked.

"There's no reason. I figured out that the only thing keeping me from being the sort of person I want to be is what kind of person I think I am. I realized that if I could change the way I thought about myself, I could change who I was: simple as that. You know what else? It's really happening. It's happening because I have people all around me who see my full potential."

For an instant I was gripped by the desire to set him straight about everything, about my name and the kind of stories I'd published and how we were charging him for his debt at a rate of about fifty times what anybody'd actually paid for it.

"Hey," barked Lear, "what's the hold up?" He had limped ahead—had lost all sensory feedback in the toe (which is how come the paramorphine anyways) and been seized by manic feelings of invulnerability. Now, our languishing in the rear was unacceptable to him. His arms were crossed and he was regarding us with open contempt.

"Colin was just telling me that he's never felt more like himself." I patted Having on the shoulder. "I've got to say, I know the feeling. What about you?"

"Who'm I sposed to feel like?" he asked. "You?" He snorted and took off, head down, slamming his bad foot robotically against the gravel path.

"What's that mean?" asked Having.

"No idea," I said.

The guide led us through a stand of birch, which opened into a clearing that had been created by cutting down every tree for half a hundred yards. It ran right up to the foot of a limestone cliff that jutted shelf-like from the forest floor. There was a broad tunnel in the cliff, and, beside it, a small cabin. Towering over the cabin was an unfinished lookout tower, pyramids of raw lumber piled at its base.

"*Mit az?*" asked McKayla.

"*Kontrola,*" said our guide.

We glanced at each other.

The guide walked to the door and I expected him to knock, but he fished a set of keys from his pocket, unlocked the door and pushed inside. He flicked on the lights and indicated that we should follow after. He took off his bright yellow hat and hung it on a hook by the door, selecting a more officious hat with a hard black brim.

He pulled the new hat snugly over his head and walked into a compartment made of big clear windows. He retrieved a broad bound book and a regal self-inking stamp. The self-inking stamp had a magnificent brass lever.

"Passport please," he said.

Colin Having sidled up and offered his passport.

"What do you think they need that lookout tower for?" I asked.

The sous-chef *cum* tour guide *cum* passport controller inspected Having's passport.

"Firewatch could be," said Lear.

"How's your foot?" asked McKayla. The bandages around the toe were wet and oozing slightly.

"Can't be a firewatch," I said. "We're in a valley."

Our tour guide recorded Having's name and passport number in the broadly bound book, lowered the stamp to the paper and compressed its mechanism. What a sound.

"You can watch for fires from a valley," said Lear. "There's special views of the surrounding hills."

"How's your foot?" insisted McKayla. She stepped to the counter and handed over her passport.

"I can't feel it," said Lear. "It's fine."

"Is there a toilet?" asked Having.

Our tour guide shook his head. "No toilet," he said.

"Why would anyone build a firewatch in a valley, when they could build it on a hill?"

"You're not dehydrated?" asked McKayla.

"Look," said Lear, "these mountains are on the border, right? All the good parts are probably in Slovakia."

Our tour guide recorded McKayla's information. He lowered the stamp and pulled the lever.

"I think I'd better go outside," said Having.

"We came over higher ground on the way here," I said.

"Are you alright?" McKayla asked Having.

"Excuse me," he said. He pushed violently past us, then sprinted through the door and into the cover of the trees.

"What's his problem?" asked Lear.

"Maybe he's going to check on those special views of the surrounding hills you were talking about."

"Chrissake," breathed McKayla. She turned businesslike to the Galician. "*Merd á türá?*" she asked.

"You pay four thousand," said the tour guide.

"Not *túra*, *türá*. *Türá.*" She pointed in the direction of the tower.

The guide hesitated. "*Tõrá*," he said.

"Right," said McKayla, "why the tower. *Merd a tórá?*"

"Not tórá. *Tõrá.*"

"*Törá*," said McKayla.

"*Tõrá*," he said, giving the first vowel special emphasis.

"*Tõrá?*" asked McKayla. He nodded. "*Merd a tõrá?*"

"Not migrants," he said.

"Not migrants?"

"Not migrants," confirmed the tour guide, "*kontrola*."

"This tower faces west," said Lear. "What good does a west-facing tower do to stop migrants?"

The tour guide gave him a blank look, not understanding.

"Slovakia," said Lear pointing in the direction of Slovakia.

"Slovakia," agreed the guide.

"Czech, Hungary, Poland, Germany," said Lear. "West."

"West," agreed the guide.

"West?" asked McKayla. "Migrants?"

The guide nodded. "Migrants."

# 26

**G**rass and bramble poked through the desiccated remains of a rail line on the tunnel floor.

"Aren't we going through?" I asked.

"Why should we?" said Lear

"What of our involuntary co-conspirator?" I prolixified, ensuring privacy against our guide as he emerged from the office wearing his yellow hat. "What if he is reticent at the prospect of abandoning our stated destination—if he is wroth or apprehensive, so makes report of us among the local constabulary."

"What if he does?" asked Lear. "It's getting dark."

"Lear's afraid of the dark," said McKayla.

"No one likes hiking at night," said Lear. "Plus, Having's sick."

"I'm fine," said Having, very pale. "I'd like to see what's on the other side."

"That's three to one and a blow against autocracy," I said.

Having cleared his throat and looked meaningfully around.

"What now?" snapped Lear.

"I just thought I should begin."

"Begin what?"

"My reading," said Having.

"What reading?" I said.

"The reading of my poem."

"Right," said McKayla, "your poem."

"Weeeeell," squeaked Lear, filibustering Having's momentum.

"What is it?" asked Having.

"Weeeeell," said Lear, "I dunno."

"Don't know about what?"

"If just now," said Lear, "if it's the right time for poetry."

"Oh," said Having. Air-bladders evacuated their animating gases and his head sank between his shoulders. His arms slackened so his hands rotated slowly out.

"It's not the worst time," put in McKayla.

"Not the worst imaginable," I allowed.

Having perked up.

Lear crossed his arms. "While we hike," he said. "It'll be dark coming back, if we don't hurry."

"Great," said Having. "I mean, if you really want to hear it."

"Of course we do," said McKayla. "Don't we?"

"Not really," said Lear.

"I don't mind," I said, "so long as we can chat a little while you read."

"Okay," said Having, "if that's what you'd prefer." He fumbled with his phone and, after producing a handful of receipts and used tram tickets, extracted the poem from his pocket and cleared his throat. "I call this, 'Poem to a Friend.'"

With that, Having began to read.

It was impossible to know how long he read, because, once he had begun to read, time seemed to stretch out.

His voice was very soft at first, almost uncertain. He even faltered once, clearing his throat again and repeating one line three or four times until he discovered the rhythm of the piece—words like footprints in snow, curving ahead into nothing. And his voice accelerated and became hoarse. It rushed up and down, doubling back and pouring into us, filling our empty bodies. It pushed us forward like a soft hand pressed at our backs and inspired visions that were projected along the tunnel walls and floor.

I realized, suddenly, that I was no longer a writer. I realized I had only ever been a writer if one expanded the definition of the word 'writer' until it ceased to be useful. I had been a writer in the way that a man hurtling toward the ground is a physicist.

I looked back at Having. His eyes were pressed close to the page—ragged teeth on the leaf where it had been torn from a spiral notebook. I stumbled and caught my balance. None of us dared speak. He was a thundering machine, billows of his engine fed by the locomotive process of his pumping extremities. The sound of his poetry was like iron, buckling the air as it gave way to some invisible mass.

He paused for breath.

There was a yelp. The words caught in Having's throat.

We heard the scrabble of feet coming up the gravel behind us. A dark shape charged past, and, for a split second, it was caught in the beam of our guide's flashlight. It was a small dog, mangy and soaking wet.

God, we laughed. Except for Having, who released a long piteous moan.

Our guide followed the dog down the track, shining his flashlight ahead. He stopped suddenly and I almost ran into McKayla, who had only narrowly avoided running into the guide.

There, in a dim halo of light stood two men.

They had been crouching in the dark, listening and watching as we approached. Their mouths were covered, one by a Vlodomerian flag, the other by an expensive LED display that instantaneously lit up. The LEDs rainbowed in the darkness, producing a frown. No one uttered a word. They reached into their coats and drew expandable batons, which flicked out from their clenched fists. They began walking purposefully towards us.

"*Sé ya,*" tried Having.

They broke into a run.

McKayla gave a shout and Lear wheeled sharply around, illuminated in the blue light from Having's phone.

I had not run, really sprinted, for months, and I was first overtaken by the guide, then McKayla, then Lear. I became aware of the great depth of space at my back.

I wished to juke, to turn or accelerate, but could not make myself do anything but charge dully ahead, further and further behind the others, surer with each passing second that I would feel the impact of a club.

A lot is made of waiting for the other shoe to drop, and I can tell you it's no fun, but don't buy all this about anticipation being the worst part. Anyone who says anticipation is the worst part has not been sufficiently bludgeoned by telescoping batons. I could be wrong about that, but in moments when I am forced to speculate about the possibility, I have taken to feeling the circumference of the undented melon that sits upon my neck. If you do likewise, I think you will feel that any amount of time spent running through the dark is preferable to one good belt from a steel mace.

I burst from the tunnel, wetting myself as I went.

I reached the others who, panting, waited in the shadow of the tower. "Are they behind me?" I wailed, patting at my clothes as though small fires had broken out all over my body.

Lear shook his head, then vomited. Having had placed one hand on the tower for support. He covered his eyes with his other arm and doubled over.

I could see the LED lights, disembodied in the shadows by the entrance. They floated there for a moment, then blinked out, concealed from view as the man that wore the mask turned and walked away.

# 27

The toe had to come off.

What a succession of slamming doors failed to accomplish had been achieved by Lear's sprint through Łupków Pass. Plus he had eaten through his supply of pharmaceutical-grade smack.

At minus seventy-two hours zilch paramorphine, fast approaching the Infamous Nadir, sweating and shitting from just three months of trying on this serious habit, he scored a meat cleaver at a junk *potrivjn* and tried convincing me to chop it off.

He wagged the toe in front of my face where it stank.

He had done a pretty good job of stitching it up with dental floss and wrapping it and changing the bandages and applying iodine, but it nonetheless looked like a peanut, roasted until cracked: strata of inflamed pink and purulent yellow.

"McKayla won't touch it," he complained.

"I don't blame her. Maybe it will fall off."

Lear shook his head. "You've got to do it." He held the toe further out and I caught a whiff.

During college, as a balloon-like freshman, I had worked at a summer camp with this beautiful girl that didn't know she was beautiful yet, and, in the course of things, someone I considered to be a friend, was my friend for all intents and purposes—this laid-back mildly far-out but undamaged guy from Monterey—

snagged the beautiful girl, instead of me, probably not just for reasons of balloon-likedness but also due to feelings of self-loathing and dovetailing quirks likewise symptomatic of an underlying condition—to say nothing of the legitimate preference of the girl—and after he fell asleep one night on my parents' living room couch, and playing the whole thing off as a joke/ dare/escalation of friendly rivalry/parable about how shit talking wasn't just talking as far as I was concerned and how I should be taken more seriously, maybe feared, produced my penis and tapped it against the side of his face while he was unconscious "like ashing a cigar" I told him, though I did not commit this violation, only told him I had in order to inspire feelings of discomfort and anguish that I hoped would approximate my own emotional state at not having snagged the girl, despite the fact that I did daring things like cop to violating someone I considered a friend; and, really, because the consensus was that, he, the good guy from Monterey, was all-around more likable than I was, so the aforementioned underlying condition in all this was maybe how I knew I was smarter than he was but people liked him anyways, so cruelty presented the opportunity to restore a karmic balance that had never existed, me as the yin to the yang of his laid-back mildly far-out undamaged existence.

This is the danger of believing you are special.

I can still remember his shock, a small unhinging of the mouth, the dilation of his pupils in fear response.

Anyway, the good guy from Monterey had found, in one of the lodges, a recycling bin with a narrow slit at the top wherein a rat had fallen and been unable to escape and starved to death. The rat had attracted a second rat and that rat had attracted a third, and so on, until it was five or six rats that had fallen in and starved to death. They were arranged more or less tail to snout, illustrating progressive rungs of decomposition. He had dumped the maggoty succession onto the floor of my big, old-fashioned

A-frame tent. The resulting smell was a hyper-intense beam of olfactory white noise which set off the receptors on the inside of my nose like air raid sirens.

"Your toe stinks," I said.

"I know," said Lear. "That's why I want you to chop it off."

He dropped his leg, grimacing with the impact of his heel against the carpet.

My phone went off in my pocket. *What's going on out there?* McKayla was getting ready in the bedroom.

*He popped the question.*

*The toe? He should go to the hospital.* "Go to the hospital!" she called, voice muffled by the bedroom door.

"This conversation is between men," shouted Lear. He turned to me, incensed. "Why'd you bring her into this?"

I could not have excluded her. McKayla and I had begun communicating constantly via text. In the reading of her messages her voice was always different, since it was the voice she used when we were alone together. It was not an incisive, prepared voice, but a natural one. It was part of a fantasy: McKayla lying sensuously atop her bed in the next room, a strap falling delicately around one shoulder. No such person existed. There was not more tenderness or seduction in her than shrewdness, than anger that threatened to overpower her mid-western veneer of cool disinterest. She was slow to forget.

*You don't want to cut it off?* she asked.

"What's she saying?" asked Lear.

*I'm afraid he'll bleed to death.*

*We can make it look like an accident.*

"Seriously, let me see."

I pulled the phone away. "She thinks I should put you under and never bring you out."

"That I believe."

*Should I do it?*

*Dealer's choice, sweetheart.*

Sweetheart. Is it possible to miss someone a few feet away? If I could have locked that bathroom so she never emerged, never looked distastefully around like we'd turned the apartment into a pig sty in her twenty-minute absence, never made some slight comment about how Lear had flushed his life down the toilet by trying on his paramorphine habit so that I suddenly blinked out of existence as they spun up in a domestic quarrel like smoke through a chimney, then I would have.

I examined the putrid foot. I imagined taking its whole front off, so all five toes scattered across the carpet like pink ears of baby corn.

"I better not," I said. "Why don't you go to a hospital? It's been a while since they disappeared the SEC man."

"What's a doctor going to do?" asked Lear. "He's either going to cut it off or prescribe an antibiotic; I've been taking antibiotics."

"Where'd you get the antibiotics?"

"Doc June," he said.

"He's not really that kind of doctor. He's not really any kind of doctor."

"I know he's not, but he had some left over from his surgery."

Doc June Sr. had suffered a spiral fracture in his wrist during the winter of that year, caused by the early symptoms of a degenerative illness.

"You should have gone to the hospital. They're not going to disappear you."

"I'm not going to the hospital." He held out the cleaver.

"I'll do it," said H. Defer, spontaneously generating from the blankets on the couch.

# 28

H. Defer was a triple albatross *wunderkind* who had majored in a sub-sub-discipline of Social Accounting at Kalamazoo City College, and, whenever he was asked where he was from, said "Kalamazoo"—no further explanation.

He was some kind of post-state syndicalist, whose beliefs were predicated on the inevitability of a total information environment governed by an advanced artificial intelligence. His conspiracy was that everyone was basically good.

Once, I asked H. Defer how it could be that everyone was basically good, what with the way people were so rotten to each other, to which he replied that it was a conspiracy.

We had agreed to give H. Defer to Having because Having wasn't making enough to pay us, and because we had a lot of new clients. But Having had been under pressure to negotiate an extortionate rate with H. Defer, because Wilder was still entitled to his 5 percent, and because Lear and I were to split an additional 5 percent on top of that, so he had botched the negotiation and they had landed at about eleven-five. In the end, he netted only that one and a half percent.

"Jesus-aitch-Chrys," drawled Lear, "who let you in?"

H. Defer had been lying on the couch blowing smoke rings, waiting to talk to McKayla about whether or not she thought the little gypsy prostitute was ever going to love him back.

"I said I'd do it," said H. He walked over to examine the foot. "Do what?"

"Chop it off. I'm thinking—and this is just me spitballing, this is not take it or leave it—but I'm thinking point one percent of Having per gram."

"Per gram?"

"Right. Per gram of toe."

"Of my end of Having?" Lear stopped and thought. There was nothing in the system to prevent someone buying the debt of an associate to whom they were a client. "That's stortionate. What do I do if my toe is fifty grams? Why, I'd never make a cent."

"He splits his end with me," I said.

"Oh," said H. Defer. "I didn't know that."

"You got any experience doing things like this?" asked Lear.

"Of course I do," said H. Defer. "How about one one-hundredth of a percent?" Lear paused and thought another moment. "It's only Having," added Defer.

The sub-sub-discipline H. Defer had majored in was the study of intertextual branding.

Intertextual branding was a sub-discipline of the study of corporate social responsibility (CSR), which, itself, was a sub-discipline of Social Accounting.

H. Defer was not the sort of guy to move to Visegrad. He only left Kalamazoo because the woman he had fallen in love with, before he fell in love with the little gypsy prostitute, had been unable to give the future the benefit of the doubt.

According to H. Defer, they had been in love but her not being able to give the future the benefit of the doubt had ruined it. She could not give the future the benefit of the doubt whether that meant giving the benefit of the doubt to life on our planet, or giving the benefit of the doubt to H. Defer's chosen sub-sub-discipline. And that really hurt.

"Everything ends," she would say. "Everything, everything." Everything ends, that was her mantra.

Being unable to give the future the benefit of the doubt made it seem to H. Defer as though she was constantly resolving not to be disappointed in those things H. Defer would never accomplish, which she was. It was exactly that sort of psychological drain, he claimed, which would have prevented him from accomplishing those things he wanted to. So, H. Defer had left the woman with whom he had been in love, and moved to Berlin to study intertextual branding.

The first thing you have to understand about the study of intertextual branding is that it treats both the human experience and the experience of corporate branding as texts. In broad strokes, it is most often the study of how brands permeate life outside the realms of industry and advertising—like if you ever have a dream about the salespeople at your cell phone carrier's retail location pointing to diverse clauses in your contract while your teeth fall out.

A better example is maybe the Halloween example.

In the Halloween example two people, Alice and Bob, wear costumes to a Halloween party. Alice wears a sandwich board, the word '*VOTE*' crudely stenciled across its top and a small cardboard square hanging off one side. Bob wears a colander on his head and a lumpy brown sleeping bag tied securely around his midsection. Both costumes are so poorly made as to be independently mysterious, but what devotees of the American sitcom will not fail to notice when Alice and Bob stand side-by-side is that each costume is a facsimile of a more famous costume from an episode of a hit TV show. The first is a "hanging chad" as worn by Ted Mosby in the episode "Slutty Pumpkin," S01E06, aired October 25, 2005: the second is "Spud-nik" as worn by Ross Geller in "The One with the Halloween Party," S08E06, aired November 8, 2001. Here, then, the subject of the costumes is intertextually identifiable, and Alice and Bob have successfully communicated with their audience. Furthermore, because each costume or text exists in reference to another costume or text, they have taken on layers of meaning neither would otherwise possess. Each character is a single male in his late twenties/early thirties, and each is unsuccessful with women. In each episode, a woman correctly identifies the obscure costume worn by the character (in the case of Ted Mosby, it is the titular "Slutty Pumpkin"), signaling that each woman is a potential romantic partner. Now Alice and Bob are not only dressed as characters in a specific episode, but have invoked a comparison. They have dressed, in effect, as a conversation about what media consumers and producers interpret to be the significance of costumes in the broadest sense, a reflection of the aphorism that we hide ourselves to be seen. Substitute television characters for the products, cultures and brand logos of major corporations, you have intertextual branding.

There was no hotter place to be than Berlin for intertextual branding.

H. Defer's thesis adviser in Berlin was the go-to guy in intertextual branding, but it turned out to be a mistake for H. Defer to try and study under the go-to-guy and not the number two guy, or, better yet, number three, because the go-to-guy was not interested in passing the torch.

H.'s queries, re: *THESIS TOPIC PLEASE ADVISE* were met with increasingly tepid responses. But H. thought the go-to-guy was being hard on him because of H. Defer's own incredible potential to affect the future of his chosen field. As a result, H.'s thesis proposals became more innovative and more threatening, and the go-to-guy in Berlin's responses became less substantive and less encouraging, punctuated ultimately by, "You are an adult person. You will study what you are pleased to study. I am very busy. I am too busy to always be telling an adult person what to study."

So H. Defer began a tour of Eastern Europe and Central Asia, photographing and documenting intertextual variations on Apple Computer Inc.'s corporate symbology.

Apple Computer Inc. was the perfect subject for a thesis on intertextual branding, because Apple Computer Inc. was obsessed with CX (consumer experience) and their obsession consistently bore out in the way their products proliferated the Eastern European and Central Asian marketplace:

In first world countries, Apple Computer Inc. opened retail locations in order to streamline CX and vertically integrate their business.

In countries where Apple Computer Inc. anticipated being unable to control the retail experience, it licensed retailers to sell Apple products at a mark-up, usually only a few per country.

For these retailers, the use of Apple Computer Inc.'s corporate branding was absolutely *verboten*. The ability of Apple Computer Inc. to enforce that edict varied based on perceived receptiveness to theoretical intellectual property claims in a given country, which correlated with government stability, levels of international trade and mean income.

In countries where Apple could not hope to enforce its intellectual property claims, Apple products were bought at mark-up and imported by third parties from licensed retailers abroad. As a result, the lower a country's average wage, the more expensive Apple Computer products were in that country (even disregarding inequalities in real cost).

This was due to status symbol/conspicuous consumption pressures that made Apple products more valuable relative to a country's wealth; a rich man in Copenhagen did not necessarily need an iPhone but a rich man from Chişinău was not rich without one.

The status symbol thing was intentional. The founder of Apple Computer Inc. had not been a computer expert, but a kind of branding savant. He had realized that products were not exempt from psycho/political interference, that— while differences in technical specifications did correlate to differences in supply, demand, and value—differences in the customer experience (subject to all the rules and phenomenon that apply to human political experience in the broadest sense) represented a sort of power coefficient in which the consumer and the producer negotiated value outside supply. Accordingly, the founder had implemented a producer fascism, through which the will of the consumer was subjugated by the will of the producer: the consumer as passively complicit in the use of the product as a citizen is in the crimes of a single-party state.

The relationship between Apple Computer Inc's way of doing business and a country's perceived receptiveness to intellectual property claims meant that, in first world countries, Apple insignias could only be found on authentic Apple Computer retail locations. This is in contrast to countries wherein licensed and unlicensed retailers utilized various clever but distinct parodies of Apple Computer Inc.'s branding—pears, whole apples, apple cores—scaling these similarities so as to appear as legitimate as possible while not stepping on toes at Apple.

In the third category, in countries where Apple Computer Inc. retail locations were unlicensed, branding tended to climb the vertex of familiarity. In these countries, authenticity, at least in the Apple consumer experience sense (we have returned, here, to our coefficient of producer willpower), should have been impossible, but in some unlicensed retailers, employees were never told that they did not actually work for Apple.

H. Defer was interested in only those countries with both licensed and unlicensed retailers—countries where Apple Computer Inc. was seeking to expand, but was treated with a certain level of derision insofar as the enforceability of its intellectual property claims.

It was common for unlicensed retailers in these countries to combine protected branding, so sometimes the Apple logo was augmented by a color-fill of the Death Star or the Golden Arches or the Disney princess *de jour*.

H. Defer went all over Central Asia and Eastern Europe taking pictures and recording instances of intertextual branding, but in Visegrad he made a discovery of such importance that it more or less forced the go-to-guy's hand in terms of nailing H. Defer to the wall.

He moved clockwise around the city, beginning in Old Town, carried by the momentum of the crowd swirling around its central tower.

He was at it all day, and the sun was just going down as he entered the gentrified gypsy quarter where we kept our apartment. Not far from us, he found the anthropomorphized Formula One race car of his dreams.

The anthropomorphized Formula One race car was printed on a vinyl decal that had been applied to a storefront window. She—it was a she—was reclining gently. Her chassis was significantly paired down, so it wasn't a chassis, but more of a cat suit with intertextually identifiable spoilers still attached at the neck and thigh. The term cat suit, itself, is misleading, since it brings to mind a full body thing that fails to convey the ratio of intertextually identifiable chassis to exposed anthropomorphized Formula One race car flesh, and likewise fails to convey the manner in which it split—beginning at the back, near the cleft of the exhaust pipe, to V around her sex, up the abdomen, bisecting each breast.

In Visegrad, breasts were a must for the purposes of advertising.

She was slapped all over with the decals of cigarette brands and cereals and motor oils, but what made her such a catch was that her pubic hair was trimmed into the shape of Apple's forbidden fruit. These peculiar little carbon fibers would have been totally mysterious under normal circumstances. On the decal they were explicit.

H. Defer had gone forth, as he believed he had been commanded, and found the bleeding edge of intertextuality. It was time for his hard-won accolades.

As a result, the go-to-guy dispatched an unpromising PhD candidate to Visegrad, who scooped H. Defer by rewriting his entire dissertation in four months, under close supervision of the go-to-guy in Berlin.

By the time H. Defer had read the now *very* promising PhD candidate's dissertation, there was nothing to do but write slanderous letters, and he could only write those to the heads of other departments and the editors of tangentially related journals, because the go-to-guy in Berlin was the head of his department and the editor of the only journal on the study of intertextual branding.

The letters were slanderous because there was no way he could describe how the go-to guy had nailed him to the wall without it sounding like sour grapes. In the letters, he said that he and the go-to-guy had been lovers.

We met H. Defer while he was attempting to physically incapacitate himself with alcohol, so he would be unable to shoot out the window with the vinyl decal of the anthropomorphized Formula One race car.

He was supposed to shoot out the window because, after setbacks in his chosen sub-sub discipline, he had capitalized on his one remaining asset: an exhaustive catalog of unlicensed Apple Computer Inc. retail locations and their forbidden product branding. And so he had contracted with a licensed, third-party retailer to shoot out all the windows of unlicensed retailers in the city.

He kept leaning over while I was discussing sogginess with McKayla and Lear, saying things like, "I have a secret, but you wouldn't understand it."

He was just teetering on the precipice of total incomprehensibility.

It is an interesting fact that before a drunk loses the ability to articulate himself, survival instinct faintly warns him he's in some kind of internal distress, which the drunk will often misinterpret as a sign of existential pain and grief. The drunk may in fact have a lot of existential pain and grief, since he is drinking.

Unfortunately, the drunk processes these emotions, which he may or may not have, by holding strangers hostage with long, structurally unsound, chronologically oblique monologues about what he thinks is the source of his suffering.

You learn to head this sort of thing off at the pass.

"I think," I said, "that sogginess overshadows traditional class-based explanations of commoditization and fetishization, and by extension these psycho-sexual theories of conspicuous consumption. Its most fundamental aspect being lumens, heat over time by saturation of feet."

Lear nodded learnedly.

"You know what your problem is?" asked McKayla. "You think you're the equivalent of moral jetsam; you have this fantasy you live in a vacuum removed from context."

"Morality's a construct," drawled Lear. "You can't argue against amorality by sayin' the existence of an amoral universe's part of an immoral fantasy."

H. Defer leaned way way over to butt in. "I can tell that my secret is relevant to the discussion you're having." He had a strong odor of onions about him.

McKayla shot him a look like he should go screw. Then, to us she said, "But to make the determination that the universe—physical universe—is amoral doesn't excuse you from all kinds of moral aches and pains you've absorbed or inherited as part of your human experience. I know that both of you, who are so committed to moral relativism, I know you both have these like moral kinks and hangups that turn you on or make you queasy."

"Your problem," I said, "is you cannot tolerate any theory that attempts to explain human behavior with really limited moral interrogation. Your ideology is so threatened by the idea of neglecting moral questions, you sort of inject them compulsively. Like if we were sitting here hammering out infinitesimal calculus with Oz Newton, you'd be accusing him of the same stuff."

"Don't get me started on the Oz," said McKayla. "He had hangups in spades."

"Right," I said. "But if sogginess bears out, we're talking about describing the physical laws that govern morality, since time spent developing kinks and hangups requires a certain unsogginess. Notice how we've all got dry feet."

"Okayokayokay," interjected H. Defer, "I'll tell you, but only if you promise to believe me."

"No," said McKayla flatly.

"I've been paid to assassinate a vinyl decal. I can't bring myself to do it. I think it might be important for posterity."

Lear scratched his nose. "How much?"

"How much what?"

"How much you bein' paid to assassinate this decal thing?"

It wasn't that H. Defer was squeamish all the time, just about certain things. For example, H. Defer's offer to cut off Lear's toe at a rate of 1/100th percent of Having per gram was exactly the kind of trading that transformed him from a dim prospect into a triple-A client and sterling associate of The American Concern.

He was highly motivated, because he wanted to make as much money as possible in order to pay the little gypsy prostitute who later turned to stone on the bank of the Volodymy.

"Can you name all the bones in a hand?" I asked.

H. Defer frowned.

He walked to the refrigerator and took out a bottle of Moravian Brut. He placed the bottle on the kitchen table and gestured for the cleaver, which Lear passed to him, handle first. H. peeled back the tin foil and unwound the wire basket. He turned away from us, shielding the bottle for a moment, then held it out for us to examine. We nodded.

He raised the cleaver and brought it down.

"One one hundredth of a percent," he said. The bottle's neck was neatly severed.

# 29

"Well then you can't complain," said the SEC man. That night he had got wind that none of us except McKayla had voted. "I don't want to hear you complaining when they turn America into a police state. If you're not going to be adult about it and make some compromises, you can't complain when they round everybody up and throw them in camps."

He was reclining in front of the wreckage of his meal, empty beer glasses pushed away from his dinner plate in diffusive rungs that were competing for space with our elbows.

McKayla was nodding to herself, coloring with crayons in a coloring book.

"If you can't do it for yourself," said the SEC man, "if you won't grow up and just pick a side, like everybody that votes, like most people, do it for him." He pointed to the bartender. The bartender hated the SEC man, because every time the SEC man paid for a drink, he took everything out of his pockets and a line tended to develop. "Do you know what he'd give to vote in a real, American election?"

The SEC man paused to take a sip of beer and allow this point to sink in.

He wiped foam from his upper lip with the back of his hand. "Do you know what it would mean to a starving African? They'd give an arm and a leg. I've been all over the world, believe me. I'd go so far to say that, by not voting, their blood is on your hands. At least the people that voted for that criminal P.O.S., at least they have the balls to look them in the eye and say, 'So what?'"

"I know what you're saying," said Having. His voice was sort of dreamy because he had been sneaking methoxetamine from a small baggy we were passing back and forth under the table. "You're talking about a moral imperative."

"I wouldn't say that," said the SEC man. "I wouldn't say an imperative, just, when roving bands of maniacs take over your neighborhood and invade your home and tie you up and rape and torture you, I don't want to hear you complain."

"Who's complaining?" asked Lear.

"I just want to make sure you know what's at stake."

"Complaining is what's at stake?"

"No," said the SEC man. "What's at stake is the future of the whole human project."

"And all you want is for us to vote?"

"Yes," said the SEC man.

"But," said Having, "if it's that important, you must have someone you want us to vote *for*."

"Of course there's someone I want you to vote for. But, listen, what I'm saying is, you don't want to be complicit. By not choosing a side, you're complicit in either one, whichever wins."

"Way I see it," said Lear, "you're the one who's complicit, on account of you're the one that's voting."

My head was rolled back and my mouth was open, so the only way I could see the SEC man was by squinting over the horizon of my face.

His hair was cut short and he had cultivated stubble around his mouth that was at once jocular and condescending. Later, after he had cut out his implant, his beard grew very quickly.

"Don't bother trying to get through to them," said McKayla. "Honestly, there's nothing you can say. They're hopeless."

"Well, don't come crying to me. Don't get all weepy when they're keeping you awake in a featureless room for seventy-two—" He stopped and stared.

"Are you alright?" asked McKayla.

"Don't come to me—" he began. He stopped again. He moved one hand distractedly. It bobbed, chased by his arm through the air. "Don't come to me when they start in on you with the nipple clamps and cheese graters. Criticism of the system is the same as support for the opposition. I do feel funny." He stretched, casting the fitted sleeve of his shirt over his head. "Have you been giving me some of whatever's in that bag?"

"No, man," said Deddy. Deddy was opposed to the SEC man on principle.

"You're more of a subordinate clause than a human being," snarled the SEC man.

Deddy looked around, surprised. "Does anybody know what that means?"

"You're a string of qualifiers."

"Wow," said Deddy. "Wow, what the fuck?"

The SEC man was blinking hard with both eyes. He had been for some time. The more I noticed this, the more he seemed to blink: the more he blinked, the more vigorously his eyelids clamped together. He put his hand on the table and pressed the wood.

"Are you sure you're okay?" asked McKayla. She touched the back of her hand to his forehead.

"I feel funny."

"You feel a little hot to me."

His face shone red. "You sure you didn't give me anything? It's alright if you did. I can take a joke."

"I'm sure," said Deddy.

We had no way of knowing he had been poisoned. There weren't little pieces of blotter paper floating around in his drink, because that's not how you poison people with lysergic acid amide. You need unfettered access to the substance itself, not consumer level access, but distributor level access. The quickest way to do it is by buying a lot of morning glory or Hawaiian baby woodrose seed and extracting it.

"Your friend looks sick," said one of the people following us.

Four of the people following us were seated nearby, but nobody had made them yet—not me or Lear, not anybody.

"Mind your own business," said Wilder. Wilder was sitting in the far corner with Doc June. "He's our buddy. We take care of him. We know what he needs."

"I'm not," said the SEC man. "I'm not your buddy. You're the subject of my investigation into violations of the FDCPA, FCRA, HEA, the Gramm-Leach-Bliley Act and the Privacy Act of 1974."

"See," said Wilder, "he's just kidding."

The SEC man got to his feet. His chair overbalanced and clattered to the floor.

I was awake, now, chin jutting out, interested in what would happen next.

"I get it," said the SEC man. "Now I see."

"What do you see?" asked McKayla.

"I know how you acquire individual debts," said the SEC man.

"No you don't," said Wilder.

"Oh, I know," said the SEC man. He beamed. If he had a cape, I believe he would have tossed it over one shoulder.

"You don't know anything," insisted Wilder.

"I know," said the SEC man. "You're in for it now. I got it all figured out. You're not exactly high man on the totem pole, are you?" Wilder wavered, just for a moment, as though one of his vertebrae had gone temporarily soft. He glanced at Doc June Sr. "There," said the SEC man, "that's been the idea all along; play your cards close to your chest. God, it was staring me right in the face."

"How does he do it?" asked Having.

"C'mon," said Lear, "spill the beans."

"Okay," said Wilder. He crossed and uncrossed his arms. "I know you haven't figured it out. But maybe we should have this conversation just the two of us, just you and me. And, if you did figure it out—and I know you didn't, but if you did—you realize there's more at stake here than my money." He gestured to us, suggesting faintly that we all might benefit from the conversation becoming more private.

"Don't listen to him," said Lear. "It's okay. You can tell us."

McKayla was less convinced. "Maybe you'd better talk in private," she said. I guess she didn't like the way we were looking at the SEC man.

Even Doc June Sr. was leaning forward, head down, staring at the table, channeling all his willpower into becoming sober enough to retain the information that might be coming next.

Wilder took a step.

"I'll tell them," threatened the SEC man. "I'll expose you."

"Do it," said Deddy.

"Don't," said Wilder, warning.

"He—how he acquires individual debts is, it's all got to do with people pretending to be somebody."

"I am begging your pardon?" asked one of the people following us.

The SEC man looked around, confused. "I mean, he's a glass man, you can see right through him."

Doc June released a puff of air that turned into a raspberry. Lear groaned and buried his head in his arms.

"What's he talking about?" asked Having.

"Don't you see? He's not a—he's a reflection. He's not real—None of this is how it should be."

Wilder sat down. "He doesn't know anything."

The SEC man began to rock back and forth on his feet. "This is fun, right?" His voice cracked. "We're having fun?"

"It's okay," said McKayla. She was right beside him and held his hand as he rocked.

"He doesn't know shit," said Lear.

The SEC man's free arm began flopping wildly.

"You've got to calm down," said McKayla. "You're hyperventilating."

None of us were making eye contact with him anymore, except Wilder. Wilder had a big smile cooking.

The SEC man attempted to wipe away tears with his swinging hand, and so struck himself repeatedly over the nose.

"Why don't you sit down?" asked McKayla, righting his chair.

"Uh-huh," he said. He plopped down and put his head in his hands. Mucus was shining on his upper lip.

"Are you alright?" asked Deddy

"I'm sick," said the SEC man. He didn't say anything else, but set his hands on the table. Then his face slackened as he lost control of his bladder and wet his pants.

"Jesus-Chrys," said Lear.

The SEC man keeled over and began to convulse. Everybody gathered around him and argued about whether to put a wallet in his mouth, everybody except the short man with the cowlick.

The short man with the cowlick walked out of the bar, through the front door and into the street.

# 30

**H**Defer became infatuated with the little gypsy prostitute when her attempts to steal his wallet catapulted him into fits of erotic stimulation.

I had met the little gypsy prostitute separately, before that, and before she turned to stone on the bank of the Volodymy. Most of us had. When we first met, she was vibrating with activity.

She steamrolled up, a foot and a half shorter than me so that the tops of her enormous breasts and the shape of her skull were all of a size, presenting a special moment of confusion as I looked down at the three dark orbs of her body.

"American?" she asked, moving dangerously in.

I nodded.

"You want sex?"

I told her I had a girlfriend.

The little gypsy prostitute cupped me in one hand. "Where she is?" I felt something in my pocket and discovered that tiny fingers were closing around my wallet. I pushed her back in time to keep her from pulling it out.

This was the number she did on you, on everybody, every time she saw you, even if she'd already tried it.

Having was so sick of fending her off, he stopped using the pedestrian underpass where the prostitute and her pimp spent most nights. I couldn't blame him; the constant aroma of fecal matter mixed with bromhidrosis made it a place to be gunned through with nostrils shut.

Bromhidrosis is what you have when your feet stink. In the months after the disappearance of the SEC man, the stench of bromhidrosis seemed to be following us everywhere we went.

H. Defer found the little gypsy prostitute to be absolutely titillating, and he coached her clumsy attempts at robbery until they became part of a fluid sexual discourse: pulling him in by the belt buckle, gripping him through his pants and slowly withdrawing the amount of *grivni* he had left for her in his billfold. But he was afraid of her pimp. He was a short, barrel-chested man with a pair of delicate, beak-like lips. He inspired H. Defer to plot radical detours even when he was heaving with frustrated potential.

Colin Having said that H. Defer's infatuation with the little gypsy prostitute was actually an extension of his work on intertextuality, since it was an ambition of H. Defer's to recreate those sexually defining moments from childhood which he could recall from film and television, though Having was hard pressed to find or name scenes from film or television that resembled H. Defer's liaisons with the little gypsy prostitute.

Lear said that H. Defer's infatuation with the prostitute was just an organized mind's infatuation with degradation.

I asked H. Defer one time, and he said, "I'm in love."

McKayla shook her head. "The question isn't, 'Why does he do it?' but, 'Why do we put up with it?'" She was scrolling through her phone as H. approached the underpass.

"Put up with what?" drawled Lear.

The little gypsy prostitute spotted H. and extricated herself. She never wore much—hot pink, plastic skirts and a lot of negative space. She walked toward him, laconic, strutting.

"Every time he does this, he makes us complicit."

"Complicit in what?"

"The sex trade."

Having scraped one shoe speculatively over the pavement. "You heard him. He's in love."

"He doesn't even know her name," said McKayla.

"That's love for you."

McKayla shook her head. "That's why we put up with it, because he's in love?"

"What's all this 'we' stuff?" asked Lear.

"I'm here, aren't I?" asked McKayla.

H. Defer had stopped halfway through the pedestrian underpass.

Usually, H. would become weak in the knees at the prospect of her contacting his member through his khaki pants, and he would sort of droop through the whole process until she retrieved the money from his billfold, but now he was standing very straight.

"We put up with it because he makes us so much money," I said. H. Defer was already beginning to establish his own super-effective pitching methodology that none of us could get our heads around. The secret of his effectiveness remained shrouded in mystery until the end of that summer, when he began grooming his own associates. It didn't matter much. He was downline from us and we were entitled to our 5 percent.

"Then he can hire someone to be his friend," said McKayla.

"*I'm* his friend," said Having.

"We're *all* his friends," said Lear. He was glaring at McKayla. She sighed. "I get it. Not in front of the kids."

"What's he doing?" asked Having.

H. Defer was down on one knee.

"Uh-oh," said McKayla.

The little gypsy prostitute had frozen, face unfamiliar in the absence of lascivious boredom.

H. Defer reached into his coat pocket.

"No way," said Lear. "He's not."

"He is," said Having.

On the other side of the tunnel the pimp had noticed what was happening.

"Go get him," hissed McKayla. "Now."

The little gypsy prostitute had her hand over her mouth. H. Defer held out a ring.

"Goddammit, I'll go myself," said McKayla.

"Shit, shit, shit," said Lear. He hobbled after her. The toe's postamputation clean-up had been conducted by a house doctor for an exorbitant fee. The doctor had not questioned either Lear's aversion to the hospital, or H. Defer's weighing of the severed toe on our kitchen scale.

The little gypsy prostitute allowed H. Defer to slip the ring onto her finger.

Yes, she nodded. Yes, yes. Tears welled in the corners of her eyes as we neared Defer from one side and the pimp bore down on him from the other. For a moment, it seemed like there would be a collision. Then McKayla and the pimp began shouting.

H. Defer was breathing hard as he got to his feet. The little gypsy prostitute waved the ring in front of her pimp's face, happy.

"You proposed?" demanded McKayla. Lear put his hand tentatively on McKayla's shoulder but she shrugged it off. "You're going to buy her? Is that it?"

H. Defer seemed not to hear. Color was flooding into his cheeks.

The pimp grabbed the little gypsy prostitute's hand, clamped it under his arm and turned away so she could only swat ineffectually at his back. He wrenched the ring off and threw it. It ricocheted across cigarette butts and urine stains. For a moment, I was afraid it would be permanently contaminated by the stench of fecal matter and bromodosis.

McKayla stopped shouting.

The pimp let go of the little gypsy prostitute and she retracted her hand, cradling her finger.

The color had run back out of H. Defer's face. He walked across the pedestrian underpass and picked up the ring, wiping it off on his shirt.

The pimp was talking angrily in Carpathian Romani. The little gypsy prostitute was crying.

Now McKayla was saying, "H.? H., honey?" as H. Defer balled up his fists.

Having was saying, "Hey, listen, man. Listen—"

Lear kept looking over his shoulder, making the people who were following us.

The pimp stopped and examined H. Defer, who was glaring at him with undisguised hatred.

We all knew the pimp had a knife somehow.

The pimp put out his hand. H. Defer looked at the upturned hand and the pimp waggled it suggestively. Slowly, H. Defer unclenched his fist and deposited the ring.

The little gypsy prostitute was begging or apologizing.

The pimp brought the ring close to his face. It was a white gold band with diamonds. He put the ring in his pocket and said something to the little gypsy prostitute, who nodded solemnly. She took H. Defer by the hand and led him around the pedestrian underpass, under the bridge over the Volodymy, where she performed two minutes of oral sex, which was all that was necessary.

Her name was Virág.

Afterward, H. Defer ate his liver at the Gouged Eye, bawling until everyone fled to suck bottlenecks in the street.

"What's wrong with him?" asked Deddy, who was combing a Vlodomerian tabloid for pictures of smoking babies.

"He's in love," said McKayla. She had given up on consoling H. Defer—he was inconsolable—and had joined me and Lear where we were eyeballing Deddy.

"Love is a beautiful thing," said Deddy. He said it loud with his chin up, but without looking in our direction. Deddy hadn't said anything when we walked in, or stopped us when we retrieved our own bottles from behind the bar; Mazur had made every payment like clockwork since our spell of home invasion in July. "Does she love him back?" he asked.

"It's hard to tell," said McKayla. She told Deddy about the ring.

The next day Virág went with a john to his apartment. When she got back to the underpass, her pimp was missing. She hung around all day, called his cell phone and his cousins' cell phones, but nobody had heard from him. At last, another prostitute told her that he had gone to meet the Visegrad Police officer he kicked up to, and they had left together.

She waited by the pedestrian underpass for three days and he never came back.

At the time, none of us thought it had anything to do with the SEC man.

Grief stricken, Virág moved in with H. Defer and began her transformation. Her tan faded, first to a cirrhotic yellow, then to beige. She stopped wearing lipstick and rouge and let her eyebrows grow back over where she had them permanently tattooed.

Without her pimp to protect her, she was attacked by another girl, who hit her with a bottle of plum spirits that didn't break, and she had to go in for surgeries. The surgeries left her head with a small indentation.

Her hair came in under her wig, thin and gray, and all that fall it seemed like she was collecting an extraordinary amount of dust. Like old couch cushions, dust puffed out from under her clothes or hair or wherever else she was touched.

We congratulated H. Defer, who was very happy.

His only cause for concern was how the little gypsy prostitute kept going back to the pedestrian underpass, even after she had been clubbed with the bottle of plum liquor.

"I don't know why she does it," he said. "I make sure she has everything."

"Maybe she misses her friends," said Having.

"Yeah" said H. Defer, "maybe."

She liked to roll her wheelchair up to where she used to lie in wait with her pimp. There, she smoked cigarettes and never spoke.

Lear was the first one to realize what was happening. "She's turning to stone," he said.

"Don't joke about that," said McKayla, "it's not funny."

McKayla was antsy because the three of us had been all over the city that day looking for the dissociative gammas in accordance with Visegrad substance abuse protocol: GHB, GBL, 4-butanediol.

"Who's joking?" said Lear. "You've heard of spontaneous combustion. This is spontaneous petrification."

We were just walking into the Albatross, a nautically themed pub that played sea shanties.

"Ha-ha," said McKayla. "That's really funny."

I bellied up and caught the eye of the bartender. "Excuse me," I said.

"I'm not joking," said Lear. "She's getting grayer and grayer, moving less and less. Eventually, she's going to stop moving altogether and be rock hard, sunk into the riverbank by the side of the Volodymy."

"What do you want?" asked the bartender. McKayla and Lear fell silent.

"That depends," I said. "You sell GHB or GBL?"

The bartender made a noise indicative of extreme distaste.

"Fucking Americans," said a man sitting at the bar.

This was an extension of my physical clumsiness, this failure of drug acumen. "But do you?" I asked.

The bartender sighed. "Buy something."

"Sure," I agreed. "Three *pivni prosivem*."

He poured them out. While we waited, the man sitting at the bar intermittently shook his head and looked at me. The bartender put the beers on the beer mat and we paid him six VRP. He placed the money in the register. Afterward, he looked evenly up at us and said, "I have speed."

"What?" asked Lear.

"I have speed."

"That's what I thought," I said. "It's the same everywhere."

"If you didn't have any, why'd you make us buy something?"

"I have speed."

"Fuck your speed," said Lear. "And you," he said to the man sitting at the bar. "What have you got against Americans?"

"Leave him alone," said McKayla.

"Go now," ordered the bartender.

"No," said Lear. "Not until we finish our drinks." He took a long melodramatic sip of *pivni*.

"You're finished with drinks." The bartender lifted the remaining beers from the mat and set them down on his side of the bar.

Lear grunted. He pointed to our beers and said, "Give those back," foam on his upper lip.

"You must leave," said the bartender.

"*Adj nikik a pivni*," said one of the people following us. He had come in to get out of the rain.

The bartender looked up and froze.

"What does that mean?" asked Lear.

"He said, give us the beer," said McKayla. The bartender glanced around.

Another person following us came in, still smoking. "*Mi ne tak?*" this one asked.

"*A bárman elvitt a pivniuk,*" said the first.

"*Adj nikik a* fucking *pivni!*" declared the new man.

"Now they're both saying it," said McKayla.

Everybody but the guy next to me was watching the bartender. The guy next to me was minding his own business with preternatural ferocity.

The bartender set our glasses on the counter.

"Thanks," said Lear, turning to the men following us. Then, experimentally, "*Dyékuyé.*"

The first man gave a stiff nod. "*Ezért płacitok nikünk.*"

"What's that mean?" asked Lear.

McKayla screwed up her face. "*Mit besiltél?*"

"*Ezért płacitok nikünk.*"

McKayla frowned. "He says, that's what we're paying them for."

The bartender was rummaging for something behind the bar.

"We're not," I pointed out. "Paying them, I mean."

"*Ne płacimy,*" said McKayla. The people that were following us made faces like it was none of their business.

What the bartender had been rummaging for turned out to be baggies of speed. He set them on the counter.

The baggies of speed signified the beginning of only getting speed in Visegrad. It was always the same speed, which was wet and clumpy from whatever they cut it with, and tasted like cucumbers.

"*Ne płacimy,*" insisted McKayla.

They shrugged.

"Tell them not to follow us," suggested Lear.

"Isn't that kind of rude?" I asked.

"I don't know the word for follow."

"Do you know, 'move behind?'" he asked.

"I think," said McKayla. "*Ne plecul minj.*"

The people following us looked at each other. They frowned and squinted. We were on the precipice of some very deep *visegradišag*; there was the possibility that their instinct for self-preservation would take over and they would become violent. Slowly, one nodded to the other.

"*Ne plecul migyek?*" said one.

"*Ne plecul,*" said Lear, x-ing his arms like an umpire. "You understand?"

"*Ne plecul,*" repeated the other, stubbing out his cigarette on the door.

It was weeks before we made them again.

They had donned elaborate disguises and were trailing us from a great distance.

"Those assholes," said Lear. "We had an understanding."

We waited around a particularly sharp corner. When the people following us rounded the corner, Lear stuck out his finger and said, "We had an understanding."

"*Merd minj plecul?*" demanded McKayla. "*Merd plecul?*"

One of the people following us tore off his elaborate disguise and began jumping up and down on it. We were taken aback, and it was left to his partner to intervene on behalf of his elaborate disguise.

"*Nemožlihatlan,*" roared the Vlodomerian as he stomped his bushy mustache flat. "*Nemožlihatlan!*"

"What's impossible?" asked McKayla.

"*Ne plecul,*" raved the man.

We worked out that the people following us had taken McKayla's words at face value, reasoning that they had been following too closely; the literal translation of "*Ne plecul minj*" being, "do not move *in back.*"

This was due to some complications arising from Vlodomerian sentence structure.[10] McKayla's mistake had been

---

[10] "Vlodomerian sentence structure is the reason that Vlodomerian is the only language whose teaching is expressly forbidden by the Geneva Convention. It has no set word order, which may strike the learner as an opportunity to sprinkle words here and there indiscriminately, arranging subject object and predicate as they see fit. Nothing could be further from the truth. Because there is no set word order, sentences may be formed in a variety of ways, but each formulation takes on subtle variations in meaning. The upshot is that it is difficult to form a sentence without putting special emphasis somewhere, and only Vlodomerians are aware of what is most natural to emphasize in every scenario. Additionally, there is no set of combinatorial rules that make up the grammar's underlying logic; Vlodomerian children have 'predicate bees,' instead of 'spelling bees,' and several of Vlodomeria's longest-running television game shows involve forcing participants to think very hard about where to place a verb. It is a common tactic in such programs for contestants to jam their fingers in their ears and go, '*Lálálálálá,*' since

to place the predicate behind the subject, thus emphasizing *plecul*, and not *minj*. This suggested to the people following us that, while we were perfectly amenable to being followed, we wished not to be followed *in back*.

The people following us were not especially bright, but they were consummate professionals, which was a frequent combination in Visegrad as a result of all the *rábotånélkülišégetlen* they played. They had been determined to abide by our stipulations, purchasing disguises at great personal expense. Our demand that they "not move *in back*" had therefore made their work very difficult. By the time they rounded the particularly sharp corner, they were physically and emotionally exhausted.

You can imagine how the finger pointing and incessant questioning was sort of the straw that broke the camel's back. We all felt so guilty about it, from then on, we allowed them to follow us at whatever distance they found convenient.

---

the complexity of Vlodomerian grammar scales relative to the amount of attention being paid it. This phenomenon is named the Vovk Effect, for the linguist who first identified it. And it was the Vovk Effect that resulted in a spate of suicides among Galician militant nationalists captured during the Polish-Ukrainian War, who were undergoing a process called Vlodomerianization: were forced to stand in a muddy field for hours at a time while belting out preferred word order. Luckily, enough POWs survived the experience that they were able to testify to the treatment they'd received in open court. Though not in Vlodomerian." (*Surviving Eastern Europe*, 432–33)

# Part 3

# 31

**C**olin Having leapt to his feet, clutching the blankets from under which he had suddenly appeared. I ripped them away to discover he wasn't wearing anything underneath.

He rushed to shield his genitals. "Lear," he begged. His nose was broken and he had a black eye.

I sat down on the couch and held my head in my hands. "Lear?" he asked again, more slowly.

I peeked up at him from between my fingers. "What do you want?"

"Could I have the blankets back, please?"

I handed him the blankets.

"Why are you naked?" I asked.

"I was all over the city, looking for you. By the time I got back, I was pretty wet." He went and picked up his clothing from the big heated drying rack in our apartment. Every apartment in Vlodomeria had one.

Doc June Sr. said Vlodomerians had big, heated racks because they had deep-seated cultural memories of never being able to get dry from when Visegrad was devastated by floods with medieval regularity. He had a personal interest in the topic, actually.

Doc June Sr. had earned his doctorate in universal history at a San Francisco college which lost its accreditation. His dissertation had been on *chemyon*, or facework, which he argued was a unique method that Koreans used to establish subjective truth as fact.

Doc June said that Korean facework determined the value of subjective experiences correspondent to the face value of each personality in any group, defined along Modern neo-Confucian lines of seniority, class, and sex. That is to say, the older, wealthier, and maler you were, the higher your face value: senior wealthy males having pretty much a stranglehold on the truth, destitute junior females being so far removed from truth that it was a miracle they were walking around without bumping into solid objects.

Example: one middle-aged man, one middle-aged woman, one *colorblind* but wealthy older man, and one destitute young woman are all sitting around a table taking an examination for color blindness that consists of red and green spots on a piece of white paper. In accordance with values of truth as determined by Korean facework, the group will most likely arrive at the conclusion that the red and green spots are various shades of the same light muddy brown, despite the fact that only one person in the group—the wealthy older man—is colorblind. This is because the wealthy older man's perception of the spots on the paper, and his corresponding face, is more valuable than the combined face of the other three; it is the job of the middle-aged man to negotiate with the wealthy older man, so as to get him to come around to the idea that he is uniquely unqualified to make this distinction, all while he and the middle-aged woman make a point of agreeing that the spots on the paper are basically light muddy brown, and of calling into question the value of the experiment—what's the difference between red and green and brown, anyhow?—while the young woman gazes at the surface of the table and doesn't speak.

Doc June Sr. theorized that Korean facework was developed to counter successive waves of invaders from the Steppe, China, Japan, and the Russian State. Repelling these successive waves always required a lot of getting outside in bad weather in order to flee or fight or farm under threat of starvation, and very little time to get back inside to dry off and put together an alphabet.

Thanks to *chemyon,* no matter how covered in blood and mud and sputum any given number of Koreans were, a protocol existed to identify who was capable of deciding the best course of action. Doc June Sr. argued that this phenomenon reflected a rolling reinvestment of truth value into informed, rational actors, capable of making decisions that scaled automatically to the number and diversity of individuals affected by a given problem.

In his dissertation, Doc June Sr. theorized that across the Eurasian plain—where there existed conditions similar to those that had produced Korean facework—there might exist a similar body of practices.

When the school Doc June graduated from lost its accreditation, he was writing about the big heated drying racks like the one from which Having was collecting all his clothes.

"We can't stay here," I told Having. "We've got to get somewhere I can scrape myself off and put my feet up."

I had excreted a thin exoskeleton of accumulated oil and sweat. I am a great excreter.

"Do you think they're watching us?" He was pulling on his socks.

I moved into the kitchen. There they were: four pink spheres caught in the funhouse mirror effect of the warped glass. "Yes," I said, squinting and bobbing my head.

"What if McKayla and Rye come back? Shouldn't we warn them?"

"They're not coming back," I said.

"Oh," said Having, pulling on his jeans.

The pink spheres disappeared from the roof of the building opposite. "Hurry," I said. "They're coming."

We descended the stairs as fast we could, hands on either rail like kids headed to recess. Colin had not had time to put on a shirt, so he was half naked. We were maybe halfway to the street when I heard the security door buzz.

"The shed," I said.

The surveillance professionals were already clobbering the steps with their surveillance professional boots. I could see the tops of their heads on the stairwell, shaved close, arteries bulging. "We won't make it," said Having.

I have always felt I am a different person when my back is against the wall.

"*Cipő zlodiy*," I shouted. "*Cipő zlodiy!*" How did I know that, when strung together, those sounds would compose the words for shoe thief? It was like I had reached into Visegrad and plucked them out.

Doors banged open and matronly Gregs were on the surveillance professionals in a flash. They bull-rushed the big men in total defiance of physical logic, their biting mouths worked to a lather, old yellow nails like goddamn mother fucking potato peelers. There were screams.

I opened the fourth story window and looked down. It was a long way to go. Footsteps, now, on the landing.

I jumped and my arms went in small loops all the way down.

I collided with the shed's roof and my whole body compressed. One knee shot into my face and knocked me silly. I listed sideways, saw Having; he was straddling the window frame, fighting with a pair of hands as they came to seize him and pull him back inside. Then I keeled over and fell from the shed to the ground. I hit my head and bit my tongue, deep.

I got to my feet and walked in a wide semicircle, aware that I was not traveling in a straight line but unable to compensate or change direction. Colin and one of the people following us teetered precariously out of the window. I collided with a trashcan and sat heavily back down.

Having shouted something to me before they fell.

They broke through the roof of the shed and dust billowed out.

I pushed myself up and walked from the courtyard to the road. There, the sun seemed brighter than it had a moment before. What time was it? A bus was arriving and I got on. I distantly hoped they were both okay, the person following us and Having.

There was a kid on the bus, an American. He was maybe twenty-two twenty-three. When he looked at me, I knew he was thinking he should do something to help. Bloody drool was running from the corner of my mouth.

"Don't worry about me," I told him. "I'd go to the hospital, but that's where they disappear you." He raised an eyebrow. "You want some advice? You'd better toughen up. You'd better get soggy. That's how you know if you've got what it takes."

I gave him a business card, which said, *Lear Fadder, THE AMERICAN CONCERN*. He hesitated, then took it.

I heaved, spine jerking my head up and down like a string attached to a balloon.

"I know it seems strange that no one wants to help," I said. I threw up, mostly blood and stomach bile. How long since I'd had anything but black *pivni* and amphetamines? This kind of comedown is like acid reflux that starts in the bowels and works its way out; you've been on such a long burn, you're digesting your own stomach lining.

The public transportation gestapo was waiting at the next stop, so I walked off the bus and across the street into a junk *potravjn*.

In the *potravjn* I bought a cheap cotton duvet and a miniature plastic bottle of rum. I also bought some antiseptic hand cleanser and a package of tissues and a sleeve of crackers. I took my belt off and wrapped the big cheap cotton duvet around my head and shoulders, then cinched the belt around my waist to keep my hands free.

I took sips from the rum and lashed my tongue around feeling the part I had bit.

When I got to the Volodymy the little gypsy prostitute was there, turned to stone on the riverbank. Her skin was gray and she was speckled with pigeon shit. One hand was thrust out in genital appraisal, another dipped into the pocket of some invisible mark. That hand, the dipping one, looked almost dainty, like she was accepting an offer to dance. I undid the belt and draped the blanket over her and got out of my clothes.

It had been raining all morning and the river was swollen.

I walked down to the riverbank. On the bank there was a plaque to commemorate where the Iron Trout had shot Jewish people. The Iron Trout shot them and pushed them into the freezing water chained together, so they didn't have to shoot each one. The people they shot dragged the others down. They killed like seven or eight people at a time this way and saved a lot of bullets.

I skimmed my toe through the water. I felt big and white. Vlodomerians catcalled me.

I climbed in and began to freeze. I rubbed the hand sanitizer all over my body and tried to rub my tongue, but it was too bitter. That's the difference between hand sanitizer and rubbing alcohol, though you can drink both.

I got out shivering, testicles retracted up into the interior of my body. I picked my way toward the little gypsy prostitute and used paper towels to dry myself off. I put my clothes back on, feeling the collected oil on the collar of my shirt.

Then I fastened the blanket back around my waist and sat down to wait.

# 32

Colin Having arrived breathlessly at the door of our apartment one morning in September. He carried with him a large flat book, a manuscript copy which he slapped down on the kitchen table.

We were puttering around in various states of undress, and the hurling of the manuscript onto the table failed to elicit much of a response. I glanced at Having, who was pointedly returning all of our looks.

"What's that?" drawled Lear. He was wearing no pants, so the trunk of his genitals peeked disconsolately from the ratty hem of his t-shirt.

"Bare-faced plagiarism is what it is, shameless academic purloinery, ideological assassination."

"Oh?" I asked. I peered at the manuscript as I passed, shirtless, into the living room. Its cover read, *The Visegrad School Press Journal Volume 1, Issue 1*. "I didn't know the Visegrad School had a press."

"It doesn't," said Having. "It's not a press, it's a gun held to the head of intellectualism. And it's got our fingers on the trigger, yours and mine."

"Aren't you being a little melodramatic?" asked McKayla. She was the most completely dressed of the three of us, in a high school track ensemble she donned whenever she suspected the remainder of the day would be spent indoors. The sun was out, and we knew that we should be enjoying the weather while it lasted, but we had been exhausted by the social and chemical demands of the Indian summer—had not come to grips with the encroaching fall.

"Here," said Having. He picked up the manuscript and flipped to its table of contents. "Intertextual Definitions of Sogginess, H. Defer; Practical Failures of Relativism, Doc June Sr.; Applications of the Hydrodynamics of Drinking Straws to Social Objectivism, H. Defer *and* Doc June Sr; they actually cite you in this one." He flipped to a dog-eared page. "Morality is predicated on special laws of sogginess and unsogginess, so its basis must be those physical laws that govern heat and time and saturation of feet."

"Hey," I said, "as long as they spelled my name right."

"L-E-A-R?" asked Having.

Of course.

"Am I in it?" asked Lear.

"Doc June has you saying some pretty damning things about the futility of discourse." Lear gave me a big thumbs up.

"Wait," said McKayla. "What are you talking about? What are you saying?"

"I'm talking about this," said Having. He tossed the floppy manuscript back onto the table, where, this time, the sound of coffee cups rattling in the roosts of their saucers was enough to make us all flinch.

I rubbed my arm. "What do you want us to do about it?"

"This is your work. Your ideas have been stolen. It's piracy."

"Don't be ridiculous," said McKayla, "who would take an idea like sogginess seriously? They're probably just throwing stuff at the wall to see what sticks: troop movements before H.'s re-invasion of Berlin."

"Think whatever you want," said Having, "but I wouldn't put my name on something like this."

"Wuzzat?" drawled Lear. "I thought your finger was on the trigger just like ours."

"Ah—" Having cleared his throat. "Well, that may be the case in a figurative sense, but obviously I'm less culpable—what with the quotes being attributed to you and Lear. My involvement is more peripheral, more difficult to pin down. Don't get me wrong, I am keenly aware of my complicity."

I gave him the once over. "This hasn't got anything to do with that terrible rate you negotiated from H., does it?"

Colin had been unable to negotiate for more than 11.5 percent from H., and, because Wilder had been entitled to 5 percent (and Lear, McKayla and I, combined, another 5 percent), Having had been operating on a thin margin even before the removal of Lear's baby toe. That transaction had been a disaster because Lear had failed to accurately gauge the quantity of fluid which had collected there. It had weighed just shy of forty grams. For a baby toe, that was enormous. Since Lear had agreed to pay one one hundredth of a percent of every gram of flesh, Lear had been reduced from holding 1.25 percent of Having (we were now splitting Lear's income stream 50-50, and he was splitting his half with McKayla) to just .85 percent. Under normal circumstances, this might have made little difference. But, as H. Defer's super-effective pitching methodology sunk in and his income stream ballooned, the remaining sliver of H.'s income was enough for Having to pay off his debt practically overnight. The absent toe, then, came to represent both a loss for Lear, and a souvenir of Having's failure to negotiate. This also meant that Lear had traded shares in what turned out to be a triple albatross client at double-S prices (albeit prices set in 1/100th gram of toe), ruining his credibility until later in the season when H. Defer's pitching methodology inflated the value of everyone's clients and there was a rush on the sparrow-rated unnecessariat.

Lear took to sighing loudly and staring down at the place his toe had been whenever it was his turn to buy a round of drinks or pick up the check.

He resented us both—McKayla and I—for failing to remove the toe, and its absence, combined with the drought of physical intimacy necessitated by his condition, resulted in the Lear Fadder sexual embargo of that fall. During this period, the growth of our downline income was exponential. By October we had so many children in the Arable UI that it became a chore to name them.

"If you think," Having began, placing one hand over his heart, "that I would act out of pettiness, when I just happened to find evidence of plagiarism, of misrepresentation of your privately expressed notions."

"How did you get hold of this stuff in the first place?" I asked. "It doesn't look like it's exactly making the rounds."

"I found it," said Having.

"Found it?" said Lear. "Where?"

"In a printer's task log," he said. "In the task log of a printer at the Visegrad School."

"Pretty weaselly," observed Lear. "What were you doing snooping around the Visegrad School?"

Having gathered himself up. "If you must know, I've been teaching there."

"Teaching at the Visegrad School?" said McKayla. "It's not a real school, Colin. It's got no students or curriculum."

He shook his head. "They changed all that. Technically yes, what's happening there would probably better be described as a sort of info-Yogism. There are very few traditional trappings of academia, sure, but a great deal of emphasis on practical knowledge and experience. I consider it more of a DIY creator-space, an anti-cafe with its meetups and bootcamps folded into the structure of a one-time payment."

"Jesus Chrys," said Lear, "imagine that. That's great. What do you teach?"

"Work-life balance."

"Come again," said McKayla.

"Work-life balance," repeated Having.

"But, Colin—" said McKayla, "you haven't had a job in months."

"I do have a job," he said. "I teach work-life balance." The sudden collective impulse toward self-restraint momentarily beggared everyone's ability to make eye contact. "I'm serious," he said. "I'm a textbook case of work-life balance and people want to know my secret."

"What do you tell them?" asked McKayla.

"I talk a lot about the power of dreams, about willpower as an instrument in defense of happiness." Lear was making a face that I was trying to ignore—eyes bugged-out, chin pulled into the armpit of his neck. Having said, "I don't appreciate the implication that there's anything funny about it."

McKayla stifled a laugh by coughing into her fist.

He crossed his arms. "Listen to me. You give this a look." He poked the cover of the floppy manuscript. "If you're one hundred percent okay with what's being said, how it's presented"—he glared around at us until, one by one, we met his eyes—"then, fine, that's on you. But if you don't like what it's saying, what your ideas are being used in service of, you'd better do something before it's too late."

After he left we gathered around the table and flipped through the introduction, Lear and I racing through each page but McKayla moving more deliberately until Lear went to the kitchen to get a beer, and, instead of returning, lay down on the couch. I finished the introduction and excused myself to the bathroom. When I came out McKayla was gone and so was the manuscript.

"Where is she?" I asked.

Lear took a sip of beer and looked at me over the top of his phone. "Sharpening her ax."

"Isn't she a beauty?" asked H. Defer. He was standing in front of an ancient off-set printer, which had been installed in the basement of the Visegrad School. Black mold was creeping down from window wells that passersby used as toilets.

"She's really something," drawled Lear. "How do you work it?"

"Oh," said H. Defer, "I don't know if it does work. We got the whole thing at auction."

"Well then what are you planning to do with it?"

"Do with it?" H. Defer looked at Lear as if he had opened a linen closet to find him eating handfuls of paste. "All our actual printing is going to be done on a scaled-down basis by a press outside the city. The margins on firing this puppy up require too many copies for it to be cost effective."

"Then why'd you buy it?" asked Lear. He was examining a machine that had been labeled "rewinder." It was last in a sequence of a dozen beige squares, each the size of a photocopier and housing one of the offset-printer's large components.

"It's part of an experiment I'm running," said H. Defer. "For the experiment to work, I think it might be important for the Visegrad School to appear more legitimate."

"Your experiment got anything to do with those people upstairs?"

We had arrived at the Visegrad School expecting it to be empty of teachers and students except those who had stopped by to pony up for tuition, or to collect a paycheck that constituted the legal minimum qualification for their work visa. Instead, we had found it brimming with activity.

It was not just the unexpected presence of strangers; there was evidence of prolonged habitation: community bulletin boards, umbrellas in a holder by the front door, a functioning water fountain that was so unexpected in a country where tap water had to be cajoled from waiters under threat of violence that it seemed faintly extra-terrestrial in origin.

Most surprising was the notable absence of Doc June's brand of action without consequence. Now, the opposite appeared to be true. There was the overpowering sense that choices had meaning, and that there existed—beyond the hedonism and ennui of Visegrad—a world to build and improve. I pointed this out to H. Defer.

"Well," he said, "that's also part of the experiment. I'm testing a theory that several businesses, when acting interdependently, comprise a sort of primitive life form."

McKayla was giving Lear the eyebrow with enough force to bend cutlery.

Lear cleared his throat. "It's just that, we, Lear and me"— McKayla swiveled her head minutely—"*and* McKayla, we all feel that some of the conclusions you've drawn, we feel—"

"They're a slippery slope," said McKayla.

"Conclusions?" asked H. Defer. "I'm afraid I don't follow."

McKayla withdrew the floppy manuscript from her bag.

"Where'd you get that?" asked H. Defer.

She opened it to a passage she had highlighted in fluorescent green. "There exists no interpretation of reality, no possible world, which is exempt from the question of water and feet; attempts in academia to popularize an objective relativistic doctrine in which real objects are interpreted relative to the individual, are, in themselves, subject to observable laws of sogginess and unsogginess, so that sogginess is a satisfying tautological meta-narrative. That is to say, every human accomplishment, every failure, all of war, culture and technology, the rise of every dictator and the unwritten history of every forgotten peasant that has ever been, or ever will be, is inscribed on the sole of a wet foot. Sogginess and its critical lens—through which we may interpret the events of the past, present, and future—constitutes a second wind for positivism, a revolution in epistemology, and a tent-pole for neo-environmental determinism."

H. Defer paused. "I was hoping to surprise you." He walked over to the window and took a pack of cigarettes from his pocket. He lit one and inhaled, blowing smoke through a hole in the glass. "There's nothing in there you haven't said yourselves. All I did was take some of your ideas and develop them toward their natural conclusion."

McKayla leaned in. "Well, *I* didn't say it, did I? They weren't *my* ideas."

"Well, *your* name won't appear in the table of contents." There was a brief silence during which McKayla visualized H. Defer being cut up and fed to dogs. "Listen," said H.

"No, *you* listen, you fucking reptile." H. shot a look past McKayla in an appeal to Lear, which McKayla correctly interpreted as a suggestion that Lear was holding her leash. Lear opened his mouth, but McKayla raised a finger in his direction, causing him to make a small wet noise as he closed it. "Don't think for a second you're fooling me, latching onto this stuff like you believe in it."

H. Defer cocked his head. "What makes you think I don't believe it?"

"You just want to stir up a hornets' nest. All this," she pointed at the printing press, "is just a photo op."

"I'm sorry," said H., not sounding at all sorry, "have I ever been less than one hundred percent above board with you? When have I ever lied or even distorted the truth? I'm addicted to the truth. I practice radical honesty." This claim more or less held water, since H. Defer's super-effective pitching methodology was, it turned out, just telling clients the truth.

So much for subterfuge. So much for the art of buying drinks until it was no longer peculiar to broach the topic of outstanding student loans.

Here is how the super-effective pitching methodology went: "Listen, I don't know the exact means by which this is done, but I have a friend who can acquire individual debt, including federally held student loan debt, for a flat rate of about $X$ percent.

"Now, I know you're not breaking the bank working in Visegrad, but consider also that over the course of the next few years you could pay down your student loans at a significantly reduced margin. So, whatever number you have in your head—the amount you can expect to save before leaving Visegrad versus the amount you can expect to save living in your parents' basement—I want you to add to that number the value of your outstanding student loans. Also, add to that the considerably reduced cost of incidentals like dental care and health care, not having to own a car or buy gas, the cultural enrichment one undergoes in exposing oneself to another way of life—the Visegrad scene wherein one lives among artists and intellectuals—and the considerable bonus of being able to afford your own apartment. Now ask yourself, 'Where do I really stand to make the most?'"

This breakthrough resulted in pixelated forests of guava and kiwis, mangoes, passion fruit and cocoa, our children playing barefoot in the shade of heavy branches, fructose-crusted smiles painted atop their chubby necks.

"Sure," said H. Defer, tapping his foot against the floor of the reeking basement, "some of this might seem like a dog and pony show—it might not hold up to vigorous examination—but take these machines." He gestured to the assembly line of beige photocopiers.

Lear shrugged. "What about them?"

"It's not cost effective to use this printer to publish books, but the overall value added to the Visegrad School through the acquisition of a press, which, I grant you, is difficult to measure, may actually exceed the cost of the equipment."

"You've got Having teaching lectures on work-life balance," said McKayla.

"So?" said H. Defer.

"He's the least balanced person I've ever met. He's a sack of neuroses with opinions attached."

"He must have something figured out; he's teaching classes."

McKayla's eyes narrowed. "You think this is all a big joke. That's why you're doing it, because you think it's funny."

H. Defer shook his head. "Look, the Visegrad School might be a three-story visa mill, but that doesn't mean it has to stay that way forever. That's the power of action. Okay, let's give me no benefit of the doubt whatsoever; today, all these people are chumps in a scheme I've worked out to claw my way back to academic relevance, only possible because I've begun to rapidly accumulate wealth thanks to the systematic exploitation of a population of young people clinging to the hope of escaping predatory financial institutions; but tomorrow, *tomorrow*, I'm sitting in my home with the windows open, the pitter-patter of *kinderfüße* in the hall, reading correspondence from my old friends: various personal professional and intellectual accomplishments tangentially or directly linked to an institution—this institution—that I helped sculpt. I'm sharing with them my accomplishments, too, the details of a position I've earned in no small part as a result of their hard work. Suddenly, a call from the little woman, 'Strudel!' Isn't that the definition of making good and paying it forward? Does it matter if my motives are not totally altruistic, that I want something for myself? You can do a lot for a lot of people if you knuckle under and find the will to carry on. Okay, let me ask you this: would you rather things kept on the way they've been going? Don't you have doubts about the purpose and integrity of the Visegrad School?"

"Of course I do," said McKayla.

"Well then, what is it you're trying to accomplish?"

"H.," I said, "just because the system's dysfunctional, doesn't mean we should be taking advantage of it."

"Well, why's that?" drawled Lear.

We all looked at him. "No, really, tell me. Why not make some hay, so long as nobody notices? I'm with H.—gather ye rosebuds while ye may, before you gotta hide them up your ass to get them out the country."

I was seized by a strong desire to side with McKayla for the purposes of demonstrating how I was perhaps, not physically or intellectually, but morally, superior to Lear. I didn't have the energy. I turned to her, contemplating a nonchalant shrug, then, seeing the look she was giving Lear, reconsidered: reversed my position on shrugging so radically my back seized up and I winced.

"What's wrong with you?" asked Lear.

I worked the meat of my left shoulder, groping for the segmented muscles along my spine. "Pangs of conscience."

## 33

For Colin Having and Lear, the success of H. Defer was a Pyrrhic windfall, for McKayla, a deep concern, for me, a cause for hushed celebration.

For Wilder, it was all still somehow about Mixed Doubles curling, and he spent a lot of his time probing the Canadian Mixed Doubles Curling Team for weaknesses.

The Canadian Mixed Doubles Curling Team was so far and away the favorite during the Olympics that any inside information about them, especially inside information that might suggest they were not everything they were cracked up to be, was primo sports betting information worth killing for.

They were a rock, a phalanx, an unshakable instrument in the hands of destiny. Wilder was giving the action on them less and less generous odds, totally out of whack with the Canadian SportsBook Assc. of Major League Curling, the only organization keeping tabs on Mixed Doubles curling prior to the Olympics. Of course, so-and-sos from Las Vegas and New York and Atlantic City were sniffing around when Wilder went to watch the team clinch their Olympic berth at the Doubles Semifinal in Alberta. The so-and-sos made him and, afterward, it was an Idareyoutofuckwiththeteam-type deal.

Wilder flew back after a couple weeks with no problems getting in or out. He had to fly back to handle a crisis that was unfolding at the Visegrad School.

The Visegrad School had accrued a staff of Vlodomerian teachers and administrators that were the absolute cream of the crop, and all great players of *rábotånélküliśégetlen*. They had poured out of the private and public sectors at the siren call of unapproachability. Of course, Anglo-sphere secretaries and contractors and lawyers and accountants were sourced for all the actual labor.

The crisis was that the Visegrad School had applied for its International Quality Accreditation through the Central and Eastern European Management Development Assoc., even though the Visegrad School was still only nominally a school, and the Visegrad School Methodology, only nominally a methodology.

In order to pass muster with the accreditation committee, H. Defer had been planning to bribe the Anglo-sphere secretaries of the Vlodomerian administrators to impersonate their bosses, it being impossible for Vlodomerian administrators to work at a caliber necessary to receive accreditation without compromising their reputation and dignity.

"How then," asked Wilder, "will the secretaries impersonate their Vlodomerian administrators?"

"What?" said H. Defer. He screwed up his face and squinted at Wilder. "I'm afraid I don't follow you."

"If it's necessary to bribe the secretaries to impersonate the administrators, because the administrators won't administrate, because they're the best administrators, won't it be necessary for the secretaries not to administrate in order to impersonate the best administrators?"

"Do you think that's why this city has so few venerable scholastic institutions?" asked McKayla.

We were sitting in a giant plaster reproduction of a Thanksgiving centerpiece in a bar called The American Dream.

"Whose idea was it for the Visegrad School to get its International Quality Accreditation, anyway?" asked Doc June.

We all held our breath, wondering if H. Defer would take the hit.

"It wasn't me," said H. Defer. "But are we sure we need to do anything?"

"What does he mean by that?" asked Doc June Sr. He rounded on H.. "What do you mean by that? Can't you see the position this puts us in? It might seem like nothing's at stake, the way you waltzed in here, but this, all this"—he waved his arm around the empty restaurant—"took time."

"What I meant," said H. Defer delicately, "is that if the Anglo secretaries aren't going to be able to impersonate the Vlodomerian administrators, why not cut out the middleman and bribe the Vlodomerian administrators?"

"You're poisoning the well with this accreditation thing," said Doc June. "You've been here five minutes and you're throwing us all under the bus."

"Accreditation," said H. Defer, "was always the next logical step." There was murmuring around the table. H. Defer may have been gunning for the go-to-guy in Berlin, but the rest of us did not want to be legitimized so badly as to brave questions of legitimacy.

"Boy," said Lear, "this must be the first time a school was built so scruple free. When you think about it, it's a model of efficiency. I don't think you could find a scruple if you turned the Ethics professor upside down and shook him."

"What are you implying?" asked Doc June. "I happen to be the Chair in Ethics."

Lear coughed into his fist. "What I mean is that, when you consider the precedent, it seems sort of irresponsible, doesn't it?"

"Not really," said H. Defer. "There's a rich tradition of self-actualization in academia, which has been subverted by a conspiracy of silence."

"Example?" asked McKayla.

"Max Pettenkoffer drank cholera."

Wilder sighed. "It seems like we've come full circle on bribing the secretaries. The problem is that the Vlodomerian administrators cannot appear to be administrating without jeopardizing their positions of *elérhetetlenség.*"

Colin Having raised his hand.

"Yes, Colin?"

"What if we bribe the secretaries not to impersonate the Vlodomerian administrators, but to hire competent administrators from another country?"

"But," said McKayla, "then the Accreditation Review Committee might accuse us of having hired incompetents, because the foreign administrators are so hard-working." She had not really come around to the idea of the Visegrad School or its press, but was caught up in the intellectual exercise of solving the problem presented by the Review Committee.

"Is the Accreditation Review Committee Vlodomerian?" asked Having. "If they're Vlodomerian, they'll just be pretending to review the school for accreditation."

"They're from Slovenia," said H. Defer.

"Slovenia!" decried Having.

"That's practically Austria," said Lear. "Austria is practically Germany."

"What's the worst-case scenario?" asked Wilder.

"Worst case scenario," I said, "is we're dealing with a lot of practically Germans that have done their research, know all about *rábotánélküliségetlen,* and are holding a competent Vlodomerian consultant's family at gunpoint so as to extract straight answers in regard to the Visegrad School and its qualifications."

"Gunpoint," meditated Doc June Sr. "*We* could ransom someone's family."

Wilder leaned back and stroked his beard.

"Ha-ha," said McKayla. No one was laughing.

Having shook his head. "What happens when the competent Vlodomerian administrator tries to pull one over on the competent Vlodomerian consultant, each fearing for the safety of his or her respective family?"

"That's what great moments in *rábotånélkülišégetlen* are all about," said H. Defer. The whole assemblage lapsed into silence. We had glimpsed the complex goings-on of another society, the reasoning that underpinned its entire way of doing things, truly foreign to our own. Yet, there was the feeling that our two systems were mutually derived from the commonsense of human beings. Such moments are few and far between.

McKayla looked around. She opened her mouth to protest, but the food had begun to arrive and she seemed to think better of it.

H. Defer rubbed his chin and grimaced. "Vlodomerian versions of American food always remind me of those Cargo Cults that build runways out of sticks in the hope of attracting supply planes. It's like they've only heard someone describe a chicken sandwich." He lifted half of a chicken club from his plate. "Like maybe they've only seen the crude intertextually identifiable shape of a chicken sandwich in a child's drawing."

"Not to nitpick," I said, "but if we're ransoming the administrator's family, and the practically Germans are ransoming the consultant's family, assuming everyone has enough family to go around, what's that leave us with? Fifty-fifty? Wouldn't it be better to get our administrator to cooperate? You can't trust people when they're backed into a corner."

McKayla crossed her legs and leaned over to take a bite of her Kálifornai Burger. The tip of her foot brushed against my leg.

She glanced at me across the table as it came to rest partway up my shin.

Careful not to disturb her, I put my fork down on my American Breakfast Platter, setting it atop a stack of crêpes.

She brought one finger to her mouth. Her full lips rounded and she pushed it in. There was the heady rush of blood to a colossal vein. She turned the finger over in her mouth and picked out a rock-hard sliver of avocado that had been wedged in her teeth.

"But we really do have the best people," said H. Defer.

"Why the skulduggery?"

"The problem as I see it," I said, "is you've done too much to cultivate an environment of tolerance and professionalism. However competent the administrators are, they're soft from all the coddling."

"Something wrong with your crêpes?" asked Wilder.

I looked down at my breakfast platter. "I find it a little disconcerting when blood sausage and whipped cream appear in such close proximity."

"I didn't know you were so squeamish." He was pulling apart a roast turkey leg, wiping his hands on his shirt whenever he took a drink.

The potentially accidental nature of the foot/shin contact with McKayla made the touch an internal question, more erotic than, say, explicit grinding. At any moment she might start and say, 'I didn't realize that was your leg,' as I might say, 'Excuse me, that's my shin you're touching.' The eye contact was testing the symmetry, psychic interlocutors grappling over our red, white and blue cutlery.

"I think I know what you're saying," said McKayla. "About the Vlodomerian administrators being soft."

Doc June grunted. "Then they'll get what's coming."

"We'll all get what's coming," corrected Wilder. "We've got, what, a quarter of our downline clientele going in and out of that place? International Quality Accreditation is not a bell we can unring, gentlemen."

"What we need," said H. Defer, "is a way to tip things in our favor, give our man an advantage over the hypothetically competent Vlodomerian consultant."

"Why not just give him a chance to save his cushy gig?" asked Doc June Sr. "They love that sort of thing." He wiped his mouth. The lion's share of the deep-fried stuff was his. Fried food made up a lot of his diet and he called himself a 'picky eater' for that reason. He would not touch anything that wasn't vaguely Americana, except maybe a slice of pizza or schnitzel which he called *donkkaseu*. "If our man knows what's at stake, he'll come ready to play."

I cleared my throat. "Only if he thinks failing the accreditation review will result in more work than dodging the review committee."

"We'll have to make that crystal clear," said Wilder. "Crystal. You understand me?"

I was no longer capable of moving the leg. Too much time had elapsed. I was afraid it would trigger an inquiry from among interested parties at the table. I was afraid of the affectionate question—"How long have you two been playing footsie?" They thought McKayla and I were dating, and she had participated in a lot of cruel, ironic flirting since the initiation of the Lear Fadder sexual embargo: McKayla calling me 'my man,' sitting in my lap while Lear glared at us over his drink. But if she wanted to make him jealous, wouldn't she have already withdrawn the foot and apologized—allowed the thing to be discovered, her leg against mine—a big show for Lear's sake?

"If we're not careful," I said, "he might think more of this type of behavior is forthcoming."

"What do you mean?" asked Doc June Sr.

"We don't want our administrator thinking he'll have to constantly be doing his job."

Everyone ate, even me. "You know," said McKayla, kissing sauce from her fingertips, "you have a real knack for this sort of thing."

# 34

éla Béla was a man who exemplified the patriotic Vlodmerian qualities that defined his moment. He was a school administrator who deserved respect, if he could be found to be respected, which he could not. It was not that he played hooky; he seldom left the Visegrad School during business hours, such was the extent of his talent and verve for the great game over which he enjoyed almost complete mastery.

He was a svelte man who wore a blazer and hot pants, tennis shoes and extra-long tube socks. He dressed this way because of how he played, which required a complete range of motion.

His style of play was this. Béla Béla would knock on the door of a person who he had decided to meet with, sit down and apologize for being late. Immediately, he would glance at his watch and spring back onto his feet. He would apologize a second time, having realized that there was someplace else he was supposed to be. Then he would race out of the door and down the hall to his next appointment, where he would arrive late and begin apologizing all over again.

His actual administrating was incidental, and involved expanding the school so as to take increasingly circuitous routes everywhere he went. His American secretary hated him because she had to work extraordinarily hard to maximize the distances involved.

We had fingered him to meet with the hypothetically competent Vlodomerian consultant whose family was being held at gunpoint by practically Germans, because he was a stellar example of the competency of our administrators, and because he might need the meetings to show up late to, anyway.

"Nothing doing," said his secretary. "Béla likes to arrive unannounced. He only tells people they have a meeting the moment he steps in. That way they don't mind when he takes off. He has to stay on good terms with these people because there's only a certain number of offices with maximum distances in between. Building the satellite campus in Strelsau is really going to simplify things."

"That's amazing," said McKayla. "It must be interesting to work for someone so talented."

"Me? I hate him. I'm the one stuck organizing the construction of a satellite campus on a secretary's salary."

"Why don't we just tie him down?" asked Lear.

"Let's give the man his due," I said, glancing at the secretary. "You heard what she said, he's a genius."

So our objective was to convey to Béla Béla the bind we were in, from which he might extrapolate the significance of the Accreditation Review Committee.

We fumbled it from the beginning.

That was understandable perhaps. It was only with tremendous luck and the application of our combined intellectual powers that we ever stood a chance of success, since none of us were practitioners of *rábotånélküliśégetlen*. We did have natural talents that lay in that direction. We had made our money without working, taught classes at the Visegrad School without teaching, and held high positions in an increasingly respectable organization that we had done nothing to earn. Most significantly, we had a great deal of time in which to think.

Lear's initial idea was to waylay Béla Béla as he jogged, since it was during unplanned stops that the man did what administrating was not conducted by his secretary. This administrating occurred when his shoes came untied or he struck up a conversation at the urinal.

I think Lear assumed, and we assumed by proxy, that the Vlodomerian dream of unapproachability was part posturing, that it did not thrum undiluted from Béla Béla's soul as he bounded between disparate points in the Vlodomerian State Consumer Electronics Manufacturing Facility. We were simply unable to conceive of a world that could not be explored through the shrewd application of money. We unfairly blamed each other for many of our subsequent failures which stemmed from this singular mistake.

Lear ascertained from Béla Béla's secretary which offices he would be running between, and, taking into account his average ground speed, calculated where he was likely to be. Unfortunately, Béla Béla varied his routes, which made it impossible to meet him along the way. Also, because he ran everywhere, Béla Béla was a man of fantastic physical endurance, prone to remarkable bursts of speed. Furthermore, he ran with his head down, noise-canceling earbuds blaring music in his ears. And everything had to be accomplished with a degree of plausible deniability, since plausible deniability characterized the execution of any great play in *rábotánélkülíségetlen*. That meant a lot of stage diving, faking emergency medical problems, congesting the hallways with hired extras that made jogging at any significant rate impossible.

Even these stratagems proved fruitless, because Béla Béla pretended not to understand a word of English, and, though we knew he did speak a word of English—spoke a great many words of English according to his secretary—there was no way to prove it.

So there was Lear, screaming at the administrator as he chugged along without making eye contact or giving any sign that he could hear what was being shouted over the music in his noise-canceling earbuds, except once muttering, "*Ne beszélek jézyk angielski.*"

The next solution to present itself was that McKayla and Béla should have some sort of collision, jettisoning from her hands hundreds of fliers like the type dropped on enemy troops during a prolonged military campaign.

In the clearest and most concise Vlodomerian, the fliers said, *Surrender, we have you surrounded. You are to meet with the Accreditation Review Committee at such-and-such time, on such-and-such day.* The gambit hinged on prejudices of ours that led us to believe a healthy Vlodomerian man would not miss the chance to stare down McKayla's blouse.

This is what I mean when I say we really had the best people, that Béla Béla was a talented administrator, who, under normal circumstances, would not have failed to pass muster with an unbiased judiciary. Not only did he not stop to help McKayla, which would have potentially undermined his position of *elérhetetlenség*, but, sensing through his tremendous physical acuity that a trap was being set, dropped his shoulder and shot through her as if smashing into a row of defensive linemen.

The collision resembled nothing so much as the crystalline bud of a dandelion being shot with an air rifle. Fliers glided to the hallway floor and we were all very taken with the poetry of the moment.

Here was a noble spirit, unbowed, refusing to acknowledge Lear's entreaties, gazing through McKayla's fliers with unfocused eyes. But once an opponent knows your methods in *rábotânélküliségetlen*, it is only a matter of time and there is nothing left for you but to meet the coup de grâce with gamesmanship and dignity.

It was my brainwave, I am not too proud to admit, that notched Béla Béla onto our belts. His undoing was that we also exemplified those properties that defined our moment, as young, active minds that had developed a revolutionary, universal, historiographical and sociological theory based on the wetness of feet.

We poured bottles of mineral water onto him as he jogged up the school's front steps, so that he would have to take off his shoes and hang up his socks. The bottles glugged as water cascaded over the second story railing, splashing down on his bald head and shoulders. His first instinct was to flee, and he pivoted, but the polished concrete steps were slippery. When he fell, he fell with his left leg beneath him. Water slapped his back and ass as he rolled around clutching his knee. It soaked into his shirt and shorts and extra-long tube socks: navy blazer turning black and flopping, catching him once in the testicles so that he stopped rolling and lay still. After a few minutes he dragged himself inside on his stomach.

"Director Béla," said Wilder, "what happened?"

"I've been attacked," said Béla Béla. The floor was covered in McKayla's fliers, and he was leaving an administrator-shaped swath as he went.

"It's a good thing you're here," said Wilder. "We happen to have a doctor handy." He indicated Doc June who was sitting nearby.

Béla Béla gave Doc June the once-over. "Someone please call for the ambulance."

"Actually," said Wilder. "It's a very lucky thing, meeting you like this. I'd like to bend your ear for a moment."

Béla Béla's eyes narrowed. "You should arrange a meeting with my secretary."

"Nonsense," said Wilder. "That would be a wasted opportunity."

Teal paramedics loaded Béla Béla into the back of an ambulance while the people following us asked them questions and smoked cigarettes.

After the administrator had been carefully stowed and the ambulance was out of sight, Doc June turned to me. For a moment, I thought he would be angry about poor Béla. He squeezed my shoulder and said, "I've got to hand it to you—not that I wasn't starting to have doubts. I was beginning to doubt that it would ever get done. I was beginning to suspect that we might be trying to fit a square peg into a round hole with this Vlodomerian thing. I was thinking we should address this problem with an old-fashioned round peg. But now that I've seen it all come together, how you've comported yourselves—is that right, comported?" I nodded. Wilder's mouth was unslung over Doc June's shoulder, pores on his chin stretching into fat ellipses. "Now that I've seen how you've comported yourselves, it's given me a real appreciation of your group prowess."

"It was all Lear," said McKayla.

Lear glanced at me.

"It was nothing," I said.

"Well, whatever the case," said Doc June, "we've decided to reward you for your efforts. We've been talking, and we decided to put together a master service agreement for all your future trades."

"Wow," said Lear. "What's a master service agreement?"

"It's an invitation to play at the big boy's table. No more approval to take on clients, and no collateral for trades up to a half million. You'll have a downline all to yourselves."

"Great," said McKayla. "More money."

"Not just that," said Wilder. He wagged a finger. "I've got something else. Follow me."

We left Doc June and followed Wilder toward the center of the building. He adopted the attitude of a man with an exciting secret, smiling to himself and drumming his fingers on his stomach. "I was hoping you'd come through for us," he said. "I would have shown you no matter what, of course, but I was hoping this would be my chance." He made a series of lefts, a dramatic right. We entered a long, thin access hall that ended in a pair of double doors. None of us had been so far toward the middle, since the middle of the building was not along any maximally circuitous jogging routes.

Wilder removed an old-fashioned brass key from his pocket and inserted it into the door lock. The doors stuck for a moment, then swung open. We were standing at the back of a large lecture hall, sun filtering down through swirls of dust that scattered across drop-cloth planes of gray and white. Racks of blinking servers stood among sheets and piles of chairs, as if their enclosures had sprouted in fairy rings from the vinyl floor. Bookshelves climbed one wall, towering over a heavy wooden desk and a rolling hospital bed. The whole arrangement was tied together with a bright green and orange carpet.

We stopped at the threshold and stared. It was like opening your refrigerator to find that your salad crisper had developed a view of the ocean.

"That's right," said Wilder, "you've never seen my apartment."

"Where do you shower?" asked McKayla. "What do you eat?"

"I don't have time to cook. I shower at the gym."

His terrible smell: mildewed towels and the fungus that lurks in the drain of men's locker rooms. Of course.

"No windows, though," he conceded. "That's why I bought my green friend." He pointed to a limp potted plant by the rolling bed. "Let me show you what I'm talking about."

We followed him to the front of the lecture hall and stood among his possessions, not desiring to disturb them. Wilder walked to the desk and unlocked a drawer. He opened it and picked through its contents. Then, selecting a small manila envelope, he took it out and set it on the desk. He shut the drawer and re-locked it, slapping the envelope against the palm of his hand as he brought it over to us.

He held it out to McKayla, who was reading the spines of books. She glanced at the envelope. "What's this?" she asked.

"Open it and see."

There was a bright red stamp on the envelope that said, СОВЕРШЕННО СЕКРЕТНО. She took it. "It's not," she said.

Wilder's upper lip paled to contain his yellow teeth. "Someone owed me a favor."

She unwound the string that was used to seal the envelope. "What is it?" asked Lear.

She turned the manila envelope upside down and a bundle of papers slid into her hand. "It's him," she said. "You did it. You found him!"

"The SEC man?" asked Lear

"The SEC man?" asked McKayla incredulously. "Who cares about the SEC man? He found Bukovni!" She held up the dossier, waving it for us to see. Pinned to the collection of papers was the fuzzy black and white photograph of a headstone.

"Where is he?" I asked.

"Strelsau," said Wilder.

"Of course," said McKayla, "that's why I couldn't find him in Visegrad." She began to jump up and down like a little kid.

Wilder nodded. "They wanted to put him somewhere no one would think to look."

"Strelsau," she squealed. Then, all at once, she leapt into his arms.

He lifted her easily and spun her around in mid-air. For a moment, it was as if they were alone in the room.

# 35

"We've gotta get out of here," said Lear. He was staring out of the window on the train. It had taken a month for us to pin down the graveyard in Strelsau and make our arrangements. "Unless we do something drastic, we'll end up being the people we were afraid we'd become."

McKayla snorted. "Successful, you mean?"

"Quasi-intellectual neurotics balding into our soup."

"Weren't we lying to ourselves, though?" asked McKayla. "Weren't we walking away from success and prestige because, deep down, we thought we'd never have any? Wasn't this self-imposed exile just to keep us from bruising our egos?"

"Success?" said Lear, "This is success?" He indicated his phone with one hand, which was new. We were making so much that we had begun to purchase things we did not need.

"Your problem," said McKayla, "is that you've spent so long broke and sneering at the system, you've begun to equate the two."

"My problem is that I have to put on a southern accent every time I see anyone. I've started to dream in that accent. My interior monologue has developed a drawl. It's like someone else is narrating everything that happens to me."

I started and got up from my seat. I stared into the corridor after the man who had just wandered past. "It's him," I said.

"Who?" asked Lear.

Without answering, I poked my head into the hall.

He was stepping through the pneumatic door at the end of the first-class car. Gone now, our days of riding economy. I held a finger to my lips and shut the door to the compartment carefully behind me. As quietly as I could, I followed him into the vestibule, arriving just as the door to the dining car slid shut. I waited for him to reach its other end, then I hurried after, plates of blanched liver vibrating as I thundered past.

When I arrived at the next car he had vanished. I checked the bathroom and found it unlocked and empty. I started back in the opposite direction, going door to door and peeking into every apartment. I found him in the third car in the second to last berth, surrounded by the people following us.

One of the people following us was reading a paperback with the cover folded over. Two more were playing cards by the window.

The man with the cowlick saw me peeking into the apartment and waved.

He said something to the man with the paperback, who slid the door open without looking up. The pair playing had the window unlatched so they could smoke cigarettes, which you aren't supposed to do on trains in that country.

With the window open it was very loud, so the short man with a cowlick had to shout to be heard.

"Rye," he shouted, "the beautiful writer."

"What?"

He turned to the men playing cards and said something in Vlodomerian. They stabbed out their cigarettes and shut the window.

"Rye," repeated the short man, "the beautiful writer. Would you like to come in?"

"I'm alright," I said.

"You might be wondering how we all know each other," he said.

"Is it because you've been following me?"

"It's because we're following you," he said.

The Vlodomerian inland rail equivalent of the public transportation gestapo walked through the pneumatic doors at the end of the hall. He wore a conductor's uniform with a round blue hat that reminded me of a *gendarm*.

"Why are you following us?" I asked.

"For your own good," said the short man.

The man in uniform began checking tickets in the next compartment.

"Did you poison the SEC man?" I asked.

The people following us all looked up at me when I said that.

"Who's that?" asked the short man.

"He was my friend, an American. Somebody disappeared him."

The short man with the cowlick frowned. "Have you reported this to your embassy?"

"Are you the ones that disappeared him?"

"Let me ask you something, Mister—"

"Just Rye," I said.

"Rye then. Rye, how much do you think you're worth? How much will you be expected to earn before your next filing?"

"Filing?"

"What about your friends? Could you ballpark the three of you sitting in that first-class compartment?"

"A lot," I said.

"And where did all this money come from? Did it just grow on trees?"

"It belongs—belonged to Americans."

"And where do the Americans get their money?"

"That's none of my business," I said. He waited politely for me to answer his question. "Working contracts—teaching, a lot of them."

"Ah," he said, "then it is really Vlodomerian money. It is really the labor of Vlodomerian people paying Americans that is being sent back to pay American companies."

"*Jegyet*," said the ticket inspector. He was standing beside me with a machine that scanned tickets. When I didn't move, he said, "Ticket."

I patted my pockets apologetically. I had left my ticket in our compartment.

"I left it in my compartment," I said. "I'm in first class."

"Go back to your seat," ordered the inspector.

"Just a minute. I'm in the middle of something."

The ticket inspector looked into the compartment. The man with the cowlick gave a discerning shake of his head.

The ticket inspector said, "Go to your seat now or I will have you taken off." Here was a man of such limited capacity that he spent all day walking up and down trains doing his job.

I shrugged and made to leave. "Mr. Rye," called the short man with the cowlick. "Have you ever been to a casino?"

"No," I said.

"You should go. You're so lucky."

One of the people following us opened the compartment window and the noise of the rumbling train drowned everything out.

"They're smoking in there," I told the inspector.

When I got back to the compartment, McKayla asked, "Did you see somebody you know?"

"I did."

"Who was it?"

"You don't know him." I said.

"Who do you know that we don't know?" asked Lear.

"Have you ever been to a casino?" I asked.

"I hate casinos," said Lear. "They really creep me out."

"My brother used to go to one," said McKayla. "He counted cards at an Indian casino outside of Denver. It wasn't to make money or anything, he just liked to get away with it." There was a mythos of intellect around McKayla's brother that I disliked. He spent his time designing toys, but not with an audience in mind, and was tremendously revered among toy designers of that type.

"What's it like there?" I asked.

"It's all right," she said. "He won mostly. Like I said, he wasn't in it for the money and spent most of it there."

"How come?"

"They make it really easy to do, comp you all kinds of stuff just to keep you from going home. Once, we stayed in a suite and he took the whole family out for dinner at the casino restaurant. They do it so you'll blow your winnings, because they know you'll lose it all eventually, as long as you don't leave."

Afterward I sat and watched the corridor and waited for the ticket inspector who never arrived.

## 36

Strelsau had not been bombed or shelled by artillery during the war and the buildings on the square were mostly unmolested but, here, the brutalist gray, there, the pale green of safety glass. And faintly discernible everywhere were the cloven serifs of Yiddish sibilants, the faded signs of a Strelsau Jewry. The skunk of beer and the aroma of frying meat wafted from the stoops of its imperial apartments.

We followed McKayla across a small pedestrian bridge and onto the side of the highway, where we walked for almost fifteen minutes while sleet pelted us as it was kicked up and turned over by semi-trucks. We were chilled to the bone by the time we found the embankment and climbed down.

Large tombstones protruded from among the collapsed remnants of a waist-high hurricane fence. We watched, teeth-chattering, as McKayla withdrew the prized dossier from an interior pocket of her coat.

"Who builds an overpass across a graveyard?" Lear asked.

"Good question," said McKayla and buried her nose in the papers.

"Ah," I said, recognizing the script. "They were Galitzners."

"What?" said Lear.

"It's a Jewish graveyard," I said. "I guess they thought nobody would mind."

McKayla looked around, taking in the old graves and the defoliated slope beneath the elevated road. Tombstones climbed the hill for a short distance, stood in highest concentration near the highway as though deposited by a retreating flood.

"Somebody's idea of a joke," she said.

Lear grunted. "Kill hundreds of thousands of Jews, get buried in a Jewish cemetery."

McKayla clapped the dossier shut and handed it to Lear, who tucked it under his arm. She threw a leg over the top of the chain-link fence and straddled it, then hopped nimbly onto its other side. She picked her way between the graves, and, reaching the cemetery's far end, began counting up the rows and columns, moving toward us as she went.

She arrived at a grave and stopped. She hesitated and glanced around. It looked like maybe she had lost count. She shook her head.

"Uh-oh," said Lear.

She started over, moving left.

"I bet all this infrastructure wasn't here when they buried him," I said.

"Probably not," said Lear.

I bounced lightly up and down on the balls of my feet and Lear blew into his hands. She arrived at the same place and stood staring, arms akimbo.

She came over to us. "Which way is north?" she asked.

Lear got out his phone and checked. He pointed in the direction we'd just come.

"That's what I thought," she said. Then she walked in the opposite direction, counting rows and columns again—this time moving right. She reached a different grave and stopped. It was large and ancient, Yiddish letters worn away by weather. She stared at it for a moment, then looked around and behind it.

She walked back down to the fence.

"Everything okay?" Lear asked.

"Can I see the photograph?"

"The photograph?"

She pointed to Lear's armpit. "There's a copy in the dossier."

"Oh," he said. He opened the dossier and began to fish around for it. He found the picture, but just as he did, a breeze snatched it out of his hand.

"Careful," warned McKayla. "Let Rye get it."

I ran it down where it had landed in a puddle and brought it back.

It was a grainy copy of a dim photograph and now it was badly damaged.

"Whoops," said Lear.

"Just give it to me," she said.

I passed it over the fence and she held it up to the overcast sky. I could discern the blurry outline of a grave, but all the photograph's other distinguishing features had been expunged. Without saying anything, she turned and strode brusquely back toward the incline.

She stopped at the far corner and held out her hand in the direction of a tree, making a right angle with her thumb as if sighting.

She turned her head this way and that, then began picking her way back up the embankment. She walked slowly, pausing along the way to examine headstones. Once she reached the top, she came back and started over.

She stopped at the gravestone she had previously considered, then knelt beside it.

Lear gave me a look of hopeful significance.

She stood up and continued walking a few paces. She stopped and, returning to the grave, hunkered down and peered around either side, seeming to make much of the angle between the tree and the headstone.

She backed up and put her hands on her hips, bent over, and nodded. She patted the grave like an obedient dog.

"Hey, alright," said Lear. "Yes."

She looked around. "Be my lookout."

We both gave her a thumbs up.

She dropped trow, backside shielded by the tail of her jacket. She held up one finger for a moment, crooking it as a gout of steam rose from in front of the grave. I turned reflexively away.

"Hah," said Lear, "you're cute."

A car swerved onto the road that ran beneath the overpass. "Hey," I said. "Hey."

"What?" said Lear. The noisy little car shot toward us. I grabbed his shoulder as he turned to look. "Car," he shouted. He took a few running steps. "Car!"

I looked up at McKayla who was still peeing, but was otherwise motionless.

The car slowed down as it passed. For several seconds the faces of children were visible as they ballooned against the glass of the rear driver's side window.

The stream abated. McKayla shook, pulled on her underwear and hiked up her pants. She was still struggling with the top button as she walked up to the fence.

"Hand sanitizer," she said. I passed her a small bottle of hand sanitizer we had acquired for that purpose.

"Sorry about the car," said Lear.

"Whatever," she said. She wiped her hands on the back of her jeans and hopped the fence.

"Well?" I said.

"Well what?"

"Did you find it?"

"What do you mean, did I find it?" She pointed in the direction of the grave. "Didn't you just see me pissing on it? Weren't you both so busy watching me piss you didn't notice a car until it was halfway up my ass?"

"Okay," I said.

She glared at me. "You think I'd piss on it if I wasn't absolutely sure it was him?" I silently recalled the grave of the late 'Bukovni F.' McKayla had despoiled in Visegrad. "You think I'd piss on the grave of some old Jew, because the man who wiped out his whole family has a marker the same shape and size?"

"That's a pretty specific question," I said.

Lear sucked in air through his teeth.

McKayla seethed. "Jesus, you really think I would, don't you? Don't you think I'd make absolutely sure before I did that?"

"Okay," I said. "I'm sorry. I guess it was sort of rhetorical."

She pushed the wet photograph into Lear's chest, then made for the embankment. Lear and I exchanged looks and he held the picture up to the light, where it was no longer possible to distinguish any characteristics of the graveyard or the surrounding hillside. She glanced back and, seeing what we were doing, lunged for the photograph. She met no resistance and snatched it from Lear's hand before stuffing it into her jacket pocket.

At dinner we talked very little and ate superb food that cost practically nothing. When either of us asked McKayla a question she gave one-word answers.

Lear ordered round after round of cocktails made with Galician honey. "Four months ago," he said, "we were squabbling over the price of visa stamps with the operator of a kielbasa stand."

"Who's we?" I asked.

Lear waved away the question and lifted a martini glass. "To our success." We stared over each other's right shoulders, happy not to be making eye contact. Lear took a drink and blew out a soft belch. "We never figured out what that tower was for, did we?"

"Who knows why anybody does anything in this country," I said.

McKayla took a sip and asked, "Did you know that everyday the caretaker of our apartment hangs a black flag outside our building?"

"Oh yeah?" I asked, relieved that she was forming complete sentences.

"Yeah," she said. "He raises it in the morning and takes it down at sunset."

"I thought that started with the bombing," said Lear.

"No," said McKayla. "It's always been that way. I've been trying to figure out why for months and I recently got up the nerve to ask. He told me it was to commemorate the loss of Vlodomeria to the Swedes."

"The Swedes?"

"Uh-huh," said McKayla. "The Swedes came down the river systems through Poland, all the way to Visegrad. They burned the city."

"Around when was all this going on," asked Lear, "this thing with the Swedes?"

"Mid-seventeenth century," said McKayla.

"So, you're saying the caretaker of our building raises a black flag every day because Visegrad was sacked four hundred years ago by Swedes?"

"Three hundred fifty," said McKayla. "But I don't think he cares about the Swedes."

"Then why's he do it? I mean, what's it accomplish?"

"It accomplishes the act of raising a black flag every morning." Lear gave me a worried look.

"I can help?" asked our waiter. He was an ethnic Pole. He had demonstrated that he was not a player of *rábotånélkülišégetlen* by being generally attentive; tourist season was over, and, except for us, the restaurant was empty.

"Can I have another of the same?" asked McKayla, lifting her drink.

"Let's ask him," said Lear.

"Huh?" said McKayla. She shook her head. "No, leave him alone."

"He doesn't mind," said Lear. "You don't mind, do you?"

The waiter shook his head in a small way, indicative of the fact that he didn't really know whether he minded or not.

"See?" said Lear. He pivoted his whole body in the direction of the waiter. "What do you know about the Swedish invasion?"

"Swedish?" said the waiter.

"*A svéd*" said McKayla, "*svéd vojnorú.*"

The waiter's face clouded. "Oh yes," he said, "*a potop svéd.* Terrible, terrible time. A very terrible time in the Vlodomerian history. Are you interested in our history? This is the historic building."

"It is?" asked Lear. "The only one?"

"Sorry, what?" asked the waiter.

"Ignore him," said McKayla.

"Would you like to see it?" asked the waiter hopefully.

"The historic building?" asked Lear.

"Yes," said the waiter.

"Now?" asked McKayla.

"Yes, I will give you it. Come with me." We got to our inebriated feet. "This way,"

He led us toward the back, where a long hallway branched off an auxiliary dining room. The hallway ended with a sign on a short stand that was in Galician, Vlodomerian, Polish, English, German, and Japanese, and said, THE JEWISH ROOM, with an arrow pointing left.

"What kind of Jewish room is it?" I asked.

"Normal Jewish room," explained the waiter. We followed him past the sign, entered a cold, dark space. "Please wait," said the waiter. He flicked a switch. We were standing in a turn of the century drawing room.

A chiffonier with cabriole legs was set against the wall to our left beside a beautifully restored velvet divan. There was a sideboard beside a washstand and a gleaming credenza. There was an ottoman, a Ming vase, and a marquetry commode. On one side sat a four-poster bed, as though it had lurched in from an adjoining room.

"This is the normal Jewish room," said the waiter. "Everything is as it appears."

We looked prudishly around.

"Come and see." He ushered us forward. "Everything from before the World War Two."

Lear cleared his throat. "And how many Jewish people were there in Strelsau?"

"Jews?" The waiter shrugged. "Less than half."

"Less than half? What does that mean? Of how many?"

"Until the Germans," explained the waiter. "Less than half from people in the city."

"Of everybody?"

"All kinds of people," said the waiter. "Hungarians, Poles, Slovaks, Jews, Gypsy."

"How much is less than half?" asked McKayla. The waiter shrugged. She pointed at the restored bed. "Why did you do this?"

The waiter frowned. He weighed the question, which maybe was not a fair question. "History," was what he finally came up with.

Lear and I nodded.

"It's ghoulish," said McKayla.

"I do not know," said the waiter. "What is ghoulish?"

She shook her head. "This," she said. "All of it."

"People like to see," explained the waiter.

Lear looked at me askance. I don't know what he expected me to do.

"That's it? Just to look at?" asked McKayla.

The waiter deliberated. "For some money, you can have the full surface tea."

"Ah," said Lear, as if this explained everything.

"Maybe we should go," I said.

"I think I'm understanding," said the waiter, "that you are one of these kinds of Americans."

McKayla stared at him. "What kind is that?"

"My grandfather was lucky," said the waiter. "He was a good farmer in Ukraine." He said this as if in answer to McKayla's question.

We traded glances. After a moment, Lear asked, "Why was he lucky?"

"He was from near Kharkiv," said the waiter. "You know Kharkiv?" We nodded. "He was very lucky because he was a good farmer, so when everyone is starfing he has food to eat. You know about the starfing?"

"The Holodomor," said McKayla.

"Good, then I will not explain. Everyone starfing, but he was a good farmer, so he had food to eat. It was very difficult for him because it was against the laws for farmers to have food to eat. Police came and they have a pole, pole?" We nodded. "They take a pole and," he gripped an imaginary spear and thrust it around the room. "In fireplace and in clothes, even toilet. If they find any potato or even some seed, seed?" We nodded. "Yes, then the police shoot him. He was lucky and hided things and they are never finding them; food was against the laws, because the farmers hided their food to not starf. Many farmers are starfing because it was against the laws to hide it, which is why they hided it."

"Huh," said Lear.

The waiter nodded. "Soon, it is also against the laws starfing."

"What?" said McKayla.

"Starfing was also illegal, illegal? Because it makes communism look bad to starf. It was illegal to eat and it was illegal to starf. This was very bad, but my grandfather was lucky. He was a good farmer so he is eating a little food every day and was not starfing. His wife and children is eating every day, so was not starfing too. Americans think starfing is like"—he cradled his stomach to mime a swollen belly and made a pained expression—"but it is worse, is sickness and is eating dead people and starfing anyway. My grandfather goes to the neighbor to beg for food for his wife and child, but he is dead. He goes to the church to beg, and the priest is dead. He goes to his parents. They are dead and the house is burned up. He goes to his brother, who is not dead, but will not let him in. Where is his brother's wife? He does not say. Later, the police shoot his brother for not starfing. At home, all his childs is starfing and dying. He buries them. His wife is starfing and dying. Finally it is time that he also dies. He goes to the church and digs a grave. Grave? But he is lucky, because the next morning the grave is full of people. Can you imagine this, people wanting a grave so much?" The waiter laughed. "He is digging another grave. He is all day digging in the grave and lies in the grave, but is raining. He tries to lie down and he floats! He tries to drowned—drown?" More nodding. "But it is hard, so he gets up and goes to some house. In the house lives a communist. The communist is making tea for him, saying do not give up and this kind of thing. He hates communists now more than anyone and he kills this one. He waits for others, but no one ever comes. He is lucky. He wears the clothes of the communist and walks to the next town and is getting on the train. The train has many soldiers going to Poland. Stalin thinks Poland will be invading. My grandfather walks from the train station to Poland and is becoming a soldier because he also thinks Poland will be invading. He wants to shoot communists, you understand? He meets a *vlodomeri* living in Poland and has a daughter. It is not Poland that is invading Ukraine but Germany that is invading Poland. My grandfather does not know any Germans. 'Why should a *ukrán* who wants to shoot communists shoot Germans?' he thinks. My grandfather shoots them all the same. Afterward, they shoot my grandfather's Polish friends. 'Polish are dogs,' they say. 'The law protects soldiers. A dog cannot be a soldier, so how can it protect Polish?' My grandfather is lucky, because he is from Ukraine. Germany is not fighting with Ukraine yet, so the Germans send him to the communists. The communists put him in the camp of Polish. In the camp, the communists shoot the Polish, but my grandfather is lucky because he speaks Polish and Ukraine. He works on the trains. Now my grandfather is very close to where he is from. He has been gone many years, but he is worried all the time he will be seen. Also, people all the time are shot and dying from working on the trains. Then Germany is also invading Ukraine and freeing my grandfather. My grandfather does not like

Germans now, but he does everything they say, then escapes. He walks to Poland, and from *Krakkó* goes to Visegrad. It is months and he is all the time hiding and starfing the whole way. When he is arriving in Visegrad, his neighbors say the Germans send his wife and daughter to a camp. Russia invades. Russia is blowing up his apartment and killing his neighbors and sending him to a farm. It is the worst farm you ever seen. All the farmers are starfing. He is very successful there as a farmer. That is why he is lucky he is such a good farmer back in Ukraine."

The waiter crossed his arms and looked at us as though he had made his point.

McKayla cleared her throat. She shifted nervously from foot to foot. "But what type of American am I?" she asked.

"What?" said the waiter.

"You said I was a type of American. What type of American did you mean?"

"You are the type that likes to watch movies about Jews in striped pajamas. You think what this is like, is Jews in pajamas, because that is what Americans find when they invade Germany."

"They didn't wear striped pajamas?" asked Lear.

"They didn't wear anything," said the waiter.

"I don't get it," said Lear.

"How many Jews are working in these camps? Zero per-cent. Half of zero percent. It is not in camps, where they are dying. It is on roads and in train stations. From the train stations they go to undress and are gassed: no pajamas. If a Jew wears pajamas, it means he is working and he is as lucky as my grandfather."

McKayla didn't say anything.

"Do you know what the Hungarians are calling Vlodomeria?" asked the waiter. "*Bohatulorság.* You know what this means?"

"God something," said McKayla hoarsely.

The waiter nodded. "The Behind the Back of God Country. Before the—What is *potop* means?" he asked.

"Flood," she said.

"The flood, the *svéd*, it was *Eperorság*—Strawberry Country. After the flood, come the Turkic, *ostrák*, Hungary, Germany, Russians, Ukraine. Then it is Behind the Back of God Country." Lear was examining McKayla, who was staring at the carpet. It was a big Persian. She was opening and closing her hands. After no one said anything, she must have realized we were watching her and turned her whole body to one side so that we could not see her face.

Lear bit his lip. "Why's it called that?"

"What?" asked the waiter.

"Why's it called the Country Behind God's Back?"

"Ah," said the waiter, who had perhaps anticipated a little more deductive reasoning on our part, "it is the Behind the Back of God Country, because God cannot see there so many bad things are happening."

"I mean, why the back?" asked Lear. "There are plenty of places God can't see, if we're going to apply that kind of logic to God."

McKayla slowly rounded on him, tears in the corners of her eyes.

The waiter leaned back and gave Lear a thorough reassessment. "I have never thought about this. It also is maybe, because what happens in *Bohatulorság* is coming from everywhere, but not everywhere else *Bohatulorság* is not, not—"

"Affecting?" asked Lear. He was making a point not to return the look McKayla was giving him.

The waiter nodded. "Yes."

"Well, that seems more like God's Trash Can, because God can turn around, you know." He smiled nervously. "I mean, wherever God's looking he can't see behind his back, of course, but if he got himself a mirror and stood in the bathroom—You understand what I'm getting at. But why would God go through his trash, like did he accidentally throw something away? Plus, there's a sort of *eau de Vlodomeria*, right?"

"I am not understanding," said the waiter.

"It could be the Country in God's Sandwich," I said helpfully. "You put a lot of things into a sandwich but you never take them out again."

"People *eat* sandwiches," chided Lear. "I think what we're looking for is more like the Country Between the Cushions on God's Sofa, or Way Up in God's Colon."

"Don't be disgusting," said McKayla. She turned to the waiter. "I'm sorry about them."

He shrugged.

"Or God's Shower Drain," I suggested. "Because it's small and wet, and the idea of anything climbing out is pretty alarming."

The waiter stood by the light switch as we filed out ahead of him.

"What about God's Perineum?" said Lear. "It's got some of the esoteric qualities of God's Back, but with fewer caveats."

"What about the Country in the Stains on God's Kitchen Grout?" I asked.

Lear shook his head. "Let's confine ourselves to God's body, so as to constructively limit our options and also to guard against tangents sure to arise from theological questions pertaining to the contents of God's refrigerator."

McKayla cleared her throat. "If we're going to do this, let's do it methodically. Working backward, what do we know about Vlodomeria?"

We returned to our table and sat down while the waiter left to calculate the margin by which we should be deprived of our change.

"It's a place with a lot of conflict," I said.

"But it's not a wasteland," said Lear. "It has a rich culture and history. If anything, it's overwhelming. Who can keep up with the invasions, what with the Swiss—"

"Swedes," said McKayla.

"It's a history that elicits damp unpleasantness. A scabby nostril, maybe."

"Let's see," I said, "dark, wet, smelly."

McKayla sat suddenly upright in her chair. "I know where it is," she said excitedly. "I know exactly where it is. But it's not on God's body."

"Where is it?" said Lear.

"It's on Rye. It's Rye's belly button."

Lear frowned. I felt a prick of deep internal wrongness, as if some small organ had begun vigorously to malfunction.

"I don't get it," said Lear.

"Rye's belly button is abnormally deep," explained McKayla. "It smells like Parmesan cheese."

I forced a laugh. "That's right," I said.

Lear cocked his head. "How do you know what his belly button smells like?"

McKayla looked at him. It took her a second to understand what he was asking.

I took a sip of water. "Why wouldn't she know what my belly button smells like?" I asked.

"*I* don't know what your belly button smells like," said Lear.

"I'm sure I've mentioned it," I said. "I tell people about my belly button all the time."

"You do not," said Lear. He rounded on McKayla. "McKayla?"

McKayla had turned bright red, chest rising and falling as she stared at the table. She said, "What do you care?"

"What?" asked Lear.

"What do you care if I know what his belly button smells like?"

I attempted to clear my throat.

He regarded her coolly. "What's Wilder's belly button smell like then?" She gawked at him, mouth open. "How about

Having's?" Her eyes narrowed to slits and I leaned instinctively back, as far as I could go. "You thought I didn't know? You cheated on whatshisname when we met—"

"Chris."

"—you think I wasn't expecting this now that every asshole in town has your phone number?"

They were locked into each other, spiraling radically out of control. I wanted to say something that would stop whatever was about to happen. What I said was, "Guys, c'mon."

"It's okay," said McKayla, "that's all he's got. He can't fuck me anymore, so it's all he's got. You know he's impotent, right?"

Lear grinned.

"C'mon, guys."

"I never loved you," said Lear softly. He said it in a way that, whether or not it was true, all three of us knew he meant it. McKayla blinked. "How could I?" he asked. "I know you. I understood you from the moment we met, trying so hard to be somebody. You've never even come close to surprising me. You're not special."

McKayla rose to her feet. I brought up a hand to my face to shield it from flying shrapnel. She reached into her bag and, in one motion, emptied her wallet onto the table.

Coins plunked into craft cocktails and hundreds of *pivni* fluttered through the air, alighting onto dirty dishes and half-finished desserts. Lear had broken eye contact, was pinching the skin on his forehead between his thumb and forefinger. I was still leaning all the way back, teetering on the hind legs of my chair.

She snatched up her bag and opened her mouth, then shut it so her teeth clicked. She shimmied out from behind the table and straightened her dress by pressing it flat with both hands, then walked out of the restaurant and into the street.

The waiter stuck his head out of the kitchen and asked us how we wanted to pay. We collected McKayla's money and paid with a credit card, tipping with whatever had fallen between the seats.

By the time we got back to the hotel, McKayla had booked tickets from Strelsau to Lisbon.

Lear handed her the sticky *grivni* notes, which she stuffed into her bag. "You've been filibustering this relationship for months," she said. "You wanted this to happen."

Lear sighed heavily. When he spoke, he was on the verge of tears. "I could never love you the way you love me," he explained. "It's not your fault. I just couldn't stand the idea of you hating me."

"I guess you'll have to get used to it," she said. She swung her suitcase down from the bed. "Fucking coward."

"You're still my best friend," he said.

McKayla looked at him and I felt hideously invisible. "Goodbye."

Once she had left, the people following us knocked on our door. "Is okay?" one asked.

"No," said Lear. "Not really."

# 37

I crouched above the toilet in the furthest stall from the door while my flight boarded and my plane took off. I crouched there for maybe an hour. I had no luggage except the overnight bag I had brought back from Strelsau, which hung from a coat hook in front of me.

I did not have a plan. If I had had a plan it would have been to go to the service desk in the terminal and buy the next available ticket on any flight out of the country. My legs were cramping and I was sweating from the effort of perching on the toilet, which, combined with adrenaline and the straightening of my intestinal tract, tinged my circumstances with brutal irony.

A man's voice called out, "Mr. Rye?"

When I didn't answer, the man walked into the bathroom. His shoes stuck to the floor so I could hear him moving around as he checked the urinals. He approached the toilets and tried each of the stalls until he got to mine. "Mr. Rye," he said again.

I cleared my throat as if he had caught me in the midst of a prolonged and delicate operation. "I'm on the toilet."

"Okay," the voice said.

I listened to his shoes as he walked away. I got stiffly down and stretched. I deliberated about whether the police would allow me to use the bathroom after I was arrested. I decided not to risk it.

After I finished, I went to the sink, where I washed my hands and splashed water on my face.

I exited the bathroom, emerging onto the concourse among a semi-circle of VDF. I nodded to them, intimating that I had performed a task of great significance. They returned the nod, heartened, perhaps, by my stoicism.

I had purchased tickets on the way to the airport, avoiding eye contact with the person following me while the Visegrad transportation gestapo paced up and down the bus, hunting for one last score before our datagram of potential revenue hit the atmosphere. I had decided to call Lear from Vienna. I knew he would understand.

I slipped through the automated kiosks at security, leaving the person following me at departures and throwing away my razor and toothpaste at security. It all seemed suddenly natural, and, as I browsed the duty free, I felt a wave of relief wash over me. I had been dreading something and it had finally come to pass. Now I was happy that it was over with. I purchased a box of chocolates and a two-liter bottle of water. I had fifty minutes left before my flight boarded, so I treated myself to an expensive beer and double-checked the name of my hotel, scrolling through a list of local attractions all of which were museums.

It was time to start over but maybe not in Vienna.

When I arrived at wherever I was going, I would be able to buy food and clothing with more than enough left over for a laptop and a safety deposit on a new apartment. As early as next week I could be back at work in the lucrative field of Fantasy Gangbang parodies. I paid at the bar and reached my departure gate, weighing the relative merits of *Catch 22 of Those 22 Lizard People that Have Just Been Banging Me, Catch Them!* and *The Sun Rises and, Thanks to This Leprechaun, So Does My Penis*—feeling that, what the former lacked in brevity, it made up for in its potential as a meditation on the absurdity of war, as well as the absurdity of participating in a lizard-person breeding program helmed by Italian fascists.

A voice over the P.A. said, "Fadder Lear, please come to the front desk," and my stomach dropped. For a split second I languished under the belief that I had booked my ticket under the wrong name. Then Lear stood up in the terminal waiting area, shouldered his bag and marched to the gate.

Two Vlodomerian Defense Forces officers were waiting for him. They wore neat berets and had automatic weapons slung across their chests, hands behind their backs so the muscles on their arms bulged. I saw them at the same time Lear did.

He froze.

He glanced between the gate and the open concourse. He patted his pockets, thinking. Then, opening his bag, he began to rifle through its contents. He shook his head as if unable to find something, then zipped it shut and rubbed his chin. Suddenly, he pivoted. His right knee came up, his left elbow back. His bag levitated for a split second as it swung across his chest, and he broke into a sprint. He vaulted a fence of rolling luggage and momentarily stunned a troop of German pensioners. He arrived at a moving walkway before the VDF realized what was happening—turned in their direction, their dumbstruck expressions beaming into his own: victorious.

A man in a short-sleeve shirt leaned over the handrail and clotheslined him.

I craned my neck for a better view as he rolled around on the slats, washing up at the feet of more VDF who had appeared through a side door. They helped him to his feet as I heard my name being called through the loudspeaker, after which I walked to the bathroom, locked myself in the furthest stall and climbed onto the toilet.

On my way out, the VDF escorted me past the moving walk and in through the side door from which they had come.

They frogmarched me wordlessly along a corridor of whitewashed cork, past the doors of temporary offices. At any moment I expected the man who had spoken to me in the stall to stop and gesture to a room where I would be held until I could be released into the custody of the Foreign Police at the Ministry of the Interior, detained overnight, and deported. The man asked, "You have baggage?"

"Only this," I said.

He nodded.

Airline attendants and luggage handlers stopped talking and watched as we passed. At the end of the hall we exited a pair of double doors and entered a small screening area. An x-ray machine stood to one side, monitored by a bored looking transportation agent. The man nodded to him, and he waved us through. Automatic doors slid back to reveal the inter-Schengen departures terminal and ticketing hall.

I looked around. The VDF had stopped in a cluster on the far side of the x-ray. The man who had spoken to me in the bathroom pointed across the terminal at the person following me, who was sitting patiently by the door to the airport shuttle. He saw me and curled up the magazine he was reading, slapped it once on the top of his thigh and stuck it into his back pocket.

On the way to the city I began to think very hard and very fast. It was difficult to concentrate because of all the dread and confusion I was feeling. Also, I was being repeatedly blasted by my adrenal gland.

The airport shuttle dropped us off in the city center, from where I took a tram to the gypsy quarter. All that time I was trying to think—the light just beginning to fade.

We arrived at the apartment and the person following me waited for me to go inside, then crossed the street and unlocked the door to the building opposite.

I stood at the entrance on the inside of the security door. The first flight of stairs loomed up, unfathomably tall. The matronly Greg with her mole hair of extraordinary length was smoking in front of the window on the second-floor landing. I walked to her and signaled her to move aside. Then I opened the window and tossed my bag onto the shed in the rear courtyard.

I lowered myself down after, and she closed the window behind me.

I estimated how long it would take the people following me to realize that I was not upstairs in the apartment while I waited for the bus. It was no good hoping for a cab, because it was rush hour and no Vlodomerian taxi worth its salt would be caught out at a time when there was such high demand.

A bus arrived and I boarded it. I settled in among glances from other passengers, airing out my shirt.

I dismounted at the international coach station and checked the departures board. BUCHAREST 17:40. I looked up the website of the bus company and bought a ticket, then I left the waiting area for the gift shop. In the gift shop I purchased a pair of sunglasses and a large wool hat that had *VISEGRAD* knit around its circumference in national colors.

The waiting area in the coach station was well lit and exposed to the outside, so I bought as much Czech lager as I could carry and escaped to the bathroom, where I drank and paid a woman .5 VRP every time I reemerged to check the departures board. Once the coach pulled in, I began to hover around inside the exit. Passengers showed an attendant their tickets and loaded their gear, while the driver performed a cursory inspection of the taillights and mirrors. There was no sign of the people following us. The attendant cast one final look around and I pushed through the station doors.

Empty cans bounced across the asphalt as I signaled frantically for him to wait. He paused, gazing at me impassively as I puffed to the door of the bus. Then, because no other option made itself available, he took my outstretched phone, scanned my ticket and allowed me to come aboard.

# 38

The cabin was mostly empty: Romanians heading home for the holidays, Vlodomerians and broke college kids traveling in the off season. I put my bag down next to me and stretched out.

There was a couple in front of me watching a 90s action movie on a netbook balanced between their knees. They were sharing headphones, occasionally leaning into one another as if beaming affectionate thoughts back and forth through their foreheads. After a while, and with nothing to do, I began watching their movie, peering through the gap in the seats in front of me. There was no sound, of course, but I had the broad strokes.

"Good movie?" asked a voice. I twisted around to see an affable European of the type that is interested in conversing with foreigners. All the hair stood up on the back of my neck.

"Sure," I said, and turned back around.

"You're American?" he asked.

"Yes," I said. Then, after a moment of loud silence, I asked, "You?"

"Moldovan. I was born in Moldova but my wife lives in Vlodomeria."

"Cool," I said. I tried to look like I was concentrating on the movie playing in the row in front of me.

"Why did you come to Visegrad?" he asked.

A police cruiser shot past with its lights on and I jumped. I listened to it fade into the distance. The Moldovan gave me a questioning look. "I followed a girl," I said.

He wagged his finger at me. "I knew it," he said.

"I guess it's a pretty common story."

"And what do you do for a living?" he asked.

I thought about that. "I guess you could say I'm a business person."

"Oh?" he said. "What kind of business?"

"I collect student loan debt."

He screwed up his face. "What?"

"School is so expensive in America that lots of people take out loans to help finance their university tuition. I collect the money they owe, the debt."

"Oh," he said. "You must work for the government."

"No," I said. "It's a private company."

The man shook his head as another police car sped past. "I think that there is a collision," said the man.

"Yeah," I said. A moment later, the bus driver applied the brakes and the coach lurched to a stop. I leaned against the window and parted the curtain, squinting into the growing dark. Traffic snaked into the distance. "A collision. Definitely."

"Excuse me," said the man. "I need the bathroom." He got up and walked to the little set of stairs set perpendicular to the corridor.

On the netbook in front of me a man with a well-developed upper body was facing down a threat to the American way of life. The beer was wearing off and I could sense a hangover coming on. I felt a stab of nausea and looked through my bag for a bottle of water. I found the one I had purchased at the airport and took a long drink, then leaned back and shut my eyes. I considered trying to order a coffee from the coach attendant, and almost didn't notice when we pulled into the checkpoint: blue and white flashers on the dashboard of an unmarked van, two squad cars positioned on either side of the road, throttling traffic.

Other passengers looked curiously out of the windows while I slouched down in my seat. Stomach acid climbed into my throat and I suppressed the urge to vomit. I begin to sweat. I looked around and briefly contemplated wedging myself into the overhead luggage compartment. No. Grace under fire. Don't call undue attention to yourself.

I stole from my seat and down the stairs to the bathroom. I tried the door, which was locked. I knocked and heard an apologetic chime of Romanian from the Moldovan who had been sitting behind me. "Hey, mister," I said, "I'm sorry to bother you but I really need to get in there." No response.

Van doors opened and slammed shut. The engine turned off and the coach driver got out.

The stairs beside the bathroom led to the bus' rear entrance. I could feel the dark exterior world breathing cold air through the rubber seal at the base of the door.

I knocked again. "You gotta hurry up in there, mister. I'm gonna shit my pants." A woman sitting across from the stairwell gave me a concerned look. I thought of my bag which lay in the open on the seat next to mine; it was too late to go back.

Outside, a raised voice was issuing commands. I could hear the sound of boots on gravel.

The toilet flushed. I cleared my throat and knocked a third time. "Come on, man."

The bathroom door opened out and I moved a few steps to allow the Moldovan access to the stairs just as the people following me boarded at the front, arguing with the attendant. I hunched over.

Miming abdominal pain, I slid past him so that, for a moment, our bodies were pressed warmly together. There was betrayal in his eyes, moisture on the coarse hair of his upper lip.

Then I was inside, hot air reeking from the Moldovan's bowel movement. I locked the door and sat down on the toilet.

Heavy feet stomped past. I listened as they reached the seat where I'd been sitting near the back of the bus. They stopped and I imagined their corresponding surveillance professional staring disappointedly down at my abandoned pack. Some muffled Vlodomerian and more footfalls, this time back toward the front. More Vlodomerian. Now silence. A single interrogative flute of Romanian. The boots made their way slowly up the aisle, halting at the top of the stairs. Fuck.

I held my breath.

Transfixed, I watched as the little plastic handle of the bathroom door began to oscillate. It found its boundary first against the lock on one side of the mechanism, then the other. Then the whole door shook as someone tried to wrench it violently open. I started, banging my head on the low plastic ceiling of the coach's toilet.

There was the sound of a muffled consultation being conducted on the stairwell. Footsteps raced to the cab. I braced against the door and, too late, I remembered that it opened out. A key went into the lock, and the handle turned. I lunged forward and tried to pull the door closed, but it was ripped from my hands.

"Help me," I screamed. "These people are attacking me."

"Shut up," said one of the people following me.

"Don't touch me, you bastard. Help me! These are maniacs. I don't know these people. Call the police. Somebody call the police!"

"Shut up," he repeated. He grabbed one of my legs and pulled it. I twisted sideways, hugging the back of the toilet.

"They're criminals! No one is safe!" My fingers slipped and I collapsed on the urine-slick floor. Spitting, I tried to pull myself up.

"*You cum,*" I said in Vlodomerian. "*You idiot peasants.*" Someone took my other ankle and, together, they began to pull me out of the bathroom. "They're cannibals," I screamed as I scrambled for purchase. "They're Nazis. They're taking me out to shoot me by the side of the road. They'll come for you next. They'll rape your wives and burn your livestock. They'll kill your dogs." I was being dragged down the central aisle. "Why aren't you doing anything to stop them? Get out of your seats and defend yourselves, you fucking animals, you primitive fucking animals. Don't you know how to stand up for mankind, for humankind?" I got my hands around the bottom of a seat and clung there. Faces poked into the aisle, watching me. I made sudden intense eye contact with the Moldovan and he turned pale. "I hope this bus crashes," I screamed. "I hope it's a bad crash and you freeze and burn at the same time, writhing as life seeps from your mutilated carcass. And I hope it means nothing." I lost my grip and my head cracked against the floor. I brought my arms in front of my face to protect myself as they dragged me down the stairs and onto the pavement.

I felt strong hands under my armpits and around my back. The hands lifted me onto my feet. I gave no more resistance.

The people following me put me in the unmarked van and shut the door. I held my forehead while they retrieved my bag, which they tossed in beside me. Then they pushed in on either side, so I was hemmed in between them. The driver got in and started the engine, made a three point turn and peeled out.

After a few minutes one of the people following me gave a little giggle. "Nazis," he said. Suddenly all of them were laughing, laughing helplessly, huge grotesque belly laughs, pawing their faces while tears streamed down their brilliant red cheeks.

By the time I returned to the city I had fallen asleep. They had to wake me up and tell me to get out. I obeyed groggily, unlocking the building and climbing the stairs to the apartment.

I expected to find Lear already gone. Instead, large scarlet curtains had been installed and drawn over the kitchen windows.

"Hey," said McKayla. She was sipping beer at the kitchen table where she and Lear were playing durak. "I think we might be in some kind of trouble."

## 39

"Hey," said a man in a suit.

He was leaning over me, talking down. I had been asleep by the little gypsy prostitute who had turned to stone on the bank of the Volodymy.

"Lear, right?" he asked.

"Weit" I said. My tongue had swollen from when I had bitten it.

"Can you talk?" he asked.

I shook my head. "Nawg wihlhe."

"But you're Lear?"

I nodded.

"You know a guy named Rye?"

"He wefd." I held out one arm and waltzed a pair of fingers across my wrist.

"Where'd he go?"

"Bewin, powy."

"Where?"

I did a little Vagner.

"Germany?"

I nodded.

He puffed up his cheeks and blew out some disappointed air. "You're not lying to me?" I shook my head. "Shit," he said. "Didn't think he'd do that."

"Hoo aw yu?"

"I'm from the Canadian Sports Betting Association. We believe Rye was part of a plot to manipulate the outcome of matches involving the Olympic Curling Team."

"Mihex Duple gurring?"

"That's right."

It took a moment for that to sink in. "Wha'de ew?"

"He tampered with some technical supporting equipment."

"Wha'dyu meng?"

"He sabotaged the boot dryers of the Canadian Olympic Mixed Doubles Curling Team. The team's boot liners would never be totally dry. They weren't dry for months. It's very difficult to concentrate when your socks are always wet, always—"

"Iz nod Why."

"Come again," said the man.

"Wyhlr, nod Why," I said.

"I don't understand."

I got out my wallet. From behind my replacement driver's license and credit card, I brought out the black business card Wilder had given me. It said, THE AMERICAN CONCERN on one side, on the other side, *Wilder Bright*. The man in the suit turned it over, examining both sides carefully. He looked at me.

"Nod Why," I said, "Wyhlr Wighd."

"You're saying I'm looking for this Wilder person?"

I nodded.

He raised the business card into the air, signaling. A so-and-so in a black leather jacket broke away from a group of men that was waiting at a respectful distance. The man in the suit pointed down at me. "Do you recognize him?" he asked.

"No," said the so-and-so.

"It's not the guy?" asked the man in the suit.

"He's just as ugly, just not as big."

"Shit," said the man in the suit, "somebody said he was the guy."

The so-and-so in the black leather jacket examined me.
"No," he said, "he's definitely not."

"Alright," said the man in the suit, "go back and wait." When
the so-and-so in the black leather jacket was gone, he asked,
"Listen, does your family know where you are?"

"Yeff," I said.

"Because you look like maybe you're in some kind of
trouble."

"Eim fwingh."

He hesitated, then shrugged. "Whatever." He withdrew a
sixty *pivni* note from his wallet and put it in my hand. "There's
more where that came from, providing you disclose what you can
about this Wilder guy. Also, as long as we're disclosing things, I
hope you'll listen and think carefully about what I say next."

I nodded.

"First, as you may have gathered, I'm only loosely affiliated
with the Canadian Sports Betting Association. I am more closely
connected to an organization that values fairness, an organization
whose whole reason for being is giving people a fair shake and
making sure everyone plays by the rules. The organization makes
sure everybody gets what's coming to them. People like Rye—"

"Wyhlr," I said.

"Right, Wilder. We make sure people like Wilder are punished
for interfering with the operation of technical supporting
equipment. Second," he said, "you should know that this
organization, the one dedicated to fairness, is not a deliberative
body. It's not an organization that responds flexibly to crises as
they arise. It's an organization that gives its people a lot of leeway,
a lot of operational discretion. It relies on people like me to call
audibles, to make tough choices. As a result, it's an organization
that has a reputation for scorched earth tactics."

I nodded.

"Third—and this has a lot to do with the first two things
I've just been telling you—the organization I belong to doesn't

assign letter grades. It's a pass/fail organization. It looks at what happened, who did what, but it doesn't qualify. It doesn't go, 'This person did a B plus job, that person a D minus.' It says, 'This person succeeded and that person did not; this person did something wrong and that person did not.' You follow?"

I nodded.

"Okay, I want to give you the opportunity, again, to tell me anything you haven't told me."

I thought for a second. I squiggled an invisible pen.

He dug his hands into his coat pockets and extracted a ballpoint. I used the bench to write down a couple of things on the back of a receipt. Then I folded up the receipt and passed it to him.

The man in the suit unfolded the receipt and read what I'd written down. The two things I wrote down were, *TRUST XBODY* and *B CAREFUL.* He looked at me for a long time.

"Are you sure you're okay?" he asked.

"Yeff."

"You can keep this," he said, passing back the receipt. He glanced up at the little gypsy prostitute that had been turned to stone on the bank of the Volodymy. "Weird statue," he said.

When he left, he left a so-and-so to watch me. The so-and-so leaned against the rail on my side of the pedestrian underpass: a fat, middle-aged guy that stuck out like a sore thumb.

After a while, he was disappeared over the rail into the Volodymy.

"Jeez," said H. Defer, sitting down next to me, "you're in rough shape." Two associate professors of intertextual branding were with him. They heaved themselves over the rail that the so-and-so had been leaning on when he was disappeared. "I admire your chutzpah, but I hope you didn't tell them anything."

"Hoo?" I asked.

"Them, them of the same kind as that one we just disappeared into the Volodymy. What are you doing out here, anyway?"

"Dyingh ouf," I said. He looked at me sideways. I mimed doing the crawl stroke.

"You went swimming?"

I nodded.

"Do you know who this is?" asked H. Defer, speaking to the two associate professors. "This is Lear Fadder." They looked at each other. "They're familiar with your contributions to the evolving field of intertextual branding." They stuck out their hands, wet and bloody from disappearing the so-and-so over the rail.

"A pwehol," I said. I took their hands, one after the other.

"All the pleasure is ours," said one of the associate professors. "Professor Lear, what is such a person as you doing out of doors by the Volodymy?"

"You see what I mean," said H. Defer, "when I talk about a failure of critical thinking?" The associate professor reddened. "Confronted with a man, an educated man, dressed in dirty clothes and a duvet, freezing by a river, he does not conclude that it is not necessary to know what he is doing or why he is doing it, since, as an educated man, he doubtless has good reasons, which—while not immediately obvious—will make themselves known in the fullness of time."

"Weesiwch," I said.

"There you go," said H. "Research." The associate professors nodded. "Lear, do you mind if my colleagues make sure you don't have a gun or a knife?"

I shook my head.

They went through my pockets. All I had was the sixty *pivni* and the note and bottle caps and empty plastic baggies that were still wet and cucumbery. H. Defer found and unfolded the receipt with my two pieces of advice.

"Can I speak to Professor Lear privately?" asked Defer, causing the two associate professors to retreat out of earshot. "I can't help but feel that this sum of currency, here, and this handwritten warning, are somehow related. Well," said H., looking around, "I can understand why you might feel like you don't have a horse in this race, like inaction is an acceptable choice. I can understand that; I've always liked you the most. You've certainly been the most resilient. But I see you in this state and I can't help worrying. I get it. Don't think for a second, I don't get it. The irony is not lost on me. But, long term, what are we talking about here? Can you imagine me not telling the others where you are? Is that something you can imagine me not doing?"

He waited for me to answer. "Yeff," I said.

"Be that as it may, I want to emphasize that, regardless of your feelings, the easier things are for the group as a whole, the easier things will be going *forward*. I respect that you didn't make a break for it, that you didn't tuck your tail between your legs and run, but I think that's because you must have known the way things would shake out. I respect that. I respect your clarity of vision, what I hope it will someday bring to my chosen sub-sub-disciple of intertextual branding. Lear, nobody in this line of work is irreplaceable. This is academia. We can go out and get someone just as smart. We'd rather not, of course. And that's not just coming from me. You're a likable guy—arrogant maybe, but likable. Who wants to deal with a question mark? Not me. Is this getting through to you? Do you understand what I'm saying?"

"Yeff," I said.

"And that's another thing. Just what do you think you're doing, jumping out of windows? Do you know what the people following you have been through? The feelings of guilt and professional inadequacy? I don't know myself exactly, but these guys talk to each other. My associates tell me that it's been a terrible blow to their self-esteem."

"Um horry."

"I've said my piece," said H. Defer. He whistled and the associate professors of intertextual branding jogged over and got into position on either side of the little gypsy prostitute that had turned to stone on the bank of the Volodymy.

"Okay," said H., "on three. One, two—" the men strained. The earth shifted as the cinder block that Virág was affixed to bubbled to the surface.

Suddenly there was a cracking noise and both of her arms snapped off. They stood beside the stumps, gawking, amputated limbs in their enormous, white hands.

H. Defer's face was pinched and his teeth bared. "You know why they put her here?" he asked.

"Nou."

"You can guess?"

"Yeff."

"Keep those," he said to the associate professors, who were each holding an arm. "We'll rent an excavator or something."

They left the little gypsy prostitute a curvaceous Venus de Milo. Afterward, I cinched the blanket back around me and crawled inside the underpass, where it smelled like fecal matter and bromhidrosis.

# 40

What you cannot learn about picking up and moving to another country without actually doing it is that, no matter how far you go, you'll be there when you land. Even if you feel absolutely loaded with the potential to become someone new, the interior you, having been carried along with the rest of your luggage, will slip its phalanges out to remind you exactly what you're made of.

If you've spent years working to seem smart or funny or good-looking, you might step off a plane in Seville and discover that you are all three, a creature of self-determination and grit to boot: learning and growing, attracting the kind of free-spirited independent person you've believed you deserve all your life. Afterward, you will pull them down as your personality reassembles itself, creeping up over your eyelids as it spreads and crystallizes and returns you to the codependent, two-faced gargoyle whose only solution was to make a break for it in Please Leave.

The fantasy that you might be someone you are not is a fantasy glimpsed through the foliage of magical thinking. It is not that you are incapable of change, only that you are incapable of being someone else.

McKayla had attempted to flee Vlodomeria, first, through the air, and again, via rail.

"They ran my passport, added up the dates on my security stamps, and told me to go back to Visegrad."

"Who's they?" asked Lear. "I mean, who did the actual stamp counting?"

"Some sort of airport security. They said I couldn't leave from Strelsau International, even on an inter-Schengen flight. I thought they were trying to stall me, so I ran."

"That's when you came back to the apartment?"

"I tried to go to Ukraine," she said, "but at the station in Yavorov a conductor asked me for my passport. He told me I had to get out, and the person following me took me off."

"What'd he say?" asked Lear.

She rubbed her forehead. "The conductor?"

"The person following you."

"He asked if we were going back to Visegrad, so I stomped on his foot, kicked him in the testicles and caught the train before it was up to speed."

"Wow," I said. "Pretty determined, weren't you?"

"Not that it mattered," said McKayla, "because they stopped it again at the border."

"The whole train?" asked Lear. She looked at him as if she had forgotten who he was. I wondered how long they had been alone together in the apartment.

I asked. "What do you mean stopped the train?"

"At first I thought they were changing the rail gauge, but then a pair of conductors found me in steerage. They radioed in, and the person following me pulled up in a van. He didn't say a word all the way into the city and he wouldn't let me listen to the radio. I thought he was going to kill me."

"What I don't understand," said Lear. "Is why go to all this trouble? Who are these people and what do they want?"

"Think about it," I said. "Who has the most to gain by keeping us in the country?"

McKayla nodded. "It's that reptile, Doc June."

Talking to Doc June Sr. made McKayla feel like she should be someone else, that they should never have met—that the overlap in their spheres of interest was a sign something had gone terribly wrong.

"Or Wilder," said Lear. "Or H. Defer, for that matter. In any case, none of us are getting out."

"Don't think I've forgotten," said McKayla sharply. "This doesn't change anything."

Lear shrugged. He went to the fridge and made a withdrawal of 1 VRP. It was to be the first of the great pyramid on the kitchen floor.

"I've got to tell you something," I said. "There's something I need to tell you and it's very important."

McKayla groaned. "Rye, please—"

"No," I said. "I've got to say it." In that moment I felt the walls of possibility pushed violently out, a sensation like I was a long way up looking down at everything else. "McKayla, I love you."

Lear grimaced and McKayla sighed.

"And I think you're in love with me too."

"Oh, man," said Lear. "Oh, buddy."

We had waited for silences, for soft, warm breaks in conversation: fingers pinching the fat of palms. There had been the smell of hair and breath. There had been not wanting anything but to be allowed to sleep as I lay, legs entwined with hers, sheets damp from sweat, before she got up and walked to the bathroom to run the shower.

I said, "McKayla?"

McKayla looked down at her feet for what felt like a long time. At last, she said, "No."

Lear shook his head and said, "It must be awful, being the last person to have your own idea."

I sat heavily down and sprang up again as the SEC man rose from the blankets on the couch, wraith-like, gasping.

# 41

The SEC man had dark rings around his eyes and hollows where the fleshy part of his cheeks had been.

He had been lying there for hours, his feet wrapped tight to keep them from stinking up the apartment.

"You're all here," he said. The smell of cheap spirits and bromhidrosis shot through the room.

McKayla shrieked. Lear's pivni foamed over. I fumbled for a book from the shelf behind me, and finding one, pitched it at him. He knocked it aside but I loaded another, blind, unable to tear my eyes from the apparition who was now blowing on his nicotine-stained finger.

"You," said Lear.

The SEC man slapped the finger against his mouth and hissed.

"Jesus Christ," said McKayla.

He caught one of my books and cocked it back, threatening to beam me. I ducked, which put me out of range of my stockpile of ammunition.

Slowly, he took the finger from his lips and used it to signal us to meet him in the bathroom.

Once inside, he turned on the sink and ran water into the bath.

Lear passed around bottles of pivni and I took one.

"All they're going to hear is water running," said the SEC man.

"What?" said Lear.

The SEC man motioned for us to squeeze together. It was an unpleasant prospect.

"We thought you'd been disappeared," said McKayla.

"I disappeared myself," said the SEC man. "I heard them getting ready in the hall outside my door, and I went out through the bathroom window."

"We thought maybe it was the doctor with the push broom mustache, the one who had us record everything."

"Aha," exclaimed the SEC man. "You admit you were recording me."

McKayla shook her head. "You told us it was okay to record you, don't you remember? You said it didn't matter and you would have done the same thing."

The SEC man squinted at her and sucked ruefully on the neck of his pivni. We were all growing slightly damp standing near the spray from the running faucets. We had great water pressure in that apartment.

"If you disappeared yourself, where have you been?" asked Lear.

"Right here," said the SEC man. "All over the place. I've been following the followers, watcher watching. Let me tell you, I have a bird's eye view on their whole operation. The secret was not to go up, but down. The exterior systems of the city are still functioning, but if you want to know what's really going on, you've got to get much deeper in. There are systems on the inside that have begun to go insane and there's no way to tell which ones they are without seeing them firsthand." The smell of his feet was eye-watering. It transcended the heady cheese-like flavor of old socks to dance playfully with notes of rancid fish and ammonia.

"Do you know who's following us?" asked Lear. "Why they're doing it and why they won't let us leave the country?"

"Yes," said the SEC man, "there's an explanation for all of it."

"Thank God," said Lear.

"I just don't know what it is."

We stood there for a moment, dampening.

"What do you mean?" said Lear. "It's just like you said, it's a conspiracy."

The SEC man shook his head. "I was way off about that."

"To be honest, I'm relieved to hear you say that," I said.

"I think what's happening here is more fundamental, has more to do with destiny than free will." He paused and looked around for dramatic effect. I nodded encouragingly. "I think it's probably the result of Atlantean DNA."

"Now hold on," said Lear.

"It's not a conspiracy if people are just acting in accordance with their DNA," explained the SEC Man. "So, what we're seeing is evidence that the ancestors of Vlodomerians intermarried with a late-Atlantean expeditionary force, probably sometime toward the middle of the first millennium, BCE."

"Uh-oh," said McKayla.

"They must have traveled inland from the Baltic," said the SEC man.

"Like the Swedes?" I asked. McKayla batted me with her hand and I flinched as if struck with a closed fist. She gave me a concerned look.

"Exactly," said the SEC man, "exactly like the Swedes. The Atlanteans probably brought workers down through Lithuania, Poland, Vlodomeria and Hungary. Did you know there's evidence that this leg of the Volodymy shouldn't exist at all, that it shouldn't fork east through Vlodomeria into the Tisza? The culprit is a series of ancient canals the Atlanteans used to trade with the Nomadic Empires and the Illyrians. Did you know there are pyramids buried in the Bosnian countryside where Tesla's Torsion Fields have been verified by independent scientific study, suggesting the existence of a cosmic internet and corroborating numerological evidence rooted in sacred geometry? At the end of the day, it's a problem for the Bosnian courts."

We took long apologetic sips of beer.

The SEC man said, "And that gets at the very heart of this thing. That the Atlantean DNA of everyday Vlodomerians is being expressed in ways that do not seem focused or cohesive, but which invariably solidify the position of political and financial elites: creating a cabal of Togetherness Party officials who will detain you until they can learn the means by which Wilder acquires individual debts and extract your money, or, failing that, never allow you to leave."

We looked at each other. "Wait," said McKayla. "What?"

The SEC man put down his bottle. "Or you can go back to your conspiracy of sogginess, how nothing is planned and nobody is out to get you, where there's no such thing as Atlantean DNA. But then you'd never know what's happening, or the danger you're in." He opened the bathroom door, as though to usher us out into the hall. Fresh air washed invitingly over us.

"Hold on," said Lear. "Let's say—let's say, for the sake of argument, some of these things are true. Just what, what— as an operational imperative, mind you, because a lot of what you're saying seems pretty far-fetched—but if, hypothetically, just hypothetically, some of this is true, then what should we do?" The SEC man closed the bathroom door, sealing us inside.

"A good first step would be to figure out what's going on in this city. We'll have to shake the people following you, which can be accomplished by leaving the apartment the same way I got in. You'll need to look a little wet behind the ears, like it's your first time in Visegrad and you have no idea what you're doing."

"We don't know what we're doing," said Lear.

"Exactly," said the SEC man. "Yes, exactly."

# 42

We cut our hair and shaved our beards.

It was necessary to appear as if we were from a place with churches and governments and families, that it was the least we could do to be clean. If we were to sweat, the smell of the sweat was to be clean sweat. It was necessary to appear unsure of what was fashionable, as though we were always working: to dress as the sort of American that eats mouthful after mouthful of Shrimp Louie. It was necessary to be seen.

We could not make McKayla look fat, so we decided to make her look successful, since that is the type of American who can afford to travel but is thin.

"I have just the thing," she said, disappearing into the bedroom.

While we waited, we drank, setting our empties in a triangle on the kitchen floor.

After a while I turned to the SEC man. "Listen," I began, "I feel like there's something I have to tell you, something for which I owe you an apology."

"What's that?" He had transformed his appearance. He was wearing, again, the watch and the very tight pants from whose pockets he would regurgitate all his expensive belongings.

"I feel like I owe you an apology for selling your debt. I let your debt go to some guy I never even met."

"Oh?" he asked.

"Only, I thought you'd been disappeared and I didn't know if you were alive or what."

"Don't worry about it," said the SEC man. "You did the right thing."

"Yeah?"

"Yeah."

McKayla reappeared in an incredible dress. She must have purchased it in a boutique on Visegrad's high street or on the top floor of a department store.

"Wow," I said.

"Uh-huh," agreed Lear. She looked unattainable, which is how Lear said she had looked when they first met. Of course, she would not have had the scar on her cheek from when May Mazur cut her.

"I bought it last week," she said. "I finally have my own money, and I thought, 'Why not?' Then when it came time to put it on, it felt like it wasn't mine."

While we were lowering her out of the second story window, the dress tore part way up its back. We hemmed and hawed about that, but she said, "At least I look like I could be slumming it with you three."

As soon as we boarded a tram a girl asked, "What happened to your dress?"

"It just now happened," said McKayla. "It's the first time I've worn it."

"Oh no, you've got to be kidding me."

"I'm not," said McKayla.

"I'm Emily," said Emily.

"McKayla," said McKayla.

"Are you just visiting?"

Emily was accompanied by what I judged to be a double goose-rated specimen, probably on contract with a multi-national.

"I just moved here," said McKayla. "We all did." Lear and I waved from behind her. The SEC man sat off to one side, flipping through a stack of Vlodomerian tabloids.

"What kind of work?" asked Emily's companion, extending a beefy hand and adding the perfunctory, "Lee."

"Programming," said Lear. They shook. "We're a startup registered in Riga, but we're looking to open an office here. Do you mind if I ask you something?"

"Shoot," said Lee.

"Do you feel safe in Visegrad? Do you ever worry about the political situation?"

Lee couldn't help but smile on account of this question was so naive. "No," said Lee.

Emily shook her head. "That's the Vlodomerian side of things."

"What do you mean?" asked McKayla.

"There's so many of us here now, it's like we have our own city inside the city. The government stuff, the nationalist stuff, that's for the Vlodomerians, the—this might sound bad, but we have a special word for them."

"Oh?"

"Gregorys."

When no one said anything, Lee asked, "Do you want to hear a joke?"

"Sure," said Lear.

"How do you make Helen Keller less useful?" Emily smiled reassuringly as he loomed over her, ready to ejaculate his punchline.

"How?" asked McKayla.

"Teach her Rusyn."

"What's wrong?" asked Emily. No one had laughed.

"That's good," I said. "Where'd you hear it?"

Lee thought for a second. "My boss. Want to hear another?"

"Sure," said McKayla.

"If you want to have some fun in this city, you only have to do one thing. You know what that is? All you have to do is walk to the top of an escalator and shout, 'Hey, Béla!'"

Emily waited to see if we would laugh, and, when we didn't, swatted Lee.

"What?" he said, massaging his shoulder.

We accepted their invitation to Bunker in order to meet some friends who never arrived.

It felt good to have given the people following us the slip, even if we didn't know what we were looking for, or why—beyond the obvious, beyond the fact that whatever it was had kept McKayla and Lear from escaping the wreckage of their relationship. We drank Bunker beer and took turns eating from a bag of watery speed.

After a half hour, Lee began his pitch, delicately at first, feeling out the edges of our cover story, then fast and sloppy once we gave him a whiff of money—young Americans working abroad due to financial circumstances beyond our control.

"If there's one thing you don't want," said Lee, "it's balance-sheet insolvency." Lee had both his arms around the back of the bench he was sitting on, so Lear and McKayla were hunched forward to keep from touching him.

"Can I ask you something personal?" asked McKayla.

Lee and Emily looked at each other. You could see that McKayla's asking a personal question was not protocol. "Of course," said Emily, "anything."

"What was your rate?"

"What?" said Emily.

Lee drummed his fingers absentmindedly against the back of the bench.

"Because I'm guessing you average out at triple-swallow, maybe a soft one-G, so I was wondering what percentage you were quoted by the associate who signed you."

Emily's mouth became a flat line. "I don't appreciate you leading us down the garden path like this."

The door to the courtyard banged open, providing a glimpse of its subterranean carob tree. A string of Germans wandered in from outside, blinking in the light.

"What's that?" asked Lee.

"They're not new," said Emily.

"What?" said Lee.

"They're not tourists; they're already associates."

"Well, what the fuck?" said Lee.

"How much?" asked McKayla.

Lear had acquired the fixings for cigarettes and began to roll. "It never would have occurred to me to pitch someone in Bunker," he said. "Pretty wild."

"High risk, high reward," said Emily.

"What was the rate you were quoted?" said McKayla.

"I was wondering that too," I said. "I mean, it strikes me as funny meeting you, what, ten minutes from the apartment?"

A traffic jam erupted as two hen parties slid past each other, each pretending the other did not exist.

"Were you riding the tram looking for Americans?" asked McKayla.

Emily had begun to tilt radically to one side like she was rounding a corner at high velocity. "This thing is big business. It's win-win. Clients win by paying less, less than they normally would."

"How much less?" asked McKayla.

"What's your deal?" barked Lee. He was pointing at me across the table, shouting to be heard over the ruckus by the door. Lear took tobacco from a pouch and sprinkled it across a canoe of rolling paper.

"I'm a businessperson," I said.

"Bullshit," said Lee. "You're a liar."

The congestion worsened. Forward momentum ground to a halt as passersby shuffled in all directions. The cheery din escalated almost to a roar. I realized what was happening. "It's the GBU," I shouted. "At last."

"How much money?" called McKayla.

"The going rate," said Emily.

"What?"

"The going rate, the normal amount of money!"

"What amount of money is the normal amount of money?"

"Sixty," shouted Emily.

"What?"

"Sixty, sixty percent."

"Sixty?" said Lear. His mouth hung open. The little boat of tobacco floated in mid-air, then dropped to the table.

Bunker patrons had given up on making any kind of headway in or out of the courtyard, had resigned themselves to loud, embarrassed conversations with whoever was closest.

"Why did you do it?" asked McKayla.

"What?" shouted Lee.

A stranger slid into the booth at our table with a bottle of *horilka*. Without asking, he began to pour us drinks in tiny plastic shot glasses.

"What made you take the sixty?"

Lee and Emily's faces scrunched up. They were hearing but not understanding. And what was it McKayla expected to learn? They had taken the sixty because it was better than zero, because they weren't supposed to be able to pay down individual debt at sixty cents on the dollar, especially not student loan debt guaranteed by the U.S. Department of Education.

The man with the *horilka* finished pouring drinks and held his up. We all cheersed, staring briefly over each other's right shoulders.

"I know how he's acquiring individual debt," I rasped.

"What?" shouted Lee.

"Wilder," I said. "I know how he does it, buying the debt, I mean."

"You don't," said Lear. "Trust me."

"I do. I figured it out."

Lear cleared his throat. "Listen," he said, "I know you've been through a lot, but you've got to be careful. The more you believe in one impossible thing, the easier it is to believe in the rest. You don't want that. It's like a bad habit, only, you don't know it's a habit—everyone else does. At least with a smoke or a drink, maybe someday you hit the Infamous Nadir and call it quits. But how can you quit doing something you don't even know you're doing? That's what happened to him." Lear pointed to the SEC man. His face was pressed so far into a Vlodomerian tabloid I could distinguish the lump of his nose through its spine.

"It's not impossible," I said, "if I know how it's done."

"See," said Lear, "it's starting already."

"Lear's right," said McKayla, she reached across the table and I recoiled. She froze and stared at me for a second, mouth open. Then she turned and looked through the doorway packed with bodies. "It's a risk that's not worth taking," she said.

The stranger with the *horilka* shook his head, having gleaned nothing. He rose dramatically and returned to the crowd. We grabbed our coats and made to follow him.

"Wait," shouted Emily. The pair was glued to their seats, indistinguishable from the throng that crowded in on all sides. "What was your rate?"

We looked at them.

A chubby young woman was sprawled in Lee's lap, and tears were running across his cheeks. He looked as if he were going to ask us not to leave him. Then he disappeared, replaced by the window of a stranger's cleavage.

"Same as yours," McKayla called. "Sixty."

## 43

"Sixty percent," said Lear outside. "Jesus Christ. How far down the totem pole can you get?"

Assuming Emily and Lee were at the bottom and Wilder was at the top and each associate was taking five percent, ten people were taking a piece of every client the couple got.

I wondered who they had negotiated with for sixty-five. I wondered if somebody out there was negotiating for seventy percent.

"The question is," said McKayla, "how would anyone make that much money in Visegrad? What's the point of negotiating at that rate, when only albatross clients will ever be able to pay it?" Of course, the system had changed so radically everyone was albatross-rated. We were the ones who were hopelessly out of touch.

The tram stopped on the way back to the apartment and there was an announcement over the PA in Vlodomerian. The other passengers groaned and disembarked.

We were near a bridge over the Volodymy. It had rained while we were inside and the temperature was just above freezing, but the windchill was enough to turn the water on the sidewalks into black tongues of ice.

At the bridge, all kinds of Vlodomerian people were lined up. Lear stopped to ask a well-dressed couple, a man and a woman, what they were doing. "What are you lined up for?" he asked.

"We are not lining up," said the man. "We are marching."

"It looks like you're standing in line to me."

"It is a protest," said the woman. "We are protesting Kárbon."

"About time," I said. "What'd he do?"

"It is what he is not doing," said the man. "He has ceased to expand the influence of business on public life, since there are so few parts of Vlodomerian that are not now controlled by the private sector. He is not doing enough to protect the criminals and oligarchs; we demand the arrests of those that might one day oppose them. We want more suppression of the media, more corruption of government and more interference from the East."

"Why?" asked McKayla. "Why do you want those things?"

"You are not Vlodomerian and we do not expect you to understand."

"Try me."

"In Vlodomeria we have a special way."

"Yes," she said, "we know all about it."

"Then imagine," said the man, "all the time it is getting more like the way of doing things everywhere else. What makes the Vlodomerian people great and makes special the Vlodomerian way of doing things is under attack. This generation of Vlodomerians is more educated and more hardworking, more likely to own property and to attend graduate school than at any other time. Something must be done before it is too late."

"And you think standing in line will fix that?" asked McKayla.

"We are not standing in line," said the man. "We are waiting to cross this bridge. The march is from one side of the bridge to the other. It's a very slow march, but we are patient." He leaned against the railing and lit a cigarette. "Our patience is a sign of our seriousness."

"We can tell you're serious," said Lear.

"This is a perfect opportunity," said the SEC man suddenly.

"For what?" asked Lear.

"It's a perfect opportunity for you to be arrested. That'll teach you what's impossible, believe me." Evidently, the SEC man had not enjoyed his stint as a cautionary tale.

"Why would we want to do that?" asked Lear.

"To prove that you can't."

We hung around the protest and got cold waiting for the outbreak of violence. When none was forthcoming, we rode the tram back and forth until the public transportation gestapo caught us and wrote us tickets for what seemed like very little money.

"No," said Lear, glancing at the ticket. "We have no money; you'll have to arrest us."

"We go to the ATM," said a woman. Her hair was the color of red velvet cake.

We shook our heads.

"ID," barked another.

"Don't have it," said Lear.

"We call the police."

"Good," said Lear, "call them. That's the point."

Police officers took us into custody at the next stop and booked us at a station not far from the apartment. It was open all night, kitty-corner to a clinic where they took suspects for medical examinations and where victims went to get their rape kits.

"I'll never forgive that sonuvabitch," said Lear. "They're going to line us up against the wall for this." He seemed about to add something, but went suddenly quiet. "Is that—" he asked.

A man was sitting in the middle of the bullpen. He was sitting directly beneath an overhead light in a chair surrounded by a makeshift ring of furniture, as if on stage. He wore a Hawaiian shirt and a pair of dark sunglasses atop his balding head. He was discoursing fluently and with great enthusiasm. It was Danylo Nawj.

We filed in silently and took our seats on the periphery.

He was relating the plot of a book that he was translating to a crowd of police officers. The book was about a heroic teenager in a dystopian future where everybody was allowed one crime. Criminals who committed more than one crime were punished much more harshly than criminals in our world, with lifelong prison terms and death sentences for even misdemeanor infractions. One consequence of this was that a great deal of respect was paid to people whose crimes were executed with panache. Another consequence was that a great deal of disdain was paid to people like the protagonist, who had stolen a loaf of bread to feed her starving family.

In the book, the story's protagonist fell deeply in love with a teenager who was famous for having executed a daring bank heist. The bank heist made him famous, because it had been executed in such a way that each member of his crew had committed only one crime. The bank robber and his criminal bourgeoisie friends took pity on the protagonist, though she inspired envy in the girls and lust in the boys. Of course, it transpired that they committed more crimes, for which the repercussions were more and more extreme.

I identified the story by the names of the characters and the timing of sound effects made by Nawj, explaining to the others what was happening as best I could. I had authored a parody of the story, but had been reluctant to publish it due to complications arising from the age of the characters. The reason I was reluctant to tackle work with minors was that it required workarounds in the form of time machines and stasis chambers and other contrivances I felt were distracting.

"Why don't we ask him what he thinks?" said McKayla

"About what?" asked Lear.

"About whatever's going on in the city."

After Nawj finished there was a round of applause and a few cheers from his arresting officers, one of whom rushed forward to refill his tea. The former prime minister looked at me, manacled to his seat, sunglasses resting among loose strands of white hair and the liver spots of his scalp. "You understand Vlodomerian?" he asked. He had been half-listening to my summary.

"I know the story," I said. "I'm an admirer of yours."

He jogged his eyebrows, "Why do you say that you are an admirer of me?"

"I admire your style," I said.

He laughed. "I have no style." He tugged on his Hawaiian shirt to illustrate his point. "Americans are confusing substance with style. Maybe you admire my substance, is that what you mean?"

"Yes, that's what I mean."

The people following us came into the police station, flanked by VDF. One of the people following us saw I was speaking with Nawj and pointed and said something to an officer in an angry tone of voice.

"Are you with them?" asked Nawj.

"I don't know," I said.

"In that case, may I ask you a question?"

"Yes," I said. "Please."

"Why are you living in Visegrad?" he asked.

"I'm a writer," I said. "I fell in love with your city."

"Would you like some advice, since you are an admirer of mine—of my substance?"

"Very much."

"If you don't know these men, then you are not with them."

"That's probably true," I said. "Thank you."

"I'll give you another piece of advice," said Nawj, "because you strike me as the intellectual type like I am, and I am fatherly to types like me." Several officers wandered over to the people following us and began to argue.

"Right," I said. "We're on the same side, I think."

"No," he said, "just because two people are of the same type does not mean they are on the same side."

I thought about that. "That's true," I said.

A Visegrad Police officer broke off from a cluster on the perimeter of the bullpen and strode over.

"Are you ready to hear what I have to say?" asked Nawj.

"Yes," I said.

"Love is a joke," said the old man. "But it's not funny."

The officer told Nawj to stand, which he did. All the other men in the room stopped talking and straightened up as Nawj got to his feet.

"Where are you taking him?" asked McKayla.

"Prison," said an officer. "He has committed serious crimes."

"What crimes?" asked McKayla.

"Treason," said the officer, "conspiracy, impersoning a priest." The officer motioned for us to stand.

"What kind of conspiracy?" she demanded.

He squinted at her, as if the question might be a trick. At last he said, "Normal conspiracy."

The people following us laughed and threw their arms around us when we came out of holding. Seeing Nawj that way had put them in a good mood. They were so happy we thought maybe they had forgiven our little excursion.

When we arrived at our building they offered us cigarettes and we each took one. Then one of them stepped back and pointed to Lear, after which another broke Lear's nose and knocked out three of his teeth.

## 44

That winter we attended the wedding of H. Defer and the little gypsy prostitute, who was slowly turning to stone on the bank of the Volodymy.

H. Defer was in a hurry to get married before Christmas, because her transformation was well underway. She was moving more and more slowly, saying less and less.

She had to be supervised at all times by a live-in caretaker who accompanied her to the pedestrian underpass, because she could no longer be trusted not to freeze.

"I got lost in the snow near Karlizensky and saw them," said McKayla. "They weren't speaking, just sitting under a beach umbrella. I wondered if her nurse hated her, because of what she's doing, going to the underpass all the time, so the caretaker has to sit with her and keep her from freezing. I never used to wonder if people hated each other, isn't that funny?"

"Oh brother," said Lear. He rolled his eyes, inspiring a look of enmity from McKayla. He was wearing a partial denture that had been fitted by a Syrian dentist for almost nothing.

The reception for the wedding was at a vineyard northwest of the river, overlooking the city. H. Defer squeezed my arm as we walked in, said, "I'm so glad you came. I invited everybody who's anybody. They all came, except Virág's family. I guess that makes them nobody." He laughed.

H. had hired a street musician to play Virág's father.

The musician was in his late forties or early fifties. He hovered over her shoulder, accepting fat envelopes stuffed with 60 *pivni* notes. In that respect it was a Vlodomerian affair.

It was also a Vlodomerian affair in that there was a man whose job it was to liven up the proceedings with pranks and songs and by encouraging everyone to drink.

One prank was that the man ladled soup for H. Defer from a slotted spoon. H. Defer had to drink the soup before it ran through the holes in the bottom of the spoon, which was impossible. Trying to do so only got soup down the front of his tux. He came over to our table afterward and wiped himself off with a cloth napkin. Lear nodded in the direction of a large man who was looming over the street musician, taking possession of the envelopes full of cash. "Who's that?" he asked. "You hire a cement piling to play her godfather?" The man had a lot of bad tattoos and absolutely no neck.

"You mean Attila?" asked H. Defer. "You've never met Attila?"

We all shook our heads. "I think we'd remember," said McKayla.

"A coworker from my time on contract with a third party."

"Shooting out windows?" asked Lear.

"Right," said H. Defer. "Well, eventually it occurred to him, to Attila, I mean—It occurred to Attila to ask, 'Hey, what's the big idea, shooting out all these windows?' Maybe shooting out the windows he understood. Maybe it was more like, 'How come you've got a book with pictures of all the windows we've been contracted to shoot out?' I can't remember. Anyway, I'll be doggone if we didn't get into some pretty good talks, in a limited sort of way, due to his English—but some pretty good talks about intertextuality. And I'll be doggone too, if he didn't grab hold of the material and do some of his own work, interesting if very specialized work—but then, it's a very specialized field, intertextuality. And I'll be doggone a third time if he hasn't been lecturing at the Visegrad School all this month."

"What?" said Lear. His mouth gaped, metal clasp on his partial denture showing dimly under the light from the hall's crystal chandeliers.

"He's my associate director of intertextuality, one of several Vlodomerians that have demonstrated an aptitude for the work. He's been bothering me about getting a word with you, actually."

"Me?" I asked.

"Sure."

I glanced at the associate director. He looked like a cross between a pit bull and a crocodile. "Why me?"

"He's very interested in some of the work you're doing on post-post-structuralism."

"All I ever did was pour water on somebody."

H. Defer smirked. "Do you hear yourself? That's your inner detractor speaking. You know, I struggled with my inner detractor for years."

"I find that hard to believe," said McKayla.

"You have to ignore your inner detractor," said H. Defer, ignoring McKayla. "If you can do that, it's a stepping stone to success, believe me. Then you won't need an inner detractor. Then they'll be lining up."

The man whose job it was to liven up the proceedings approached H. from behind and goosed him on the tuchas. H. spun around, both hands up. There was laughter from the tables in the reception hall.

"Now?" asked the wedding clown, slightly abashed.

H. Defer examined the procession that had formed to give Virág envelopes. "Not yet."

"Not yet for what?" I asked.

"We're mixing things up," said H. "Traditionally, the envelopes come after the kidnapping."

"The kidnapping?"

"It's a Vlodomerian tradition to kidnap the bride in the middle of the wedding," said McKayla. "The groom has to visit places all over the city until he finds her and brings her back."

H. Defer tapped his nose. "That's when guests hand over their envelopes in exchange for a last dance. But I thought, under the circumstances—" H. Defer puffed out his cheeks. The soup had been a thin tomato bisque and had totally saturated his shirt and pants. We could see his chest and nipples and belly, all stained the color of the tomato bisque.

"Well, I suppose we'd better get in line," said McKayla. "I don't know if I've said this yet, but congratulations." She kissed him on the cheek.

We handed over our envelopes, together, passing them to McKayla, who gave them to the street musician. The musician wobbled slightly and passed the envelopes to Atilla while McKayla pecked Virág on the cheek and said, "Congratulations."

"For what?" Virág asked.

We were half taken aback. None of us had heard her speak English except when she was attempting to prostitute herself and rob us.

"For marrying H.," said McKayla.

"*Hah*," she said. She leaned over the side of her wheelchair and spit on the floor. "He does not want a wife. He wants a price."

"You mean prize?" asked McKayla. Attila eyed us from behind the man moonlighting as Virág's father.

"He wants, what are you saying? He wants me to turn to stone by the Volodymy."

We were stunned. "We aren't saying that," said McKayla. "Who told you that's what we've been saying?"

Virág shrugged. "It does not matter. He wants only his price."

"Then why did you marry him?" asked McKayla.

"I want a price also," said Virág. She grinned and her face shone suddenly happy and feral beneath her gigantic wig.

Attila cleared his throat and signaled for us to keep moving.

We each stooped and planted a kiss, then Attila put a fleshy hand on my shoulder and said, "I would like to speak to you. Do not leave."

I nodded dutifully.

"Jesus Christ, would you look what the cat dragged in?" said Lear.

May Mazur and Deddy were waiting in line at the bar. Deddy looked like he was not sure where he was or what was happening. Mazur looked better than we had ever seen her; she was wearing a strapless dress, and her usually substantial figure was nowhere apparent except her cheeks. The dress was accompanied by a mink shawl that must have cost about as much as her apartment.

"Looks like she's been working hard for us," said McKayla.

"Has she?" I asked.

McKayla nodded.

When Mazur saw us she gave a light wave, rings sparkling over the backs of her fingers. She traipsed over, leaving Deddy at the bar. Her and McKayla kissed each other on both cheeks.

"You look fantastic," said McKayla.

"So do you."

"No, you really look fantastic," said Lear.

McKayla nudged him and he gave a nervous laugh, but Mazur said, "Go on." She primped a little, showing off her haircut. "I thought it was time I spoiled myself. You spend years looking for something, you know—you're not sure what—then you find it; you've got to take care of yourself. "

"You mean Deddy?" I asked.

She smiled. For a split second, she was in her kitchen, accusing us of putting the kibosh on her plans to flee to Germany. She said, "Maybe just some place I belong."

"A place to belong," said Lear, as if toasting. None of us had a glass and the moment stretched awkwardly out. Then, as if unable to control himself, he added, "I wanted to say sorry about our mix-up."

"What mix-up was that?"

"The uh, the whole—"

"Misunderstanding," finished McKayla, taking him now at the inside of the elbow.

"We've had a little trouble since then, ourselves," I said.

Mazur smiled. "Something happen?"

"It doesn't matter," said McKayla.

And just like that the specifics were minutia in the protracted separation of Lear and McKayla. Mazur cast a dark look my way, as though the fact of my irrelevance were part of her revenge. And, since it was her that had taken Lear's toe, the toe that had inspired Lear's paramorphine habit, the paramorphine habit that had taken McKayla's sex life, and McKayla who had taken me, this was more or less the case.

"How's Deddy?" I asked.

"Oh, he's fine."

"He seems fine. Tell him I said hi."

She nodded, smiling again, and retreated to the bar.

We began the business of tying one on.

The business of tying one on was becoming our bread and butter. We had entered a long hot season of drinking. We were waiting for something, the end of drinking, perhaps—drinking to pass the time. It had become a chemical and social correspondence: black beer at breakfast, a digestif, a glass of rosé mixed with soda water, a shot of spirits to make up for the rosé, amphetamines in a bathroom stall—swallowed in casings made of toilet paper—a celebratory brandy, an ocean of beer beginning after lunch that carried us through dinner, a coffee, more digestif to quiet the spasms of our writhing colons, more beer, an ill-advised pack of cigarettes, speed from a little baggy—licked from wet fingertip or sucked from under dirty nail—shots. Physical and spiritual crisis loomed. We were in danger of being overwhelmed by our consumptive habits.

Some time after midnight I staggered onto the veranda.

"Cigar?" asked Wilder. His was already glowing in the corner of his mouth.

He had shaved for the occasion, and his long hair was pulled back into a pair of braids.

"Thanks," I said. I took the cigar and ran it under my nose as I had seen men do.

He retrieved a cigar cutter from his jacket pocket. "Here." The cutter snipped.

"Where have you been hiding?" I asked.

"Keeping busy," he said. I followed his gaze out over the skeletal vineyard and the Volodymy. An enormous Vlodomerian flag had been draped across the rampart of Vlodo's Seat where the bomb had exploded. We could see its colors, illuminated in the ultrabright beams of fat outdoor spotlights.

The only other source of light between the veranda and the city were the people following us. They had decamped at the front gate and were eating hors d'oeuvre and drinking champagne, the waitstaff running a supply train down to them from the party.

The door to the veranda opened and shut.

The short man said, "I never would have believed it could happen in a country like this." He walked up to the rail and leaned over, as though all three of us were old friends. "When I moved here with my parents in ninety-two it would have been unimaginable: armed uprising maybe, nuclear holocaust sure. It goes to show how far we've allowed things to backslide."

"Excuse me," I said, "shouldn't you be down there with the rest of the help?"

A low fire was burning on the shoulder of the road. One of the people following us crouched down and stirred the contents of a hanging pot.

The short man with the cowlick said, "I was invited, same as you—same as anybody."

"Oh?" I asked. "Why's that?"

The short man put his hand out for a cigar and Wilder ponied up. The little guillotine snipped and Wilder struck a match. The short man puffed and let the smoke unravel from his mouth. "Mr. Defer is what you might call a pragmatist in this. Like you, he has been careful not to pick a side."

Wilder laughed. "We'll see how long that lasts."

I put my fingertips against my eyelids and rubbed my eyes. "What are you talking about?"

"I hoped I had made myself clear at our last meeting, Rye. My position is that your people should pay their way, same as everyone else."

"They're not my people," I said.

"Very clever," said the short man, "attacking the question."

"He's not being clever," said Wilder. "He really doesn't get it."

"Get what?" I said.

"He's muscling in," said Wilder.

"Not at all," said the short man. "No more than any government that raises a tax. Make no mistake, a tax loophole is all The American Concern represents."

Wilder snorted. "What's the difference between paying taxes and lining the pockets of the Togetherness Party?"

"Well, since you're a non-voting alien operating a collection racket, I'd say the difference is none of your business."

"What's Doc June say about all this?" I asked.

"A very good question," said Wilder.

The short man examined his cigar. "He'll be dealt with." I looked at him askance. "Don't give me that. The man is a fascist. Surely, he's at least as bad as I am."

"Doc June isn't holding people up at airports," I said.

"He's not?" asked the short man. "Who do you think gave you that scare at Łupków Pass? Why do you think Wilder has been allowed to keep abreast of developments in the world of Mixed Doubles curling?"

The masked men with expandable batons. It was Wilder who had told us about Łupków in the first place.

"Thanks for the cigar," said the short man. He sidled off, and, as he left, raised his hand in a casual farewell. "Don't forget to have fun. It's a celebration."

"You're shooting yourself in the foot," Wilder called after him. "You're playing a game no one else is playing."

When the short man was out of range, I rounded on Wilder. "That's your friend in the Togetherness Party?"

"We are no longer in close collaboration."

"Great. That's great. And Łupków, whose idea was that?"

"You don't understand how delicate this whole thing is. The idea with Łupków, the idea was to impress on you, to impress on you subconsciously maybe, some of the limitations of life at the top of the pyramid, in case you considered putting us in the lurch." He turned his head to look at me, "Doc June heard about Mazur and got cold feet. It was the little prick who put you on to that, by the way; that's how deep this guy goes, gives you Mazur so Doc June will overplay his hand and he can stick me with it six months after the fact."

"How come he lets you fly out then?"

"Who knows?" said Wilder. He stubbed out his cigar. "I guess he knows I'll come back."

The door opened and Attila poked an intertextually identifiable appendage onto the veranda. I stiffened.

"I said do not leave," said Attila.

Wilder patted me on the back. "Take it easy. He's just now swallowing a tough pill, the big one."

Attila nodded solemnly. "You come both with me. The bride has been kidnapped."

H. Defer was pacing back and forth in front of Virág's empty chair. Behind him, guests spilled down the front steps, coats and gift bags pressed into their arms as they were shoved into the night.

He pointed to us as we came in. "You," he said, "where have you been?"

"Smoking cigars," said Wilder.

H. Defer rounded on me. "Is that right? Can you corroborate that?"

"Sure," I said. "We lost track of time talking to this short guy that wants us to pay some kind of Vlodomerian tax."

Wilder groaned and shot me a look.

"Him?" asked H. Defer dramatically.

"Yeah," I said. "You know him?"

Lear perked up. "Who wants us to pay what?"

"It was *him*," said Defer. "Or else it was the two of you and the human lamprey in a conspiracy together."

Wilder snorted. "Christ on a cross. It's you versus everybody, is that it? How convenient."

"What's that supposed to mean?" There were notes of hysteria in H's voice. They carried across the venue and caused the waitstaff to apply increased pressure to stragglers. Everyone sensed that the moment for privacy had arrived.

"Lower your voice," hissed Doc June Sr. "Maybe she got cold feet."

"Cold feet?" asked H. Defer. "She hasn't been out of that chair in months."

Doc June crossed his arms. "Then she probably needed the exercise." I found myself examining him carefully. He had bags under his eyes and the beginnings of a wispy mustache on his upper lip, which he was generally at pains to keep shaved. "What are you looking at?" he asked.

"Nothing," I said.

The last of the wedding guests trickled out and the reception hall doors slammed shut. The street musician made a small noise of discomfort, readjusting himself against the shoulder of the wedding clown where he was fast asleep.

H. Defer pointed to him. "Find out what he knows."

Attila started forward and the wedding clown flinched. For a moment, Virág's father sat upright under his own power. Then Attila took him by the ankle and pulled him out of his chair. He writhed, and, in his panic, struck a lucky blow, rapping the bigger man's knuckles.

Attila dropped the leg and stared at the hand for a moment, as if it had betrayed him. Slowly, he wrapped it into a fist and delivered a series of methodical punches, first, to the offending leg, then to the musician's stomach, after which the musician allowed himself to be dragged onto the veranda.

The waiters had all stopped to watch.

"Little harsh," observed Wilder.

H. Defer looked up, seeing everyone again for the first time. "Of course," he said. "It's just, it's supposed to be the happiest night of my life but the woman I love has been disappeared. Associate Professor Hunor," he called, "please make sure the Associate Director doesn't overdo it."

A tall, thin man stood up from reading a newspaper. He crossed the room, opened the door to the veranda, and stepped outside.

"I think the thing to do," said Doc June Sr., "is to revisit this problem at a later date."

"She's bound to turn up," said Wilder hopefully. "How far could she get?"

"Yes," said H. Defer, lost in thought. "Let's all be very careful." He stared across the dance floor for a few seconds. He got to his feet.

There was a scramble to collect coats and gift bags, then we were cast out, as other, less privileged guests had been before us.

Once we had piled into a taxi, I filled Lear and McKayla in on my conversation with Wilder and the short man.

Lear frowned. "How could anybody enforce a tax on money moving between bank accounts in another country?"

In the front seat McKayla put her head against the window and muttered softly, "Romania."

"What's that?" said Lear.

She looked back at us. "Do you know any Romanian history?"

"No," I said.

"Ceaușescu was a monster," she said. "Mass surveillance, repression, politically engineered famine. He actually made it illegal to keep your thermostat above sixteen degrees Celsius, claimed it never went below ten in winter. His predecessor was a hardcore Stalinist that worked people to death on the Danube canal. They have a whole tradition of home-grown fascists; there's a man named Antonescu who led pogroms in the forties. Vlad the Impaler left hundreds to die on wooden spikes. Vlad's father, Vlad the Dragon, enslaved gypsies. He had estates all over the pristine wilderness of Transylvania. Can you imagine? You'd have to get each one just to be sure."

"You mean," I said, "this is about pissing on dead Romanians?"

"I've been putting off Romania for years," she said. "You can find the places these people are buried. They're heroes. A few years ago there was a poll to see whether they would reelect Ceaușescu and forty-six percent responded, 'yes.'"

"Nobody's keeping you," said Lear. "After this, I mean. It's not like they can trap us here forever."

She pivoted her body so that her reflection was shielded from the light of the dash. "I think we're getting better at not leaving with practice."

Lear and I looked at each other.

"We're not staying," I said. "I'll think of something."

# 45

"The way I see it," said the SEC man, "there are multiple obstacles to getting out of the country. It seems to me that these obstacles are not insurmountable, as they might appear, but that their insurmountability is rooted in what we do not understand. Despite that, we can be sure that they stem from an underlying condition."

"The money," said Lear. "The underlying condition is we're rolling in it."

"More precisely," said the SEC man, "your problem is how much you stand to make and for who, whether it's for Doc June Sr., Wilder, or the secret cabal within the Togetherness Party."

"Ah," I said, nodding. "Why's that?"

"It's like Lear's toe," said McKayla. "He didn't get burned for what it was worth, but because it showed him to be short-sighted and unreliable." Lear gave her a look. "The amount of debt collected so far is immaterial; the real question is the amount of debt they might extract from us given a much longer period of time."

"That makes sense," I said. "They've been paying people to follow us. That's a substantial investment. They must be expecting a return."

"Right," said the SEC man, "I've never known a reptilian humanoid to work for free."

"Hold on just a second," said Lear. "You think the people following us are lizards?"

The SEC man paused. "It's possible they're just useful idiots. But, yes, in all likelihood they're reptilian humanoids."

"How can you tell the difference between a reptilian humanoid and a middle-aged surveillance professional?" I asked.

"In my experience," said the SEC man, "it's a very difficult distinction to make. Sometimes the middle-aged surveillance professional is not aware that he is actually a reptilian humanoid with Atlantean DNA, at all."

"The Atlanteans were lizard people?"

"Mmm-hmm." The SEC man nodded, staring unfocused rays of paranoid blue. "Reptilian humanoids."

"Passports," said Lear.

"What?" asked McKayla.

"Passports. When they caught you at the airport, was it after you showed your passport?"

"I guess," said McKayla. "Why do you ask?"

"And that's how it was with Mazur, right?"

"Yeah," I said, "I remember that."

Lear snapped his fingers. "That's it. They stopped your train before the border too. They can't stop us properly, because there's no restrictions on inter-Schengen travel. They must be tracking us using our passport numbers."

"They pulled me out of a bus to Romania in the middle of nowhere," I said. "But I had to give them my passport information to book the ticket. They must have us flagged on some sort of automated system."

"This all sounds pretty thin," said McKayla.

"It's not," said Lear. "Think about it. They won't be using names. There's only three names in this whole country. Plus, they'd be stopping travelers all the time for having the names of associates. They'd have to use numbers, since it's the only thing that distinguishes us from the Shrimp Louie eaters."

"There are an awful lot of Shrimp Louie eaters," conceded McKayla.

It was the beginning of a period of prolonged self-confinement, undertaken to inspire feelings of complacency in the people following us. The effect of our self-confinement was the completion of the pyramid of empty *pivni* that rocketed up from a corner of the kitchen; we had lost the impetus to recycle, but we could not permit ourselves to throw away bottles.

No one except the SEC man was allowed into the apartment. If he made judgments as we grayed and fattened behind the red curtains, swilling *pivni* and eating wet speed, he kept them to himself.

Christmas passed without celebration. By January, time had taken on a static quality. All the lights seemed turned down, muffled, so only neon colored the frozen sidewalks. The weather ran dry and rashy, too cold for precipitation. It felt as though we were living beneath power lines that gave off a low, monotonous buzz. I left a trail of dander wherever I went, and dust accumulated at an alarming rate all over the apartment. No amount of vacuuming seemed to break its advance.

The drugs made us paranoid and the beer made us surly. We bickered over card games. We slept too much or not at all, and became gripped by a strange paralysis. It was a particularly American paralysis, since it was a paralysis whose only symptom was a ceaseless debilitating hunger for television. For months after H. Defer's wedding, there was no amount of television that could satisfy us and we watched whole shows in chronological order, every episode of every season, back to back to back. Some of these were so old that we had to download them piecemeal from torrents that limped along at 50 kb/s, or else streamed them in low resolution from websites whose aging moderators worshiped vintage television.

We watched television for roughly sixteen hours a day, from one p.m. to five a.m., ordering our food and beer to the apartment so we would not have to cook or do the dishes. We did not pause the television if one of us showered or used the toilet or took out the trash, but performed these private tasks, whatever they were, privately. We watched television like it was our job, like we were middle-aged bureaucrats waiting to cash in on pensions from lives spent watching television. We became alternately fat and thin, ceasing to exercise, then to eat. The television we watched ranged wildly in quality and in point of origin. It seemed to radiate outward from an epicenter in the cultural consciousness, so that we went backwards and forwards, saw the whole form shift dramatically: the influence of vaudeville, of radio, of P.G. Wodehouse and science-fiction: of older, more regal ideas of what television could be, until it was a pair of dogs racing up a frozen riverbank on a stormcast afternoon. And none of it was observed or consumed with an ounce of attention. We were on our laptops. We lounged around, turned upside down on the blankets on the couch, learned to knit and went shopping and played video games against non-human opponents set to ultra-low difficulty, so that we could still win while watching TV.

There was a passive entertainment zenith out there, a climax that we yearned to reach, that we felt in our bones must exist despite all evidence to the contrary, and the summiting of which would finally, finally liberate us from our debilitating hunger for television.

One day I realized that the television was not even on, but that we were playing the audio of an episode with the screen off. I had been awake for two hours and was warm with coffee and my second beer, listening to an episode of something, not realizing the monitor was dark, smoking a cigarette, mechanically navigating a game of colossal scale I had whittled down to joyless routine.

After I realized the TV was off, I got curious about what the others were doing. I discovered that McKayla had become invested in an enormous puzzle, which she was exploring with closeness and agility under the influence of wet speed and the half-hearted supervision of the SEC man. Lear was watching pornography on half of his screen and a movie on the other half. The movie was a superhero movie, and the pornography was superhero pornography. A third part of the screen, the bottom third, was partially eclipsed by an empty markdown file, as though Lear had been seized by the desire to create or express something that had escaped him. He sat in the lotus position and showed no sign of concern or embarrassment that I was leaning over behind his shoulder to view the markdown prompt and the superhero movie and the superhero pornography.

The doorbell rang.

"After you," I said.

"Me?" said Lear. "I'm not fucking touching it."

"I'll get it," said the SEC man gamely.

"You're supposed to be disappeared," I reminded him.

Lear shook his head. "If he wants to answer the door, then let him answer it."

"I'll do it," said McKayla tiredly. "I don't care." We stopped what we were doing and watched as she walked to the entryway. Was that the scuffle of jackboots on the landing?

"H.," she announced.

He barged into the apartment: no Hunor, no Attila. "Which of you did it?" he demanded.

The pyramid of empty beer bottles vibrated precariously as he stomped past.

"Did what?" asked Lear.

"Put her there." His nose was red and his lips were chapped to bleeding.

"She volunteered, actually."

"Volunteered?" he stared at Lear, his eyes bugging out of his head.

"Sure," said Lear. "We didn't hold a gun to her head or anything."

"What the hell are you talking about?"

"McKayla," said Lear. "She answered the door. That's who we're talking about, right? Who are *you* talking about?"

"I'm talking about Virág!" H. Defer's chest was puffed up and his fists were clenched. "I'll tell you another thing, there's nothing funny about it, hitting a guy while he's down like this."

"Hello," said the SEC man.

"Hello," said H. Defer. "Who are you?"

"I work for the SEC," said the SEC man.

"Oh," said H. Defer, "everyone told me you'd been disappeared."

"I'm in and I'm out," said the SEC man.

"You found Virág?" asked McKayla, picking her way carefully around the tower of *pivni*.

"Found her?" he decried. He registered our expressions of cowed-eyed incomprehension. "You mean, you haven't seen her?"

"We're spending a lot of nights in," I said.

H. Defer collapsed into an empty chair. He put his face in his hands and a nexus of eye contact formed in the air over his head. McKayla ventured forward to rest one hand on his shoulder.

It hitched once, then relaxed. When he sat up, his eyes were red and there were tears on his cheeks.

"I thought it was you, because of what you called her. You know, that she was being—that she was turning to stone by the Volodymy."

"Jeez," said Lear, "I wish people would shut up about that."

"What happened?" asked McKayla. "Where is she?"

Virág had appeared in the night. From where? Let it remain one of the great unsolved mysteries. Her body was a densified cement mixture that had been polished with a metal-bonded diamond and was set in a freshly dug alcove by the pedestrian underpass on the bank of the Volodymy. A plaque by her feet read, *IN LOVING MEMORY.*

It has always struck me as unfair that the more heartbreaking and sudden a twist of fate, the harder it is to come up with something nice to say. That is, the more someone could use a kind word, generally, the harder it is to come by.

After a cup of tea and refusing our offer of some cucumbery speed, H. departed. The audio of the episode was still playing. McKayla turned it off. It was the final straw; he had been one of us and, in a way, so had she.

That night we pulled up the Arable UI and set things into motion.

The small brown bodies of our children waited patiently inside the doorway of our hut while older siblings frolicked among groves of lilac and coconut. We had toyed with the possibility of writing a script to expedite the naming process, but none of us had the chops. In the end, we input the names manually, squared off in thirty-five-character chunks.

The guests began to arrive as soon as we left invitations in their mailboxes, mostly in intertextually identifiable DLC costumes that Wilder had made available on a microtransactional basis—celebrities, athletes, video game characters. As they flooded through the gate, we began naming our children. We had not named our children in months. They popped out of thin air as fast as we could copy and paste their names from a Word document.

We staggered naming each child by about six seconds, so they would have time to wander away before we introduced the next. They all had the same names, and each name was part of a message. The message read:

*There is group inside VLD gov't 1/?*
*actvly stpping assocs exting VLD2/?*
*4 purposes of extortion & theft 3/?*
*They track us w/ old surv. tech 4/?*
*& w/ passprt #s @bordr & @airprt5/?*

*Top assocs alrdy undr surv. 24- 6/?*
*7 & Xable 2exit VLD &so trapped 7/?*
*Top assocs alrdy in dir. conflct8/?*
*W/ crim. group inside VLD gov't 9/?*
*Both are dangerous so any &all 10/?*
*assocs Xwant conflct leave ASAP11/?*
*Clients also @ risk, plz warn 12/?*
*w/o causing panic. Best way is 13/?*
*2 use land brdr w/ new passprt 14/?*
*2 every1 reading stay safe&GL 15/15*

# 46

We had conceived of our escape as instantaneous and dramatic. Triumphant, we would lead an army over the border into the rest of their lives. Nothing doing.

One thing did change, and that was the oppressive static under which we had lived for months. It was replaced with the expectation that at any moment something important was going to happen, and under the surface of each moment there was a negative mass of unexplored potential, as if a tremendous pot was set to boil. It was a sense of wrongness—the feeling that we had either miscalculated or something had malfunctioned within the apparatus of reality itself.

"I don't get it," said McKayla. She was refreshing the Arable app on her phone, farmstead polluted by the wandering tribes of our gorging progeny.

"Relax," said Lear, "people need a little time to pull their hair out and make arrangements."

"Something's definitely wrong," said McKayla. "Are they still out there?"

"Last I checked," I said.

"Please check again."

I parted the curtains and eyeballed the roof of the building opposite. There they were: pink orbs through warped glass, right where bobbing my head up and down had the most interesting effect. "The heat is still on."

"Maybe they know what we did," said McKayla.

"You're being paranoid," said Lear. "How would they know?"

"Anything's possible," I said. "Somebody might have tipped them off."

McKayla stood up and began to pace. "It's not just us. It's everybody. By everybody I mean nobody, because nobody's leaving—us included."

Lear's phone chimed.

"Having's on his way up," said Lear.

I went to the door, buzzed him in and threw the deadbolt. He appeared on the landing, rosy-cheeked. When he saw me he clapped me merrily on the back.

I leaned into the hall to make sure he had not been followed, then shut the door and locked it.

He took off his gloves and scarf, stepped from his boots and hung up his coat. He clapped me again on the shoulder, as if he had just heard some piece of good news. Then, peeking around the corner, he waved gingerly to Lear and McKayla who stared at him. "Well?" he asked.

"Well what?" drawled Lear.

"Did it work?"

"Did what work?" I asked.

"The plan," said Having. "I've been filled in."

"You have?" said McKayla.

"Sure," said Having. "You scared the hell out of me for a minute there, but Doc June came around and gave me the skinny. I don't think I would have figured it out all by myself. Why didn't you tell me? I could have been a big help." No one knew what to say to that. We looked at each other. "I know it's a secret," he continued. "That was the whole point, but you really scared the hell out of me."

"Okay," said Lear slowly, "what did Doc June tell you?"

"The plan," said Having. "I know all about the plan."

"You know that—" prompted McKayla.

"I know that you were stress-testing the Arable app and its social architecture. All that stuff about being stopped at the border and a government cabal was pretty good. I seriously considered making a break for it." He gave a hollow laugh. "Jeez, that would have been embarrassing. Of course, my better half won out. How many clients did you poach and hook into that direct line of yours? Brilliant to cut down on risk like that, turning overvalued assets into triple AAA prospects and paying down their debts at the same time. I would never have thought of it, really."

"Neither would we," I said.

"Oh," said Having, "whose idea was it?"

"No, I mean we didn't scoop up any uncapitalized debt at a reduced rate in order to minimize risk."

"What was the point of the stress-test then?"

"There was no stress-test," said Lear. "It's real."

Having rolled his eyes. "Yeah, okay." He looked around.

"He's telling the truth," said McKayla. "We're under twenty-four-hour surveillance."

Having stepped back. He made a sour face. "Ha," he said. "Ha-ha-ha."

"Don't believe me? See for yourself." She gestured to the curtains in the kitchen. I obliged her by getting up and beckoning Having over.

Frowning, Having moved from the kitchen table to the windows and peered out at the building opposite. He was silent for a moment, then he said, "What am I supposed to be looking at?"

"What do you mean?" I asked. "Aren't there a lot of middle-aged surveillance professionals out there?"

"Not that I can see."

I pushed Having out of the way. The people following us were still there, but instead of peering back at us through binoculars they were turned in different directions and doing their best to affect an air of disinterested nonchalance, hands stuffed in their pockets—whistling.

"Those guys," I said. "That's them."

"Those guys?" said Having. He considered them where they loitered on the rooftop. One kicked an empty can. "It doesn't look like they're up to anything to me."

"Are you kidding? You think they just happen to be waiting on the roof across from our apartment?"

"Okay," said Having, "you've either lost the plot, or—for whatever reason—you won't cop to your brilliant risk minimization strategy." He put up his hands. "I appreciate modesty as much as the next man, but what I'm picking up here is mistrust; you're saying you can't trust me with this stuff, and I find that really insulting."

"Listen," said Lear, "we're telling the truth. Sorry we didn't bring you in sooner, but if you keep pretending nothing's wrong, you'll have nobody but yourself to blame for what happens next."

Having flushed. "I guess you really think I'm an idiot."

"Of course we think you're an idiot," cried Lear. "How can we not when you won't understand?"

Having looked imperiously down at him on the couch. "What is it I'm supposed to be understanding? That you're locked in an apartment hopped up on speed. It reeks in here, by the way—smells like old feet."

"This," Lear waved around the room, "all this. Haven't you figured out something's wrong?"

"How so?"

Lear stood. "There's no real weight to any of it, just saps on the line, trying to put the next sap on the line, playing like there's some kinda future. There's not."

Having snorted. "That's just impostor syndrome talking. You feel like the money's not yours because you've done nothing to earn it."

"You've got that right," said Lear. "But it's no syndrome. We really are impostors. We're floating on a wave of impostors somewhere toward the top. You, you're right below us. You're so close to drowning you don't even know it. Why do you think they gave you that cushy teaching job? They're trying to make it look like there's something to all this when it's dumb luck that got us here in the first place. Hey!" Having had broken from Lear's tirade and was headed for the door.

"What?"

"Answer me this, do you know a single Vlodomerian? I mean to talk to, not a bartender or an old lady runs a *potrivjn*. Do you know a Vlodomerian that's not a dead prostitute or some kind of hired muscle?"

"What's your point?"

"The point is we've been trapped. We went on pretending everything was okay and now they've got us right where they want us."

Having paused for a second, then shook his head. "You think I don't know that?" he asked.

Lear looked at him, momentarily speechless. "I need this to work, okay? I've put a lot of time and money into this, taken a lot of risks. I didn't get into this because it was just something cool I was doing with my friends." He collected his belongings, piling them in his arms. "You think you're so far ahead of everyone else," he said. "You're not. You're just assholes." He opened the door and walked out without lacing his boots.

After a minute, McKayla said, "Someone should go after him."

"Why don't you?" asked Lear.

She didn't say anything but shrugged obliquely and turned away, as if she couldn't stand to look at him.

"I'll go," I said. "Just, let's not fight about it." I put on my coat and left the building through the front.

I went to the Gouged Eye and the El Matador Café: to the Galician Whale, the Fubliner, and Garden. I visited the Ritual

Sacrifice, the Superior Mind, the Albatross, and the American Dream. I walked through Bunker, which was almost deserted, and up to the Mausoleum of Electric Teeth. A frowny-face scrawled on an A4 piece of paper was hung on its door. I realized with shock that I hadn't been there since the bombing and didn't know if it had ever reopened.

It was nearly midnight by the time I gave up and went home, deciding to stop in at the bar that had replaced His Cups. There, I found Wilder nursing a cocktail.

The bar was called the Monologist. It was staffed by men with luxurious beards who wore wooden bowties and chipped perfect spheres from blocks of ice. It was totally out of whack with the *pivni* scale, and the secret of its continued operation was to pretend that it was not a bar in Visegrad, but in Brooklyn, Taipei or Berlin.

Before I could leave, Wilder saw me and waved. "He'll have what I'm having," he said. I sat reluctantly down beside him. "Can you believe the prices in this place?" he asked.

I took a used tissue from my pocket and blew my nose. "No," I said.

"Cheer up. You can afford it. You know what?" He signaled to the bartender. "Let's do shots. Put it on my tab."

"Yes, sir," said the bartender.

"You've gotta hand it to these people," said Wilder, "they catch on eventually."

I looked at him.

"What's eating you? Sour grapes?" He took a drink. "We'd be crazy not to plan for something like that—like what you did. June was making house calls five minutes after you sent your invitations. Now everyone's trying to keep you from poaching their clients instead of fleeing the country."

"That doesn't bother you?"

He laughed. "Why should it? Oh, cheer up. One day you're going to look back on this and it's going to be the thing you're most proud of. All those communications majors who married at twenty-five, got their real estate licenses and spent their lives breaking their backs, they're going to be haunted by this. On their deathbeds they're going to think of all the times they rolled over and took it. They'll know there was something else. They won't know exactly what, but they'll know they missed out."

Our shots arrived. He held his up to the light, its contents sloshing against the tips of his dirty fingers. "Here's to us."

"It's killing McKayla," I said. "It's killing Rye, too, but it's killing McKayla right in front of me."

Wilder snorted. "She'll be fine. You know, I used to think that you and I were a lot alike. Don't ask me why, but I saw something in you. I thought, 'Here's somebody with real potential, a specific kind of potential.' It's too bad, in the end our similarities were only skin deep."

"I couldn't agree more," said the SEC man.

He was all the way down at the far end of the bar. I hadn't noticed him when I came in and I guess Wilder hadn't either, because he looked surprised.

"Yeah," said Wilder after a moment, "why's that?"

"He'd never let all this go to his head."

"That's not true," I said.

"When I first met him," continued the SEC man, "what puzzled me most was how he got him mixed up with you in the first place. You know what it was? It was that he's a reptile. He's not a bad reptile, as far as reptiles go, but he's a reptile all the same. You can't fight your reptilian nature, believe it."

Wilder scowled. "You know this guy, Lear?"

"Sure." I looked between them. There were deep lines in the SEC-man's skin from sun damage and no fat left on his face. His hair had gone gray at his temples, and he was wearing a jacket that was fastened across his chest with loops and teeth. He gave the impression of someone who had been a long time in the desert. "Don't you recognize him?"

"No. Should I?"

"He's an associate," I said.

"Huh," said Wilder, "I thought I knew them all."

"I guess not," said the SEC man. He finished his drink and stood up. "Would you do me a favor, just in case it doesn't hit you out of the blue and you've got time to reflect while you're lying on the floor? It was because of you I had to do it." He placed a hand on Wilder's shoulder, and Wilder stared back at him, dumbstruck. "It's nobody's fault but ours."

It was the SEC man who had purchased his debt after he disappeared himself from the hospital. He had posed as a glassblower unable to pay down the private loans he had taken out while enrolled in correspondence courses.

He had successfully mortgaged his original AAA position at a much better rate than I had, in order to buy a battery of AA prospects, which he had traded for debt one sub-tranche lower. He had repeated this maneuver several times before he began signing clients, which, while conventionally rated, secretly belonged to a special category all their own. That category never received a name, but I grew to think of it as Cuckoo-rated, because its clients were brood parasites whose purpose was to destroy the reputation of whichever associate held their markers. This was accomplished by the SEC man via a unique signing bonus. The signing bonus was to offer his clients debt from other clients that did not exist. He used the imaginary debts as additional markers to be filled at a later date, and which constituted a reduced rate. In effect, many of his clients signed for amounts they could not pay and the SEC man paid himself the difference. Once he traded them, he funneled the income from the swaps through the same imaginary clients. It was a zero-sum game, except for this: except for he had created a giant, red, self-destruct button in the middle of the market and nobody else knew it.

He would have dismantled the entire system before December, had it not been for the intervention of H. Defer and his super-effective pitching methodology, which further inflated the value of his clients and continued to hide the bad bets he had created.

After our meeting in the Monologist, he never paid another dime.

Over the following days, Albatross-rated humps everywhere watched as their children collapsed into desolated fields. The children, who they had christened and nurtured, who represented the downline earning potential of their clients, clutched their bellies and writhed with hunger. The pixelated bodies convulsed for hours—sometimes days. This had all been built into the UI to encourage associates to extract money from clients that, it turned out, did not exist. By the end of the week, the bottom had fallen out of the Visegrad debt market.

## 47

I awoke to Colin Having, who looked very much the worse for wear. One of his eyes was covered with a mound of gauze that was tinted the color of iodine or dry pus.

He pointed to one of Virág's stumps. "What happened to her?"

"Aitch Defew," I said.

"He's crazy," said Having.

"Yeff," I said.

"Rye," he said, naming me, "do you know how bad you look?"

I shook my head.

We stopped to observe a small commotion at a boat launch that was situated downriver from the pedestrian underpass.

A group of mourners were sprinkling ashes and laying wreaths in the Volodymy. As they did, a large amphibious bus pulled into the launch, swirling the ashes and pushing the wreathes to either side as it climbed the slipway onto land. Tourists pressed their noses against the glass, misting it with their breath. Unshakable, the Vlodomerians stared disinterestedly back.

"Ever since I found out who you are, the same question has been going through my head, over and over. Can you guess the question?"

He waited for me to guess.

"It's a simple question," he said. "The question is, 'Why?' What was the point of all of it?"

When I did not reply he said, "Never mind, I don't want to know, seriously." He gave a sharp laugh. "Seriously." He sat down next to me and, after some time, said, "I read your work. Not every word, but I got the idea pretty quick. You know, maybe it's not fair for me to nail you to the wall when you can't say anything."

"Yeff."

"But I thought you were capable of more. I still think—I thought for a moment during *A Portrait of an Artist Being Penetrated By a Lot of Centaurs* that you were more than equal to the task, that you might be *read*, that dream word. But you always fall back on graphic, juvenile depictions of sex. You're so desperate. You're so—" He shook his head. "You're such a disappointment."

I didn't say anything; what could I say?

A stork glided in and landed on the riverbank. It stood on one leg, cleaning itself.

"You could have told me and I still would have paid," said Having.

"I didng kno dadt."

"Is that supposed to make me feel better?" He took a breath and looked out over the Volodymy. "You had every opportunity. You still do."

"I dyo?"

"Sure you do. There's no one in a better position to press pause on this thing before the wheels come off. Doc June lacks the capacity, nobody can find Wilder, H. is only worried about getting what he wants. But you, believe it or not, you're someone people trust. You're someone that people would listen to if you just said, 'Hold on, let's stop and look at what's going on. This might be a big missed opportunity. Lear, McKayla: they ran. You stayed, because you know you might be able to help clean up this mess—that no matter what else you've done, it's up—"

Having was interrupted by a bark.

A dog sprinted toward us from the other side of the pedestrian underpass. It was a black sheep dog with hair over its eyes. Its tongue hung from the side of its mouth like a pink windsock.

A giant hand collared it and pulled it from view. It yelped, then whimpered pitifully as one of the people following us broke its neck.

A woman screamed in the distance.

Having turned very pale. "I'm sorry," he said. "They told me they'd go easy on you."

"Id oghey," I said.

The people following us emerged from their dens and lairs. They crossed the road, stopping traffic.

They discarded the dog's body and came through the pedestrian underpass. They pulled themselves up on the rail, over which the so-and-so had been disappeared by H. Defer's associate professors of intertextuality.

"I told them it wouldn't work, but they didn't believe me," said Having. "God, I wish I was gone already. I'd never come back."

One of the people following me put a bag over my head, then they half carried me to the sliding door of a van. A middle-aged security professional palmed my skull, so I wouldn't hit it on the roof; I guess they felt they knew me, having surveilled days, weeks, months of my life. I was not proud of that time myself, but maybe it was my flaws that had endeared me to them.

As we rolled through traffic, one patted my knee. "It's going to be alright," he said. The voice sounded familiar.

"Hyou," I said.

"Me," said the short man with the cowlick, "luckily for you. You know, you're not indispensable: far from it. The others were probably minutes behind."

"Dey awl weady heen me."

"Already seen you?" asked the short man. "What does that mean?"

"Who's that? Who's talking?" asked Lear.

"Lear?" I lisped.

"Rye, is that you?"

"McKayla?" we said at once.

The short man grunted. "Unfortunately, no. We think she got off near Terebes and went the rest of the way on foot."

She was one step ahead of us to the very end. It was the final confirmation of her exit from the city and from my life, as though the arguments she left unfinished, the indignities of Visegrad and the determined weariness of her resistance were dress rehearsals for this ultimate escape. Under the bag, I managed a smile. "Goohd."

"Good for her," said a new voice. "Not so good for you two. You two are between a bullet and a hard place."

"Deddy?"

"Yeah," said Lear miserably. "He's been in on it the whole time."

"En ond whad?"

"Everything," said Lear. "You name it. He finked on me to Wilder, kept tabs on Mazur, told them when we left the Gouged Eye; the car that picked me up took me straight to a windowless room with nothing but books on Vlodomerian word order."

"Like I care what you think," said Deddy.

"Of course you don't," said Lear. "You're a picture of self-esteem."

There was a wet thud, a crack.

"Enough," said the short man.

Whoever was driving turned up the windshield wipers.

"Fuck you," said Lear. He spit into his bag.

"Habing?" I said.

"I'm here," said Having.

"Habing, I'm horry."

"Sorry for what?"

"He's sorry we dragged you into this," said Lear. "The way Deddy dragged us."

"Nobody dragged anybody," said Deddy. "Everybody got here as a result of his or her own choices."

"Rye," said the short man, "who did you mean when you said they'd already been to see you?"

"Erybudee."

"The Americans?"

"Yeff."

"That doesn't make sense," said the short man. "You're worth a lot less than you were before your little stunt, but that's still a lot."

"Listen," said Deddy, "if you want to keep what's yours, it's time to join the winning team. It's time to play baseball."

The rain was pounding against the windows, so that everyone had to raise their voices to be heard.

"What team is that?" asked Lear.

"Isn't it obvious?" said Deddy. "Their team. They're the ones trying to make sense of everything, making sure it's done fairly."

"What's with this sudden intense interest in fairness?" asked Lear. "I'm sitting here with a bag over my head and you're asking me if I brought enough gum for the rest of the class."

There was the sound of a brief, intense scuffle.

"Hey," protested Having. "Hey. Hey!"

"I said, that's enough," shouted the short man.

The scuffle stopped. "You must think you're pretty funny," said Deddy.

Lear spit again, coughed. "Not really."

Traffic ground to a halt and our driver laid on the horn.

"Wer ar we goingk?" I asked.

"We're going to end this ridiculous operation," said the short man. "We're finishing it tonight, before there are any more colossal fuck ups that reduce its value by half."

The van took a sharp right and I slid across the bench, was shoved violently back. After a while, the road surface pitched up. It felt as if we were driving a long way, but I couldn't be sure because I so seldom rode in cars. I imagined the scenery, the city in the distance, the castle on the hill.

"You know what all this means?" asked Lear.

"Whad?"

"They knew who I was the whole time and I was still speaking in that goddamn accent."

We turned onto a gravel drive. I could hear branches slap against the window. The van dipped once or twice, then pulled over and stopped. The driver set the parking brake.

I was helped carefully from the van into the pouring rain. They pulled off the bag and I squinted around, blinking and spitting. Lear stood beside me. He had deep rings around his eyes and his nose was bloody, but he was otherwise intact.

The van was parked near the treeline. In front of us, a gravel driveway opened onto the lawn of a two-story country house. Another van pulled up, and more of the people following us spilled out.

There was a flash of lightning and thunder rolled.

"Jesus," said Deddy, "it's really pissing."

A flagstone walk led to a set of stairs that forwent the first story of the house and climbed to the second in a distinctly American architectural feature. A boy was jumping in the puddles on the porch.

The front door opened and a woman stepped onto the deck. She said the boy's name and he stopped and looked at us, then went inside. After she guided him in, she called over her shoulder into the house. We waited in the parking lot, getting soaked. Lear coughed and hocked up blood and a piece of his partial denture.

The screen door banged open and Doc June Sr. walked onto the porch.

"Lear," said Doc June Sr. "Rye." I waved. "We've been looking for you."

"See?" said the short man. "What did I tell you?"

I looked at him, tired, feeling for the first time in a long time like I could manage a solid bowel movement. "See what?" I asked.

"Where is he?" called the short man.

"Not here," said Doc June.

"Then you won't mind if we take a look?"

Doc June paused for a second, then shook his head. "I don't think so."

A few men came out to the porch behind him, high level associates of the type I had seen on the first night we met, before the straight-dope pitch and the era of wet cucumbery speed. They were old hands, burn outs. The only sure thing they'd been handed in their entire lives had probably been given to them by The American Concern. "What are you planning on doing with those two?" asked Doc June. He was pointing at me and Lear.

"They've decided to cooperate," said Deddy. "They're going to name names."

"Is that true?" asked Doc June Sr. Everyone—people following us, short man, Doc June Sr.—turned to hear what we would say.

"Nog wily," I said.

"We can't," said Lear. "We didn't have anything to do with what happened. It was a coincidence that everything fell apart when it did."

"Bullshit," said Deddy.

"It's not bullshit," said Doc June. "They don't have any real names. They only have the names of the clients they sign. They have a lot of usernames maybe—a few of H. Defer's, which he probably gave you. Mostly, what you need are his clients' clients. You're trying to draw water from a stone with these two."

The short man with the cowlick turned to Deddy.

"He's lying," said Deddy. "That's not how it works. Even if it was, these two have an inside line."

"Why do you think he came to you?" continued Doc June. "He's the worst associate we ever had. He couldn't pull the trigger. We paid him in lump sums, *lump*." The men on the porch laughed. "Uh-oh, your new boss doesn't look too happy, Ded."

"All the more reason I should talk to Mr. Bright," said the short man. "Where is he?"

"What?" called Doc June. He cupped his hand around his ear, as if he couldn't quite hear the short man. "What's that you're saying?"

"Where's Wilder Bright?"

Doc June looked around at the guys on the porch like, 'Wilder Bright? You know a Wilder Bright?' They looked at each other, hands out. 'Any of you guys know Wilder Bright?'

"It doesn't matter," said the short man. "We're getting wet out here. We're coming in." It was really pouring.

"You're sure as shit not, you *jjangkkae* bitch." There's something about a racial slur you can feel from about two language families over.

"Let me make this easy for you," said the short man. He walked to one of the people following us and put out his hand. He received a small revolver, which he pressed to the back of my head. "We're coming in."

Muscles tensed among the surveillance professionals. One of the men on the porch pushed open the door and ducked back inside.

"You have until the count of ten," said the short man.

"You ain't gonna do shit," said Doc June.

"One."

I looked at Lear who was doing the math insofar as the minimum number of hostages the man with the cowlick needed to continue to apply pressure. He looked back at me, very sorry.

"Two."

I thought about my mother and how disappointed she was going to be about this whole thing.

"Three."

My mother is one of those mothers that would show up in court if I were implicated in a series of grisly murders and lay it all on society.

"Four."

I thought about McKayla, and hated myself for that.

"Five."

Time began to move slowly. I felt the rain on my back and the sweat on my hands and my own heartbeat. I didn't think about the future.

"Six."

Then I was betrayed by time and the count sprinted ahead, as though it were trying to catch back up with itself.

"Seveneightnine—"

I opened my mouth to say how unfair it was, how maybe I should get some of my last seconds back, because of the extraordinary rate at which they had passed. Only, I realized I would be dead by the time I said it. For a single, intense moment, I vividly regretted having watched so much TV.

There was the clang of a screen from around the back of the house.

A figure sprinted across the back yard toward the treeline.

"There," shouted Deddy. "There!"

It was Wilder, head down, long hair billowing out behind him, each step raising a crown of water.

Thunder crashed.

A headlight exploded on the van at the end of the drive.

There was a man with a rifle standing on the other side of the property. I squinted. It was the man who had given me 60 VRP by the Volodymy. He was wearing a trench coat and aiming his rifle at Wilder. A so-and-so was standing next to him, holding an umbrella over his head. The man with the rifle let off another shot.

Suddenly there were gunshots all around, as the people following us returned fire.

Wilder was still running across the open field at an incredible speed. He was too big to miss. It was all those lateral pull downs that did it.

## 48

Wilder had been a smoking baby. There had been pictures of him in the back of a magazine that carried articles of interest to the kind of people that read magazines with pictures of smoking babies.

He smoked his first cigarette when he was two years old. He said he'd been chomping at the teet for one, ever since.

What they don't tell you about smoking babies, what the lucky bystander that snaps the picture or records the footage never tells the parents of these objects of curiosity, is that, with the publication of said photographs, the intervention of law enforcement becomes an inevitability.

Afterward, the state removed Wilder from his mother's care and gave him to his mother's father.

Wilder's grandfather did not seem like the type of man to raise a daughter that thought it would be all right to let her baby smoke, but it turned out he was.

His whole life, Wilder collected pictures of smoking babies, and it was a great way to get into his good graces, if you unearthed one he'd never seen. He tracked down smoking babies and sent them letters. The letters were basically the same, and went,

"Dear Mr./Mrs. _____, are you the smoking baby from the enclosed photograph? My name is Wilder. It may interest you to know that I myself am the smoking baby in the other photograph, here enclosed. I saw your picture and wanted to reach out to you, since we have so much in common. I am a Pisces. Do you still smoke? If so, what is your preferred brand? I still smoke but only when I exercise. I prefer menthols. Any brand. Were you removed from the custody of your parents after a picture of you was published as a smoking baby? I was. I was taken from my mother and given to my grandfather who raised me. I think I would have been happier with my mother, even though she allowed me to smoke cigarettes. As you can see, I know how complicated it is, having been a smoking baby.

In the event that you would like to further our correspondence, you may contact me at:

Wilder Bright

Care of The Visegrad School

The Museum of Vlodomerian State Electronics Manufacturing

Zygmunta Krasińskiego ut. 18

Visegrad, Vlodomeria 99853

or email me at:

WB@theamericanconcern.to"

He kept the letters from all the people who answered, which was almost everybody. None of them had ever heard from another smoking baby, but afterward it seemed like they met or otherwise got in touch with nearly every smoking baby who had ever lived.

Wilder said being a smoking baby was one of those defining experiences people take for granted. He said the world was divided up into groups of people with defining experiences they were taking for granted, that the defining experiences had to be really damaging before you'd reach out to others, like being a substance abuser or an incest survivor or a lottery winner. Wilder said that, if you could find a group of people whose dads all made the exact same off-color joke over and over, or who had also asphyxiated their childhood goldfish with their bare hands, that the force of that commonality would drown out everything else, that you would probably fall in love.

He was dead serious about the smoking babies and felt like he was closer to them than he was with hardly anybody. He encouraged them to write to each other and to get to know one another, which many of them did.

He fell over in the standing water in the back yard, a few feet from the cover of the treeline. He was dead as a linguist.

# 49

A stray bullet removed two fingers on Having's left hand. It was the goddamnedest thing I ever saw, like the fingers had got up and samba'd out, sticking him with the check.

The offending bullet might have been fired by the man with the rifle, or by the so-and-so holding the umbrella, who had drawn a pistol from a shoulder holster and was firing across the lawn. Or it might have been fired by the people following us, who were all around us, shooting at the man with the rifle. The men on the porch, I absolve from culpability; they had gone indoors to retrieve their guns.

The short man with the cowlick was shouting, but I couldn't understand him over Having's screams. He was probably shouting for everyone to cease firing, because he was afraid that Wilder would die if he did not receive emergency medical attention, but nobody was ceasing.

There was a human-shaped puff of air where Lear had been.

That clinched it. I'm not a man of action. I'm the calm and collected type. Doctors have trouble finding my pulse, which rests at fifty beats per minute. That's slow for a pulse.

There was a burst of automatic gunfire as I ran into the woods. A bullet thumped into the trunk of a pine beside my head, and, somewhere, a long high-pitched scream sounded. It was like an air raid siren. It was still sounding as I tacked right and emerged partway down the drive.

One of the vans tore past. It was being driven in reverse and its windshield had been shot out. It barreled down the driveway and over the road, where it landed with a deafening crash in a ditch on the other side.

There was water in the air it was raining so hard, coming down all around in the trees and bouncing off the mud.

I ran out to the van. Its front wheels rotated lazily, suspended a few feet above the drainage ditch. A remaining headlight illuminated sheets of rain.

The person following us who was behind the wheel was the man who had jumped up and down on his elaborate disguise and pulled me out of the international coach to Bucharest. By then, I had known him a long time, months. His eyes were closed and he had one hand clamped over his stomach, where blood was coming out. The blood was running over his hand and past his seat belt in between the seat and the parking brake. His airbag had deflated and he was getting wet because the rain was coming in through the windshield.

He looked tiredly up at me and said something in Vlodomerian. I thought maybe he was saying, *"Mem a numered."* He said it a couple times: *mem a numered.* It meant, "I've got your number" in Vlodomerian, but in Vlodomerian the phrase is not idiomatic like it is in English, where its meanings are compounded from "I know you are bluffing" and "I'm calling you out" and "I understand who you really are." In Vlodomerian, *numer* also means "song" (as in, play that number, boys!), so maybe he was saying, "I have your song; I have your song." Maybe he had heard it in a movie and was giving me the old reverse literal translation while I stared at him in such bad shape, blood running out of his stomach over his hand. Maybe I heard wrong.

The screaming had finally stopped. Doc June Sr. had defended the house and the people following us were retreating up the drive. A pistol cracked insolently from the woods nearby.

I hopped down and jumped over the rising water, pausing for a moment to wonder if the man in the driver's seat would bleed to death. Then people began to trickle out of the woods and onto the road.

One of them saw me.

He pointed in my direction and shouted something that was lost to a roll of thunder. I realized it was the short man with the cowlick. I hadn't recognized him because one side of his body was caked in black mud, appeared burnt as if he were a cartoon character that had stood too close to a launching rocket.

I kept my head down, moving as fast as I could. I found a creek that had overrun its banks and made up my mind to follow it to the river. I don't remember being cold. The only time I had been warm since leaving the Gouged Eye was with Lear, and I had not thawed completely.

I jogged, lifting my knees to keep from turning an ankle. Every now and then I stopped to listen. Nothing was audible over the rain and the sound of the rushing water. I went on like that for a long time and soon it was dark, so that I had to pick my way hurriedly along the banks of the swollen creek. It met a road, culvert stuffed with debris from the storm. Its drainage ditch was full and lapping over the pavement, and I waded across, slipping over the tarmac and down the trench on its other side. From there, the creek passed beneath a fence.

I stopped, uncertain. Then I followed the fence back and forth in both directions, gave up and started to climb. I had to scramble for traction against the boards, leaving streaks of mud on the wood. Straining, I hoisted myself onto the teeth of its pickets, which bit into the soft, pink flesh of my stomach.

Lightning flashed as I swung my leg over the top. For a moment, the whole world was brightly lit.

The man with the cowlick stood in the road. He saw me on the fence, shouted something and raised his hand.

Thunder rolled and a cascade of orange sparks showered across his sleeve and the fence shuddered. I lost my balance and toppled over.

I landed in a foot or more of muddy water. I patted myself, searching for bullet holes. His shot had missed. Scrambling to my feet, I found I was on the perimeter of a large private estate. It was enclosed by the wooden fence, which was concealed here and there by rows of dwarf pines.

In the center of the estate was a house. The house was made of squares of glass and concrete and all the lights were on inside.

I saw that someone was standing on the top floor, silhouetted against the lights of its master bedroom: a Vlodomerian woman, the most incredible Vlodomerian woman I had ever seen.

She was completely naked, and I couldn't tell if she had seen me—was watching—or was observing her nude reflection in the glass. She moved one hand to her face and tucked a lock of hair behind her ear. She wore heavy golden earrings and she was smoking a cigarette. The light of the cigarette did not quite reach past her high, symmetrical cheeks, sockets black.

I heard the man with the cowlick begin to climb the fence. Crouching down, I circled the house, giving it a wide berth to stay out of the light.

An outbuilding stood a few hundred feet away. A tarp had come loose from a heap of cinder blocks and was flapping, making a racket that I could hear over the rain. I glanced back at the fence and saw nothing. The short man with the cowlick might still have been climbing or he might have been watching for movement, pistol drawn. I considered the house. It was a lot of time in the light on my way to the door.

Lightning flashed again and I threw myself down, heard the pistol fire. Then I was on my feet again, running as fast as I could.

A man in boxers and a tank top sat at a table in the kitchen. He got up from the table at the sound of the gunshot. As I ran past, he walked to the window and tented the glass with his hands. Thunder. He was gray-haired and stout and struck me as somehow familiar.

Then I was at the outbuilding, moving around its furthest wall. I stumbled on a hard corner, a ledge, which gave me an idea.

I extended my hand, touching the surface of a metal door. I searched for a knob and found it. The knob turned. The door swung open.

I stepped in and closed the door behind me, so the sounds of the pounding rain and the flapping tarp were shut out. I walked blindly forward with my hands outstretched, kicked something—a can maybe—which rolled through the darkness. It bounced off something else, something big, and stopped. The outbuilding smelled like dirt, I thought.

Groping, my hands found the long, smooth side of the object, then canvas. A big sheet was fixed to the smooth thing by little brass snaps. I thought it was part of a convertible or jeep. I unsnapped the canvas and crawled underneath. Everything was pitch black inside. It was big, maybe the trunk of a hatchback.

Now I felt the cold and the damp. And I had time to tremble, though not so long to wait.

There was the sound of rain and the flapping tarp as someone opened the door. It shut and the noise of the tarp was instantly rendered distant, muted.

Footsteps moved around the cement floor. They paused, as if thinking, then lifted the canvas where I had unfastened it.

I withdrew, pulling myself silently into the far corner. The brass fasteners tapped as they played against the side panel of the hatchback. The canvas ruffled and they slipped underneath. I could hear them breathing. This was when Lear would have leapt forward, when he would have wrestled the short man with the cowlick, killing him, saving his own life.

I waited for his groping hand and the shot.

# 50

I don't know when I fell asleep or how long I slept. When I awoke I had no memory of where I was.

The sounds that came to me were the sounds of birdsong and the sounds of water.

My breath had collected against the bottom of the canvas during the night and now it smeared my face and shoulder as I stuck my head into the fresh air. It was too bright to see, and I had to squint my eyes. The sun was being reflected back at me from the gently lapping surface of a body of water.

I was on a boat.

I stood all the way up, canvas unsnapping as I rose. Rain had puddled on the boat cover and it sloshed over the side.

The boat was drifting, caught on the shelter of a bus stop. Evidently, the river had burst its banks during the night, picked up the boat and carried it out of the garage until it had been snagged on the shelter's roof.

A woman stood above me on a second-floor balcony. She observed me nonchalantly—looked to be in her early sixties, thick in her arms and around her center. She pointed behind me with the two fingers she had clamped around her fuming cigarette.

A shape tented the canvas on the bow and I froze. Slowly, hideously, it began to move.

Recoiling, I considered jumping into the water, which was dark and muddy with detritus from the flood. I put one foot on the side of the boat, and glanced back at the shape. It moved again. The woman on the balcony watched with total impassivity.

A head stuck up from beneath the cover on the bow. It was Lear Fadder.

"Hey," he said.

"Jesus Christ, where did you come from?" The swelling in my tongue had gone down.

"I thought it was you," he said. "I asked myself, who else would climb into a boat and be swept out onto the Volodymy? And I'll tell you something else: look at this." From beneath the cover he withdrew a laminated booklet. He tossed it to me and I caught it.

I flipped it open to see the caterpillar eyebrows of the man who had been sitting at the kitchen table. Under his portrait was printed, *Kárbon Vidor.* The Togetherness Party's patriarchal cross was emblazoned on the center of the canvas, still half submerged by accumulated rainwater. We were in the prime minister's boat.

I held up the booklet for the woman on the balcony to see. "Kárbon," I explained, only, I couldn't make the palliative 'k' yet.

The woman on the balcony went into her apartment to call the police.

"Oh well," said Lear, "all the more reason for us to get underway." We unsnapped the cover and stowed it in the bowsprit where Lear had spent the night. Also in the bowsprit was a spare key attached to a bright orange fishing lure you couldn't miss.

The engine started, and, with very little fanfare, we pushed away from the bus stop and idled into the street.

The smoking woman had returned to her balcony, began describing our approximate speed and direction to the police.

"You beautiful, old Greg," cried Lear. He was standing in the stern, his arms stretched wide apart. "I love you! I know there's somebody that you love, too!" She lowered the phone, shocked, and watched us as we puttered away.

There was some light traffic, a paddle board and a pair of kayaks, a raft of wooden pallets. We discovered miniature Vlodomerian flags folded down at each corner of our windshield. They flapped patriotically as we idled past a submerged VDF cruiser.

The current picked up as we neared the Volodymy.

Suddenly, Lear gave a shout and grabbed the wheel, wrenching it to the left. "Stop," he commanded. I threw back the throttle and Lear ran to the other side of the boat. He shoved his hand into the water, from where he retrieved a green, ice cold bottle of *pivni*.

A delivery truck was wrecked nearby. It had been the victim of a crumbling Art Deco facade and was bleeding fat, green cells. I put the boat in neutral and Lear clambered overboard to pry loose a crate.

He grinned. "Food calories and clean water: enough to keep us lubricated until we make landfall."

Once our plunder was safely onboard, I gunned the engine and the bow rose from the surface of the water like the beak of a giant bird. It was our first shocking breath of freedom, and it was exhilarating. But no sooner had we gotten underway, then there came a terrible grinding noise. Two trees had been washed into the river during the storm and had collided in midstream. They sheared off branches on contact, rotating slowly, until they met with a large piece of floating asphalt. The asphalt breached and crashed into the river with a splash.

Lear gave me the eyebrow. I slowed down as something ricocheted off our starboard side. He had opened another *pivni* and this collision caused it to foam over, so he had to put it into his mouth. He had found sunblock in the glove compartment and applied a thick sheet of the white stuff to his nose.

I considered taking the boat back to shore, but it was all or nothing now, and the spilled beer seemed to have given Lear insight into the seriousness of our situation. We shared a grim look of mutual recognition.

Soon, the vomiting began.

When we arrived at the last major city north of the border, we were bruised, but whole, and severely dehydrated.

The city was built well above the waterline so its levies had held. The resulting strength of its current necessitated that we disembark, so I steered the boat to ground and clambered onto the prow. I found the bow rope and busied myself by tying a knot.

"What's that?" asked Lear. He was standing behind me, scrutinizing the rope.

"Figure eight," I said.

He shook his head. "You want the double bowline. You're fooling yourself."

"What's wrong with the figure eight?" I asked.

"Too hard to untie," he said. "Trust me, you'll be happy you listened."

"Why's it matter how hard it is to untie? We're abandoning the boat."

Lear opened his mouth, but our argument was cut short as it slammed into the riverbank and began taking on water. "Oh well," said Lear, "I'm sure he has insurance."

The boat listed badly as we clambered onto shore, scraping our knees on the edges of jagged rocks. We stood for a moment, watching as the escape craft was tugged away by the current. On its stern was printed '*Soft Populist.*'

"The beer," Lear exclaimed. He ran a few steps as if he might dive into the water, but I caught his arm in time and he stopped short. It was too late. One moment the boat was drifting free, a few feet downstream, the next it was in the center of the river. Then she was gone. "What a goddamn waste," said Lear. "Life in a nutshell."

We closed out a bar called the Bloody Shepherd, which was full of people with push broom mustaches. Its name was spelled once in English, once in Vlodomerian, and again in runic

Hungarian. Afterward, we trudged into the *centrum* and slept rough on benches underneath the train station.

We hit an outdoor supplier as soon as it opened, buying boots and all-weather gear and Slovakian backpacks. We also bought a pump with a water filtration system.

"Not in Volodymy," said the sales manager. He was supervising the assistants whose job it was to ferry stuff between our pointed fingers and the cash register. "Microparticulates."

Lear went next door and used the browser on a device in a third-party Apple retailer to check the Arable UI. It was a desert in there. Only a few shoots remained—two or three stalks of green in a forest of wilted husks—as if an invisible plague of locusts had descended overnight.

Payments that had been made by our remaining clients were *status: processing*. They would never be confirmed and, soon, that inconsistency would be reflected on the websites of the various agencies that owned and monitored student debt in different states. Then those last, sparse rods of green would vanish.

We took a bus to a town on the border, which consisted of little more than a combination pub, hotel and pizzeria where we ate lunch.

"There's one thing I don't understand," I said.

"What's that?" asked Lear.

It was a local place that had never seen Americans, so the whole staff was holed up in the kitchen arguing over the margin by which they should stiff us.

"Why did Deddy poison the SEC man?"

Lear looked at me.

"I mean, if he was working for Doc June and Wilder, and if Wilder wanted to hide that he was getting squeezed, not letting anybody out of the country, why'd he do it? It makes no sense to me. The psychiatric specialist, I get. I mean, who knows what the SEC man had figured out by then, but why put him in the hospital in the first place?"

"I've got something to tell you," said Lear.

"Okay," I said.

"You're not going to like it. You might even think poorly of me."

"Was it you?"

"It was me," said Lear.

"You poisoned the SEC man?"

"Whoops," he said.

"Whoops?"

Lear shrugged. "I never liked him. I thought—I thought it might be good for him. You know how you teach a kid to ride a bike?" I stared. "You take them up a hill and let them go. If they crash, well that's why we wear helmets. Worst case scenario, they learn a valuable lesson about stick-to-itiveness. The thing is, nine times out of ten, they learn to ride. I thought, 'Okay, I have the hill. He has the bike. What the hell are we waiting for?'"

"He was hospitalized."

"Whoops," said Lear.

"He's a babbling idiot. He's incapable of distinguishing fantasy from reality."

Lear crossed his arms. "Can you tell me—I want you to look me in the eyes and tell me you don't like him better this way."

I faltered. "You're not sorry?" I asked.

"Of course I'm sorry. The day he was disappeared I was on my way to confess." He indicated the door to the pizzeria with a nod of his head. "Thank God it all worked out. You know, I bet he'd agree that he's better off."

"I don't think I'll ever see him again." We were standing up, putting on all our stuff.

"It's not like I didn't do anything to him I wouldn't have done to myself. The amount of time I spent wallowing in guilt, letting so much good go after bad; I don't think I'll ever get the taste of that wet cucumbery shit out of my mouth."

"That's what you feel guilty about?"

"You know, you're not some innocent bystander in all this."

"I know," I said.

He finished his drink.

I must have looked pretty down, because Lear said, "Listen, in a few months you'll be somewhere else with new people. A few months after that, you'll hardly even think about it. A year or two, you're not even the same person. There's a statute of limitations on this kind of thing. Did you know your body replaces all of your cells every seven years? The highest court in the land is your capacity to live with regret."

After a few kilometers we stepped off the road and turned west. We crossed acres of partially frozen farmland, slipped a wire fence, and disappeared into the trees at the base of a hill. We leaned in, cracking through the brush, fingers going numb as silence closed in around us.

At the top, we came to an access road, which we followed until it veered suddenly east. Only the twin engines of our breath reminded us we were not alone in the shrinking light. By 4:30 p.m. it was too dark to walk, and snowing.

We came to a hunter's blind and pitched our tents. Dinner was canned stuffed peppers with bright white slices of bread and tubes of liver paste, chased down by a fat plastic bottle of plum liquor. The plum liquor tasted like diesel and we passed it back and forth until it was gone.

"Why do you think the garage door came open?" I said.

"The garage door?"

"Of the, uh—boathouse?"

"Oh," said Lear.

"You don't think I was shot to death while cowering in the stern and this is a long sanguine hallucination?"

"Who knows," said Lear, "maybe I opened it." Lear jogged the empty plastic bottle at the end of his knee. "I wish I had more to drink."

"I'm sick of drinking," I confessed.

After a while, he said, "Do you think we'd have ever left, if they'd given us just a little more rope to hang ourselves with?"

I thought about it. "I know I wouldn't have. Even once things got bad, I would have stuck it out." Suddenly, I was crying.

Lear watched me as the snow came down in drifts. "Are you okay?" he asked.

"Sure I am," I said. I wiped my nose. "I'm an idiot."

Footsteps crunched up the path to the hunter's blind. We exchanged looks. I stood up as three men in cold weather gear appeared around our fire.

They had black hoods and wore black jackets. One had a rifle slung over his shoulder. "*Ahoj*," said the foremost man.

"Hello," we said.

All three seemed taken aback.

"Why are you here?" asked the front man.

Lear and I looked at each other. "Camping," Lear said.

The men turned inward and spoke in a huddle. One leaned out and asked, "British?"

"American," said Lear. The man gave a short nod and went back to the others. After conferring a few seconds more, they broke into a loose arrowhead formation.

"Papers," said the first man.

I turned to Lear, surprised.

"Who're you?" asked Lear.

"Papers," insisted the man.

My passport was back in the apartment. "I don't have mine."

"Not good," said the man.

"Hold on," said Lear. "Just who do you think you are?"

"Protectors of Vlodomeria," said the man.

"Protectors of Vlodomeria?" asked Lear. "Who is it you're protecting Vlodomeria from, exactly?"

"Migrants and Jews," said the youngest of the three. His boots were particularly large.

"You get a lot of Jews through here?" asked Lear.

"Everyone knows it is the idea of the Jews to destroy the white races with migrants," said the young man. We looked at the other Protectors of Vlodomeria in order to determine if this was indeed the case. From their expressions we gleaned that it was.

"Papers," said the first man.

"You should be thanking us," continued the youngest of the three. "We protect weak Western men. We protect your wives and daughters from rapists."

"We're from America," said Lear.

"So what?" asked the kid.

"Negroes," intoned the center man. He held the hunting rifle.

The youngest Protector looked at us with renewed interest. A strange emotion washed over his face. If I had to say what the strange emotion was most like, I would say it was most like ravenous hunger. "Then you understand because the Jews and the Blacks are destroying America."

"Who told you that?"

"Only look," said the young man. "It is obvious."

I realized we had taken the wrong tack. "Hey," I said. "But what's the big idea, hassling a couple of guys like us, who aren't Jews or migrants?"

"We are also looking for Globalist spies," said the youngest of the men. "Globalists are the same as Jews. They are useful idiots of the Jewish conspiracy to promote race-mixing." His English was quite good.

"We're on vacation," I said. "I can't help it if I lost my passport."

"We're not Globalists," said Lear. "Everyone knows that Globalists are Maoist, postmodernist, homosexuals from Paris and Frankfurt."

"So what?" said the young man.

"We're not from Paris and Frankfurt for starters," I said.

"Not all Globalists are from Paris and Frankfurt," said the young man. "That is a stereotype."

"Well, we're not homosexuals," said Lear.

"You are together in the woods," pointed out their leader.

"So are you," I said. I thought I had them with that one.

The young man shook his head. "If we were homosexuals, Danylo would shoot us." He thumbed in the direction of the man with the rifle. Danylo nodded that, yes, this was the case.

"Okay," said Lear, "but we're definitely not postmodernists."

"That's right," I said. "It's a matter of public record. We're published."

"In what sort of things are you published?"

"In those fields dealing with the study of sogginess."

Disbelief gripped the soft features of the youngest Protector's face. "Sogginess?" he asked. He turned to the others. They traded excited looks.

"Visegrad School?" asked the front man.

"You've heard of it?" I asked.

"Heard of it?" he asked. "It is very popular with us."

"Is that so?" said Lear. He gave me a sideways look I pretended not to see. It was not the time for a rigorous moral inventory.

"This is Lear Fadder," I said, "as his passport will attest."

"Lear Fadder," exclaimed the youngest. "You have done great work." The work he was referring to was mine, not that, under the circumstances, it mattered. "Always happy to meet a fan," I said.

"And this," said Lear, "is Rye."

"I only heard a little of you," said the front Protector. "You are not so famous."

"He's done some very good work," insisted Lear.

"It's alright," I said. "They know who you are, that's what's important."

"It's not alright," said Lear. "Some of your views on the application of sogginess to Heidegger are totally indispensable." I cleared my throat. Lear looked at me, then around at the Protectors of Vlodomeria.

"Heidegger was from Frankfurt," observed the youngest.

"That's why he was such low-hanging fruit," I said.

Lear sighed.

"I must tell you, Mr. Lear," said the first man. "I am a great admirer of yours. Your work is very popular with the Protectors of Vlodomeria as well as all defenders of the Christian Faith."

"Is that so?" asked Lear.

"But Mr. Lear, what are you doing out in this weather? We saw your fire from the tower,"—he gestured to the dark beyond—"and we are imagining you are puppets of the international crypto-Marxist conspiracy."

"We're doing research," I said. "There is a lot of demand for original research."

"Oh," said the youngest, "I think we should not interrupt."

"That's right," I said. "It's private research."

"It is a shame," said Danylo with the gun, "because there are so many people who are happy to meet you. I see you are not having much food and we have here the warming hut not far. We have hunter's stew and beer, and many men and girls who would be admirers of yours. You also would be invited," he said to me.

I nodded my thanks, perhaps a little stiffly.

I could see the gears turning in Lear's head. "Ah," he said. He seemed to be undergoing a titanic struggle. "Of course I—" He broke off.

"Would you like to come with us?" asked the youngest Protector.

Lear looked at me, pleading.

# 51

I came down on the Slovakian side, crunching over the frozen prints of a tractor tread, which I followed to a strip of road.

I walked along the road until I arrived at a bus stop. There, I read, "*ZASTÁVKA*" on a sign, and knew that I was no longer in the country where I had spent the last year of my life.

I had nothing to do and so I sat down and waited.

While I waited, three people came down the hill on the other side of the road.

I watched them coming toward me from a long way off, visible at first only as they moved against the landscape, finally animate by the plumes of their breath and whites of their eyes. Their skin was dark and they carried their things in bright plastic bags.

They were all young men.

They came down just before the bus arrived—must have known its schedule but preferred to spend the night in the cover of the trees, though their clothes were inadequate and their hands were exposed to the cold through holes in their cotton gloves.

When the bus pulled up to the stop, they allowed me to get on first, after which, the driver, a woman with short hair, tried to close the doors and pull away.

One of them had his foot in there, and the door wouldn't close, so the driver had to stop. The whole bus lurched.

The men got hastily on, but the driver would not leave without their tickets. She had not asked me for mine, and I waited groggily nearby to purchase it.

While I waited, the men offered her money. She repeated something in Slovak at them, shaking her head. They stank of bromodosis now that they were no longer in the fresh air.

I dug into my pocket and found the big VRP note that had been given to me by the man who had shot Wilder. It was crumpled from getting wet in my pocket. The bus driver and the three men grew quiet.

"*Vlodomarsky*," she said at last.

I nodded.

"No *Vlodomarsky*," she said. She rubbed two fingers against her thumb.

"Keep it," I said, waving it around a bit.

She looked at the bill. It was worth about sixty tickets.

She shrugged theatrically, as if the price I was paying were none of her business, and took it.

I glanced toward the men waiting by the door. They watched me in return, silent. The bus driver punched some numbers into a little machine and it spat out a ticket, which she handed to me.

"For everybody," I said, indicating the others by drawing a circle with my finger.

She frowned. Her nose bunched toward her heavy brow in an expression of profound distaste. Then, shrugging again, she turned to the machine and punched in the numbers to produce three more tickets.

She handed them to me without looking, and all of us went together to the back of the bus while Slovak morning commuters clutched their messenger bags and briefcases.

We sat apart, the three of them on a bench at the back, and me in a seat with my bag beside me.

We were young and cold and hungry, but otherwise not much alike.

# Afterword

One of the most interesting things about Vlodomeria was the ways in which it did not exist. It could not, for instance, be found on any map before its separation from Yanukovych's Ukraine, having always been included in the neighboring regions of Galicia and Volhynia—beginning in 1198 with the rule of Roman the Great—and, despite its non-existence, passing nominally to the Kings of Hungary with Andrew II's victory at the Battle of Visegrad in 1205.

The Hungarians lost Vlodomeria in 1221 to the Mongols, and, though the region comprised no territory, it wasn't formally abolished until its absorption into the Polish-Lithuanian Commonwealth in 1399. Despite this, the Hungarians continued to style themselves kings of Vlodomeria up to their own absorption into the Hapsburg dynasty at the end of the sixteenth century.

The Austrians inherited the title, and, though it was not real, pressed their claim to the region during the first partition of Poland in 1772. They then used the claim to cordon off part of Vladimir-in-Volhynia, naming it Austrian Galicia in New Cisleithania and, after the Austro-Hungarian Compromise of 1867, a slow process of liberalization began. From 1873, Vlodomeria was de facto an autonomous province of Austria-Hungary.

World War I brought the collapse of the Austrian Empire, and Volodmerian was subsequently incorporated into the

Czechoslovak Republic, first as Carpathian Vlodo-Ruthenia, then as Subcarpatho-Vlodomerian Rus, and, finally, from 1928 on, as Subcarpathoruthenian Vlodomeria.

Vlodomerian patriotism, however, did not begin to cast sparks until the prospect of re-invasion by Hungarians in 1939. Fed up with this sort of thing at last, Vlodomerians of every stripe rose as one and declared the Republic of Vlodomerian-Subcarpathia to be a free and sovereign nation. Visegrad was taken that afternoon.

The resisting Vlodomerians, including their newly minted president, were pushed into Poland, where they were shot. What followed was Vlodomeria's rapid annexation by the Ukrainian SSR, which briefly lumped Vlodomeria into Drohobych Oblast, before rapidly losing it to Hitler's Germany in 1941.

After World War II, Vlodomeria was temporarily returned to Czechoslovakia and steps were taken to grant it sovereignty. Then, in 1945, the Red Army's National Committee of Transcarpatho-Ukraine gifted it lock stock and barrel back to the Ukrainians. Vlodomeria remained therein, through the collapse of the Soviet Union, until the unfolding of the Orange Divorce, which produced its peaceful separation in early 2004.[11]

I was lucky enough to move to Vlodomeria in March of 2015, nearly a decade after it joined the Schengen Area. Like many other Americans, I did not know anything about the language or history of the country I was moving to, had only heard of Visegrad, though not well enough to place it in Vlodomeria. Neither could I locate Vlodomeria on a map. I remained in the city through the following winter and into early spring.

---

[11] Leybl Gorie, the preeminent ethnic Galitzianer philosopher, wrote, "The only real divide in the country existed between Visegrad and its attendant fantasies—Visegrad that was imagined by Germans and Poles as a bulwark against the enemies of Christendom, and later, against Ukrainians and Soviets, and by Jews and Ukrainians as an obstacle to the spread of fascism. By its past failures we measured the verisimilitude of our hopes." (*My Poor Country*, 76)

Lear left around the same time, about two weeks after me, through a checkpoint on the Ukrainian border. It was the most heavily controlled border and the last place he thought they would look. He purchased a guitar in Kiev and thumbed his way south. Photographs surfaced of him in Antalya, where he looked tan and villainously happy. We have remained close friends.

McKayla remained in Prague for a little while, then returned to Akron. I see her whenever I am there, which is once in my life so far. She used her money to start a non-profit, fulfilling her nascent destiny of ascension to the moral elite. She married a Vlodomerian whose parents got him out as a baby and raised him in Ohio, and I stayed at their place during my visit. On the second night I came downstairs to find them whispering to each other in Vlodomerian, so I guess she really did learn to speak it eventually.

H. Defer lives and teaches in Berlin, where, as far as I know, he uses the bleached skull of the former go-to-guy in intertextual branding as a paperweight. Deddy and May married and divorced. I heard Deddy got clean after that. Having never left, but had three kids with an incredible Vlodomerian nurse he met during his recovery. I never saw or heard from the SEC man again.

I have returned to Visegrad twice, and it is less and less recognizable. It is cleaner and less free, quieter in the daytime and darker at night. Perhaps I wrote so much about it because I felt a need to preserve it—sensed what was in the offing, the breakdown in those final levers of democracy. Or maybe Visegrad has simply passed through me and into someone else: a little wild, stepping off an overnight bus, one passport check away from deportation, someone for whom failure seems only a distant possibility.

But if there is one thing I want you to understand about all of it—who we were and what we were doing there—it is this: we were not lost. When you are lost, there is someplace you are supposed to be, someplace you belong. What made our generation so dangerous was that we discovered it was not possible to really belong in America—that the search for belonging had trapped our parents and driven them crazy. We were looking for something else, something cynical and hopelessly naive. We did not live to live, only accumulated potential never to be spent. We were the accelerated generation, rudderless, always traveling at night; invisible, we passed through the lives of strangers that might have made us who we hoped to be.

This brings me to my last point, which is that the strangest of the myriad ways in which Vlodomeria has been said not to exist and is flat out ignorance. For some reason, Americans always have trouble believing it is real. This is maybe not surprising, since the citizens of that nation are often surprised to learn that Slovenia and Slovakia are both countries, but Czeckloslovakia is not. Some Americans have accused me of making it all up, which is ironic, because this book and its description of the Vlodomerian people—their idiosyncrasies and eccentricities— was written partially out of a desire to fill a dearth of information on the subject. I am happy to say that it is my crowning literary achievement, so far.

Why, you may ask, if so many Americans are ignorant of Visegrad—doubt its very existence—did I choose to write about it? Why have I not written about a better understood city, like Budapest, Krakow, or Prague?

I cannot answer these questions because I do not totally understand the answers myself. Many Americans and Western people will cringe at my descriptions, and suggest that they are colored by prejudice, that they smack of a petite Orientalism. Some Vlodomerians will say, quite rightly, that I have mocked much that I do not understand and that I am too ignorant to articulate the rest. They will be particularly displeased by mistakes in the Vlodomerian language, despite the fact that the Vlodomerian in this book is almost always being spoken (and written) by people without a firm grasp of its grammar and syntax. In my defense, I *can* say this: while Budapest, Krakow, and

Prague all bear a resemblance to Visegrad in some respect, none of them alone captures its magic—the magic of being a stranger as one is a stranger in Visegrad, the magic of falling in love as one falls in love with Visegrad. I am not able to plot a course through those cities, eyes shut, as I am with Visegrad. I cannot so easily recall their people or their customs, the pitfalls of their respective cuisines.

That is not to say that this book is a perfect record. I am not a perfect-record kind of guy. Here and there, a detail is unintentionally exaggerated, a street is forgotten, or a word misspelled. But only in Visegrad would it be possible to recall those finer points that make this book what it is.

For that reason, if you have a conversation with someone, or happen to overhear a conversation between others, during which the events of this book are mistaken for fiction, please set them straight. Get right up in their business. Tell them, "Look, I happen to know the events of that book are absolute fact." Tell them that. Also, if you notice this book has been mishelved in a library or bookstore and placed in any section besides Narrative Non-Fiction or Travel, I urge you to take matters into your own hands.

Finally, I would like to encourage the reading of books of every kind, but especially of the kind that I have written. I consider relaxing with a book by a fire, socks off, toes curling and uncurling, to be among the chief pleasures of life. This is never more the case than when the book in question is one of mine.

Yours dryly,
Duncan Ryely

# ABOUT THE AUTHOR

**Duncan Robertson** is an American writer who has lived abroad, both in South Korea and Eastern Europe, since 2011. A native of Seattle, Washington, which he still visits regularly, he currently resides in Budapest, where he edits *Panel*, a magazine of English-language literature produced in Central and Eastern Europe. His work has appeared in *Expat Press Online*, *North Dakota Quarterly*, and *Unlikely Stories*.

CPSIA information can be obtained
at www.ICGtesting.com
Printed in the USA
JSHW042027300122
22405JS00003B/3